PRAISE FOR

HELL HEIST

"Written with insane energy and packed with conceptual fireworks, *Hell Heist* reminds me of Stephen King at his most freewheeling. Very rare for a horror and thriller novel."
Imraan Coovadia
author of *A Spy in Time* and *Tales of the Metric System*

"A delightful romp through comedy, horror, and hell that will leave you grossed out, chuckling, and uplifted. The novel boasts a menagerie of characters that spit sparks off the page. Peterson ensures every moment is bubbling, popping, zinging, alive!"
L.C. Barlow
author of the Jack Harper Trilogy

"Picture a night spent playing Lovecraftian RPGs and marathoning all the *Ocean's Eleven* and *Mission Impossible* movies with Clive Barker, Kathryn Bigelow, James Gunn, and Wes Craven. Robert J. Peterson channels that same thrilling energy into *Hell Heist*. and I couldn't get enough of it."
Dale Halvorsen
author of *Girls of Little Hope*

"*Hell Heist* is a hell of a ride. Dark, campy, and witty through-and-through, this is a great pick for fans of classic heists or the good old slasher film. I couldn't put it down."
Quinlan Grim
author of *The Ghost of Danny McGee*

HELL HEIST

HELL HEIST

Robert J. Peterson

A California Coldblood Book
Nevada City, Calif.

THIS IS A GENUINE CALIFORNIA COLDBLOOD BOOK
Nevada City, Calif.

californiacoldblood.com

Copyright © 2025 by Robert J. Peterson

ISBNs
Paperback: 978-1-955085-30-4

Ebook: 978-1-955085-31-1

Set in Minion

Cover design by Dale Halvorsen

Printed in the United States

Publisher's Cataloging-in-Publication Data

Names: Peterson, Robert J., author.

Title: Hell heist / Robert J. Peterson.

Description: Nevada City, CA: California Coldblood Books, 2025.

Identifiers: ISBN: 978-1-955085-30-4 (paperback) | 978-1-955085-31-1 (ebook)

Subjects: LCSH Cults--Fiction. | Multilevel marketing--Fiction. | Hell--Fiction. | Supernatural fiction. |

Occult fiction. | Horror fiction. | BISAC FICTION / Horror | FICTION / Occult & Supernatural

Classification: LCC PS3616 .E84749 H45 2025 | DDC 813.6--dc23

Also by Robert J. Peterson

The Odds: A Post-Apocalyptic Action-Comedy
The Remnants: A Post-Apocalyptic Picaresque
The Odds: The Audio Drama
Strong Bones

Prologue, 1993:
The Seven Maxims of Starchild Ranch

STARCHILD RANCH AND COMMUNE SPRAWLED across a hundred acres of hilly woodland in upstate New York. The commune was home to some several score souls who had fallen into its orbit—and by association, the orbit of its matriarch and ecclesiastical leader, Athena Starchild—along a myriad of the usual paths lost souls take to find such a home.

Some were displaced, unhoused, homeless, desperate.

Some were wandering the world looking for their purpose.

Some had no purpose until Athena uncovered them and gave them one.

Everyone who came to the ranch was welcomed by the same view: a faded wooden sign. The sign had once announced the ranch's previous tenant, the Starview Bed and Breakfast. When Athena Starchild bought the land in '85, the old Victorian inn was the only structure. She and her acolytes had spent the last eight years adding twenty buildings, but they left the sign standing. Instead of taking it down, Athena ordered her Starchildren to sand away the inscription, *Welcome Traveler! You've made it to the Starview Bed and B-fast!*

Across the smooth surface they etched the following:

You are entering Starchild Ranch. Welcome.
Forever while you're here, you must honor the Seven Maxims of Starchild Ranch:

One: The Starchild Family is your only Family.
Two: Speak with no one who lacks the Starshine or who comes at you strongly or with malice.
Three: Secrets are forever. Protect them even into the afterworld and past all the Infernal Downfalls.
Four: Oppose all Invading Notpers with viciousness and finality, for this is the way to triumph.
Five: You are permanently and axiomatically an entity-object in time and space.
*Six: **
Seven: Hold true to the Seven Maxims.

It was that sixth maxim that roped in most of the waverers, the fence-sitters. They'd arrive at the threshold, knapsack slung over a shoulder, and contemplate the sign. Two or three Starchildren would flank them—one watching the way they'd come for any greedy-eyed notpers. The ghost of the original inscription was still visible, like someone moaning through foggy glass. Something about those faded letters always unsettled the new arrivals, who would peer past the sign into the thicket of overhanging willows and cedars that hugged the dirt pathway leading into the ranch proper. Setting sunshine would sparkle and flash over the treeline, while voices would echo from above—some laughing, others barking orders. The newcomer would consider a quick about-face … but the need to know would win out.

"What's the sixth maxim?" they'd ask, jerking their chin at the penultimate line, which bore only a single five-pointed star. The souls escorting the wanderer would share a knowing look and a smile.

"That one's only for her Starchildren."

That was usually all it took.

A woman, British accent: "All you ever think about is money."
A man, Scottish brogue: "All anyone *ever* thinks about is money."
The little girl hugged her knees close and giggled. The movie wasn't

rated R, but it sure felt like it was. Sean Connery sat shirtless in bed, surrounded by fine silks, an ornate brass clock ticking on his side table, smoking a cigarillo. His mistress, a brunette with mounds of hair, pulled on hose and garters while they both plotted one of the greatest robberies in British history.

They'd only had the VCR at the Ranch since last year—contraband smuggled in by Nicky Starchild. Their Foundation, Athena, had grudgingly allowed it so long as everyone shared and her little Letta got it to herself for at least two hours every weekend.

Little Letta Starchild. Athena's daughter.

Letta sat in what had once been the old Inn's mudroom. During the long winters, it remained so, but for the summer months, it transformed into a center for relaxation. Starchildren brought in couches, futons, beanbags, and blankets. Nebbie had teamed up with Alastair and Byron to carry in the television, a seventies behemoth that was housed in a wood cabinet and radiated heat like an electric burner. The VCR sat next to it, surrounded by tapes. Most were instructional videos Athena made them all watch (*Maximizing Your Truth Potentiality, How to Fend Away PsychoSentionisms*), but Letta had conspired with Frith and Nicodemus to sneak in some good ones: *Star Trek II: The Wrath of Khan, Tron, Return to Oz, The Goonies, Raiders of the Lost Ark, Batman, The Breakfast Club, Supergirl, Ghostbusters, IT, Dick Tracy, Blade Runner,* and Letta's personal favorite, *The Great Train Robbery.*

She'd played the tape almost to breaking. Snowy speckles danced across an image that gave occasional flips. She didn't care. Every weekend, Nicodemus would try to persuade Letta to spend her two hours of VCR time on another movie, but every weekend, Letta would pop in *The Great Train Robbery* and lose herself. She always watched it from start to finish, only pausing to let her beloved pit bull, Marjorie, out the mudroom's screen door to relieve herself.

The only time she failed to finish was the weekend she saw the Sunflower. That also happened to be the day Marjorie died.

It happened fast.

Onscreen, Sean Connery and Donald Sutherland walked along a cobblestone street bathed in fog. Marjorie had conked out awhile ago; Letta hadn't noticed. The screen door squeaked, and a shadow fell over Letta—a tall one.

She was six feet tall and seventeen years old, though she always seemed older. When she crossed her arms, bands of muscle rippled across her torso. A blonde ponytail rested on her chest, which was covered only by a white tank-top. She had undone the top of her jumpsuit—standard Starchild Ranch work clothes—and tied it off around her waist. Sparklepoints of sweat dotted her brow. Tomorrow was the Fourth of July, and everyone was getting ready for the big night. Her feet were crossed. She leaned against the doorjamb, her bulk barely fitting between the joists.

This was Winifrith Starchild, known to her fellow Starchildren as Frith.

"How you doing, big girl?"

"Shh! I love this part."

Onscreen, Sutherland asked: "You didn't do the Barclay Hills job, did you?"

"Barclay Hills?" Connery said. "Shit job!"

Letta mouthed along to every word, stopping to giggle at the profanity. Frith jokingly waggled a finger at her. Marjorie snorted in her sleep and jumped to her feet so fast she jostled Letta. Frith stepped in and leaned over.

"Marge? You okay, girl?"

The door flew off its hinges in Marjorie's wake, the screen bearing a dog-sized hole. Letta sprang to her feet in pursuit, squeezing past Frith into the dusk. The little girl pelted down a brick pathway that encircled the old inn. The brick path sloped down and around the house, curving under a canopy of trees. Fireflies danced in the scent of honeysuckle. Several fellow Starchildren blocked the path, all of them carrying folding chairs, tables, and decorations.

"*Gaaaaangway!*" Letta yelled. They parted to let her through, but one lingered, a wiry teenager covered in tattoos. She'd pushed her chunky horn-rim glasses over a mop of ginger hair to make way for a camcorder she kept perpetually jammed to an eye. She gesticulated wildly.

"Cheat out for the camera, guys! Let's see those muscles! Cheat out—oh, hi Lets!"

This was Nicodemus Starchild, known to her fellow Starchildren as Nicky.

"Hi Nicky! Gotta run Nicky bye! Marge! Marjorie! Wait!"

Marjorie's muscular backside vanished around the side of the inn and under the trees. Letta sprinted to the end of the house, set her hand on chipped red clapboard and white wainscoting, and peeked around the corner. It felt like looking into a cave. Somehow, she'd never come this way before, so she hesitated a moment before going farther. Darkness enshrouded her. The temperature dropped several degrees. Ahead, a pet door swung open and shut with a *fwap-fwap-fwap*. Letta crept forward, Frith's voice calling behind her:

"Don't go in there!"

She sounded a thousand miles away. The pet door was set into a regular one, which Letta opened. More darkness awaited her inside. She patted the wall in search of a switch: click. Fluorescent light the same sickly yellow as an infected fingernail splashed the scene, which her young brain failed to perceive at first blush. It wasn't her fault. No one could have understood the sight, except their Foundation, Athena.

It glistened and wriggled, whatever it was. About four feet tall and two feet wide, it was a beige-pink cylinder of … something. Hundreds of strips of the beige-pink stuff had been sculpted into a column capped with a bulb that sprouted dozens of nubby protrusions, all of them undulating in an endless circular wave. Binding it together was a slick sludge the same color as blooming violets. Letta stepped closer, mesmerized, her brain still processing the images. It took her a moment to realize the beige-pink strips were human flesh, the nubby protrusions fingers.

Someone had sculpted a sunflower out of a person. And it was still alive.

But as shocking as that revelation was, she didn't scream, not at first, because her focus had narrowed around the sunflower's center. Instead of seeds, the bottom half of a human face rested in the center of the fluttering finger-petals. A Doric nose sat over pursed lips. No, not pursed—trembling lips. The nostrils flared and wheezed breath into lungs that didn't exist.

Maybe ten total seconds had passed since Marjorie ran from the mudroom.

In the eleventh second, Letta heard two things: Frith's heavy footfalls approaching, and the *lap-lap-lap-lap* of Marjorie's tongue. She was worrying at something on the sunflower's base, slurping down the purple sludge until she'd freed another protrusion—in this case, a toe—which she swallowed whole.

The sunflower screamed in response.

It sounded unhuman; like speaker feedback wailing from every direction. Letta slapped her hands over her ears, backing away from the horror and into the waiting arms of Frith. Commotion followed; Frith was shouting and pulling Letta aside, more people crowded into the space, a red light blinked—Nicky's camcorder—and several bodies blocked the sunflower. Nicky squeezed in next to Letta. Nebbie Starchild wrangled Marjorie into the corner just as she swept in. She was shorter than her reputation suggested, topping out at five-foot-three. Her outfit rarely changed: jeans, workboots, and a succession of paint-spattered sweatshirts. Tortoiseshell aviator glasses gave her an owlish look.

This was Athena Starchild, known to her Starchildren simply as Athena, or more commonly, as "our Foundation."

She scanned the room, performing some calculations in her head. Everyone held their breath; everyone, that is, except Letta, who kept craning her neck to get another look at the sunflower. Athena stepped before her, blocking the view and glaring down with green eyes magnified to silver-dollar size. Letta's insides turned to stone.

"Who failed to secure this door?"

"Starchild" wasn't Athena's actual last name. Miller was. Susannah Josephine Miller was born in 1948 and gave birth to little Letta thirty-three years later. Because it was a geriatric pregnancy, the doctors applied fetal monitors in utero, leaving Letta with two scars on the crown of her head. When asked to name her daughter, Athena read the nurse's nametag—Emily—and gave it, knowing her child would need a legal alias.

But she never called her Emily. Not once.

No one answered Athena's question.

The only voice was Nicky's, speaking in a low whisper: "It's a macabre scene here today, dear viewers. We're in what appears to be a storage room underneath the old Starview Inn, home to the Ranch these many—"

"Enhancements are forthcoming."

Athena had only whispered, but she may as well have slapped everyone in the room. Her Starchildren all exhaled as one—some sighing, others wheezing, others emitting a faint yelp. They all stood, shoulders rolling forward, a single collective wince spreading across their faces in anticipation of Athena's "enhancements" and who was doomed to receive them. Nicky fell silent, too, but kept her camera trained on the scene. Athena stared at her daughter but addressed Nicky.

"Stop filming. Now."

Nicky lowered her camera. Athena turned away, giving Nicky an opening to prod Letta. The camera's red light was still flashing, but she'd hidden it out of their Foundation's sight. They shared the briefest of grins, though Nicky's complexion had turned to paper. Stanton Starchild, a former college wrestler from Rutgers who'd arrived at the ranch a year earlier, was transfixed by the sunflower. He dipped a fingertip into the purple binding agent. It sparkled as if shot with quartz.

"Foundation, what is this?" he asked.

"I hereby invoke the Sixth Maxim."

It had always been a perfect summer day, Letta thought.

Letta couldn't remember how she'd come to be sitting on the retaining wall by the northwest gardens, but she was happy to be there.

You didn't finish it.

The voice was her own, a reminder from the recent past ... but of what? Her mind searched for the answer, but none came—only feelings. She'd been in the middle of something. Something she enjoyed and did at regular intervals. ("Regular intervals" was the exact, bookish turn of phrase her young mind conjured. She was only eight, but she always read ahead in her lessons and asked enough questions to annoy her 'marms.) Someone had been with her, too, but a different kind of someone.

A person who wasn't a person?

Shadowy images filled her mind's eye: A talking box, couches, a companion. The thing she hadn't finished was associated with that box, somehow. She squinted, trying to bring the memories into focus, but instead, the companion—a creature sleeping next to her in the mysterious room—stood on his hindlegs and sprouted thousands of prickly-waving frond-blossoms. The apparition hissed, its blossoms curling into a set of makeshift jaws that lunged at her.

The voice echoed from a distance: "Big girl?"

Letta gasped. It had always been a perfect summer day. Overhead, the sun suddenly spanned the width of everything, hurting her eyes. A few of the retaining wall's stones shifted under Frith's mass as she sat. She touched Letta's knee, leaning in to speak in a comforting whisper.

"Are you okay?"

"Head hurts," Letta said, checking the sky. The sun had returned to its normal size. "What was I doing?" Suddenly, her memories lurched into view, clicked into place, and leaped out of her mouth: "Marjorie! Where's Marjorie? We were … watching something. The box. Watching a movie!"

"Nicky's taking Marge away."

Letta's heartbeat slowed. "Where?"

"Something happened." Frith looked as confused as Letta felt, but she pressed on: "Something bad, and Marge got hurt, big girl. Nicky said it was her fault—something about a door? So she has to take an enhancement."

"Oh, no." Tears were coming. "What door? What did Nicky do?"

Letta stood, her head swiveling in search of her friend and fellow Starchild. The retaining wall stood at the northernmost and highest boundary of the ranch, giving view to the rest of the property as well as the surrounding forests. The Adirondacks stood on the horizon to the east. About fifty yards down the hill, a few bigwigs, Athena's strongest Starchildren, escorted Nicky to the edge of the grounds. Marjorie strained against a leash Nicky held.

"Nicky!" Letta was jumping up and down. *"Nickyyyy!"*

Frith laid a gentle hand on her shoulder and eased her back down.

"It's okay. Marjorie got sick, and Nicky's taking her to get help. That's her enhancement."

Letta's lower lip trembled. "I'm not stupid. I know what it means when we take animals away. They took away Abraham's little kitty and never brought her back."

Frith wrapped a massive arm around her and squeezed. "You're right. I'm sorry."

Letta was crying in earnest by then, the sobs quiet but strong.

"Where's your mommy?"

"My mommy?" Frith asked. "Athena's my mommy."

"No, I mean your mommy-mommy. Where is she? Why isn't she here with you?"

"Oh. Well, not everyone who lives here was born here."

Letta's face clenched. "I *know* that." She cried harder. "Sorry I yelled."

"It's okay," Frith said quietly. "You've had a bad day. Feel what you need to feel. Do what you need to do."

"I just don't understand …"

"What?"

"Why anyone would want to come live here."

Nicky could tell they were going to leave bruises on her arms. They always did, the bigwigs. Her feet scrabbled on gravel as they passed outside the ranch's boundary onto the unpaved road that slashed past it. Poor Marjorie whimpered with every yank of the leash. All over the Ranch, Starchildren were setting off early fireworks: *Bang bang boom!*

Remember, remember, remember, Nicky Starchild chanted to herself, willing and wishing her mind to rewrite the previous half hour. The Sixth Maxim had done its delirious and dirty work like it always did, plus she'd lost track of her camcorder again. Without it, she'd have no way to remind herself of what the Sixth Maxim had deleted.

Franco Starchild, a kind soul who had done terrible deeds, tightened his right fist around her arm, his other arm in a sling.

"Come on, Nicky. You know we all hate doing this."

Bang boom!

Down the road from the ranch stood a wooden structure, about ten square feet wide and high. A remnant of an 1870s coal mine, it bore a single door they kept padlocked most of the time, only opening it for occasions like this. Franco swung it open, the motion drawing forth a breath of coal-scented musk from the depths of the earth. Marjorie lunged away from the smell. Did she know what it meant? Franco pulled a small pistol, one he used only for this task. He raised it to check the chamber, wincing as he jostled his left arm. His right forearm was stained with graphite—Franco was an avid sketcher.

"It's a long way down," he whispered. "Come on. You don't want her to be awake. The echoes will never go away."

Nicky kneeled and hugged Marjorie close. "Maybe there's no bottom."

The other bigwigs shared a look with Franco. *Boom.*

"Why'd you forget to lock that door?" he asked.

"I didn't. I don't even remember what's in that room."

Bang! "None of us do. But Foundation says the dog's tasted blood, so she isn't safe to be around Letta anymore."

Another bigwig, Bayard, motioned for the gun. "We're losing the light. C'mon. I'll do it if she won't."

"No!" Nicky cried. "I'll do it. Just … let me be alone with her."

"Fine," Bayard said, already walking back to the Ranch. "Let's go, guys!"

Franco lingered. "You sure you're okay to do this on your own?"

Nicky nodded.

"Okay," he said. "And keep a watch out. Foundation told the bigwigs we've got a burrower."

Burrower. A spy.

Boom bang!

"I will," she said. He turned to leave. "Franco?"

He stopped, looked over his shoulder.

"Yeah?"

"How's your arm?"

He glanced down. His fingers were gnarled like talons, his knuckles covered with bruises that were fading from deep blue to red and yellow.

"Oh, it's fine. Just banged up some."

"When did you hurt it?"

He frowned, and for a moment, his face stretched, like he was about to cry. Or scream. It passed.

"Dunno. Drank too much roughhousing with the bigwigs, I guess."

"Hope you feel better."

"Thanks."

Franco heard the gunshot a few minutes later from the top of the ranch. Fireworks swallowed the sound.

After a silence, Letta spoke again: "Mommy is so mean sometimes."

The early fireworks punctuated their conversation: *boom boom bang!*

Frith nodded. "Yeah, she can be mean, that's for sure. But she's smart, too. Everyone here has different reasons for wanting to be here."

"Why did you come here? You just got here, right?"

Frith smiled. "Well, I wouldn't say *just*, but it's only been a couple months, yeah. I ... wasn't happy at home. My dad was awful. Maybe the only truly evil person I've ever known. If you think your mom's mean, she's got nothing on my dad. I'd had a bag packed for weeks. I knew I wanted to blitz out as soon as I got the chance. It took forever to work up the nerve. He'd go out for hours at a time, but sometimes he'd come back early. One time he said he was going out all day, but the son of a bitch came back ten minutes later. 'Surprise!' He said. I still think he was testing us. See if we were going to try and leave him."

Bang boom bang!

"We?" Letta asked.

"Me and my mom. Sorry, my mom and I. She always said she wanted to leave, but I knew she never would. So I had to leave her. I was so scared I'd run into him as I was sneaking out. To this day, I still get the fuckin' willies whenever I hear a garage door opening. Because that meant he was home. I left everybody, everything. My name, my family, my whole life. I met Athena at a festival, and she saved me. The moment she looked in my eyes, I knew I'd come home."

"Even though she's scary?"

"Honestly, big girl, her being scary is a big reason why I feel safe here. She may be mean, but she would die to protect all of us. She built all of this from nothing. Brought us all together."

Letta had stopped crying. "Do you have two names?"

"You mean, did I have a name before I came here?" Frith said, standing. "Yeah."

"What was it?"

She smiled. "Cindy. But don't tell anyone."

Part One
Thirty Years Later: Camp Crimson Lagoon

THE CHATTER OF CHILDREN WAS a comforting constant across the camp.

They scampered everywhere, darting from cabin to cabin, some flying kites, others stitching wallets, still others playing games improvised from found props. One child used a switch to aid his efforts in a game of *Tag*, another chucked water balloons, while still another balanced on a piling in a curious game called *Tip Over Lewis*. All of this unfolded against the backdrop of a broad field that sloped down to a lake that sparkled under magic-hour light. The camp took its name from this view: the sun always looked like it was plunging directly into the lake, its rippling reflection like a pool of newly spilled gore.

A banner strung between two oaks read, *WELCOME TO CAMP CRIMSON LAGOON CAMPERS!*

A dozen cabins sat scattered around the grounds, each bearing a different name: WARBLER, RACCOON, ROBIN REDBREAST, and so on. Two counselors, a man and a woman, stood on the porch of the largest cabin, GREAT ELK, leaning against its wood railing and watching the scene with wary eyes. They were both dressed for the August heat—khaki shorts and T-shirts. Hers bore the camp's logo, while his delivered the warning, *WHEN THE HAND GOES UP, THE MOUTH GOES SHUT.*

But while they may have *looked* the part of camp counselors, closer inspection revealed curiosities.

First, the cabin. The door was locked with a numeric keypad, while a pair of small satellite dishes had been mounted to the roof.

Second, although Crimson Lagoon counselors had to pass a fitness test, these two could've passed Navy SEAL BUD/s training. The woman stood six-two and combined an hourglass figure with a bodybuilder's muscle mass. She was a dead-ringer for Brigitte Nielsen in her badass 80s prime: short silver hair, flashing eyes, and a chiseled jaw. Crows feet and smile lines carved up her face.

She had two names, but tonight Winifrith "Frith" Starchild was going by Cindy Hastings.

The man had two inches on the woman along with a similarly outlandish physique, with muscles jumping across his forearms and chest. Except for a dusting of gray along his temples, he could've been a body double for Carl Weathers.

Frith discreetly passed him a flask. "Take a pull, Trax."

The man was Bowden Traxler, but his wife always called him "Trax."

He took a sip and winced, but not at alcohol. The drink was a cocktail of Red Bull and Adderall with a dash of smelling salts. It tasted like antifreeze and was mandatory for everyone on the detachment. He nodded at the lagoon.

"Sun's almost down."

On cue, a pair of older kids ran by, teenage counselors-in-training. Both wore the same Crimson Lagoon uniforms and were in the flush of young love: the girl's long auburn hair glittering in the sun as she trailed a hand to her fling, a lanky boy with a kind face and a knowing grin. They checked in with some of the younger campers before setting their sights on the darkness of the forest beyond.

"Right," Frith said. "Time to sharpen our knives."

She punched in a code and opened the door.

Inside wasn't a woodsy cabin but NORAD.

A half-dozen soldiers sat at several workstations, all tapping into laptops, monitoring readouts, and exchanging hushed words about telemetry coming in from several satellites in geosynchronous orbit. Frith strode across the room to chat with one of the solders, a fit middle-eastern twentysomething, while Traxler stood with the door ajar. He was about to close it when a small child appeared outside.

"Mister Twaxler, I accidentally eated a booger."

Traxler stooped to speak face-to-face. "Oh, that's okay, Billy. Go on and—"

"Are boogers poison?"

"Boogers aren't poison, buddy. They're just gross."

Frith smiled and gave her husband an approving glance. "Honey?"

Traxler nodded and sent little Billy on his way. "Go have fun before the sun sets!" He shut the door and crossed over. "Still want kids?"

"More than ever," she said as they shifted focus to the mission at hand. They flanked a solider who manned a station: a thermal readout displayed bright yellow splotches that danced across a topographical map of the camp. Frith tapped the screen. "There they go."

Traxler nudged the soldier. "How's the perimeter, Siddig?"

"Overwatch is in place around the SZ, sir," he said with a faint English accent. "Subjects have been retreating to the same area every night." He indicated a drop in elevation half a mile west. "This glen right here."

Frith shook her head. "I swear those two are gonna need vitamin-B shots before the summer's out."

"At least he's wrapping it," Traxler said. "Any sign of Blue Hen, Siddig?"

"Not since—wait," Siddig stopped short. "Look."

A new color blossomed onto the monitor, not yellow but purple. It materialized in the middle of the lagoon and tracked a steady course toward the two canoodling kids. Frith and Traxler made eye contact.

"We've got movie sign," she said before addressing the room: "Let's motorvate!"

Their names were Christy and Blake.

They'd met eyes on the first day, when those two enormous counselors had confiscated their electronic devices and invited them to "live like the old days," before iPhones, messages, and constant alerts. They promised a summer's worth of fulfillment—and they'd delivered. The two of them had never met someone like the other— Christy with her easy laugh, Blake with his surprising intellect. The work was challenging and fulfilling, guiding the kids to their little triumphs, consoling them after the death of the camp parakeet, dealing with a pack of bullies who kept challenging the others to a strange game: *Tip Over Lewis.* The long days and endless nights felt like they'd go on forever.

But when the calendar turned over August first, they knew the end was near.

The days were getting shorter, the shadows longer. The temperature dipped into the forties on some nights, making everyone cuddle closer. They'd discovered a secluded glen close to camp where they shared secrets and confessed their love for each other.

They were eighteen and immortal.

On the night the red lightning started, Christy and Blake dashed down a darkening path, hand in hand and hearts racing as the sun set behind them … and cast a figure in silhouette. At first glance, it was a comforting shape: rotund and big-hipped, unmistakably female, with a mop of frizzy hair. The figure advanced at a steady pace, following the kids into the forest, her posture betraying a hostility at odds with her homeliness. She *stalked,* shoulders hunched and head tilted forward. As the kids arrived in the glen, she hovered on the periphery, watching them spread a blanket on a warm tuft of grass. Cicadas hummed underneath their giggling and flirting and small negotiations. Shorts came undone, a belt was unlooped, a shirt pulled over a head to reveal lacy treasures underneath. They rolled over each other, bathed in the scent of grass and honeysuckle and late-summer haze.

On cue, the moon emerged to reveal a gray-haired woman in her sixties or seventies. She looked like your mom, their mom, everyone's mom. Her waistline had expanded over the years to a comfortable spread, while she'd frosted her hair until it shone like silver. About five-foot-three, she wore baggy, stonewashed jeans and a cobalt blue hoodie that read, UNIVERSITY OF DELAWARE FIGHTIN' BLUE HENS. Something reedlike bristled from her back like the stalk of an anglerfish.

About half a click behind, Frith and Traxler gave chase, backed up by a platoon outfitted for otherworldly combat.

Frith halted her men with a raised hand. Traxler pulled up beside her. Everyone's equipment looked like a combination of riot gear and a child's Halloween costume. Some, like Frith, wore special purple glasses, while others wielded billy clubs that glowed purple and spat the occasional red and orange spark. Other men were armed with plain old assault rifles, but they were in the minority.

Traxler prodded his wife and communicated with a silent language only they knew.

What's the plan, boss? He asked.

Look, she said, nodding. *Target acquired.*

Her men maintained perfect noise discipline behind her, silently filling in the space and taking aim at the seemingly harmless old woman on the far side of the glen. Traxler gave the slightest gasp at the sight of a woman he'd only heard about in clippings and briefings.

"My god," he said, audibly this time. "That's Claudia Castle."

Claudia Castle had been the chief counselor at Camp Crimson Lagoon until her son, Lewis, fell from a nearby dam. Her son attended the camp every summer but never quite fit in with the kids or counselors. Local legend held that the other kids had dared Lewis to walk across the dam. An unexpected surge in the river carried him over the side. The counselors, all drunk and partying, didn't even hear about it until the next morning. Lewis Castle's body was never found.

What happened next is also the purview of local legend, the incident having been covered up. The file sat in a cold case locker for decades until someone requested it.

A chill breeze signaled the sun had set. Christy and Blake cuddled closer, unaware of the threat looming in the greenery. It stepped out of the shadows and put a hand to its heart.

"He's calling for you, y'know."

The two teenagers whirled over, clutching each other in alarm. Christy grabbed her top and held it over her chest, while Blake scrabbled for his pants.

"Hey! How long you been standing there, you creep?!"

"I'm no creep, dears," she said with a smile. "I'm Miss Castle. I work here."

Blake stood, holding his pants over his privates, and put himself between Christy and Miss Castle.

"I've been here all summer," he said. "I haven't seen you once."

The old woman was looking at him but also *through* him. She spoke as if addressing a roomful of kindergartners.

"I've already forgiven you. All of you. It wasn't anyone's fault. My little Lew's death. That terrible spill he took. That's what they told me in group. A circle of sympathy, sitting all around me with their sad, stupid little eyes."

Moonlight caught the reed jutting from her back, revealing it to be a longbow. Miss Castle drew it, reached into a quiver and nocked an arrow, the bowstring's creak like a death rattle. Her teeth came together in a grimace. Blake and Christy blanched.

Frith's voice was a siren: *"Claudia Castle! May I have your attention!"*

Silence settled over the scene. Wind whistled. Branches creaked. Leaves rustled. Chests heaved. Frith's men, including Traxler, held fast, weapons at the ready. Frith stepped out from the trees, hand raised.

"My name is Cindy Hastings. May I speak with you?"

Traxler, barely audible: "If she fires that arrow …"

The old woman defused the moment by lowering the bow. Christy cowered behind Blake, both of them gaping at the sight of their supposed counselors strapped like black op ghostbusters. They both wore what looked like Kevlar vests that sprouted sets of wires, both capped with vinyl gauntlets. Orange, purple, and red lights blinked and flickered all across them. Red light from the chestplates' insides cast their faces in spooky shadows. Castle peered at them with bleary eyes, as if through a mist.

"Who is that? Is that Jessica? Aren't you Cabin mother for Robin Redbreast?"

Frith took a tentative step forward, signing to Traxler: *Flank her.* Aloud she said, "That's right, Miss Castle. I'm the cabin mother for Robin Redbreast, and I was hoping we could talk about something."

"Whatever is there to talk about?" she asked, honey-toned.

Christy whispered, "Let's get out of here."

Frith, still smiling, shook her head. "Stay there, Christy, just for a minute. Miss Castle and I are having a talk."

Castle's smile flickered. "Don't talk about me like I'm not here, sweetie."

"No, no, of course, Miss Castle," Frith said, her smile hardening. "It's just that we've been looking all over the camp for you, wouldn't you know, but we couldn't seem to track you down. We're here to help."

Castle nodded. "They all wanted to help me. After it happened. They thought they understood. What it felt like. They thought they could empathize with me, them with their sorry little cups of coffee and powdered doughnuts and their pamphlets, pamphlets, pamphlets—'Don't grieve alone! Cultivate a support network! There are others like you!'"

As her volume increased, the top and bottom halves of her head seem to decouple, behaving independently of each other; her mouth smiled while her eyes bulged, her pupils turning to catlike slits, her whites filling with blood. Blake and Christy held each other.

"Oh, my god," he hissed.

Frith teetered on an inflection point—which was broken by an unexpected visitor.

"Mister Twaxler?"

Everyone spun toward little Billy, who had maintained his own perfect noise discipline all the way from camp. He stood on the edge of the glen, his attention focused on Traxler and not the strange scene unfolding.

"I eated another booger."

Traxler's face fell. "Billy—"

The monster's movements were lightning-fast and feral; she lunged for the teenagers. Christy and Blake screamed. At the same instant, Frith hurled herself across the glen and delivered a crushing punch across the creature's jaw. It landed with a subwoofing *thoom* underscored with staticky crackles and snaps. Castle staggered back as Frith drew herself up to her full height, her bodyarmor fluorescing purple and orange in the dusk. She was about to rush to Billy's aid, but Traxler had already scooped him up. Christy and Blake were stuck in their terrified tableau. Frith's decisionmaking mind processed the possibilities but was interrupted by yet another unexpected development.

Castle ran.

Frith's next orders came in a series of voice-cracking barks to her men:

"*You two, secure them!*" She indicated the teenagers. Two of her men ran over while she took off back toward camp. "The rest of you, follow me—she's headed for the lagoon!"

Her first encounter with a preternatural entity happened in rural Kentucky.

The Bureau had sent her out solo, a Mulder without a Scully, to investigate reports of a goat-headed demon that was tricking kids into walking in front of speeding trains. Frith had busted her ass to join FBI, but the Bureau never seemed to want her around. She was too big, too assertive—just *too much*—so they kicked her upstairs with the weirdos who washed out of Behavioral Science.

Frith was determined to build something from the scraps they gave her, though, or as she put it, "Make lemonade from dogshit."

Her first batch of dogshit lemonade came in those backwoods of Kentucky, loping over undergrowth in the dead of night, her flashlight slashing across the retreating form of a hunchbacked creature running on reverse bowlegs and covered with a layer of kinky hair like steel wool. Its musculature and physiognomy were mostly human, but its head—with horns and a dark black mane—was decidedly not. Either this was an elaborate prank, or she was chasing a half-man, half-goat through the forests between Louisville and Lexington. When she bagged the beast and presented it to her superiors, they freed up funding and assigned her a partner:

Bowden Traxler.

They all stampeded off, Traxler handing off a bewildered Billy to another soldier before he pulled up next to his wife.

"How do you feel?" he asked.

"Like I just got shot with a twelve-gauge, but the Hauberk held! The Faraday tech's good!"

Like her, Traxler was a bit of a misfit. He'd solved some well-known cases but was constantly getting sidetracked with engineering projects. When Frith told him she wanted to build tech that could "trap and hold entities that might see the laws of physics more as guidelines," he dove into the work that would eventually bring about their unusual arsenal—the enclosures, flytraps, and cattleprods, as well as the suit of power armor they'd later wear during the Crimson Lagoon operation.

Traxler nicknamed the armor the Hauberk of Havoc.

Frith nicknamed this new class of technology they'd cultivated "Faraday tech."

Back at camp, her men were ready.

She'd cautioned them that the subject, like her cohort class of preternatural, was stuck in what she called a *djinnlike loop,* a moment from her past that she relived in perpetuity.

"But unlike a level-four free-repeater," Frith briefed her men earlier that week, "she's no ghost. A level *five* free-repeater like Castle has a physical form, as the unlucky citizens of Crimson Lagoon have learned over the years." Frith was referring, of course, to the periodic bursts of violence around the area, always perpetrated on unsuspecting campers, and until this day, unexplained.

So when Claudia Castle came sprinting back through the camp, her men had already erected a wall to guide her into the water. A line of soldiers stood between the cabins and the water, each armed with a glowing purple shield that spat red and orange sparks. A few curious kids and teenagers stood on porchfronts watching the mayhem unfold. Castle loped out of the woods, tripping on undergrowth, and staggered down the beach, her shadow pistoning behind her as she, silhouetted, splashed into the water.

Frith's platoon followed close behind.

When Frith and Traxler, newly engaged, presented their Faraday tech to their superiors at the Bureau, he asked them where they came up with the name. They made eye contact and nodded, both of them waiting for the other to answer before they spoke as one:

"Michael Faraday," Traxler said.

"The time-traveling mad scientist from *Lost,*" Frith said, prompting a playful jibe from her soon-to-be husband.

"Are you kidding?"

But their superior was already smiling. "It's a good name, regardless."

Castle walked with the awkward, arm-swinging gait of someone waist-deep in water. Frith and her platoon emerged from the forest close behind. After ordering them to hold back, Frith followed Castle into the lagoon, Traxler at her elbow, both of their hauberks glowing and crackling. Castle approached a piling that separated the lagoon into two sections. The piling terminated in a crumbling heap that dissolved into the surf. The sun was as blood, the scene a darkroom. Castle laid a hand on the piling, where not half an hour before, kids had been playing *Tip Over Lewis.*

"It was unseasonably warm," Castle said. "Even for the summer. A hot snap, they called it. A glacier broke off thousands of miles north and it all cascaded down." She faced Frith, who eased her way closer, as if approaching a rabid dog.

"It wasn't your fault," Frith said. "It was an accident."

Castle turned, nodding. Water had soaked her clothes black to the chest. "Of course it wasn't my fault. That's what the people in group told me, over and over." Her tone dropped to a pleading wheedle. "They tortured him all summer. Relentless. Just because he was different. They told him they'd stop if he'd climb up here when the tide was up. You watched it happen all summer, and when he needed you most, you abandoned him." Her voice trebled in volume: "You a-*BAN-DONED HIM*. YOU LEFT HIM YOU LEFT HIM YOU LEFT HIM ALONE WHILE YOU DRANK AND LAUGHED AND RUTTED IN THE DARK! LIKE LIFE'S JUST ONE BIG HOOTENANNY!" Her pupils suddenly dilated to full width, her focus locking on Frith and Traxler. She continued: "Well, I'm here to tell you: *life is not a hootenanny.* YOU'LL PAY! YOU'LL ALL PAY!"

Traxler whispered: "So are we building this thing or what, boss?"

"Not yet—we need ocular proof on this." She turned to her men and screamed: "*Lock 'em in!*"

Steel shields rolled down across every window of every cabin across the camp, locking the children safely inside and blocking their view of the horrors to come.

Frith cried, "*Light 'em up!*"

Floodlights blasted the lagoon from every direction; it felt like a Hollywood premiere for Miss Castle, who squinted into the sudden glare.

"You ready?" Frith asked her husband.

"Yep. Deep breath."

Frith called, *"Open fire!"*

They whooped a deep breath and dove underwater, holding hands. Muzzleflashes lit the lagoon overhead in dreamy, splattering ripples, the blasts beating out a drum solo: *thudda-thud-thud-thud.* As planned, her men fired for five seconds and stopped. Frith and Traxler rose from the water, still hand-in-hand. Siddig waded up next to them. He stood silent, awaiting orders.

Castle had collapsed against the piling in a Renaissance portrait of gore: one hand draped over her chest, the other stretched to her side. Gunfire had splayed her open like a dissection project. Flaps of skin hung loosely across her body, giving view to pulsating organ meat. Steam rose from her in a curling cloud. Cicadas buzzed.

Frith and Traxler approached, the former giving her next order in a hushed tone.

"Swap out. Ready the enclosure."

The cadre guarding the cabins ran splashing into the lagoon, arraying themselves around Castle. Frith and Traxler waded back a few paces.

"Just like we practiced at Quantico, guys," he said.

The soldiers deployed their glowing shields, bringing them into contact and kicking off volleys of red-orange sparks and purple dust-light. As they built the enclosure laterally, their shields gradually expanded vertically, closing into a dome over Miss Castle … whose eyelids started to flutter. Some unearthly power hoisted her aloft and set her upright. Shoulders hunched, she bared a set of red fangs, lowering her brow to glare forth with feline-slit eyes. That she was gushing blood from a hundred gunshots didn't faze her.

Frith and Traxler watched from behind, their senses at high alert. He handed her a pair of thick purple rubber gloves that she pulled on—just as Miss Castle attacked. She practically quantum-leaped across the divide, but the instant she made contact with the shields, the reddish-purple barrier repelled her. She flew back, cutting a pair of waves in her wake, her body smoking, her hoodie charred. Snarling, she struggled to her feet … and waited.

Frith exhaled for the first time in a minute.

"Perfect containment field," she said. "Nice job, sweetie."

"Thanks. I'm about thirty percent surprised it worked."

Castle waded forward. "You love him, don't you?" She leered at Traxler. "He's next, dearie, and he won't go well."

Traxler: "Don't listen to her."

"I'm not," she replied before addressing her men: "Lock her in a coffin!"

She'd made her men study bee migration and ballet dancing to master their next move: to shrink the dome. Men deactivated shields in perfect tandem with others who slightly increased the gain on theirs, the dome shivering and flickering smaller and smaller until Miss Castle only had a scant few feet to move. Frith herself joined the lineup, her gloved hands raised and ready.

"Give me a hole."

The soldiers opened a hole in the dome just large enough to admit Frith's arm. Miss Castle seemed to sense what was coming next, because her monstrous appearance instantly evaporated, leaving behind a tired and terribly wounded old woman. She fell to her knees.

"I'm hurt. I'm hurt. God almighty. Call her, please, call my sister. I need to tell her—"

Frith's fist shot through the dome and plunged into Castle's chest.

Purple and red light-dust showered everywhere. Miss Castle's shriek was unhuman—like speaker feedback wailed from every direction—and it stirred Frith's memorybanks. Forbidden images and ideas bobbed to the top of her mind like bloated corpses:

A sunflower.

A scream.

And the Sixth Maxim of Starchild Ranch.

She dismissed the thoughts and focused on the mission: extracting the target from Miss Castle's chest. It felt like pulling a clot of roots from bone-dry earth. Her bicep ballooned as she bared her teeth. Veins popped out across her body. Traxler stood behind her like a baseball catcher.

"Need me?!" he yelled over the racket.

"Yes! Pull!"

He hooked his arms under hers and heaved them both backward. A rending sound, like inch-thick burlap giving way, accompanied the action. Miss Castle's unhuman wail stopped at the same moment. Frith and Traxler fell backward in a splash underlit with a bioluminescent purple. The scene was suddenly silent but for everyone's breathing. The soldiers maintained the Faraday enclosure's integrity, but there was no need; Miss Castle had collapsed. Frith and Traxler rose amid a cloud of purple light-dust.

Frith held their prize. It looked like a beetle carved from pure amethyst. About the size of a toy football, it wriggled in her fist, its six legs flailing. Sparkling purple-quartz sludge coated the creature, which snapped at them with a jaw full of razor-sharp fangs. A five-pointed star shone like neon from the thing's back. Traxler shook his head in disbelief.

"You were right," he said. "This is it?"

Frith nodded. "This is it. Claudia Castle's soul."

At least "soul" was Frith's shorthand for what she'd hypothesized lay within creatures like Miss Castle. Such beasts had taken on many names throughout history. Some were simply serial killers with no preternatural trappings. Others were completely preternatural and could only be seen (or interacted with) in certain locations or certain states of consciousness, like dreams.

Others were like Miss Castle: a hybrid of natural and preternatural.

Frith's task force hunted them all. Her research took her to the dankest corners of the Dark Web and some of the strangest, most remote libraries and holdfasts on earth. A hooded, one-eyed man had first told her about the beetles in the back room of an illegal casino near Fort Munro, Pakistan; only he didn't call it a "beetle."

He called it a "whirligig."

"I need the hat-box!"

Off her order, another pair of soldiers waddled forth carrying a litter that bore a round container about the size of its namesake. They kneeled, setting it in the shallow water before Frith, whose fist ached from holding the whirligig. Traxler donned purple gloves and tapped the box's center-top. Threadlines of light carved the lid into five sections, which the two soldiers opened like leaves. Inside boiled a pool of the same purple-quartz sludge. Purple and red light-dust danced around them. Frith's soldiers drew back from the sight, some of them taking off their helmets to gape, while others muttered prayers or crossed themselves. Frith shoved the whirligig into the hat-box, retracting her hand just as her men slammed the box shut.

Breath fogged before everyone's faces.

Traxler nodded at the hat-box. "You sure this thing's gonna hold?"

She shrugged. "Yeah, of course it—" *SLAM.* The box jolted, everyone jumped. Frith's forearms made an X over her face. She slowly lowered them, sharing a cockeyed grin with her husband. Everyone watched the box like it was about to explode. But it didn't move again.

"Jessica? Is that you, dearie?"

The old woman's voice was tiny, like she was speaking through a tin-can telephone. Frith's soldiers had been maintaining the Faraday enclosure the whole time. None of them moved until Frith gave the all-clear. They nodded and pulled back. As they watched, her bullet wounds completed sealing themselves shut, her blood separating itself from the water as it rushed back into her body. Frith got an impromptu survey of her team's religiosity as muttered prayers circled the group:

"God and sunny Jesus."

"Ya Rab."

"Oy Gutt."

Another guy just said, "Fuck me friendly."

But despite her miraculous healing, Miss Castle was still dying. Fat and healthy weight evaporated from her, her hair falling away in clumps, her skin wrinkling into a neverending network of crannies and crevices.

Frith and Traxler approached, waist-deep in water.

"Jessica?" Miss Castle said. "Jessica? It's Claudia. I'm here to read to you."

"Miss Castle?" Frith said. "Can you hear me?"

"Hear you? Why, of course. Jessica, it's time to read."

"Ma'am? I'm here, but I need you to concentrate. Can you tell me what year it is?"

"Year? Of course. Don't be silly. What year? My goodness. It's 1983."

More prayers from the peanut gallery. Traxler gave a small sigh. Miss Castle continued to deteriorate, her skin translucent enough to give view to her underlying musculature. Once again, memories— forbidden memories—bubbled up in Frith's mind, spurring her to remove a glove and take the old woman's hand. Gentle waves sighed as they broke against them. Frith spoke in a tentative whisper, like she was gently reminding an ailing relative they'd told the same story twice in a row.

"Miss Castle, do you remember … what you did?"

Miss Castle's breath hitched at the question, like she'd been caught off guard. She opened her eyes to reveal a pair of empty sockets. The men murmured in alarm. Miss Castle's grip tightened slightly as she answered.

"Yes. Yes, I remember what I did. All those people I murdered. We started with children, my adherents and I, but it wasn't enough. It was never enough. All those children. Those teenagers. Those naughty teenagers." Her grip was growing tighter. "Those filthy, depraved, decadent, libertine teenage *sluts! And whores! And sluts!* Yes, I remember what I did—*and it wasn't nearly enough!*"

"Frith!" Traxler shouted, pulling her hand free and yanking her upright. They held each other and watched Claudia Castle age a hundred years in a single time-lapsed moment: her skin, blood, and guts all withered to dust and bled into the lakewater in a spreading paddy. Her death rattle was an insane cackle, her final words on this plane of existence a self-proclaimed mission statement.

"Life … is not a … hootenannyyyyy …"

She was gone in a *whoosh*, her remains scattered to the four winds like a mandala upset by an unseen deity's errant sneeze. They say you can still hear her cackles echoing across the lagoon.

Frith and Traxler continued to hold each other. The camp's banner shook loose and fluttered across the water: *WELCOME TO CAMP CRIMSON LAGOON CAMPERS!* Traxler nodded at it.

"You know I want to add a comma to that, right?"

She smiled and kissed him. The soldier Siddig waded closer, taking off his helmet.

"Special agents, when we write up our reports, can we say 'fuck,' as in, 'what the living fuck just happened?'"

Frith and Traxler chuckled. She was about to answer when the first earthquake struck.

The Guildmaster

A METEOROLOGICAL STATION IN SHOAL BAY, Australia, detected the first disturbances, which manifested along the Pacific Rim. A hundred-mile bank of atolls vanished and was replaced by a network of volcanoes that burst from the sea in a matter of seconds.

In east Tennessee, a massive earthquake shook the region and unseamed a new faultline that snaked across the southland like a dark lightning bolt. The earth opened wide and swallowed several small towns across Appalachia.

In Japan, a tsunami smashed the island of Hokkaido in one of the worst humanitarian disasters since the Okushiri earthquake.

Hundreds of such natural disasters followed Claudia Castle's death, most of them within ten minutes of her passing. No two regions were victim to the same calamity, but everyone on the planet saw the red lightning and hot hail.

The hiss of a snake woke him from deep slumber.

He lurched upright with a gasp, his skin tingling in a way it hadn't since he was a young man. He wore a black gown and slept on a wooden cot covered with a single cotton quilt, an extravagance in days past. His pillow was a rectangular stone he'd worn a groove into over his many years of service. He'd shaved his head some years earlier, he couldn't recall when, and grown a white beard that lined a face that looked like it was carved from dried gray cedarwood.

This was the Guildmaster, though his Christian name was Matthias.

He'd been dreaming about the motley cart, as he always did. By royal command, it rolled through London, taking care to crisscross every street and pass by every storefront and home. A statue of bloody sorrow was perched on the cart, lashed upright to a post. He looked like a Renaissance anatomical sketch: his skin had been flayed away—"while he was still most alive and breathing," the criers made a point to say—leaving his muscular system exposed to the elements, his head sundered from his body by executioner's axe and secured to the post with a black-iron stake that had been driven through his mouth.

The King had demanded that all Londoners of good standing watch the cart and pummel its occupant with insults and hurled trash.

No one did. Everyone watched in silence as the poor soul rode past, his body defiled, his crimes known to all, though not a single Londoner of good standing or otherwise, thought his actions to be crimes.

That was seven hundred years ago.

But the snake, Matthias. You heard it in your dream. It hissed and coiled around your ankle.

Matthias scanned the room. Cataracts made his pupils ghostly gray, though he could still see. White stucco and beams of wood composed his personal apartment, which included the cot, a washbasin, a chamber pot, and nothing else. There was no way a snake could've found its way into the Fortress; not unless it could fly, of course. Something caught his attention by the door, a wisp of smoke. He rose, his knees crackling, stepped into his wooden sandals, and shuffled across the room.

A black hole, two inches in diameter, sank into the hardwood floor, radiating enough heat to warm his ankle. Muttering, he kneeled to investigate. A pellet of blood-red ice was melting at the hole's center. The ancient man's eyes grew wide.

"Morningstar be kind," he said.

Something hit the outside of the building, immediately followed by another snakelike hiss. Matthias hurried to the window, which was blocked by a pair of wooden shutters, and threw them wide. The view he revealed, though commonplace to him, would've struck anyone else instantly silent with awe.

The Fortress was hewn from a hectic mix of beige mudbrick and woodfired red. Historians eyeballing the structure would place its era anywhere from circa 1100 to 1350 in the common era. It was roughly octagonal, its eight sides dotted with dozens of smaller outhanging turrets and ramparts. Matthias' apartment was a jetty that swelled from the tenth (and topmost) story. Such buildings can be found all over the world, most of them monasteries or libraries, but the Fortress didn't make its home on land—but sea. Looking down its length would reveal a stone foundation that tapered into an underhang of dried moss and vines.

Below that, nothing.

Matthias the Guildmaster's home floated two hundred feet in the sky. Roiling oceanwaves surrounded it and converged in a mile-wide whirlpool that spun into eternity directly below. It resided at the geographic center of a region whose informal (and to him, risible) name Matthias had heard on the winds in recent memory: the Bermuda Triangle.

What he saw outside confirmed it: the Guildmaster was already out of time.

Black stormclouds loured overhead, their insides blooming with flashes of red light. Crimson lightning bolts blazed into the sea and kicked up hazy gouts of water. Blood-red hail—steaming and white-hot—rained down everywhere, pockmarking the Fortress' exterior.

"It's happened," Matthias whispered, slamming the shutters and turning on a heel. "I've been so blind. My folly had doomed us all." He rushed to his door and flung it open to reveal a massive, ten-story atrium. Wooden guardrails encircled an octagonal room, each floor packed with thousands of ancient books, documents, maps, etchings, reliefs, and other artifacts.

At the center of it all stood the Apparatus.

It was at rest—for now. If someone had sculpted a hundred-foot rainbow eucalyptus from a thousand interweaving bands of wood, stone, and steel, it would've resembled the Apparatus in its inert state. From the bottom floor to the stained-glass ceiling of the Fortress did it stretch, awaiting the call from one of its two masters.

Matthias stepped to the railing and cast a magic spell. Over the millennia, he'd heard this turn of phrase used in all manner of silly or unusual ways, but there was no better name for the act. Casting one required no special props or movements, only concentration and a fluency in ancient Aramaic. He'd been trained to always utter magic phrases in his head, but in his elder years, he'd fallen into the habit of whispering them. Hearing himself speak helped keep his pronunciation tight while reminding himself that he hadn't lost his mind.

The spell, when complete, activated not only the Apparatus but also the Fortress itself. Paneling, tiles, struts, joists and buttresses all shivered to life, springing from their places and folding over and around each other. The Apparatus unfurled in glimmering, sunflower-like radial of wood and steel, its hundreds of leaves and fronds interweaving with the rest of the Fortress like one massive organism, which in a manner of speaking is exactly what it was. The Fortress transformed the Apparatus from its default appearance—that of a tree—into a simulacrum of the earth.

It was a globe.

The cartography would look quaint to modern eyes, with chubby continents frozen somewhere in the 1500s or 1600s. Small apertures shuttered open around the globe, from which slid hundreds of steel emitters that spewed blue flame. Seen from a distance, the pattern of flames would resemble the earth at night: cities smoldered with dozens, while rural areas flickered with only a few. As the globe spun, glowing, spectral letters materialized over each of the flames, bearing strange designations: THE BROWNSVILLE BUTCHER. THE VESUVIO KILLER. DEVIL FACE. MAD DOG. THE TSATI-DAISY SLAUGHTERER. THE SHROPSHIRE SLASHER. THE PHANTOM RIPPER. THE MARIETTA MANGLER. THE MANIAC OF TWIN PALMS. THE CAPRICORN KILLER, and so on.

When the last flame was marked, the Apparatus rumbled, its north pole breaking apart like a wooden eggshell to allow the passage of a four-digit counter that bore ancient glyphs. Simultaneously, the counter ticked down one digit as a flame in eastern Pennsylvania flickered out.

The flame was marked: CLAUDIA CASTLE.

An ear-splitting volley of cursed lightning cast the Fortress' interior in a gloomy pall that was the deep red of an old scab. More hot hail peppered the stained-glass ceiling, which only held because it had been fortified by a ward cast by Matthias' predecessor. An earthquake shook the ocean nearby and triggered a massive wave that smashed into the building and sent plaster and dust raining from the ceiling. Matthias held to the railing with white knuckles, his teeth bared.

He knew this was happening all over the world—and he had to act fast.

Overhead, Claudia Castle's name faded, replaced by a word in Aramaic.

"D'taniynoa," Matthias said, nodding his head as if to say, *Of course.*

But the Apparatus' work wasn't done. Another name, this one

written in English, replaced the Aramaic characters: WINIFRITH STARCHILD. Two more names shimmered to life underneath it, both of them alternating with more Aramaic text.

LETTA STARCHILD.

ATHENA STARCHILD.

"Very well," Matthias said, stopping to note a sight that was, to him, curious. All three names flickered in and out of view before suddenly starting to spin like rollers in a massive slot machine, cycling through all manner of ancient tongues. Matthias watched this unfold without realizing he was no longer alone. A shadow fell over him, cast by the Fortress' other occupant.

The Cartographer.

"That is what they are called, but those are not their names," he said, his voice a rasping rumble that shook the air round them. Matthias clutched his gown closer; his companion's presence always reduced the ambient temperature by twenty degrees.

"No, Cartographer, they aren't." Matthias closed his eyes and cast another magic spell. The Apparatus fell suddenly dark, its marker-flames extinguishing in an instant. With a few more whispered words, Matthias called forth one more flame—a new one—that sprang forth from the southwestern United States. Matthias' eyes rolled to whites, his lips pursing in concentration. The name "Letta Starchild" reconstituted itself into a different one. The Cartographer drew closer, his armored skirt scraping along the hardwood floor.

"Well done, my master."

Matthias nodded an acknowledgment, his focus narrowing around the name.

"So, Emily Miller. It falls to you. But who are you?"

The Lodestar Express

SHE HAD TWO NAMES, BUT today Letta Starchild was going by Emily Miller.

Her stage manager was counting down the final seconds with her fingers: five, four ... and time slowed like it always did, the smells of sawdust and theatrical makeup bringing her back to the plays they performed on the Ranch. She stood just off stage, gripping the curtain, her heartrate increasing as she rehearsed the opening she'd delivered a thousand times.

One more finger ticked down: three.

Lights rose onstage, warming her cheek.

Another finger: two.

The applause sign illuminated, prompting wild cheers.

Last finger: one.

An announcer blared: "Get on your feet and get on board for the woman of the minute, the hour, and your life!" Letta flung the curtain aside and strode onstage, her veneers glittering, as a train whistle hooted and a smoke machine simulated a blast of steam. The set was at once comfy and garish, a Victorian train station by way of Liberace's mansion. A wooden ceiling vaulted over black and white tile floors, all of it against the backdrop of a locomotive engine fashioned from pure crystal. Script letters across its hull read:

THE LODESTAR EXPRESS: HOW TO EXCEL AT EXCELLENCE.

Letta's appearance, the product of a personal trainer recruited from the SEALs, belied her thirty-eight years and had been enhanced with several subtle surgical interventions. She was carved from granite, with flaming red hair that bounced with her jaunty steps. She always wore flats, embracing her diminutive height, which she inherited from her infamous mother. Like Athena, Letta rarely wore skirts, instead opting for a succession of slacks-and-vest combos.

She arrived at the set's focal point, a wide credenza, where she stopped and soaked up applause that continued for a full five minutes. It felt like someone had piped aerosolized cocaine into the audience of The Price is Right. Her acolytes, mostly women, packed the theater, all of them wearing imitations of her outfits or Lodestar Express T-shirts ("LodEx" for long-timers). They held up signs—WE LOVE YOU EMILY! LODEX FOREVER! YOU CHANGED MY LIFE—jumped up and down, and wept openly. Most were locals, but hundreds had made a pilgrimage to Stamford, Connecticut, to see their parasocial mentor and thought leader.

"Welcome aboard the Lodestar Express, carrying you straight to your rightful accomplished destiny!"

More thunderous applause. More mugging for the camera. Another hoot from the train whistle. Stagehands rolled on several shelves bearing the day's snake oil, which were wrapped in powder blue LodEx gift boxes adorned with gold ribbons. Letta opened one on the credenza, peering inside like a child with a Christmas present. She whipped her head back up, eyes closed, biting her lower lip.

"Wait till you see today's bounty, everyone."

She pointed inside the box and produced a bright pink implement that looked like a leatherman branded for Barbie dolls. The audience ooh'ed and aah'ed.

That's when Letta's head split in two.

Metaphorically, that is. The pain was immense and all-encompassing. She clapped both hands to her temples.

A stagehand rushed over. "Emily? Emily, what's wrong? What's— *oh, my god.*"

Emily? Who's that? My name is Letta. Letta Starchild. The pain temporarily wrecked her long-term memory, unmooring her from the moment. Her head was suddenly a harmonically perfect receiver for otherworldly agony.

But as bad as the pain was, it was nothing compared to the visions.

They blazed across her consciousness: maimings, dismemberings, beheadings, entrails splattered in every direction, war crimes and body horror from every chapter of history paraded before her, culminating in a review of an incident she'd read about online: The Massacre at Camp Crimson Lagoon. Claudia Castle—yes, that was her name— never stopped killing, popping back up around the camp every few years to claim a new crop of victims. Until suddenly, it stopped.

Twenty seconds ago.

Somehow, Letta's internal clock registered that Claudia Castle had been finally and definitively killed only moments ago, at the very instant her thermonuclear migraines started. But how could she know such a thing? *Why* would she know such a thing?

She vaguely sensed that something was amiss in the studio. Havoc had erupted. People were pointing and screaming at … something, she didn't know what. Letta swallowed and girded herself to speak through the pain.

"What's … what's happening?"

She spoke to an empty theater, because everyone had already bolted out.

Letta stumbled into the hall, where her stage manager almost bowled her over. Her headset dangled around her neck, her hair a frizzy mess. She was trying to make a call.

"Pick up, pick up, mom, pick up," she said through clenched teeth.

Outside, something howled. All the windows flashed red, while hail battered the building and left steaming pockmarks in the glass. Letta, her eyes narrowed in anguish, grabbed her stage manager's shoulders.

"What's going on?"

"Wave, wave," the young woman said. "This way. It's coming."

She wrested herself from Letta's grasp and sprinted away. Dozens of people—audience members and crew—crowded into the back hallways, ducking into dressing rooms and bracing themselves in doorways. Letta shouldered her way to the end of the hall, where a window stood next to a staircase leading down. *Funny, I don't remember a stairway here,* said a confused voice in her mind. Outside was a gobsmacking view: a hundred-foot wall of water inexorably advancing from the ocean. Cars overturned in its path, while thousands of people fled screaming. Letta backed toward the staircase, reaching out to grip a wrought-iron guardrail that was hot to the touch. That same confused voice from her mind asked, *When did we install wrought-iron?*

The wave had almost reached the studio. She had to move.

And move she did, plunging down the mysterious new stairwell, which clanged under her feet. The light around her quickly extinguished as she descended, the wrought-iron growing hotter and hotter as she ran and ran, farther and farther, the stairs neverending, the building suddenly a thousand stories tall, screams echoing from above as the wave struck and hundreds perished, but still she clambered down, down, down the endless stairs—until they seemed to vanish from underneath her, and she crashed to a cold, hard floor. When she looked up, she realized two things: the headaches had stopped … and she was no longer in the studio.

The place smelled like waterlogged paper.

The studio had hardwood floors, but these were marble. Her fingers left tracks through a layer of dust. She got to her feet, eyes widening. She stood on one of ten mezzanine-balconies that encircled an atrium. Wood railing, inlaid with intricate carvings, lined each floor, each of which held hundreds of bookshelves that overflowed with tens of thousands of volumes. Their pages had swollen with moisture over the years, giving the place its musty smell. It brought her back to her college days when she practically lived in the stacks at the University of Montana. The only sounds were the crash of ocean waves outside and the activity of some kind of massive engine; wood and metal scraped and slid against each other.

Am I dreaming?

"You are not dreaming, Letta Starchild."

The voice emanated from everywhere, a thundering bass that rattled her brains. She spun around in search of its source, but the voice wasn't coming from behind but below. From the center of the atrium rose a horror that sent her senses into a superhot hard freeze. It looked like someone had taken the dismembered remains of a man and reassembled them around a superstructure of boiling black metal.

Or wrought-iron.

It hit her in a flash—the creature was made of the same material as the strange staircase that had brought her here. He—she called it a he, for its appearance approximated that of a man—floated over the railing and came to a silent landing before her. Up close, Letta realized that the creature's metallic innards weren't boiling but *moving.* He was a seven-foot clockwork machine powered by millions of tiny insectoid gears, servos, ratchets, pivots, and coils. What remained of his flayed flesh was pale white, stretched across his body, and held in place by those same seething insectoids. He wore a black armored skirt and a chestplate that bore strange runic symbols. His face was a white mask, his eyes a pair of onyx stones set in his skull. Letta backed away.

"Where am I?" she asked in a strangled whisper.

"Welcome to the Fortress of Maximum Suffering, Letta Starchild. Your initiation begins now."

Part Two
1993: The Starchild Players Present
William Shakespeare's Othello

MEMORIES ARE CURIOUS COUSINS AND strange bedfellows. We live our lives one moment at a time but remember them in totality, so that unrelated incidents are suddenly drawn together due to commonality in theme, sensory perception, or the players involved.

For everyone who emerged from Starchild Ranch unscathed after October 1993, the days preceding that fateful night are both a keystone and a Rosetta Stone for the remainder of their lives.

Nicky Starchild insisted on taping every rehearsal. Her everpresent red light blinked away from the bleachers as they rehearsed. A late-running summer had blessed the region with a warm enough October to perform Athena's all-female *Othello* outdoors for one more encore weekend.

They'd reclaimed an abandoned house located a few miles south of the Ranch and transformed it into a moneymaking destination for concerts and theatrical performances. The house was a rambling, redbrick masterpiece from the seventies with a thatched wooden roof and metal-inlaid windows. They'd renovated the place over six back-breaking weeks in the summer of 1991, installing bleachers and rechristening the property as the Starchild Players Amphitheater.

"Give me the ocular proof!" Celestia, one of the Ranch's few Black members, thundered away at Frith's Iago. It was Tuesday of tech week before Athena's *Othello* made its debut. Thankfully, Athena was a pretty good director. Her first few productions, *Twelfth Night* and *The Winter's Tale,* drew huge crowds. She even staged a serviceable all-female *Waiting for Godot* with Nicky as a manic Lucky, but this year, she decided to venture into tragedy—not for the first time, it turned out.

As the two leading ladies performed, Letta wandered the grounds of the amphitheater. Athena wasn't due to arrive for another hour, so everyone took the opportunity to let their guards down a little.

Around back, someone was playing the new Hole album. Folks were unfolding tables and setting up a grill. (The Ranch served a groovy menu of counterculture vegan and vegetarian food, although Frith insisted on grilling some meat, "for the less-groovy locals who eat normal food.") The sun was setting at the start of a busy Halloween week.

Letta thumbed her place in a book, *The Magician's Nephew*, and strolled along the house's rear, where a door sat ajar. More stagehands were at work inside, the thump of hammers and various chatter floating out. Forbidden memories from the previous July flashed across her mind—chasing Marjorie, Frith following close behind, her mother invoking the Sixth Maxim, and … nothing. She was about to peek inside when a familiar voice spoke behind her:

"This is Nicodemus Starchild of SRTV News, reporting to you live from backstage of the Starchild Players Amphitheater, where future star of stage and screen Letta Starchild is overseeing preparations."

Letta spun around, already smiling. Nicky wore a clashing combo of purple denim (jeans she'd unsuccessfully tried to dye red), a Hawaiian shirt, and a long sleeve T-shirt. She'd pinned her unruly hair back into a bun, but several rebellious ringlets bounced by her ears. She'd pushed thick tortoiseshell glasses onto her head to make way for the camera.

"Letta, what can you tell us about this revolutionary new production of *Othello?*"

"Well, my mom likes doing plays with all girls, which is cool because we don't get to play a lot of these parts."

"An all-female production is certainly unique and somewhat 'boss,' wouldn't you say?"

Nicky made exaggerated air-quotes around the word "boss." She seemed to live on a stage of her own making, constantly clowning around, assuming voices, dropping quips, and generally being a goofball. Letta giggled.

"Yeah, it's pretty boss."

"Is it more boss or bitchin', would ya say?"

Letta's giggles became laughs. "I'm not supposed to say that word."

"So you're saying it's bitchin', then?"

Letta nodded, still laughing. Another person came around the side of the house, a woman with close-cropped black hair wearing jeans and a Buffalo Bills T-shirt. Letta didn't recognize her. Nicky lowered her camera so she could crack wise at the new arrival. "Stop the presses! We have—" her voice caught. Nicky and the strange woman stared at each other in silence for a moment before Letta finally spoke up.

"Can I help you, ma'am? Backstage is only for Starchildren."

The woman kept staring at Nicky. Her eyes jittered. Her jaw flexed. She chewed on silent words before answering.

"Sorry. Lost my way. Is the play tonight?"

Nicky didn't answer, so Letta responded: "Tech rehearsal. We open Halloween night."

The woman broke eye contact with Nicky and looked at Letta. Letta thought she looked familiar but couldn't place her. The woman turned around and left at a brisk jog.

"Thanks. Good luck this weekend!"

Nicky seemed to reactivate. "It's 'break a leg,' if you please!"

But the woman was already gone.

"Who was that?" Letta asked. "Are you two friends?"

Nicky hesitated. "Never seen her before. But back to our interview! Stop the presses, everybody, because we have confirmation of this production's 'bitchin'-ness!'" She leaned in to whisper: "Pretty sure we can make the bulldog edition with that late-breaker." She replaced the camera. "What else can you tell us?"

Behind Letta, some stagehands emerged from the house carrying a series of bizarre props fashioned to resemble natural features: mushrooms, willow trees, shrubbery, and several different kinds of flowers.

Nicky's attention shifted to the props. She zoomed in on a sunflower being carried by Franco Starchild.

"Beg pardon, ladies," said a smiling Franco, his sleeves rolled up to reveal bulging biceps and his trademark graphite-stained forearms. His left hand was out of its sling, but the hint of bruises still stained his knuckles. Franco's stubble was starting to take on streaks of gray, while friendly crow's feet flared from his eyes. Nicky panned to his face and prodded Letta.

"Care to field this interview, Lets?"

Letta assumed a silly baritone: "Yes, this is Letta Starchild of SRTV News interviewing Mister Franco Starchild of the Starchild bigwigs."

"Hi, Lets. What's up?" He always spoke to Letta like another grown-up, which she appreciated.

"These props sure are cool! What can you tell us about them?"

Bayard and some of the other bigwigs filed past with more trees and flowers. Franco's gaze grew distant. He looked at some of the other men, but everyone either shrugged or shook their head.

"Not sure, honestly," Franco said. "Foundation said she stitched them out of …" he trailed off and looked to another bigwig, Stanton, the former college grappler from New Jersey.

"Different kinds of leather, I think?" he said, heading around the house with his arms full of fabricated garden plants.

Franco nodded. "That sounds right. Foundation's been talkin' 'em up for months, saying she's gonna revolutionize the theater."

Stanton, having deposited his cargo, came back around the house: "Yeah, she said she's gonna 'link man and nature in a way heretofore unimagined.' All I know is they're fuckin' heavy!"

He laughed, but no one joined in. Athena stood just behind his shoulder, having somehow materialized backstage. Stanton swallowed his laugh with an audible gulp and pressed his palms together.

"Foundation, forgive me. I didn't mean to mouth off about your incredible—"

"Nicodemus?" Athena said, ignoring Stanton. "Hand over your camera."

"Sorry. Lost my way. Is the play tonight?" Athena watched the video playback through the eyepiece, frowning. They'd stopped the rehearsal. Everyone stood arrayed around Athena, who interrogated them with her owlish eyes.

"I saw a notper leaving the grounds when I arrived, the woman whose voice is caught here." She indicated the camera before addressing Letta and Nicky: "You both saw her?"

They nodded.

"Why didn't you sound an all-hands?" Athena asked her daughter, referring to an "all-hands call," which was Starchild parlance for "emergency."

Letta shrank under her mother's gaze. "I don't know."

Nicky took her hand. "We're putting on a play. Don't people come to see plays?"

"Are you angling for an enhancement, Nicodemus?"

"Foundation …" his voice cracked.

"Do you wish to speak, Franco?"

He swallowed a lump in his throat. "Expunging seems like overkill."

"You look well-rested," she said. Franco grew suddenly still, his face pale. Athena continued: "Memory recountings of your last enhancement are close at hand. What did you do, again? If memory serves, yes, let me see, if memory serves, you stayed awake, standing at attention for … how long was it?"

"Sixty hours, Foundation," he said, barely a whisper.

"Of course. You enjoyed your last enhancement, Franco."

It wasn't a question, and Franco didn't answer.

But Frith did: "It's an open rehearsal, Foundation. So some townie wandered back here. We should've fed 'em a burger and sent them on their way. Might've been a nice opportunity to evangelize. We've got nothing to hide. Right?"

Unease rustled through the crowd at Frith's boldness. Setting sunlight turned Athena's glasses into featureless gold discs.

"Are you the one angling for an enhancement now, Winifrith?"

Frith shrugged. "I'll take the enhancements for this one. You tasked me and the bigwigs to keep eyes alive for notpers, and I dropped the ball."

Athena shook her head slightly. "You're not a bigwig. Women can't be."

Frith hooked her thumb at Franco and the rest of his men. "I built half the set we're playing on, carried most of the big-ticket items, and I bet I could go twelve rounds with any of these lunkheads. No offense, Franco."

A visibly sweating Franco managed a smile. "None taken."

"If security's so important, they could use the help. I'm taking the enhancement for this anyway. Might as well revise the book so I'm a bigwig. And go easy on Nick, huh?"

Athena stared at her in stony silence before turning her focus back to the camera. She replayed the video a few times, frowning, and looked up with a curious smile.

"Rehearsal is canceled. I'm calling an immediate all-hands back at the Inn. Franco, get your sketchbook. We have a burrower among our ranks, and whoever it is knows this woman. Winifrith, you're right. You should be a bigwig, and in fact, tonight will be your first night on duty."

Thirty Years Later: The Successor

LETTA SCREAMED. DARKNESS ENCROACHED ON the periphery of her vision, but she staved off unconsciousness through sheer, terrified will and turned to run; run where, she had no idea, but she sprinted away from the pale horror and around the mezzanine. Something behind her cracked like a lashing whip—no, not one whip but two. The cracks stung her inner ear just as red-hot metal gripped her ankles and yanked her backward. She landed hard on her forearms, crying out, and hurled herself onto her back, crossing her legs in the process. She shrieked at the sight.

A pair of wriggling insectoid tentacles had coiled around her ankles.

The tentacles' origin, naturally, was the black-armored man. They snaked from his midsection, a pair of inky-black pseudopods that clicked and whirred and chittered and chattered. The man gently waved a hand and uncrossed her legs. A flick of his wrist, and two more tentacles lashed around her shoulders, pulling her upright. He pressed a fist into his palm and rotated it. The tentacles retracted, *clank-clank-clank-clank-clank,* dragging her closer and closer, her soles squeaking along the marble. They stopped, leaving about a yard between them. He radiated more heat than an open flame.

He glanced to the side. "This is she?"

Someone else had joined them—a man in a black robe. He drew back his hood to reveal a face so ancient Letta thought he was wearing a mask. His flesh was a patchwork atlas of gray scoring and chapped cracks, his voice a whisper from another era, his accent unplaceable.

"Letta Starchild is thy truename?" He mashed the two words into one: *truename.*

"No, no," she said, tears trailing down her cheeks. "My name's Emily. Emily Miller. I don't know how I got here, I—"

He raised a palm and made a fist, the act cinching her throat shut.

"We haven't the time for subterfuge. It has already begun, the succession. Thou art Letta Starchild, yes?"

She nodded.

The black-armored creature sneered. "Such an unworthy successor, my lord. Let us dispense with the Initiation. Allow me to unskin her instead. Make her my plaything while we watch reality unravel together."

"Silence, my old friend. I haven't stood sentry these seven hundred years only to let Old Father's dream end under my watch." He addressed Letta: "I am Matthias, the Guildmaster. We must exchange words. I am going to instruct the Cartographer to release you, and thou wilt not run."

She nodded. The tentacles released their grip, leaving angry red rings around her ankles and shoulders. Letta winced and looked around, catching her breath.

"Listen, I'd like to be able to tell my friends about this dream after I wake up, so now that 'thou' knows my truename, how about you tell me what's happening?"

The old man's smirk rearranged a hundred archipelagos of wrinkled flesh around his mouth.

"We don't speak with the familiar any more, do we?" he asked.

"Come again?"

"'Thou' is the familiar form. You use it with children."

"Or your inferiors," said the Cartographer, emitting a rhythmic rumble.

Letta pointed at him. "Did that … *thing* just chuckle at me?"

"Indeed he did, but time is short. Letta Starchild, it is time for me to show you the universe." The skeletal remains of a hand emerged from his robe. "Come with me."

She took his hand, and the world shimmered apart into a million shining shards.

Frith had once shown Letta a "photo" of the universe. The scientists who'd composited the image had colored the universe's mass—its stars, galaxies, and dust—a bright purple, everything else a darker blue. The end result was a crosslike shape, its single vertex situated just center-left of frame, with thousands of smaller glowing struts offshooting from the largest structure. Scientists would later compare the image to that of a single neuron. When she took the old man's hand, Letta learned one of the first secrets of the universe:

That picture was dead-ass wrong.

As she telescoped out a zillion settings to the edge of all observable reality, what came into view wasn't a cross but a series of roughly concentric ellipses.

Matthias' voice echoed in her mind: "Behold the totality. The breadth. The all. What do you see?"

Shimmering "above" and "below" the sea of concentric ellipses were a pair of Aurora Borealises, one the bright blue of the earthen sky, the other the smoldering red of embers.

Letta thought and spoke at once: "I" *I* "see" *see* "balance" *balance.*

"Yes. Balance. Maintaining order within the universe has been my charge for the last seven hundred years. All across the universe, two great armies wage war for Old Father's dream, but they rarely meet in open combat. No, we fight our war using Old Father's greatest dream, humanity, as our proxy."

Across the "roof" of the universe, the sky-blue Borealis, an army of silhouettes stood forth, all of them clad in various forms of armor from across the ages: Roman Centurion, Terra Cotta, Aztec, medieval. Some bore wings, others not.

Matthias continued: "The forces of Heaven believe they act through benevolent means, serving as sources of inspiration, whispering secrets from Old Father himself, all in an effort to win their hearts and minds."

The old man gave a wry chuckle.

Matthias guided her attention down to the universe's "floor," the glimmering red Borealis, where another army of silhouettes appeared, this one a parade of horrors. All manner of monsters and serial killers shimmered into view, some of them armed with melee weapons—axes, pikes, chainsaws, butcher knives, meat cleavers—while others were creatures from mythology and folklore—a lumbering grotesque with a Jack O'lantern's head; another a tall, slender man with willowy arms; still others bore the trappings of deviltry: horns, wings, cloven feet.

"Our forces, the forces of the Downfalls, wage war with temptation, vice, hedonism, guile, resent, rage. For the last seven hundred years, I have been Guildmaster of Lord Morningstar's Menagerie. These warriors prey on the sinful, marking the days on the calendar with their kills. The demons tempt them, the Menagerie slaughters them, and then the demons torture them in a grand cycle of suffering. The realms of hell are one massive furnace underlying all of existence, and we keep it burning."

R-r-r-ummmmble! Suddenly a quake that spanned planets, solar systems, galaxies, everything shook all of reality. Below, the so-called furnace's light flickered on and off. Simultaneously, one of the silhouettes vanished, that of a portly middle-aged woman. Letta recognized her instantly.

"Claudia Castle," she said. "Someone finally killed her."

"Indeed. Which is why you're now here. The Menagerie's numbers must always equal or exceed that holy sum of six hundred and sixty-six. When Claudia Castle perished, the number fell below that threshold for the first time in seven hundred years. When I replaced my predecessor."

Snap.

She had returned. The pan-galactic view, the sense of peace, and the ecstasy of ego-death all rushed away from her. She was once again surrounded by the musk of a million ancient tomes, her body subject to the rigors of headaches, bad backs, and bum knees.

"I'm here to replace you," she said.

Matthias nodded. "Precisely, but to do so, you must complete an initiation, a sacred ritual to prove your worth and your mettle."

"I get that now. But why me?"

The old man beckoned her to the railing. Earlier, she'd heard what sounded like a giant machine; now she saw its source. A thousand-thousand wooden and steel panels, struts, leaves, and lattices all interlocked and interwove like a massive mechanical lotus as conceived by Leonardo DaVinci, expanded upon by Jules Verne, and constructed by Frank Lloyd Wright at the height of an acid bender. The library's bottom floor exploded, thrusting skyward a massive column that blossomed into an intricate, thousand-piece puzzle that assembled itself into a globe that spanned the atrium's width. Matthias raised his hands in exaltation.

"This is the Apparatus, and when Claudia Castle died, it delivered unto us thy name, Letta Starchild. It listens to the stream of whispers that runs between the realms of pleasure and torment, eavesdropping on Lord Morningstar's dreams and Old Father's nightmares. It chose you—chose you to claim your mantle of leadership through one of two challenges."

"One of two? I get a choice?"

"Your free will is part of the ritual. You must elect to undertake the initiation, or all will cease to exist."

"Seems fair and totally sensible. What are they, the challenges?"

"The first is the most difficult, the most treacherous. You must replenish the ranks of the Menagerie by retrieving the soul of a fallen killer from Hell itself."

Letta's senses, still swimming from her trip to the edge of existence, had started to fade back into focus. She touched the wooden railing, felt its age and grain, the slight prick of a splinter. Outside, lightning splashed bloody light against the windows. Hot hail peppered the Fortress in an endless, rapid drumbeat. And the smells. Letta had once toured a five-hundred-year-old adobe in Baja, Mexico, and Matthias' scent brought her back to it. The Cartographer, whatever he was, radiated an industrial-technological aroma and warmth, like a steady-state machine that was running hot.

Letta had never had a waking dream, not once, and she didn't believe this was one.

"Okay. I haven't the faintest notion of how I would accomplish such an objective, but tell me more. Who would I be retrieving? That Miss Castle person?"

"No," Matthias said. "The Apparatus revealed the identity of your 'objective' as well. It is a woman, one of the most infamous killers of the last century. Her name of record is Susanna Josephine Miller, but her truename is Athena Starchild. Your mother."

She was screaming before she realized it. Her words poured forth in a torrent of invective, her face turning instantly red. She balled her fists and advanced on Matthias, her posture aggressive enough to draw a protective tentacle out of the Cartographer that whirred and clicked between them. Some moments later, maybe a few seconds, Letta could hear herself again:

"How dare you, how fucking *DARE* you say her name to me, that monster, that fucking *BITCH!* Spent half my life climbing out from under her poisoned fucking shadow after what she did, to me and my friends, my sisters, Frith and Franco and Nicky, oh poor sweet Nicky, my family, my fucking *FAMILY HOW DARE YOU!*"

Her last words echoed through the library: *dare you … dare you … dare you …*

Matthias took a breath. "I suppose you'll be electing for the second of the two rites, then."

Letta, still winded from her outburst, nodded. It only took Matthias a few seconds to describe the second rite.

It took her even less time to decide between the two.

"Fuck you. You son of a bitch. Fine. I'll do it. I'll get my mom out of Hell. I'd sooner do that than—fuck you. Fine. I'll do it. But I'll need help, and I need the two of you to swear something to me …"

The Catalyst

THEY PARKED IN THE POURING rain and jumped out, one of them wrapping a raincoat over her head, the other opening an umbrella that the wind immediately inverted and carried away. Emptyhanded, he wrapped an arm around his beloved as they splashed across their apartment complex's parking lot. They stopped under the entrance overhang and turned around.

"My god," Traxler said.

"I know," Frith said.

Inclement weather had grounded all flights, forcing them to drive back from Pennsylvania. They'd returned to Washington DC with the intention of stopping by the FBI, but flooding downtown sent them home with a trunk full of evidence along with Frith's "Faraday" ghostbusting equipment. Red lightning had punctuated their two-hour crawl home through bumper-to-bumper traffic. The hail had abated for the time being, but the rain hadn't stopped since the moment Frith killed Claudia Castle. She fumbled in her fannypack for their keycard.

"They're saying this is happening everywhere," she said, but Traxler didn't answer. Something had caught his eye. Across the parking lot, a head came bobbing into view, rising up from behind a car. He thought of mime routines where they pretended to climb a flight of stairs. The bobbing figure rounded the car and approached. About five-foot-three, it was a woman wearing slacks, vest, and a blouse. She might've looked stylish except for the addition of hooded monk's robe that kicked up more dust than a construction site, despite the downpour. Even with her face shaded, Traxler clocked her. When he spoke, his voice dropped a full octave.

"Winifrith, we've got movie sign."

Frith dropped the access card and stood shoulder-to-shoulder with her husband. She'd rehearsed this moment so many times over the years, but of course when the time came, she wasn't ready. Her heart raced, her mind went blank. What came out was borderline word salad.

"It's our distress code, that thing Trax was saying, distress code. In case of danger, break glass."

Letta lowered her hood. "Are you having a stroke?"

A smile threatened to break Frith's defensive posture, but she stifled it.

"What are you doing here?"

Letta took a step forward, which brought Traxler out from the overhang.

"That's far enough," he said, rain pelting him.

Letta twined her fingers and smiled. "You must be Bowden!" She could've been socializing at a backyard cookout.

"Yeah," he said.

"Your name's come across my transom so many times, did you know that? Stories of your derring-do. 'The Hero of Atlanta,' they called you. But that one—" (she indicated Frith) "—has never mentioned you to me, not once. It defies belief, I say."

"That's enough!" Frith shouted, reaching out to pull Traxler back under the overhang. Across the parking lot, her peripheral vision detected a new arrival: a tall, dark figure who seemed to stand up from behind a car. Ignoring the figure for now, she addressed Letta: "What do you want, Letta?"

"Can I come inside?"

Competing impulses warred within Frith. Her instinct to be polite was screaming, *Your old friend is drenched, invite her inside!* But her better judgment was calmly telling her that after all these years, Letta had returned to wheedle her way back into her life. After Halloween 1993, they'd crossed paths one last time in 2011 and hadn't spoken since.

"Honey?" It was Traxler, touching her arm. Frith gave her head a small shake.

"Right, listen, Letta, you can't—"

"No, not her," he said, jerking his chin at the parking lot. "Who's that?"

The dark figure had somehow crossed the lot without her noticing. He was about six-six, with stark white skin, no hair, and the blackest eyes she'd ever seen. A duster-length, double-breasted pea coat enshrouded the man, who seemed to float instead of walk, his very presence repelling the rain. If Murnau's Nosferatu looked a little more like Ryan Gosling, he could've been this guy. Letta startled slightly upon noticing him; was she not expecting him there? His eyes bore into Frith, who fidgeted under his gaze, her reaction split between *turned on* and *creeped out*. She gave a nervous chuckle.

"Who's Lurch?"

Letta exchanged a series of whispers with her tall companion, the rain pelting them both. Frith was sure she heard him hiss something about "boiling barbed wire," whatever that meant. She waited, sensing her husband's growing unease.

"Let's get inside, sweets," he mumbled.

"*Wait!*" Letta said, holding up a palm. "Give me five minutes. That's all I ask."

"Five minutes for what?"

"It has connection and many parallels with what you do for the Bureau."

Frith crossed her arms. "How would *you* know what I do for the Bureau?"

"I read message boards."

"So?"

"You understand me well enough," Letta said. "You know about the *un*known, and that's the help I need—someone who's seen what goes bump in the night."

"I don't know what any of that means, Lets. I really don't."

The tall man, Lurch, bared his teeth. "Time is waning, Successor."

Frith exhaled harshly. "Who *is* this asshole?"

Lurch's eyes flashed. *"Thou shalt meter thy tone—"*

Letta cut him off: *"He* … is my Uncle Dick."

The rain eased up. Silence fell like a portcullis between the two women. In the distance, car horns bleated as the storm pitter-pattered its way to a pause. The tall man's nostrils were still flaring from his outburst. Letta's cheeks flushed red. Traxler was on high alert, his body temperature rising in concert with his temper. Steam rose off everyone present. Violence was in the air.

Until Frith started crying.

She hadn't planned or anticipated it, but nevertheless it came, a quiet outburst of grief. Her face clenched, her shoulders shook. She covered her eyes. Letta leaned forward.

"Frith?"

"What is this?" She gestured vaguely. "What are you doing? Is this some kind of prank? Getting back at me for throwing you out of my apartment? The stuff they're saying online, it's terrifying. It's like the world's ending."

"That's because it might be. It's why I need your help."

The two women, old friends who had fallen out, stared at each other. For a few seconds, Letta thought she'd won her over. Frith's eyes, normally icy green, warmed a few perceptible degrees … right before she shook her head and pointed toward an unseen exit.

"Fuck off, Letta. I'm not interested."

Two things happened at once: Frith turned to go inside—and Richard *activated*. He unhinged his jaw and let loose with a window-rattling, subwoofing wail:

"ENOUGH!"

Frith and Traxler gave each other a look and smirked.

Traxler: "What the fuck's your problem, man?"

Richard rose into the air, his innards boiling forth with his dark host of millions of insectoids that slashed through his flesh, pulling and stretching it back to its original monstrous appearance. Black armor slid out of his skin like breeding dragon scales. His eyes filled with black ink. Frith and Traxler cowered, eyes gogging.

But they only cowered for a moment.

Traxler jerked his chin, yelled "Left!" and sprinted toward their car, dodging under one of Richard's insectoid tentacles. Frith broke to the right, but incredibly, Letta—all five foot three inches of her—tackled her. They both splashed to the pavement. Across the parking lot, metal groaned and something beeped. A car's trunk stood open, and Traxler emerged from behind it wearing a glowing red-purple backpack and wielding some kind of cattleprod that spat red and orange sparks. Richard moved so fast he looked like a smear of black watercolor, hurling himself directly at Traxler, who jabbed the cattleprod into his seething midsection, propelling the ancient hell-lord back a few yards.

Letta jumped to her feet and screamed: "Take us back to the Fortress, now!"

The creature—named Richard, apparently—nodded in acknowledgment and unfurled a black tentacle that it whiplashed into the earth. There it remained tethered as the creature spun in a circle and unseamed a massive ring around them. The newly cut disc of earth teetered like a dancing dinner plate before crumbling to bits underneath them and revealing a bottomless pit whose walls teemed with black insects.

Frith screamed.

They all plummeted into a darkness that shrieked with the chatter of those endless insectoid creatures, the pit narrowing into a cone that funneled them toward a light below. She slammed into the wall, readying herself to fight off a swarm of insects, but instead of attacking, they took gentle hold of her and lowered her through the opening, eventually setting her upright amidst a sight that made Frith feel like she was dreaming.

But Frith knew she wasn't.

Richard lowered them to the hardwood floor, his palms upraised like an orchestra conductor at the end of a movement. A wriggling webbing of insectoids connected them to the ceiling, where the passage back to their apartment parking lot stood open, giving view to a sky thick with clouds and lightning. With a flick of his wrist, Richard retracted his tentacles. Everyone tottered for a moment before Traxler rushed to his wife and hugged her.

"Oh, my god! Baby, are you okay?"

"I'm fine, I'm fine." She released her husband and looked around, slowly pacing along the railing. Her eyes widened at the sight of the Apparatus, but she kept calm. She gripped her wrist behind her back, like she was out for a Sunday stroll. Richard floated closer, but Traxler raised his weapon.

"Back! Stay back, motherfucker! I don't know if I'm dreaming or what, but you're not laying a single … tentacle or bug or *whatever* on her!"

Richard raised a palm. "I'd advise you to move several feet to your left."

Before anyone could ask why, pavement and earth rained from above. They all looked, gasped, and leaped out of the way just as Frith and Traxler's car came crashing down through the passage.

Traxler tackled Frith out of the way just as several square yards of street, grass, and dirt came sliding through the passage under the weight of their Prius, which smashed through the wooden railing and teetered on the brink of falling before Richard's dark host—his insectoid innards—lifted it upright. He floated closer and wrenched its trunk open to reveal more of Frith and Traxler's unusual weaponry.

Traxler: "Hey! What're you doing?"

Ignoring him, Richard beckoned to Matthias, said: "These have learned to channel the iridescent ether." He indicated the trunk full of devices.

Matthias gave an approving nod, asked: "Some manner of enchanted armory they've fashioned?"

Frith stepped closer. "Watch it! That stuff's expensive!"

Richard channeled a network of insectoid pseudopods to lift one of the flytrap devices out of the trunk.

"Where is its wick?"

Traxler, holding close to Frith, seemed to understand. "You mean, how do you turn on the light?"

"Yes."

"I can show you, but I don't think you want to be holding it when its wick is lit, man."

Richard nodded and set the device before Traxler, saying: "Demonstrate for me."

Traxler checked in with Frith, who nodded. "Don't have much choice."

"Right," he said, unstrapping the cattleprod backpack and pulling on the flytrap. He flicked a switch on its barrel, activating a network of blue, red, and orange lights across the device. Red energy radiated and orange sparks spat from the bear-trap-like jaw that capped its end. Richard squinted and raised a hand to shield himself, as if someone had just opened a raging furnace. He floated back a few feet, a smile spreading across his starkwhite face.

"Remarkable. Hast thou ever crossed swords with a Prelate Centurion?"

Letta hissed, "*Formal* form, asshole."

His lips curled, but Richard obeyed: "*Have you* ever crossed swords with a Prelate Centurion?"

"Not sure what that is," Traxler said.

"An angel, basically?" Frith said.

The old man nodded his approval. "I can see why you've called on her to assist in your initiation, Successor."

Frith sighed. "Okay, enough. Tell us everything, starting with this initiation."

Letta explained it all in less than two minutes, using the plainest language at hand. She dispensed with formalities, pithy jokes about the absurdity of the situation, and told Frith and Traxler the unvarnished truth: She had to travel among the several realms of hell to revive her own mother, damned to eternal torment.

"Or else … the universe explodes?" Frith asked, checking the door. Matthias had let the three of them into a small study chamber adorned with a few illuminating easels and stools. The door stood open but empty.

"Yeah. All of existence will unravel. Every universe, every reality goes away. Nothing'll be left."

Frith and Traxler leaned back, absorbing the information.

"And you came to me because of my work. My experience with preternaturals."

"Yeah, something like that," Letta said, avoiding eye contact. "All your knowledge, plus I think your ghostbusting tech'll come in handy."

"Yeah, Lurch and Obi-Wan seemed pretty impressed with it," Frith said with a hard gaze. "Is there … any *other* reason why you came to get me?"

Letta was silent. For a moment, she considered telling Frith the truth.

Earlier, Matthias explained the *second* rite of succession.

"The second rite is much simpler. It requires only that you sacrifice two souls. The first would be your nearest and truest comrade. In modern parlance, your best friend. The second would be the Catalyst, or the person who triggered this cataclysm. In this case, the woman Cindy Hastings, better known to you as Frith Starchild."

After hearing this, Letta agreed to attempt the first Rite of Succession, revealing to Matthias and Richard an unusual coincidence: the Catalyst and her best friend were one and the same person.

"I need the two of you to swear something to me," she said. "I need to ask Frith for her help, but you cannot tell her about the second Rite. Ever."

Letta was about to tell Frith the truth when Richard interrupted them:

"You're still living on primate time, you sons of Adam and Daughters of Eve. We must move quickly before the powers of Heaven strike against us. Come. I will explain to you the nature of the Rite of Succession."

They followed him out, Letta still holding onto her secret: She could end all of this by killing Frith.

The Five Infernal Downfalls

THE FORTRESS SPRANG TO LIFE all around them. Richard and Matthias led the way around the atrium. Letta, Frith, and Traxler marveled at how the massive globe disassembled itself, its million myriad parts retracting and ratcheting apart and sliding together into five roughly elliptoid discs, two about ten feet in diameter, the others about two feet. Richard waved a hand, his innards hurling forth hundreds of black tentacles that formed connecting bridges among the wooden discs. More activity followed, as thousands of slivers, slices, blocks, and bricks of metal and wood slid, shinked, clicked, and clacked together into hundreds more discs, all of these much smaller—some only a few inches across. More tentacles connected these discs to the others like a glittering network of spiderwebs. Letta and Frith both sat, while Traxler remained standing.

Matthias nodded his approval. "Well done, Cartographer. This is somewhat comprehensible to mortal minds."

"What're we looking at?" Traxler asked.

"It's a map," Letta said, standing. "Right?"

"It is," Richard said. "Behold, the many realms of the Infernal Downfalls."

Letta and Frith shared a look of unease, the latter asking: "The what?"

"The Infernal Downfalls."

Traxler sensed their disquiet and asked: "What's wrong?"

Letta crossed her arms. "That's one of the maxims." To Traxler, she added: "Mom's—well, *Athena's* seven maxims for the ranch. That's from number three: 'Secrets are forever. Protect them even into the afterworld and past all the Infernal Downfalls.'"

"I remember that," Traxler said. "Huh. That *is* weird."

Frith: "Richard, where could she have heard that phrase?"

Richard: "It is laid down in much of the ancient infernal literatures. But time is short."

"Got it," Letta said. "So are these downfalls a bunch of circles, like in Dante?"

Richard nodded. "Indeed, your Dante Alighieri had some perception of Old Father's dreams and the iridescent ether when he wrote his *Inferno,* but the structure of damnation is far more complex. It is borne of belief and changes with the times. When he wrote his masterwork, he was able to peer into only nine of the Downfalls, but at the time, there were actually some nine hundred million."

Matthias said: "But for the purposes of your initiation, Letta

Starchild, you'll need only concern yourself with a half-dozen or so of the Downfalls. Richard, if you would?"

The Cartographer waved his hands across the map, dismissing thousands of the smaller discs and bringing five into focus. Letta noted to herself how his gestures recalled those used on smartphones.

"There are five primary Infernal Downfalls, each of them arising from what humans would call 'sins': rapaciousness, acedism, fraud, barbarism, and vainglory. The world's various faiths all feed into these realms. Most of the damned have no knowledge that they've been put in the same hell as someone from a different faith, if they're conscious at all."

"What are the five realms called?" Frith asked.

"The realm of fraud is known as Stercorebubulus. The apathetic and slothful are condemned to Phaegor. The downfalls of—"

"Wait, what was that one name, the one for Fraud?"

"Stercorebubulus. It is an ancient tongue of your own, mortal—"

"Yeah, Founda—I mean, *Athena* made us all study Latin back in the day. There's an actual, official hell that's called *Bullshit?*"

Richard's answer was a silent glare.

Matthias cleared his throat. "That is an imperfect translation, but … yes."

Letta and Frith shared the briefest of smiles, and for a moment, Letta felt like she was back in the TV room at the Ranch, ready to pop in *The Great Train Robbery* and waste a Sunday afternoon.

Smiling, Letta said, "Okay, noted. Go on."

Richard continued: "The downfalls of avarice and rapaciousness will send a soul screaming to the pits of Balaam. The largest and most treacherous of the realms, Leviathan, is home to all the unrequited rage of existence. Much to your good fortune, you needn't traverse its boundless plains of chaos. But your mother, O Successor, will not be found in any of these realms. For her immeasurable pride in the betrayal of her charges, the several voices of the iridescent ether, singing in honor of the great pretender, Old Father, summoned her soul to the realm of Asmo. Dante saw this realm with clear eyes: the deepest circle of hell is still reserved for mutineers, as well as the prideful, whose sin goes hand in glove with betrayal. The vainglorious find their torment in the depths of Asmo, which cannot be reached directly."

"How do we reach it, then?" Letta asked.

Richard extended his arms and made a diamond with his thumbs and forefingers before bringing his hands apart. The gesture "zoomed in" on three of the hell domains, while the others shrank into the background. Matthias helped with the show, too, muttering words that magically generated an array of tiny silver letters over the wood-metal elliptoid discs.

The three domains highlighted were Stercorebubulus, Balaam, and Asmo.

Letta's mind wandered to the past again, back to *The Great Train Robbery*. As Richard continued—he waved away the insectoid bridges that linked the domains to illustrate something—she stood and absently wandered to the railing, recalling a scene from the movie. Sean Connery had to run along the top of a speeding train to reach an armored car that carried millions of pounds-sterling in gold.

Richard continued: "Asmo is only accessible via one of two ways. The first lies so far afield from the realm of possibility, I shan't mention it, leaving the second: a passageway from the realm of Balaam."

"Fair enough," Letta said. "So how do we get to Balaam?"

"Balaam is only accessible from the Downfall of dishonestly, Stercorebubulus."

"Let me guess—we're not going to be able to just *walk* from Bullshit to Balaam?"

Richard's jaw flexed against his tight-stretched skin. "That is a sacrilegious moniker for what is a thrice-glorious realm of eternal torment, but no, you won't."

Once Sean Connery reached the armored car, he had to unlock a strongbox holding the gold with a set of four keys. Letta's eyes glittered as she replayed the scene in her mind.

"So what's the trick for getting into Balaam?" she asked. "Do we just say, 'Open Sesame'? Or are we going to need a key?"

Richard pivoted on his dark host to face her. "You are correct. Though it isn't a key but a key*stone*." He zoomed in on Stercorebubulus, and as he did, the wood disc came alive: buildings and bridges and dark rivers all bristled into relief across the disc. Letta started smiling a curious smile, which drew Frith's attention. She rose and crossed over, bending down to whisper:

"What's going on in that brain of yours?"

Letta shushed her. "Don't bother me. I'm thinking."

Richard zoomed in further and brought a structure into focus that looked like a Gothic cathedral hewn from millions of sorrowful faces. Its entranceway was a vaulted arch—one that was missing its keystone. Letta thought of the strongbox from *The Great Train Robbery* and its four keyholes. Connery and his partner, Donald Sutherland, had purloined two of the keys through trickery, while the other two they'd been forced to duplicate with wax molds. Richard indicated the dark cathedral.

"From the endless ranks of perjurers and deceivers arises the Temple of Dissemble. Every thousand years, the very grounds of Stercorebubulus vomit forth the faces, souls, and beating hearts of the most perfidious, the most fraudulent to compose its nave, buttresses, and columns. All those who visit its mournful spires are greeted by the Arch of Scourgian Mists. For lo these last several hundred years has its keystone been missing. When complete, the Arch will open a gateway into Balaam, but the keystone itself will be well-nigh impossible to retrieve …"

Letta had turned away from the map, her hands clasped before her, her smile widening. A chuckle rose from her chest and quickly grew into a laugh. Richard, who was in the middle of explaining something called an "infernal vault," stopped talking. Matthias frowned and leaned to the side to get a better look, and Traxler stood, crossing closer to the two women, the smaller of which was openly laughing now. Frith twined her fingers before her, the patient posture of a caregiver dealing with someone unwell.

"Hey big girl, wanna clue us in on what you're laughing about?"

Letta faced them and assumed a goofy British accent. "All you ever think about is money."

Traxler glanced back and forth between them. "What're you two—"

A voice boomed: "You would do well to mark her."

All three of them jolted. Richard had somehow snuck up behind them. He regarded Letta with a look of grudging approval. Frith still hadn't put it together.

"Can someone please tell me what's going on?"

Richard lowered himself to the ground, his armor scraping the hardwood. When he addressed Letta, he was almost smiling: "There are keys."

Letta nodded. "And a vault."

"The act must be carried out under cover of darkness, away from the watchful eyes of state."

Frith frowned a moment before making the connection. She smiled and quoted back to Letta: "All anyone *ever* thinks about is money."

Traxler raised a hand. "I'm still a step behind here."

Frith nodded to Letta, who pointed at the map.

"This is a heist."

Part Three

MEMORIES ARE CURIOUS COUSINS AND strange bedfellows. We live our lives one moment at a time but remember them in totality. In our elder years, if we're lucky enough to live that long, our memories converge and collect, like a delta of tributaries into an ocean.

All are one, intermingling and coexisting.

1993: After Tech Rehearsal

FRANCO ALWAYS HAD GRAPHITE STAINS on his forearms.

They'd returned to the Ranch, a heavy atmosphere of paranoia attending the move, which happened in the chill of a new night. Athena had ordered the bigwigs to re-open a small storage room under the main house. They hesitated at first, though they didn't know why.

"Isn't there something ... important under there, Foundation?" Stanton asked.

"Of course there isn't," their leader said in a singsong tone. "There never has been."

Stanton nodded, fumbling with his keyring, and let them in. Athena entered first, pulling a cord to illuminate a single cone of light. Everyone else huddled on the small pathway, peering into the room. Frith had instinctively taken Letta under guard when Athena gave the order to break rehearsal. They stood near the back of the group, the younger bouncing on the balls of her feet.

"What's going on, Frith? Are we in trouble?"

"No, big girl, we're fine. Foundation's just taking some extra precautions."

"Who was that girl Nicky saw?" Letta asked at full volume, prompting a *shush* from Frith loud enough to draw attention. A few Starchildren looked their way before glancing over at Nicky, who hovered on the edge of the crowd, clutching her camcorder in both hands, her head hung. They couldn't see her face, but Frith could imagine how she felt.

Athena's voice was a foghorn: "Where is Franc-*ooooooo?*"

"Here, Foundation, here!" He came running from the topmost crest of the property, an 11x17 sketchbook in hand, his pocket packed with an array of multicolored pencils. The group parted, making a path for him into the storage room. He paused at the head of the small path, next to Nicky.

"Nick?" he said, barely a whisper.

She looked up, lips trembling, and nodded. He offered his hand. She took it, and they walked together into the room, stepping over the threshold. Athena nodded at the wall, where dozens of collapsible chairs stood folded.

"We'll need five chairs set up. Now."

"Five?" Franco said. "But isn't it just—"

"Winifrith, Letta? Come in, please. The rest of you, begone."

They closed the door, shutting themselves into a space redolent with sawdust and other reeks they couldn't place—sickly sweet stenches that reminded Frith of rotten chicken and moldy vegetables. The five of them sat in a circle. Franco was fussing with his sketchbook, flipping through pages, pausing occasionally to admire his work, considering and rejecting several pencils until he settled on one, which he sharpened with a pocket knife, wincing as his gnarled left hand curled around it. He puffed on its end, folded his leg into a makeshift easel, and looked up.

Right into the smiling face of Athena.

Her words were kind but her tone brittle. She spoke barely above a whisper: "Francis, you're one of the most talented of my Starchildren. I want you to know that. When time's in tune, I want you to take all the time you need to organize and fuss over all your wonderful trappings and implements of art. Please. But when it's out of joint, it's incumbent on you to *be … more … mindful.*"

Franco's face turned bright red. "Sorry, Foundation."

She leaned over, touching his knee. "Please don't apologize! There's no need! Though for wasting everyone's time, you'll be due an enhancement that'll be carried out tonight. But don't trouble yourself—it won't be a large one. Or small. Not small, not large. But it will exist."

He nodded, actually seeming relieved. "Should we get going?"

"Quite so. Nicodemus?"

Nicky looked up, her face streaked with tears. "Yeah?"

"Tell Francis what the woman looked like and, Letta?"

"Yes?" she whispered.

"Act as overwatch to this endeavor. Observe Nicky's behaviors and actions, monitor her descriptions, and not only help her if she can't remember something, but help *us*—and myself, your mother and matriarch—by alerting us if she should fail to disclose, or perhaps *modify,* any details. Do you understand?"

Letta nodded. Frith squeezed her hand. Athena sat back and twined her fingers.

"Nicky, begin."

Her descriptions came in halting spurts. She gave Franco the basics fairly quickly: it was a woman, about five-seven, with short black hair who wore a sports T-shirt (Letta corrected her to say it was "the one with the Buffalo"), and jeans. After that, her memory seemed to evade her. The room's air grew heavier and heavier with their collected heat. Frith had to fight the urge to gag. Over thirty agonizing minutes, she described a woman with high cheekbones, blue eyes, and a beauty mark under the right corner of her lip. Franco sketched away, graphite stains migrating up his forearm to the heel of his hand, all while Athena's impatience grew. Finally, just as Nicky was in the middle of describing the woman's ears, Athena slapped Franco's sketchbook, her hand closing into a fist that crumpled the paper.

"Enough of this subterfuge, Nicodemus."

Nicky's face stretched in fear. "I don't know what you mean, Foundation. I'm telling the truth. Letta, tell her."

"That's what she looked like, mom." Off Athena's steely stare, Letta amended: "Mother."

Franco's sketch paper *pop-pop-popped* off its coiled wire binding as Athena tore it away. She uncrumpled it and brandished the likeness in Nicky's face.

"I'll have you in enhancements for the next month if you don't come righteous with me, young lady. Tell us the truth."

Nicky sat back, holding up her palms. "That's what she looked like!"

"You simply described *yourself* to Francis, Nicodemus! Own it and be done with this charade!"

Frith raised her hand. "Foundation, can I see that?" She indicated the sketch. Athena handed it over. Frith examined it, frowning, before looking at Franco. "Didn't you and Stanton run into this woman in town?"

She returned the sketch to Franco, who nodded. "I'll be darned. You're right."

Athena's eyes narrowed. "Is this true, Winifrith, or are you trying to cover for Nicodemus?"

Franco answered: "No, she's right. Dang, can't believe I didn't notice it before." He stood and opened the door, admitting a gust of cold night air that, although welcome, made everyone shiver. "Yo! Stanny! Get in here!" Hurrying footsteps preceded Stanton's breathless entrance. He stood in the doorway, leaning in slightly, waiting to be invited.

"Hey, what's up?" He dipped his head in lieu of tipping a hat: "Foundation. How can I help?"

Franco showed him the sketch. "You remember this lady?"

Stanton lingered in the doorway until Athena nodded. He stepped in and took up the sketch, his eyes widening.

"Yeah. Aw, man. We saw this broa—this woman the other day down at the store."

Athena sprang out of her seat and marched past Stanton out the door.

"The general store closes in one hour. Get the truck."

Athena stood with Frith, Letta, Nicky, Franco, and Stanton at the general store's counter. Business was mostly done for the evening, and the incursion of a passel of folks from "that cult up the hill" sent the remaining patrons hurrying out. The store was a Norman Rockwell painting: wood paneling and floors, a hand-painted picture window that proclaimed WEST OF ADIRONDACK GENERAL STORE, and shelf upon shelf of dry goods, hardware, and cleaning supplies. A liquor cabinet stood locked behind the counter. The store's owner, a burly, white-haired woman named Cherry, shook her head at the sketch.

"Never seen her, but—" she called: "Tyler?"

Her assistant, a lanky teenager from Syracuse who spent his weekends working the store, emerged from the back holding a clipboard. "What's up, Cher?" He pronounced it like the pop star's name.

"You ever see this lady in here?"

She handed over the sketch. He hadn't looked at it more than a second before he nodded.

"Yeah, that's the J-school lady."

Everyone stared at him. Athena spoke in measured tones: "Her name is Jay School?"

"Journalism," Nicky said under her breath.

Tyler shook his head, chuckling. "Nah, that's right. *Journalism* school, sorry about that. My buddy Jason's studying broadcast over at Syracuse, and she's an adjunct there. Brought her in from New York."

"She's a reporter?"

"Yeah. For one of those Sunday night shows. *Twenty-Twenty* or whatever."

Athena snatched the sketch back and led everyone out of the store.

Outside, they regrouped at the pickup truck. Red brick and wood-fronted buildings composed an idyllic town square. The sole streetlamp clicked on a few yards away. A waning moon crested over the treeline. Athena indicated the sketch.

"This woman? She? We must find out who she is, what her intentions are, where she's staying, and most important, what she knows." She addressed Franco: "Prepare to canvas the town, and be ready to deal with—"

A new voice broke in: "I know her name."

They turned. It was Tyler, the teenager from the store. He'd put on a light coat, a bookbag slung over his shoulder. On instinct, Franco, Stanton, and Frith arrayed themselves between Tyler and the weaker folk, Athena, Nicky, and Letta. Stanton crossed his arms.

"You gonna tell us, kid?"

Tyler shrugged, glancing up the mountain. "Can I visit sometime?"

Athena shouldered her way past the bigwigs.

"Of course, child. All are welcome at Starchild Ranch. Are you interested in learning the Seven Maxims?"

"I guess. I heard it was like one big orgy up there. Is that true?"

Moonlight turned Athena's glasses to gold-glowing discs. "Whatever you want to be true *is* true at the Ranch, child. Was it Tyler? She named you as Tyler?"

He nodded. "Yeah. When can I come up?"

"Why don't you come up tonight?"

The bigwigs rustled. Frith leaned forward. "We're kinda busy tonight, Foundation."

"We never too busy to welcome a new acolyte to the fold. But first, Tyler, can you tell us her name?"

"Sure. Ashley Culpepper. I think she's staying at the Super 8 in Gloversville."

Nicky gasped slightly. Athena's glasses flashed in the moonlight again. She flicked away a lock of hair and took Tyler's hands with a sigh. Even in the darkness, they could sense him blush. Athena radiated a strange, alluring mix of motherly and seductive in times like these.

Times where she was roping in another convert.

Her hand glided up his forearm, drawing gooseflesh.

He looked like he was sinking in quicksand but excited to find out what was under the surface. His expression was a combination of turned-on and fascinated and frightened, which of course was the point; those three feelings emanated from the same wellspring, and Athena was always tapping the trio in tandem to enthrall her adherents. She caressed his cheek with her thumb.

"Who do you despise?"

Tyler's brow knit. "Despise? Well … there's someone, but I'm afraid to tell anyone about it."

She drew him into a sudden embrace, her head nestled under

his chin, their bodies pressed together. Athena always wore formless clothes, but she had a womanly figure. She guided Tyler's arms around her and helped him settle into a deep hug. The teenage boy burst into tears.

"You're safe, you're safe," Athena said. "We're returning home, everyone, with a new friend. Tyler, meet your new family. Oh, and Winifrith? Tyler's going to be in the play. I'm carving out a special role *just* for him, in gratitude for his help in finding Miss Culpepper—who we'll be visiting very, very soon."

"Copy that, Foundation," Frith said, a flash of white in her peripheral vision drawing her attention. Nicky bore a wolfish grin, her teeth bared.

Is she up to something? Frith thought.

Thirty Years Later: Assembling the Team

Y OU SAID I COULD CARRY out the initiation however I wanted, right?"

Matthias nodded. "The precepts as laid down are broad and vague. Their vagueness might be the only thing working in your favor, Successor."

"Then we're going to need more help, and a lot of it."

Richard once again rose on a dark cloud. "I had yet to finish my explanation of the Infernal Downfalls."

"We can finish it later. First, we need to line up the most basic-y basics for a good heist. Frith, Bowden, what do you think?"

"Uh, maybe you should keep calling me Traxler," he said quietly, crossing his arms.

Letta noted the pushback with a small salute: "Got it and will do, sir yes sir." His brow creased, but he remained silent. Frith stepped over and laid a gentle hand on his shoulder.

"We could use your insight, sweets," she said, then addressed Letta: "One of the first things we lock down before going in the field is comms."

Letta snapped her fingers. "Of course! We need a Nameless Numberhead Guy."

Matthias, who'd been listening with growing confusion, spoke up:

"What means that curious metaphor, Successor?"

Frith smiled at Letta. "You're thinking of *Ocean's Eleven,* right? The Eddie Jemison part?" Letta nodded, and Frith turned to Matthias, saying: "There are these things called movies, right? And one of our favorites—well, *two* of our favorites—are the remake of *Ocean's Eleven* and another movie called *Schizopolis.* This guy named Eddie Jemison was in both, and—"

Traxler stifled a smile. "Baby, I actually *know* what you're trying to say, and you're not making any sense."

Frith and Letta looked at each other … and giggled. Letta felt like they were getting gently scolded in class or maybe at a sleepover. A lingering warmth for her old friend once again welled up in her—until she remembered that night in 2011, the last time she and Frith had spoken before the current crisis. Frith seemed to sense the change in Letta's mood and responded accordingly; she banished her smile and propped her arms akimbo.

"So we'll need a comms person," she said, turning to Richard. "That means *communications.*"

"I gathered," he said dryly, flames flaring within his inesectoid innards.

Letta: "And if this heist is anything like the ones in *Ocean's Eleven, Twelve, Thirteen* or *Eight*—"

"Or the original," Traxler said.

"Or the original," Letta agreed. "We might need to split up."

Frith: "Richard, is it possible to communicate between hells?"

"It is possible, but only to a select few of the Menagerie."

Frith: "Let me guess—are there members of this Menagerie who can … I'm not sure how to put it. Who can see into other dimensions or universes?"

Richard cocked an eyebrow. "There are."

"Great. Follow-up question: When we *dream,* are we seeing into other realities?"

Richard's expression warmed. "You are."

Letta and Traxler spoke simultaneously: "We are?!"

Frith shrugged. "That theory's been bouncing around the message boards for as long as I've been hunting preternaturals. Nice to have it confirmed." She addressed Richard: "By any chance, is there a member of the Menagerie who possesses incredible power in the dream realm? A creature who haunts people's nightmares and feeds on their terror?"

"I will surmise you already know the answer."

"Yeah, I do."

Letta leaned over. "Well, don't keep us in suspense. Who is it?"

"All in good time," Frith said. "Richard, I need you to open one of your portals."

"As you command, Frith Starchild. Where shall the portal lead?"

"Stillwater, Louisiana."

Number Twenty-Seven

ABOUT TWENTY MILES FROM NEW Orleans, the twenty-seventh Stillwater Death was poised to unfold.

Inside Stillwater Mental Hospital's rec room, a seventeen-year-old girl sat in a foldout chair, her foot tapping a rapid-fire drumbeat, her hair slicked to her head with sweat. A half dozen empty coffee cups sat on a nearby table alongside some empty NoDoz wrappers. Her dishplate-wide eyes glanced around the room, trembly and twitchy, her fellow inmates all fixated on various activities—games, books, the TV—and not her. They'd already learned to ignore her chanted litany, which had been going on since she arrived:

"Don't fall asleep, don't fall asleep, don't fall asleep …"

Her name was Hester Mackenzie.

She white-knuckle gripped an iPhone, which was playing a podcast. A bouncy voice that would've been familiar to Frith and Letta spoke:

"Hey there, Nicksters! Welcome to episode eight hundred ninety-seven of Nicky Nicodemus's *Believe it … Or Maybe TOTALLY Believe it?* podcast. This week we're looking for proof of the afterlife—again!"

Hester had voluntarily committed herself the previous week after her friends started dropping off one by one. The first death happened at a kegger they'd thrown in the backwoods off Interstate Fifty-Five. She'd been dangling her legs off the bed of a pickup when her friend Lenore wandered off into the darkness, muttering to herself.

She'd been reciting a limerick:

There once was a girl called Lenore.

Who truthfully, was a sick whore.

While having a fuck,
She forgot to duck,
And her head rolled onto the floor.

They'd lost track of her near the woods. A farmer driving a tractor spotted her body the next day, stripped naked, cleaned, exsanguinated … and beheaded. They found her head a few miles away, impaled on the spike of a wrought-iron fence that surrounded an abandoned bayou manor. Hester's friend James went next, followed by Avery and Lisa, all of them vanishing into the night before being found cut to pieces.

They called these violent ends the "Stillwater Deaths."

After Lisa died, Hester's parents checked her into Stillwater Mental Hospital. She hadn't slept in a week and was repeatedly listening to the same episode of a certain podcast. This episode recounted the exploits of a legendary killer reputed to haunt—and *hunt*—the greater New Orleans region:

He was known only as Francois.

Said Nicky: "No one knows where he came from. Supposedly he immigrated to the States sometime in the eighteen hundreds, possibly from France or the Catalonian coast. He picked up English in the French Quarter and worked running a water taxi up the thousands of rivers that cut into the Louisiana mainland. That's where he racked up his first few victims, and if you're weak in the tummy-tum-tum, Nicksters, you might wanna tune out now, but here's where it gets graphic … and weird.

"Francois terrorized children and teenagers all across the Gulf Coast, ranging as far as Panama City and Corpus Christi. The list of victims grew and grew until one day, a group of parents convened at a Biloxi casino, got boozed up, tracked him down, and—as one of the mothers said—'sent his soul to hell.' The report of Francois' death shocked the state and was even featured on *Twenty-Twenty*."

But according to Nicky Nicodemus, that didn't stop him.

"Reports of Francois appearing in people's dreams started turning up on the early BBS systems back in the nineties, followed by more detailed accounts in the aughts and teens. Nicksters, you know I've been searching for proof of the afterlife for years, and with Francois, we may very well have uncovered it. We believe that he's been harvesting souls from the great beyond—"

Hester paused the podcast, her ears pricking up.

Someone in the rec room was singing a limerick.

"There was a young girl named Hester …"

Hester jumped to her feet just as something *banged* to the floor next to her. She staggered back a step before realizing she'd dropped her iPhone. A nervous laugh slipped out of her. Crouching down, she scooped it up, searching the room for the source of the singing. Nothing was moving. For a moment, she figured she'd been imagining things, but then she realized that *absolutely nothing was moving.*

Her fellow patients were perfectly still.

The TV image had stopped in the middle of a news story about the bizarre weather.

Dustmotes hung in the air.

FRRR-ZZZKKT! Hester clapped her hands to her ears. The earbuds flared to life at an impossibly high volume, blasting Nicky's continuing narration: "They call him the Specter of Stillwater, Louisiana. Could heee beeee ze proof of ze afterworld vee've been looking for?" Nicky's accent melted from American to French. Hester snatched out the buds and slung them to the floor, where they bounced once, then froze mid-air, emitting wet, slurpy laughter before a new voice spoke:

"Bon soir, mamzelle vingt-sept."

He was right over her shoulder. She whipped around to find no one there. She backed up, moving toward the TV, from which Nicky's voice suddenly barked:

"They say he wears a bowler hat and has eyes of smoke."

Hester spun around to find only her fellow patients, all of them still as statues.

"Where are you?!"

Shink.

It thudded without a bounce, like someone had dropped a steel weight. Hester skittered back a step, thinking she'd dropped her iPhone again. She kneeled to retrieve it, seeing that yes, she'd dropped it, but she couldn't pick it back up because her still-twitching right hand was wrapped around it. She slowly stood, too terrified to raise her arm but knowing she had to.

It didn't even hurt, the cut was so clean.

Steam rose from the severed cross-section. A doctor would've recognized the cut as having come just below the ulnar styloid process. Some kind of heat source had cauterized her wrist, but she couldn't feel it. She couldn't feel anything.

All she could do was listen … and watch.

He rose, as if on an elevator, from their center. He looked dapper, wearing a vest, cravat, spats, and a bowler hat, all of them various shades of burgundy or a bloody-dark purple. His skin was an inter-latticing network of burns and scars, and his face was just as Nicky—and the local legends—described: empty eye-sockets that spumed endless billows of smoke. He stopped rising, jostling slightly as if he actually *was* on some kind of enchanted lift, and ripped off a series of tap-dance moves, muttering the tempo to himself:

"Five, six, seven, eight …" *Five, seeks, sevuhn, aight …*

He ended with a flourish, producing a straight razor from his lapel. With a flick of his wrist, he expanded it into a fan of blades, freshly stained with blood—*her* blood. Hester backed away, looking for help, only to discover that every window and door were bricked shut.

Francois tap-danced closer and closer, his scarred skin bubbling like griddling cheese, melting down his face and unveiling his skull, which ballooned to twice, thrice, four times its size until it bobbed on his neck, comically huge, the rest of his body quickly following suit as he lurched forward onto all fours as his skin sprouted thousands of prickly, quill-like hairs, a tail snaking out of his backside, his smoky eyes flaring red from within.

As he transformed into a giant rat, Francois extended his unholy reach into Hester's mind and made her sing the limerick he'd personally written for her:

There was a young girl named Hester,
Whose stepfather was such a—

The voice—a new one to Hester's ears—boomed from below:

"FRANCOIS, MASTER OF DREAMS, MUSTER TO THE FORTRESS OF MAXIMUM SUFFERING."

This terrible voice seemed to enchant the white floor underneath Francois. Blackness bled through the tiles, their surface bubbling and seething and creeping over Francois' four rat feet like boiling pitch. He returned to his original form with an audible *snap* and re-sheathed his fan of blades. With a shrug, he tipped his bowler to Hester.

"Stay of execution. Until next we meet, mamzelle, adieu."

The black oozed farther and farther up his legs, and Hester realized it wasn't pitch but an interlocking network of millions of bizarre black bugs that swarmed him from head to toe before savagely yanking him down through the floor. A puff of black insects marked his exit.

The TV crackled back to life: *"Unusual weather reports continue to pour in from around the world ..."*

Everything had restarted, as if some godly force had un-paused reality. The other patients went back to talking or murmuring or playing games or reading books. Trembling, Hester raised her right arm.

Her hand was back.

The Master of Dreams

HE ERUPTED FROM THE FLOOR like a fountain of black blood, and even though they'd all seen sketches of his likeness, Frith, Letta, and Traxler still yelped when they saw him in the preternatural flesh. Francois didn't mark them at first, his ire directly solely at Matthias, who he approached while smacking insectoids off his sleeves.

"Lord Matthias, what on earth! You robbed me of my dinner!" *Dee-narr.* "My transmogrification was a—" (he kissed his fingertips) "—work of art: a giant, bloody-eyed rat, and for an encore, I was to swallow her feet first. Her screams of agony would've sustained my dark soul for a century. Or perhaps a few days." Finally, he noticed they weren't alone and tipped his hat to Richard: "Great Cartographer, I am honored." His smoking black eyes turned toward the three newcomers. "What is this, an intervention? Believe me when I say I haven't hit rock bottom yet."

Richard began: "Master of Dreams, the Rite of Succession has begun."

Francois touched his heart in mock surprise. "*The* Rite of Succession? To replace Lord Matthias?"

"There is no other such rite."

Richard looked at Letta and appeared to take a deep breath.

Did he roll his eyes? she thought, stifling a smile.

Matthias indicated Letta. "Meet the Successor, Letta Starchild."

"No. *Her?*" Francois's eye sockets narrowed at Letta. "She is so … little." *Leetle.*

Letta put her hands on her hips. "Well, at least I'm not a fucking pederast demon with smokestacks for eyes." She jerked her chin at Frith. "She told us all about you."

Francois scoffed at the insult and addressed Matthias: "Who fell? Was it that coward from Cincinnati, the doctor with the pickaxe? What was he called?"

"Doctor Pickaxe," Matthias said. "No, he's still slaughtering his way along the Ohio River."

"Then it must have been the Lunatic of Ten Thousand Lakes!"

"Neither was it he. It was Claudia Castle."

Francois fell silent and doffed his bowler. "The Scourge of Camp Crimson Lagoon. A true titan. And *this* is your replacement?" he said, sneering at Letta. "Who *is* she?"

"The daughter of Athena Starchild. And her friend, the strapping redwood, is the Catalyst."

Francois teleported next to Frith and swept her hand into a kiss.

"*Mam'zellllle!* Well done! I suppose it *would* take a bull like you to fell the great Claudia Castle."

"Christ," Frith said, snatching her hand away.

Traxler's nostrils flared. "How about I put your head through that fucking wall?"

Francois made a sound like someone pumping a rusty bellows. Laughter.

"Awww, the loving couple. Husband and wife, are you? Your great heifer has already doomed the universe to eternal chaos and destruction!" His tongue extended from his mouth and forked. He hissed. "Is that a fear of snakes I sense in you, mamzelle? Perhaps I can slake my lust on *that.*"

Matthias heaved a heavy sigh. "Richard, if you please?"

"Gladly," said Richard, who clenched his fingers like talons and whipped a tentacle around Francois's arms, binding him in place.

"*Putain!*"

Richard beckoned to Traxler, who was still wearing his flytrap backpack.

"Master Traxler, would you be so kind as to demonstrate that remarkable device for Monsieur Francois?"

"Say no more," Traxler said, firing up the flytrap with a *whump*. He approached Francois, who hissed and bared his fangs. The trap's fanged maw spat orange sparks that sizzled along his brow. Francois whipped his head back and forth, emitting a canine cry of anguish.

"What is this?! What is that thing?!"

Frith: "It's a Faraday Flytrap, and it's specifically designed to handle bad guys like you."

Matthias: "So you should mind your tongue, Francois. We're not dreaming. You're vulnerable here."

"You would tell these mortals my weakness?!"

"Letta Starchild is the Successor. She is about to learn *all* of your weaknesses. But to matters: Francois, we need your help—and your magic."

Keeping Francois bound to a chair like a preternatural Hannibal Lecter, Richard directed his attention to the massive map that floated in the atrium's center. With a wave of his hand, the map zoomed out from the Downfalls of Stercorebubulus, Balaam, and Asmo, bringing the totality of hell into view. On the far side of the view floated one tiny hell domain, about the size of a golf ball. Richard executed a few arcane gestures and zoomed in on it.

"This is the lynchpin to the whole 'heist,' as you so cannily named it, Letta Starchild: this is an infernal vault."

Francois chuckled. "You'll never breach an infernal vault. It's impossible."

Richard raised a clawed hand and slowly closed it into a fist. In tandem, his insectoids closed tighter and tighter around Francois, who grunted in pain.

"You … wouldn't dare … expunge me, Cartographer," said the Master of Dreams. "You need my magic to carry out your little task."

Letta stepped forward. "Richard? Mister Mallestratos? Can you stop expunging him or whatever? I think he's right."

Francois whooped. "Of course I'm right. Not only do you need my magic; you also can't risk another death among the Menagerie. Another death means you'd have to find *another* creature to take my place."

The three newcomers looked to Matthias and Richard.

"Is that right?" Frith asked.

The old wizard nodded. "This is a precarious time. As long as the Menagerie's number hovers under the unholy sum, not only is all of earthly existence destabilized, all of *damnation* has become unstable, as well."

"Define 'unstable,'" Traxler asked.

"When the Menagerie's ranks fall below six-hundred-sixty-six, a great upheaval unseats Lord Morningstar from his throne. Leviathan swells to omegafold its size, calling to it and absorbing all the unchanneled and untrammeled rage of existence. The damned become jailmasters, overthrowing their demonguard. All of it—all of this chaos—is merely preamble to the dissolution of existence, which can only be forestalled by one of the Rites of—"

"Dogs and cats, living together," Letta interrupted. "We get it." She addressed Francois: "So … you know you're going to help us, right?"

A gleeful Francois answered: "Exister ou ne pas exister, it matters not to me, mon petit Successeur. I accept payment in the form of cash, credit, and delicious young souls."

"You want us to bring you kids to … do whatever it is you do to them?"

"Vraiment."

Letta, Frith, and Traxler looked at each other.

"I'm not doing it," Frith said.

Letta sighed. "Frith, the *good* outcome of this clusterfuck is that I'd take over an army of murderers, right? Existence itself is on the line. We're gonna have to *cross* a few before this is done."

"You sound like somebody we used to know," Frith said. Letta had no comeback.

"I'll do it," Traxler said.

Frith crossed her arms. "You'll do what? Kidnap someone for him to kill?"

Traxler ignored her and addressed Francois: "Got any particular flavors you like? Young, old, black, white?"

"Yes, oui, yes, and oui," Francois said.

"Deal," Traxler said. "You get started on the comms center here, and I'll work with the big guy to track down some … uh, souls for you." He indicated Richard, who nodded in acknowledgment and addressed Francois.

"This is agreeable to you, Master of Dreams?"

He wriggled in his seat and made an *mmm-mm* sound. "I'll need to feed before sunrise."

"Understood," Richard said. "I shall release you now."

Richard the Cartographer unwound his tentacles and floated slowly backward. Traxler kept a bead on the Master of Dreams, who winked at them with his smoking eyes before turning his attention to the map. He wheeled around and made a "call me" gesture with his thumb and forefinger.

"Premier: you will need to confabulate. Do the mortals all have—what is the name—cellular telephones?"

Letta, Frith, and Traxler all nodded and produced their mobile phones.

"Genial," Francois said, summoning them to his hand.

"Hey!" Letta said.

Fire flickered and crackled within Francois's sockets. He bared his fangs in a cheshire-rictus grin and waved his hand over the four devices, which all flashed a sudden bright red before shooting back across the room into their owner's hands. He bowed.

"Your devices are now linked, mortals. You may simply, how do you say, *phone home* to any of your little friends while you traverse the Infernal Downfalls."

Letta examined her phone. "It doesn't look any different."

The ridge over one of Francois's sockets rose; he was cocking a nonexistent eyebrow.

"Are you certain?"

Her phone shook as two whirlpool-like apertures swirled open on its face. Unseen hands scooped and sculpted one of the apertures—where her ear would go—into a grotesque, desiccated mouth, while the other aperture puckered into what was unmistakably an asshole. Her face curled in revulsion just as the mouth's chapped lips parted to release a slithering red tongue.

"Ew! What the fuck?!"

Francois's voice fritzed forth: "How about a nice wet *bese,* mamzelle?"

Frith raised her phone. "Do they *have* to do that shit?"

"Of course they don't," Francois's voice warbled from a newly formed beak that lanced out of her phone. "But isn't it so much more fun this way?"

Traxler, unruffled, was already inserting his earbuds. "I'll just wear these."

Francois chuckled.

Traxler yelped and snatched out the buds, which had both turned to little penises. "Christ, man!"

Thunder rumbled and red lightning cast the room in a scablike pall.

"Enough of this foolishness," Matthias said. "Master of Dreams, please proceed. I suspect the Eyes of Argus shall be enchantment enough to give you view into the Downfalls."

"The Eyes of Argus?" Frith asked.

Richard answered: "It is a spell of seeing, Frith Starchild."

"Ahh, yes it is, O Cartographer," Francois said. "But in order for me to see into the Downfalls, I will need to sound the greater morpheal depths of anyone who wishes to receive my help."

Frith blanched. "What does that mean?"

Traxler: "He wants access to our subconscious."

"Fuck that," Letta said. "We'll figure out another way."

Francois's eye sockets started to emit smoky puffs in a sort of tune: *puff-puff-puff, puff-puff-puff.* His feet followed suit: *tap-tap-tap, tap-tap-tap—SHINK.* Red lightning flashed off his blades as he brought them out and slashed the air one, two, three, four times, each time unseaming a glimmering opening in reality itself. The openings were "blank" for now, showing only blinding white light. Using his fan, Francois *flicked* the four gashes over to the quartet Infernal Downfalls in play: Stercorebubulus (aka Bullshit), Balaam, Phaegor, and Asmo. He spun on a heel and stowed his fan.

"As of now, my windows are blank, empty, *raza.* If you grant me access to your depths, your very minds will act as antennae, as receivers, as broadcasting nodes for my magic. I mean no disrespect to his eminence, the Great Cartographer, but although he can provide you with an overview of hell itself, only I can provide you with detailed maps and schematics of the hazards you will face, as well as your *telebavardes*." He indicated the cellphones, chuckling at his portmanteau. "Without me, you haven't a—what is the expression? A snowball's chance in hell?"

Richard: "Unless, of course, you're referring to the outer wastelands of Leviathan, where the damned sensation of temperature drops from several million to a scant degree above your absolute zero, in which case, a snowball would fare quite well."

Everyone gave him a funny look. "Thanks, Dick," Letta said.

The Cartographer cleared his throat. "Successor, you must decide. Will you allow the Master of Dreams access to your subconscious?"

"What happens if we do?" she asked. "Will you, like, pull us into some nightmare realm and swallow us whole?"

Francois held up a hand, shaking his head. "You would only be vulnerable to my charms … if you fell asleep."

The temperature seemed to drop several degrees.

Traxler mumbled. "We *have* to sleep. How long is this gonna take? A day or a week?"

Frith: "Matthias, how long did your hell heist take?"

Matthias' brow darkened. "I did not elect for that rite, so I do not know."

Frith frowned. "How many of these Rites are there?"

Someone chuckled. Someone *new*, his voice digitized. Everyone stirred.

Traxler held up his phone. "That sound came from here." He addressed Francois: "Was that you? Are you fucking with us?"

Francois shook his head. "Non, non, not I, not I—I swear it."

"Fools." The voice rasped, gravely and grave, from all their phones, the utterance immediately followed by a sharp blast of static—then silence.

"Who was that?" Letta asked, her face pale.

Frith folded her arms, her brow furrowing. "Hmmm."

"What?" Letta asked.

"I dunno. That voice rings a bell. But we need to keep moving." She addressed Francois: "Hey, Dream Master, I volunteer. Let's do this. Trax?" He was lost in thought and didn't answer. Frith prodded him. "Trax?"

He nodded. "Me too. No looking back."

Richard floated forward. "Successor Letta Starchild? Do you agree to the terms of the Master of Dreams?"

"Yeah," Letta said. "If that's the price, I'll pay the cost. Francois, what do we have to do to make this happen?"

Francois stowed his fan and took a few steps closer. The three newcomers all backed up in tandem, to his visual amusement. "There is nothing to fear, mortals, at least not yet. Non, all you must do is tell me about your most vivid recurring dream. Mon petit Successeur, may I suggest you go first?"

Letta nodded. "Do I tell you here or ..?"

"Here would be ideal. You must all hear about each other's dreams for my magicks to take hold."

"I started having these dreams in my twenties. But they were based on a real memory, a memory from when I was a kid at the Ranch. One day I was sitting in the schoolhouse doing homework, and someone … whispered to me. And I recognized the voice. It was *my voice,* but older. Anyway, that was the dream. I was a grown-up, and I was trying to talk to my younger self."

Frith: "What did you say?"

"Run."

Francois giggled, adding, "How did this dream make you feel, mamzelle?"

"Full of regret. I wish I'd shouted." She cleared her throat. "You get what you needed, perv?"

"Most certainly," he said. "And now, the … big one will reveal her depths to me?" *Beeg one.*

"You can call me Frith or *ma'am,* ya fucking degenerate."

Francois cooed. "Oooh, of course, mon grande mamzelle. Proceed."

Frith nodded. "Sure. Mine's pretty cheesy, but it scared the hell out of me. I dreamed of a man with a plaid face. He wore Darth Vader's helmet, but he had a patch of plaid fabric—like from an old, old set of pajamas—staple-gunned to his face. I'd always try to yell for help, but I couldn't talk, and I couldn't breathe."

"Ah, yes—Le Homme de l'tissue écossais. One of the first of our kind, but he ascended long, long ago. And how did those dreams make you feel, mamzelle?"

"Terrified, for one, but more than that … like I'm a failure. Like I'll never be strong enough, never be good enough."

Francois's sockets narrowed to slits that emitted sheets of black smoke. "Mmm-*mmm*, mamzelle Frith. Merci, merci, merci." He opened his eyes and addressed Traxler: "And you, monsieur? What is your recurring dream?"

"You."

Everyone fell silent. Francois's eyes stopped spewing smoke. The charred backs of his sockets came into view, where a pair of embers smoldered like burning rubies.

Frith spoke first. "Honey, are you kidding?"

He shook his head. "Yes and no. Here's how it works: I've never dreamed about you directly, Francois, but I've watched you at work more times than I care to remember. Ever since I was a kid, I'd have these dreams about people getting hurt … or killed … by this guy with smoking eyes. Only you didn't always wear that outfit or look the way you do now."

"Of course not, monsieur."

Traxler's brow darkened. "I'd open the papers the next morning, trying to find out where you were—where your victims were. I hear those screams every night, all those people you hurt."

"That I *consumed.*"

"Right."

"And how did those dreams make you feel?"

Traxler propped his arms akimbo. "Honestly? Really, really fucking pissed off."

Frith made an empathetic scoff. "Baby, it wasn't your fault."

"Not at me." He addressed Francois: "At you."

Thunder rumbled. Crimson lightning splashed the windows. A wave crashed by outside. Violent expectation hung in the air. Francois produced his fan and *flicked* it open.

"Merci beaucoup to you all. I have what I need. Shall we proceed?"

Richard's onyx eyes caught flashes of red. He hovered forward. "Letta Starchild, with your permission?"

"You are hereby permission'ed. Let's talk about this infernal vault."

"Very well," Richard said, executing a series of arcane gestures that zoomed in on the tiny hell dimension while also bringing forth a model of the planet earth. Matthias muttered magic words that generated a silver pin, which sprouted from the center of Italy's west coast. Frith pointed.

"Is that Rome?"

Matthias nodded. "Vatican City, to be precise."

"What's the Pope got to do with this?" Letta asked. "I thought we had to break into one of those infernal vault places? Isn't that where we'll find the keystone?"

Richard nodded. "Indeed, but gaining access to the vault is only part of the quest to find the keystone to the Arch of Scourgian Mists. The keystone won't be found in the vault, but in Heaven."

Silence greeted his words.

"Heaven?" Frith asked. "It's real?"

"It is," Richard said. "And to be perfectly specific, you won't be infiltrating the Empyrean itself—the abode of Old Father—but rather the vestibaric outrealms of Heaven, a way-station for newly blessed souls to prepare themselves to join with his essence for eternity."

Matthias sneered at this. "A load of horse-drivel."

Richard ignored him and continued: "Regardless, it is known as Base Primum."

"How do we get there?" Letta asked.

"I will explain later, but—"

"Why not tell the little Successor *now?*" *Leetle.* Francois had doffed his hat so he could pirouette his way across the mezzanine. He leaned into Letta's face but addressed Richard: "Don't you want her to know that *I* am the only way into Heaven?"

Letta: "*What?*"

Richard waved away the words. "That is a problem for a later hour, and if the Master of Dreams is wise, he will aid our cause without question."

Francois clicked his teeth and replaced his hat. "Very well."

After watching Francois return to his station, Richard continued: "Back to the matter at hand." He executed a series of arcane gestures that sent a shockwave through the Apparatus, which shivered apart and reconstituted itself into a massive upward concavity, a conelike crater that funneled toward the ceiling, a mountain in reverse. In contrast with his previous models of the downfalls, which bristled and brimmed with detail, this rendering was all smooth generalities. A yellow circle floated at the top of the cone, labeled simply, *GATEWAY*, while below, an orange hoop clung to the cone's bottom.

Richard raised a hand in apology. "I beg your pardons for the crude nature of this model. I haven't had the opportunity to research the appearance of Base Primum, for the tomes in which its nature is recorded are barred from my gaze."

"So how are we planning on infiltrating this place, if your map's for shit?" Traxler asked. "No offense."

"That is a problem for a later time. What I *can* tell you is the strongbox housing the keystone is located here," he zoomed in on the funnel's bottom rim, where glittering barnacles clung: a city. "Somewhere within the contemplative bazaar that is Base Primum is hidden this strongbox—and yet, it is a safe with no keyhole."

Letta: "Where's the keyhole?"

As something rumbled in the distance, Richard dismissed the map of Base Primum and brought back the map of the Downfalls, zooming in on the infernal vault. "Here. Within this minuscule hell."

"And the key?"

"I shall explain that later," Richard said. "For now, we must find someone who is a believer in the religion that sired this infernal vault, for only they may access it. Once we purloin the key, we must sneak into the infernal vault, place it in the keyhole, and turn it. Doing do will open the strongbox in Base Primum."

"Do we know what religion created the infernal vault?"

"Lord Matthias?"

He stepped forward, the distant rumble growing less and less distant. "It is an obscure, cultlike faith known as the Magesterial Nominalists. That is all I've been able to uncover."

"Never heard of 'em," Frith said, prodding Traxler. "You?"

"Negative."

Letta: "Matthias, how do we even know one of these Magesterial Nominalists is still alive?"

"We not only know the person is still alive but that he, she, or it is a member of the Menagerie."

"We do? How?"

"Cartographer, would you please bring the vault into greater focus?"

He zoomed in until the vault was the size of a basketball scoreboard, filling the atrium. An intricate network of ridges and canals around its circumference revealed itself to be a bizarre series of characters:

"Matthias, can you tell us what that says?"

"I know not," the old wizard said. "It is an imprimatur, a signature of belief, generated by the person or creature who adheres to this faith's mythologies.

"'Mythologies,' except that this hell actually exists," Letta said.

"Well met, Letta Starchild," Matthias said. "Only a believer may read this word and thereby unlock the infernal vault."

"Okay, so aren't you the leader of the Menagerie?" Letta asked. "Don't you know which of your own killing crew believes in this hell?"

"As the Infernal Cartographer said, I have made efforts to learn everything about every Infernal Downfall, as well as the Menagerie, but in all my thousand years of study, I've never figured out which of the Menagerie belongs to this faith. The person, or creature, must hold their beliefs very close. The library's stacks may yield some information, but it would take us centuries to study them all."

"What about calling everyone back, like you did with Francois? Couldn't we just do a straw poll?"

"We haven't the time," Matthias said. "What we need is someone with a vast and comprehensive knowledge of the world's serial killers and mass murderers."

Letta looked at Frith. Their eyes widened as they came to a joint realization, and once again, Letta could sense the icy wall between them starting to thaw, ever so slightly. "Are you thinking who I'm thinking?"

Frith nodded. They spoke simultaneously:

Letta said: *"Nicky."*

Frith said: "Whoever wrote the Wikipedia page that lists all the world's serial killers and—oh, Nicky. Right. She was totally gonna be my second choice, but—" (she jabbed a finger at Letta) "—there is *absolutely no fucking way we're asking Nicky.*"

Frith slammed the door to a side room. A half dozen easels dotted the chamber, all of them set up for manuscript illumination. The unholy storm raged outside, casting them both in stark red silhouettes. Frith loomed over Letta, who sat on a stool and seemed to shrink even smaller.

Frith stared at the floor. "You never actually told me if you did it."

"I know," Letta said.

Frith looked up. "So? Did you tell Nicky what happened … y'know, that night?"

"No, I never did."

Frith let loose with a long and very relieved sigh. Tears glittered in her eyes.

"Really?"

Letta shook her head.

Frith forearm-wiped away her tears and leveled a finger at Letta: "You said you were going to tell her. You *swore* you were going to tell her."

"When I considered the factors and parameters at hand—"

"Speak fucking *English!*"

Letta sat back, blood draining from her face. "After you threw me out, I thought about what you said. And I changed my mind."

Frith took a stool and sat, her knees bent up to her chest.

"Why didn't you come back and tell me?"

"Well, I didn't change my mind right that instant. I went back and forth. I even called her, but I got her voicemail."

"Did you leave a message?"

"The greeting warned she'd post your social security number on the Dark Web if I did … but it didn't matter. I just sat there staring at my phone like an idiot." She paused. "I still think it's wrong to keep it from her. But you were right. It wasn't my place to tell her. I'm sorry."

Frith nodded an acknowledgment, her lips trembling. "I appreciate you saying that. And I think you're right. We *do* need Nicky's help with this, and I think we're supposed to ask for it." She stood, paused. "Letta, Richard and Matthias said something about another Rite. Another way to—"

Thunder exploded from everywhere. Letta jumped up and hustled to the door.

"We need to keep moving. C'mon, let's go get Nicky."

The Eighth Maxim

S HE'D BEEN ON THE VERGE of a nervous breakdown since the first bolt of red lightning.

A dozen computer monitors covered one wall. Some theorists— she hated the word "conspiracy"—like herself maintained elaborate corkboard collages to track their obsessions. So did she, but hers was virtual, not physical, packing the dozen monitors with a constant flow of information. She'd written her own computer program to manage all the media she tracked. Some arrived as growl alerts leading to Twitter threads and Dark Web message boards, while others took the form of scanned classified listings in old-school newsprint.

She'd shaved off most of her frizzy red hair in favor of a punky sidecut she'd dyed green. Chunky, bright blue glasses clung to the tip of her nose as she spun back toward her battle station. She wore a full-body jumpsuit (the print: an artsy, psychedelic mishmash of rainbows and unicorns rendered in military-standard camouflage tones) with the sleeves rolled up to reveal flesh covered with hundreds of tattoos.

Her digitized corkboard had borne many titles over the years. Its most recent asked a simple question: *IS SOMEONE TARGETING THE STARCHILDREN?* Other subtitles hovered underneath it, including:

ARE WE IN THE END-TIMES?

DOES THE AFTERWORLD EXIST?

Thunder rumbled outside. Immediately below the monitors stood stacks of old media players: VHS, Betamax, Super-8, and more. Dozens of videos were playing, some of them copying from tape to tape, others delivering signals to the monitors above. Archival footage of both Emily Miller, aka Letta Starchild, and Cindy Hastings, aka Winifrith Starchild, played, showing Letta on her Lodestar Express program and Frith on various local news channels speaking for the FBI.

She spun to face the wall behind her, which she'd covered with media of a different kind. Hundreds of old video tapes sat before her, all of them marked and organized with a strange script only she knew. Hung over the tapes was a photo: *The Cast and Crew of the Starchild Players' All-Female Othello, 1993.* Athena, her Foundation, stood in the middle, one hand propped on a hip, the other draped around little Letta's shoulder. The two were flanked by the bigwigs—including sweet Franco, whose left hand had only recently healed up—Stanton, Bayard, and the newest, Frith. The autumn sun shone over the treeline and carved everyone's faces in shadow and light. Taped underneath the photo was a paper bearing handwritten words any Starchild would recognize immediately—the Seven Maxims—but Nicky had added an eighth:

> *Eight: Show kindness, remember, and speak honestly, for these are the triune paths to friendship.*

The Eighth Maxim of the Starchild-Nicodemus Fellowship belonged to her and her alone, for she was its founding and sole adherent, a splinter sect of one. Athena Starchild was her First Patron Saint, but another monster stood in the same pantheon. Headlines told his story:

GOLDBERG, THE SOUTHSIDE'S AVENGING ANGEL, KILLS AGAIN

DIABOLICAL TRAP VIVISECTS OIL BARON

GOLDBERG STRIKES AGAIN! INFAMOUS PEDERAST DRAWN AND QUARTERED

Nicky slid a microphone through a drift of papers and notes. After launching her audio app—another of her custom builds—she spoke:

"Welcome to episode eight hundred ninety-eight of *Nicky Nicodemus's Believe it … or Maybe Totally Believe It.* This week, we're exploring the mystery of the bizarre astrological and meteorological phenomena plaguing the world: red lightning, hot hail, tsunamis. Against this backdrop are the mysterious disappearances of FBI Special Agent Cindy Hastings, and famed magnate of the Lodestar Express multi-level marketing empire, Emily Miller—except we know those aren't their real names, don't we?"

Nicky Nicodemus kept talking, unaware that a black portal had opened through the floor a few feet from where she sat.

Ambient light caught on what appeared to be a churning escalator composed of millions of interlocking black insects. Two figures climbed up out of her floor, both of them moving with great care. They hadn't seen Nicky in three decades and didn't want to startle her.

Nicky continued: "But you may know both of these women by their aliases. Cindy was once Frith and Emily was once Letta. Both used to hold the surname *Starchild* … just like your intrepid Nicky Nicodemus. We were all children of the Starchild Ranch, and now someone is kidnapping us one by one. Could there be a connection between these disappearances and the bizarre celestial events we're now witnessing? Could the mysterious mastermind Goldberg be behind it all?"

Looking over the apartment gave Letta the same feeling as walking into a greenhouse that had been left alone for decades; Nicky's obsessions had swarmed over every wall, every surface. Letta's eyes drifted to the photo from *Othello*. She sighed loud enough to draw a rebuke from Frith, who slashed a hand across her neck to say *shut up!*

But an oblivious Nicky prattled on: "You've heard me speak about our great mother, our Foundation, before. Athena. You've heard me speak of the things she did. Terrible things. Things that your Nicky Nicodemus didn't agree with. But behind the horrors of her failings was a remarkable woman, and an inspiration to me and so many others. I've tried to keep her spirit alive, spread her teachings as I can."

When Letta saw the eighth maxim, her reaction was instinctive and sincere:

"Oh, I *love* it!"

This time Nicky heard her.

Nicky's reaction was instant: she swept her desk clean, leaped to its far side, flipped it over, and had a gun trained on them. Despite the situation, Frith actually gave an approving nod and held up her hands.

"Nicky? It's Winifrith and Letta. We're here to talk, and we need your—"

"Who sent you here to swoop?! Was it the Truth?! The Purse?! The Scuzzin' Dozen?! Who blabbed?! Was it Leetmeister47? TheTaintofSauron? The Almighty Mason?! Who?! *I'm no prairie dog, and you're not Letta and Frith!*"

"Nicky? Nicky, please put down the gun. You've probably got the safety on any—"

BANG! Papers kicked around in the wake of the bullet, which punched a hole through the *Othello* cast photo.

Nicky's hands were shaking. "Tell me who you are. Or *what* you are. I know someone's picking off the survivors from 1993, and I'll be gosh-*damned* if they're getting me next."

"Nicky, how many six-foot-two women do you know?" Frith asked.

"I know enough. Your next answer better be good, or I'm killing you both."

Anger rose within Frith, but she said nothing, out of ideas. It was Letta who saved them, and she did it in a manner that made Frith's skin crawl.

"My words could support a continent, Nicky," Letta said, her voice dropping into a sing-song drawl. "They don't always. I don't speak in this manner or in this way with those who lack the starshine. Your new maxim is worthy and righteous. I love it."

The gun wavered in the air. Nicky's eyes glittered with incipient tears.

"Really?"

Letta nodded. "We always needed another one. One with *heart.* You were always the heart of the Ranch. The bigwigs were its mighty arms, Frith its conscience, *Athena* its soul—" The mere utterance of their old leader's name made every muscle on Frith's chest contract. Letta continued: "But you were its heart. You always stayed true to the maxims."

Nicky's lips quivered as she dissolved into tears, but still she kept the gun raised. Slowly, though, the barrel lowered and lowered until it dropped to her side. She buried her fingers in her hair, sobbing. Neither Letta nor Frith dared to move. Finally, Nicky looked up, gesturing with the gun.

"Do you guys wanna be on my podcast?"

"You sure about this?" Frith whispered. "She looks bad."

"Um."

Nicky seemed to quantum-leap over to them. "How'd you guys get in here, anyway? I almost plugged ya!"

Frith kept her body between Nicky and the portal, which was still running like an escalator behind them.

"We need your help, Nick, and—"

Nicky shouldered her way past them both, nearly stepping right into the portal, and crossed to a bookshelf overflowing with Manila folders, papers, legal filing boxes, and dozens more videotapes. She pulled out a small tape and strode back across the room, absent-mindedly side-stepping the portal. She kicked her chair out of the way to make room for her desk, which she righted. Onto it she plopped a newly cracked computer monitor. She crawled under the desk, where she slid the tape into one of a dozen players. Her hand snaked over top of the desk, holding a mouse. Somehow, she remembered the locations of all her computer windows perfectly and brought up a video feed that depicted a creature Frith recognized immediately:

The Kentucky Devil.

"Oh, my god," she said, stepping closer. "This … this is—"

"Your first field kill, amiright?" Nicky said, her head bobbing in and out of view. She continued chattering away, her hand gesticulating over the desk: "Word on the boards is you're the living Mulder, the *real*-real Ghostbuster, the spiritual daughter-descendant of Abraham Van Helsing."

Letta leaned in. "Hey, we're in a bit of a hurry, so—"

Frith held up a humble hand. "I work with a great team at the bureau—"

Nicky jumped to her feet. "So that *was* you! It *is* you hunting all these enmity-entities! Busted!"

"Hunting all these whats?"

Letta tried to break in again: "Frith, don't you think we should bring Nicky up to speed on the whole 'end of the universe' thing?"

Nicky gasped and covered her mouth. "I was *right!*" She blundered her way across the room, once again narrowly missing the portal, and pointed at her digital corkboard: *ARE WE IN THE END-TIMES?* "I'm right, aren't I-I-ayyyyy-*what the heck?*" Nicky had finally noticed the portal. She stepped closer and stared. "Is … is that an escalator? Made of bugs?"

Letta: "Nicky, there's something happening. Something bad. And we need to call on your expertise. There's a lot to tell, but—"

"Don't say another word. I'm in." Nicky rushed around the room, gathering up several stacks of books, files, tapes, equipment, and other media, all of which she crammed into a backpack. She crossed to the portal, teetering on its precipice as she struggled to pull on the pack, which threatened to topple her backward. She waved a wild finger at the descending stairs. "Can I just ride this thing down? Where's it lead?"

"It's hard to explain," Frith said. "It'll be easier to show you."

"Well that's good, because I'm literally from Missouri. 'Show Me State,' *represent!* I mean, wait—I'm not *literally literally* from Missouri. I wasn't born there or anything, ha ha! You guys know that, sheesh. I just think I've got the hardy spirit of a Missourian—oh, wow, these stairs are cool!"

The Protestant

RICHARD AND MATTHIAS WERE DEEP in discussion when they returned. From the back, neither Richard's monstrous appearance nor Matthias's ancient one were apparent. Traxler and Francois were nowhere to be seen. Nicky spilled out of the passage first, her balance thrown off by both her enormous backpack as well as the sensation of suddenly climbing *up* stairs when she'd entered the portal climbing *down*.

"Whooaaa!" she said as she dropped her pack and took in the sight, failing to notice the two ancient beings before her. Above, red lightning blazed through the stained-glass dome, while before her floated a diagram of the visible universe. Nicky had no idea what she was looking at, of course, but the sight was nevertheless breathtaking, as millions of star systems, local groups, and superclusters all spun in harmony, each of them rendered in varying shades of wood, brick, stone, and steel. Nicky sighed, giggling quietly.

Frith and Letta staggered up out of the portal.

"You okay?" Frith asked.

"Yeah. The re-entry's a little rocky." She checked the room. "Where's your fella?"

Traxler's voice floated up: "Down here, guys."

Across the atrium and a few floors down, Traxler waved. He was leaning against a shelf, reading a leatherbound manuscript.

"Guys, guys, guys!" Nicky was running over. "Show me some newsprint!"

Letta's eyebrows rose. "Newspaper? What year do you think it is?"

Nicky waved away the confusion. "No, no, no! Just show me your iPhones, pull up the Conspirinormal Podcast and show me the screen!"

Letta obliged. "I don't know what podcast that is, but here's the New York Times homepage."

Nicky snatched the phone from her hand and scanned it, mouthing words to herself.

"I can read it. I can *read* it. This isn't a dream!"

"Non, it is not, mamzelle, but I can make it so." Francois materialized from a cloud of black sulfur a few feet away, his eyes billowing smoke, his mouth a steampunk beartrap composed of thousands of razor-sharp tines. "Mon cheri, can I write you a song?" He doffed his bowler and tap-danced his way over to Nicky, his moves straight out of Bob Fosse. Ending with a flourish, he tossed his hat aloft and caught it on his skull.

A half-fascinated, half-terrified Nicky gawked. "Who are you?"

Ignoring her question, Francois sang: "There was a young girl named Nicky, whose sis—"

Frith stepped between them. "Nicky, allow me to introduce Francois, who's gonna back off a few feet?"

Francois chuckled and obeyed. Letta crossed to Richard and Matthias as Frith continued:

"I guess we should start here, Nicky. You saw the footage of the Kentucky Devil. That was a level one corporeal preternatural—a mutant, basically. I'd characterize Francois here as a level five, free-repeating preternatural with vast powers in the subconscious realm. He—"

"Oh! Right! Wow! Francois, the Specter of Stillwater! I was just talking about you on my podcast!"

He bowed. "Enchante."

"Holy bejeebers! You're a peerless shapeshifter, but you're *hellllllllla* vulnerable in meatspace. *How* many times have you been ritualistically killed and revived? I can't reach my notes right now."

Francois's sockets narrowed at her. He bared his teeth, his posture stiffening enough to put Frith on full alert, but then the *clock-clock-clock* of footsteps broke the tension. Traxler was heading their way, the same leatherbound book tucked under his arm. A low hiss rose from Francois's innards upon seeing Traxler, while Nicky just smiled so big.

"Well, what the heck. Sheesh! Bowden Traxler. Frith's XO. The Hero of Atlanta. You've caught just as many, if not more, enmity entities as her." She strode over and gave him a big, unsolicited hug, which he returned. Releasing him, she continued: "It's been a minute since … well, since we first met. I go by Nicky Nicodemus now, not Starchild, pleasedtameetcha. I think cops're pretty much are all jackbooted avatars of the Invisible Establishment—aka the Scuzzin' Dozen—but mister? You're A-okay in this girl's book!"

Traxler smiled. "Uh, thanks. Winnie talks about you all the time. Should we—"

Nicky propped arms akimbo and rotated at her hips, her jaw hanging slack.

"*Winnie?*" she said in a tone of mock shock, while unbeknownst to her, Richard and Matthias were approaching with Letta. Nicky pivoted on her heels and marched toward Frith, hands still on her hips. "Since when are you a *Winnie?*"

Letta leaned in to get Nicky's attention: "Hey, we've got a lot to cover, and—"

The others were quickly learning that Nicky's brain worked differently than theirs. The aperture of her focus would narrow around one thing at a time, shutting out everything else, only to snap wide at seemingly random times as her internal processes blitzed through datasets. In this case, Nicky was one hundred percent focused on razzing Frith, which made her unaware of the seven-foot hellborne colossus floating toward her.

But when she *did* finally notice Richard, everyone saw it happen.

Nicky raised a finger, ready to wag it at Frith, when she froze into a perfect statue of herself. Her eyes slanted sideward, presumably registering Richard's presence, and slowly grew wide. She pivoted on her heels—a common move for her—turning first her body, followed by her head; the whole act like something from a mime's comedic playbook. Richard floated on his usual dark host of insectoids, his onyx eyes trained down on her, his jaw clenching, his innards chattering away.

"Greetings, mortal. I am the Anti-God adherent most magnificent, his unholy eminence the Lord Tormentos Mallestratos, master of anguish, prince of pain, and infernal cartographer. Welcome to the Fortress of Maximum Suffering."

Nicky's arms fell to her sides, limp. She giggled once, a high-pitched *yip* that echoed through the atrium, and waved to him.

"Hi, I'm a good person who has a lot to offer."

Richard growled and addressed Letta: "*This* is your expert? I'd sooner lash her to a cart for All Fools' Day, or attire her in motley and send her to court."

Nicky nodded rapidly: "You can do that, you can do that. I'll wear whatever you want." Her voice dropped a sultry octave. "Sir."

Frith, Letta, and Traxler all exchanged concerned looks. Letta hurried over and escorted Nicky away from an unamused Richard, saying: "Sooo, that's Richard the Infernal Cartographer." She called: "Matthias! Get over here!" To Nicky: "It sounds like you're already up to speed on monsters and magic being real."

"Oh, I'll say I am." She waved to Richard over Letta's shoulder.

Matthias ambled over and was about to speak but stopped—Nicky struck him silent. His look slowly turned into a gape.

Nicky pointed at her face. "Do I have a booger? Oh, my *gawd*, the first time I meet sorcerers and anguish-masters, and I've got a booger!"

Letta: "You don't have a booger."

Matthias cleared his throat and blinked. "Forgive me. You reminded me of someone, although she didn't have emerald hair. I am Matthias, Guildmaster of Lord Morningstar's Menagerie." He indicated Richard and added: "Are you and the Cartographer … acquainted?"

She stage-whispered: "Not yet we're not," then blurted: "Oh, hi, by the way! Nicky Nicodemus, paranormal podcaster, expert on the occult, obtainer of rare antiquities, and eternal nemesis of the Scuzzin' Dozen. Are you, like, a sorcerer? Or a wizard? Wait, are those the same thing? Shit, did I just commit a faux pas?" She covered her mouth. "Ohmigod, sorry for swearing!"

Red lightning flashed. Matthias gave Letta a withering look, said: "Successor, we haven't the time."

"I know, I know. Nicky, *Nicky,* I need you to pay attention. Here's what's happening …"

They explained everything. Letta, with Matthias's input, broke down the details about the Menagerie; Frith and Traxler told her about the Claudia Castle killing. ("Busted for destroying the universe, Frith!") Francois showed off his comms systems. Because she refused to carry a smartphone—"weird fucking humors emanate from those things"—Matthias provided her with an intricately carved wooden message tube, circa 1250s, which Francois enchanted.

"Do not turn that thing into a fucking cock," Frith said.

"Mamzelle has my solemn oath I will not turn it into a cock," he said, chuckling.

Finally, they got to the meat of it. Richard's diagram of the infernal vault once again hung in the air, big as a scoreboard, complete with the strange script unique to its owner. Letta took over the briefing, speaking elliptically: "The overall mission has several steps, starting with this tiny hell. We have to figure out whose hell this is, then break into it, and—"

"Waitaminute! Is this a *heist?!*"

Richard, who had been regarding Nicky with thinly veiled contempt, allowed himself a grudging nod of approval. Letta joined in.

"Yeah," Letta said. "That's how we're planning to attack it."

Nicky practically squealed. "Of *course* that's how you should attack it. Wait a second—" She surveyed everyone in the room. Slowly, she walked toward Richard, pointed at him, and said, "You're intelligence and our wheeljack." To Francois: "Eye in the sky." To Frith: "Yours is so obvious, I won't even say it." To Traxler: "Early entry or *mayyyybe* subjugation, given your background." To Letta: "And you're the great owl, *obviously,* though of course only *I* know your real codename."

"What the hell's *that* supposed to mean?" Letta asked, sharing an inscrutable look with Frith. They could've been concerned parents fretting over a child.

Frith: "You don't mind helping? You don't mind that we're … well, bringing *her* back?"

"Of *course* I don't mind! She's my First Patron Saint, and I mean, I mean …" For the first time since she'd arrived, Nicky's mood grew calmer instead of more animated. She quietly said: "Listen, I need to ask an important question. It's a very important and intense question, and I need everyone to be cool about it. I'm not trying to embarrass anyone. I don't mean to put anybody on the spot. I really don't want to—"

"What's the question?" Letta said.

"Is … everyone here cool with the Doobies?"

Silence, stunned silence. Frith hid a smile behind her hand.

Finally, Letta crossed her arms, said: *"What?"*

"Does everyone here know the Doobie Brothers? Oh, sheesh—I guess you two wouldn't." She indicated Richard and Matthias. "But Matty, I think you'd dig 'em. Frankie, I dunno about you, but to quote the Doobs: 'This is it.' And make no mistake, this *is* it. We're the trump card, we're the final countdown." She pointed at the infernal vault. "And I know who created that hell."

"Nicky, you really brought a slide projector?" Frith asked.

"Of course! 'Never leave the house without a slide projector,' that's my motto!"

Francois raised a hand. "Would mamzelle like my help with the presentation? Simply look into my eyes, and I can deliver your images to everyone's mind like *that*."

He snapped his fingers and tapped out a quick beat. Nicky got a faraway look for a moment before Frith stepped in.

"No thanks, man. Nicky, carry on."

Nicky scrambled around the mezzanine setting up her presentation. Matthias had provided a sheet from his quarters, which a grousing Richard hung using his insectoid powers. ("No need to be such a grump about it, cutie!") A wooden stool provided the projector's base, and within minutes, Nicky had prepped the carousel and started the show. As she ran over by the screen, she gave Matthias a big, theatrical thumbs-up. (In addition to her insta-crush on Richard the Cartographer, Nicky had clearly taken to Matthias; she was continually sharing facts and jokes with him, all of which went over the old wizard's head.)

"Matty! Lights, please!"

A muttered incantation from Matthias cast the Fortress in darkness. Nicky activated the projector. The first slide was a glamour shot of herself, wearing a midriffy, low-cut leotard, holding pom-poms and executing a high-kick against a neon-streaked background.

She covered her mouth. "Oh, sheesh! How the heck did *that* get in there? Sorry, guys, give me one second ..." *Click.* The next slide was also of herself, but bending toward the camera to show off her cleavage. She slapped her forehead. "Aw, jeez! Where did *that* come from?!" She shot a glance at Richard and lowered her voice: "Sorry. Did that shock you, Master of Anguish?"

An unearthly growl rose from Richard's insides. "Your mortal affections *bore* me."

Nicky touched her stomach. "I'm pregnant."

Letta rubbed her brow. "Nicky, if you get us brought up on some interdimensional sexual harassment suit, I'm gonna kill you myself before the universe explodes."

Nicky made an *aw shucks* wave and laughed it off. "Sheesh, y'all, sorry about that! Let's get down to business, but—" (she jabbed a finger at Richard) "—I've got my eye on you, mister." She clicked to the next slide, which showed a woman, circa 1975, with big, frizzy hair, a flowing purple blouse, and bell-bottom jeans. She stood outside, pointing at a chalkboard while lecturing to a group of people who all sat on a hillside. The backdrop was some kind of rural compound. She'd written the sentence: "Power of the Firsts."

The image aroused an array of conflicting feelings in Letta and Frith: kinship and hardship, fear and familiarity. The woman could've been their Foundation, Athena, from a parallel universe. She looked like your typical mom of the 1970s. Frith shifted her posture.

"Damn, she looks familiar," she muttered.

Nicky looked over. "What was that, Miss Hastings? Speak up, so the whole class can hear!"

"I said she looks familiar."

Letta nodded. "Reminds me of you-know-who. Matthias, can we spring this one from hell instead?"

"That is not the nature of the Rite, Successor," Matthias said dryly.

"I was joking."

Nicky raised her hand. "Frith? Tell us why you think she looks familiar."

Frith shrugged. "I dunno. I feel like I've met her before."

Nicky bounced in place and leaned toward Matthias. "Matty, think I should tell her, or let her get her *mind totally fucking blown* later?"

"I'm afraid I don't understand your idiom."

Letta sighed. "Nicky, just tell us. Who is the Dark Nightingale?"

Nicky advanced the carousel. The next slide was an age-advanced sketch of the Dark Nightingale.

Frith gasped slightly. "Holy shit."

"Hell heisters, meet the Dark Nightingale, age sixty-seven, leader of the Magesterial Nominalists from their founding in 1974 until the feds busted 'em up in the mid-eighties. Born Wanda Jane Fredericks, she managed to elude the authorities, escaping up the eastern seaboard, where she adopted a new alias—an alias I believe you know, Frith."

"Yeah, I'll say. The Dark Nightingale is Claudia Castle."

"Are you kidding?" Letta said. "Does this mean we have to spring *her* out of hell now, too?"

"Nope," Nicky said. "And it wouldn't do us any good if we did, because the infernal vault isn't her hell."

Matthias nodded. "I can confirm this. Whenever a member of the Menagerie perishes, the Apparatus reveals to me not only where they died, but to which of the Infernal Downfalls their soul is condemned. Claudia Castle was called to *D'taniynoa,* or Leviathan, where she faces an eternity of chaos for the pain she wrought on earth."

"So whose hell is it, the vault?" Traxler asked.

Nicky: "The vault belongs to the Dark Nightingale's Franco. To her muscle king."

This turn of phrase sparked an array of reactions: Richard, Matthias, and Traxler all exchanged confused looks; but the other women—Letta and Frith—both looked suddenly dejected, gut-punched, forlorn, like parents who'd learned they'd lost a child in combat. Frith swallowed a sob. Francois's posture perked up at their discomfort—he twined his fingers under his chin like he'd just heard something delightfully whimsical.

Frith whispered: "You … can remember all that?"

Nicky frowned and propped her hands on her hips. "Of course I can! I'm not losing my marbles just *yet*, Winnie! I can remember lots from back then. I figure it's *you* who might need to start counting your marbles before the rest of us, right?"

Frith didn't respond.

Traxler cleared his throat and raised his hand. "Could you explain what a 'muscle king' is?"

Nicky practically bounced in place. "Oh! I'm sorry. Heck, look at me using Starchild innerspeak. A muscle king is, like, your lead enforcer, your heavy, your puncher, your B.A. Baracus! Which reminds me …" She pulled out a notebook and jotted something down. Holding up her notebook, she said, "Remind me to tell you guys about this later, *before* we start the heist! *Any*way, back on the Ranch, a guy named Franco was our muscle king for certain … um, missions, I guess." Her brow creased, and her eyes danced like she was tracing the splatters of a Jackson Pollack. "I can't quite recall, but the muscle king for the Magesterial Nominalsts was a man named Johnathan James Bradley. A longtime drifter, he fell into the cult's orbit as a teenager and quickly became its most ardent believer. He became *such* a fanatic that he clashed with the Dark Nightingale."

She continued: "Bradley had been party to dozens of robberies, assaults, and killings at the Nightingale's behest, but in 1977, she had a vision that convinced her the end-times were nigh, and that the anti-God was to be born sometime between the years of 1977 and 1983. She claimed it would be the firstborn son to a family located in the southwestern United States. She had instructed her acolytes to kidnap every firstborn son they could, starting in New Mexico and working their way west. When she turned her sights on babies, Bradley rebelled."

She continued: "Bradley started his own splinter sect of the Nominalists, called the *Neo-Nominalists,* and they dedicated themselves to hunting down anyone who hurt or exploited children. He brought almost a third of the cult with him, and over the next several years, the Dark Nightingale waged war against the Neo-Nominalists, picking them off one by one."

She continued: "But she could never catch Bradley. He was too wily, too cunning, and according to local legend, the Dark Nightingale entered into a pact with the devil to curse Bradley ... by imprisoning his body in an inanimate object."

"An inanimate object?" Letta asked. "What the hell *kind* of inanimate object?"

But Nicky's presentation had already spurred Richard to activity. He surged skyward on a cloud of insectoids and, in concert with Matthias, re-ignited the lights and rearranged the infernal map back into a scale model of the earth. A few whispered incantations brought the state of Arizona vaulting into focus, where a silver pin marked a location outside Phoenix. Richard nodded to Francois, who waved his fan and brought up an enchanted window that displayed the inanimate object in question.

Letta laughed—somewhat hysterically.

"You gotta be fucking kidding."

Part Four
1993: Casting

E VERYONE ON THE RANCH ANSWERED an immediate all-hands the moment they arrived back from town, crowding into the schoolhouse. Bodies jostled against one another as the last few Starchildren filed in. Brass light fixtures cast slanting cones of dust-sparkling gold. The space bore a musky odor and energy, like a summer camp meeting.

The bigwigs carved out some space in the room's center, rearranging the desks into a makeshift perimeter-stage for their Foundation. Tyler stood in the front row with the bigwigs (including Franco), while Nicky hopped on a desk, her camera running like always. Athena nodded to Frith, who raised her voice.

"Yo! Listen up!"

The crowd fell silent. Athena took center-stage, hands on hips. "We have a critical-red situation, and it requires immediate actioning. Starchildren, mark me: our fates teeter on the brink. Teeter, teeter." A few Starchildren covered their mouths or stifled chuckles at the words *teeter, teeter,* but they didn't dare laugh openly. She continued: "We're staging an impromptu, *emergency* production this week, with rehearsals beginning tonight. We may have to invoke the sixth maxim, but I pray we won't. Pray, pray, I say." Mention of the sixth maxim sent flutters through everyone's stomachs. The acrid scent of fear filled the air.

Nicky, for one, had never been around when it had been invoked.

Or so she thought.

When Athena told them they were starting an "emergency production," Most of the bigwigs had repelled "notpers," before—people who the Ranch deemed not to exist—and it was always unpleasant work. (It took months for Franco's hand to heal from their last emergency production.)

Athena sensed the change in mood and raised a hand.

"Starchildren, rejoice. Rejoice despite the tough times ahead, for we have a new potential child." She beckoned. "Tyler? Come forth." The kid blushed and shuffled forward a few steps. She continued: "I am our Foundation, and for the purposes of tonight's production, I will take my usual role as great owl." She doled out titles: "Winifrith: wheeljack."

"Got it."

"Stanton: early entry. Bayard: subjugation. Our newcomer Tyler is intelligence. Franco, you're muscle king, as usual."

"Understood."

"And Nicodemus? Eye in the sky."

She saluted. "I'm right on top of that, chief!"

"Very good. Starchildren, the rest of you may return to your work, but for the cast members just announced, muster to me." Everyone else cleared out. A visibly uneasy Tyler edged his way toward the door, only to get cut off by Stanton.

"Hey there, fella! Where ya headed? We've business tonight, and we need your help. You're intelligence!"

Tyler turned to Athena, said: "Listen, I gotta get going before my roommates—"

Athena: "But don't you?"

He scrunched his face in confusion, her words having short-circuited his thought process.

"Don't I what?"

"But don't you want to know what happened to him? Your most despised?"

Everyone else exchanged looks, some excited, some trepidatious.

They'd all heard this before. Nicky sat on the desktop, while Stanton and Bayard both took seats next to Letta.

Athena shushed them before turning her attention back to Tyler. Her eyelids fluttered. "There's … an opening. A small one in the conveyance that carries me. Like a porthole. I'm hurtling up, up, up, but … not up. I'm not traveling in any one direction that humans could understand. I'm being transported across a strange landscape, filled with tombs. And I can see him. It's your … older brother, yes?"

Tyler's face grew pale. He nodded.

"A creature of rage he was until that rainy night last year, yes? You were driving over to your aunt's, already dreading him and his constant explosions, but the trees were alight with red and yellow. Men in turnouts ran past, trailing hoses. It was a rural area, so they didn't have the Jaws of Life yet. Lucky for you." She smiled wickedly.

Tyler nodded. "They might've saved him otherwise."

"What a pity then that he burned alive. The hydrants were too far, the firefighters' suppression tanks not enough to extinguish him. Know that he suffered. He suffered about as much as one man could suffer in the space of fifteen agonizing minutes. It's a curious reality, isn't it? To think of those poor firefighters, watching a man burn to death, screaming until a hiss from his throat marked the moment of his passing. They felt such pity for him, unaware of the horrors he had delivered unto you and yours, Tyler." Her eyelids fluttered again. Frith stepped forward, beckoning to Letta.

"I'll get the big girl out of here, Foundation."

"There is no need, Winifrith. I want her to hear this." Frith frowned and returned to her place. Athena continued: "Tyler, here's an axioma you'll appreciate: he blamed you for his death. He blamed you for not getting the brakes fixed on his car, even though he'd never asked you to. The firefighters heard his last words on this plane: 'Tyler's fucking dead,' he said. Stirring final words, don't you think? His suffering and rage followed him into the hereafter, where the singers called his soul to a boundless realm of chaos. He plunged into its fiery oceans like a meteorite burning up in the atmosphere, hurling himself out of those seas and onto an arid plain teeming with unearthly, infernal vehicles, demonguard taunting him with a simple, repeating truth: *Tyler's glad you're dead.*"

Tyler was sobbing.

Athena took him in her arms and let him weep into her shoulder.

"When you pulled up to the wreckage, your sister, your stupid, simpleminded sister, came struggling up the shoulder, tears streaming down her face. She'd borne untold hardship at his hands, and yet still she mourned his passing. She leaned in your car window, the tear-streaks on her face strobing yellow, red, yellow, red, and said, 'Charlie's dead.' And you were relieved, Tyler. No more pain, no more dread, no more fear. Fate snatched him away, punished him with an infinity's-infinity of suffering, and revealed unto him your deepest truth: You hated him and were happy to see him gone."

Silence, except for Tyler's sobs. He looked up.

"What do you need me to do?"

Thirty Years Later: The Birthday Party

SHINING SILVER LETTERS PASTED TO a banner read, *HAPPY 6TH BIRTHDAY, MARY!* They might've looked festive if they hadn't been spattered with blood. The banner hung in the archway of a kitchen that was frozen in the late seventies: faux red brick and wood paneling were the backdrop for a fridge and an electric oven range, all of them yellowing with age, the stove crusted with burned sausage and dried-up sauces.

A digitized voice spoke: "Hello, I'm Bixby Bear! Do you want to be friends? Hello, I'm Bixby Bear! Do you want to be to be—*KZZZKKT!*"

An oval table sat in the room's center, bearing a birthday cake—also wishing Mary a happy sixth—and a cardboard package, surrounded by ripped-up wrapping paper. The package resembled a throne: something had been sitting in it, a toy bear whose name adorned the side:

BIXBY BEAR!
YOUR NEW BEST FRIEND. HE TALKS! LAUGHS! TELLS
STORIES!

Only moments earlier, Mary had unwrapped the gift without so much as a smile. The two adults who had brought her to this house were confused.

"Isn't this what you asked for, sweetie-pie?" the hairless adult man asked. From the moment she met him, Mary thought it strange he had no hair. He could *grow* hair, but he always shaved it off. She'd accidentally walked in on him once when he had been shaving his eyebrows. He had seen to it she didn't make the same mistake again.

The adult woman who wore too much makeup was also confused. She took Bixby from his package and pulled his string.

"I'm Bixby Bear!" the toy said.

"See, sweetie-pie? He's a Bixby Bear. He talks!"

She always wore too much makeup, Mary thought. She looked like a clown, but not the funny kind. Mary didn't know how long she'd been in the house. She'd always gotten her days confused even before she got here. (The names "Saturday" and "Sunday" always tripped her up. They sounded so much alike to her!) But she'd soon learned to act in ways that pleased the two adults, or else they'd lock her away with her tummy grumbling.

When she walked in on the adult man shaving his eyebrows, he'd locked her away with her tummy grumbling *so bad.* She'd cried and cried, but all they did was beat on the box until she stopped.

So Mary forced herself to smile. Just about anyone else would've seen a child contorting her face into a terrified, frozen grin, but the two adults saw a happy shape, so they thought it was okay. Mary reached for the Bixby Bear. A notch had been bitten off one of his ears, and his eyes were crossed, but besides that, he was good as new.

She really had wanted one. She had a faint memory of a playmate who had one, and she seemed so happy.

"Thank you, mom and dad. I really like it."

The two adults, the man and the woman, looked at each other and nodded in unison. They did that a lot, and it had the effect of putting Mary temporarily at ease. She lacked the vocabulary to describe it, but she had the sense that the gesture meant they were happy, and when they were happy, they left her alone with her toys and storybooks and coloring books.

For a little while, at least.

Mary, whose wrists were handcuffed, reached across the table to pull Bixby's string again.

"Hello, I'm Bixby Bear. Do you want to be friends? Hello, I'm Bixby Bear. Do you—*KZZZKT!*" Bixby's voice dropped an octave: "Do you need help?"

The adult woman frowned. "What did that thing say?"

Mary ignored the stranger and answered: "Yes, I need help."

Thankfully, she didn't fully understand what happened next.

Despite the form that trapped him, he retained his human strength and agility, as well as his skill with various melee weapons. He'd have found a way to end them no matter what was in the room—he'd torn out throats using only his toy paws—but they'd been stupid enough to use a butcher knife to cut the little one's birthday cake.

What Bixby left of the two adults would shock the crime scene investigators.

He escorted the little one up and out of her cell. The two adults had apparently bought a house, kept it empty, and converted the basement into its own little world. A miniature house stood surrounded by a ring of Astroturf. An array of movie lights provided sunshine, while tufts of cotton hung from thread and simulated clouds. There was even a rainbow.

"Where are we going?" she asked.

"Outside." He sounded like he was rasping through a faulty microphone; static clawed at his vowels.

He stretched on his tippy-toes to unlock the front door. Dark thunderheads awaited them outside.

"Is the sun gone?" Mary asked.

"It's still there, little girl. It's just hiding behind the clouds."

Crimson heat lightning flared across the sky, followed by a thundercrash that made Mary jump.

"So loud."

"It's all right. It's only thunder." But he had a feeling something was wrong. Lightning shouldn't be that color. He surveyed the street; drought-proof lawns, succulent plants, stucco walls, and red tile roofs suggested they were somewhere in the American southwest. He had no memory of how he wound up in a package again. It happened from time to time. He would awake, punish those who deserved it, then fall asleep for months at a time.

"Where are we?" she asked.

"I'm not sure. Do you know where you live?"

Across the street, an otherworldly sound heralded the arrival of a familiar sight: the ground boiled forth with millions of Richard's dark, chattering host. Reedlike banisters assembled themselves alongside the opening, which he knew was a staircase leading down. The voice of an old friend boomed from the heavens:

"JOHNATHAN JAMES BRADLEY, MUSTER TO THE FORTRESS OF MAXIMUM SUFFERING."

He knew had to obey, but he wasn't about to leave Mary alone. Luckily, a police cruiser rounded the corner. He took her hand.

"See that car? Ask them to take you home."

She nodded. "Okay. Where are you going?"

"Someone else needs my help."

"Are you a guardian angel?"

He looked down. "No. I wish I were."

The police cruiser slowed, its window lowering. An astonished woman looked out.

"Oh, my god," she said, activating the car's beacon lights. Rain started to patter down, accompanied by more red lightning. By then, Bixby had already scampered across the street and into the portal. The police officer stepped out and kneeled.

"Honey, what happened to you?"

"Bixby Bear saved me."

Clement's Scrotum

NO ONE NOTICED BIXBY'S ARRIVAL, because the supernatural equivalent of a fire alarm was going off. Richard was suddenly aswarm with his dark host, which carried him over to the atrium, where his entire map of existence was shaking like an earthquake was rattling all of reality, from one edge of the multiverse to the other. Multicolored lights exploded everywhere like fireworks, while crimson lightning flashed and crashed outside. The ruckus shook Letta off her feet and into Frith's arms.

"Richard!" Letta shouted. "Richard, Matthias—what's happening?!"

Matthias clung to a railing and held up a hand. "Do not disturb him!" To Richard, he said: "Cartographer! Is it Leviathan?!"

"Yes!" He dismissed the map of the universe and zoomed in on the Infernal Downfalls. Leviathan, the largest of the five major downfalls, had swollen to twice, thrice its original size. Its edges bumped into other, smaller downfalls, which got absorbed into its whole. With each downfall consumed, Leviathan flared as bright and red as neon—and you could *hear* it happening. Leviathan scooped up another downfall, and from an unseen direction—roughly *underneath* and *without*—something roared in protest, shaking everyone's internal organs and making their teeth sting.

Then it stopped.

Plaster drizzled from the ceiling. Sunlight shone for a fleeting second before cloud-cover retook the sky. A few licks of lightning slashed by the stained-glass dome. Everyone took a breath. Matthias crossed to Richard, whose eyes were clenched shut in concentration. Nicky, incredibly, had been filming the whole thing. Francois was chortling with glee.

"Will you still be needing my assistance, Cartographer? Or can we agree this is a matter for Sainte Jude?"

"Be silent, wight!" Richard barked over his shoulder before slowly zooming back away from Leviathan. The other major infernal downfalls remained untouched. Matthias stepped closer.

"Well done, Master of Anguish. Which realms did we lose?"

"None of consequence. Some trivial domains left over from ancient times."

Nicky appeared over Matthias' shoulder. "Dateline: Bermuda Triangle. This is Nicky Nicodemus, reporting to you from the Fortress of Maximum Suffering, where Tormento Mollytartarus—note, get his name CQ'ed—has just pulled off a miraculous feat. Mister Mollybumpus, can you explain what just happened for everyone watching at home?"

Richard glared into the camera. "This is not a time for japery, mortal."

She touched her stomach. "I don't know what japery means, but it just made me pregnant with triplets."

Matthias's face lit up as he finally noticed Bixby. "He is here."

Everyone turned toward the tiny toy bear, their reactions ranging from Francois' disinterest to the humans' wonder. A slack-jawed Nicky trained her camera on him, muttering to herself. Richard received him as a fellow colleague.

"Jonathan James Bradley," he said. "You arrive at our time of greatest need."

Matthias kneeled to address him at eye level. "Greetings, old friend."

"Hi, Matt," Bradley said, surveying the scene. "Who are all these people?"

"The Rite of Succession is underway," Matthias said. "And if our research is correct, you are the key to its fulfillment."

"It's Scutum Clementiae, isn't it?"

"I was a fool not to see it before."

Letta: "See *what* before?"

Matthias nodded to Richard, who said: "I have stemmed the tide, but we have, at most, one night and one day to retrieve your mother from Asmo. Come sunset tomorrow, all is lost."

"You're going to need to unpack that for us," Letta said.

Richard nodded. "As Master of Anguish, I am the sole conduit, and—what is the contemporary word?—*capacitor* for all energy, emotion, and feelings passing to and from the multivariant downfalls."

Nicky was awe-struck. "You … *feel* everything in all the hells?"

"In a manner of speaking. For all intents and purposes, I am the living avatar of hell. When a certain Downfall begins to absorb too much of the iridescent ether, I must find a way to re-balance the equation." He indicated Leviathan. "As you can see, I sacrificed several smaller infernal downfalls to the appetite of Leviathan."

Frith: "That was *you* doing that?"

"It was. If I hadn't acted quickly, Leviathan might have grown too fast to control. But I cannot maintain this equilibrium indefinitely. The longer we take, the more it will sap my strength." He turned to Bixby. "Master Bradley, we need to gain access to Scutum Clementiae, and we need your help."

Letta: "What's that you're saying? Clementy something?"

Matthias enunciated: "*Scutum Clementiae* is the formal name for the papal vault housed in Base Primum. It loosely translates to—"

Nicky raised her hand: "Oh, oh! I know! I know what that means! We all had to taken Latin at the Ranch; that means … Clement's scrotum?"

"*Shield*, Nicky," Frith said. "Clement's Shield, right?"

Matthias nodded. "Correct. The vault was commissioned by Pope Clement V, not long after his and Philip IV's slaughter of the Knights Templar. Fearing for his spiritual safety after the curse of Jaques de Molay on his pyre, Clement V enacted unprecedented security measures around Vatican City, going so far as to conspire with occult agents to construct Scutum Clementiae." He addressed Bixby: "My old friend, I cannot believe I failed to remember your part in all this."

"What part?" Frith asked.

Bixby: "I helped build it. Well, the current version at least. They change the locks every few hundred years, right? After I was cursed, the Vatican asked my help to secure the vault. They agreed to help sunset my damnation, if I can ever get separated from this fucking toy prison."

"Sunset your damnation?" Nicky asked, skirting her way across the room, around Richard, and back to her place between Letta and Frith.

"Right. Put an end to it. If I ever die, I'm going to hell. For most people, that's a 'forever' kinda deal, but mine'll cut off after the first billion years. Or trillion. I can't remember the fine print. But compared to eternity, a trillion years is nothing. They asked me to hunt degenerates who exploit children, an irony given the church's sorry fucking history."

"It is also a further irony, given our mission," Richard said.

"Meaning what?" Frith asked.

"First we must purloin the key to Clement's Shield, which is held by Tate Terrence Arbogast, the Papal Camerlengo."

Traxler: "I'm not Catholic, and I've never heard of a whatever that is."

"Quite so. The camerlengo has, for many hundreds of years, acted as the guardian of the key to Clement's Shield. His public position is mostly a subterfuge, but he handles certain administrative duties and also pronounces the Holy See officially deceased and acts in his stead between his death and the election of the college of cardinals. But the protection of the key is his signal occupation and concern. Heaven itself has assigned ... what the deuce?" Richard sensed something amiss on his unholy person. Patting himself down, he produced a small card adorned with pink hearts and an illustration of a curvy, scantily clad woman with long blond hair and a smattering of spots across her athletic frame. An icon representing a lion roared from one corner of the valentine. He read the card aloud in increasingly high dudgeon: "I want to be your Cheetara … *your SECRET ADMIRER?*"

Nicky threw up her hands: "Oh my god, guys, can you believe it? Richard has a secret admirer! Who is it? Fess up! Matthias, is it you? I bet it is, you old sea dog."

Richard narrowed his eyes and held the card between his thumb and forefinger. Suddenly, the surrounding air seemed to double in density; everyone felt like they were breathing redhot sand. Mad words emanated from Richard's mouth, which quavered like a heat mirage as he called forth his dark insectoid host. They swarmed around his hand and consumed the valentine atom by atom until it vanished in a column of red flame that scraped the ceiling. He overturned his palm and rubbed his thumb and forefinger together. Glowing red embers rained to the floor.

Nicky pointed at her midsection and mouthed, *Quadruplets.*

Letta slapped a hand over Nicky's mouth and said: "That'll be the last outburst from the floor, everyone! Nicky, please stop flirting with the ageless hell-lord for ten seconds while we map out the rest of this Hell heist, okay? Richard, you were saying that Heaven had assigned the camel-bingo some kind of bodyguard?"

Richard still looked pissed-off, but he glanced at his hand—which had held the valentine—and shook his head slightly. Was in it annoyance?

Or admiration?

He continued: "Yes, Letta Starchild. The heavenly host has assigned Camerlengo Arbogast a dedicated Prelate Centurion as his personal protection."

"So he has a guardian angel, got it," Letta said.

Matthias held up a hand. "Oh, goodness no, no, no. Not at all. There's no such thing."

"You just said he has a personal angel bodyguard. How is that not a guardian angel?"

"A *true* guardian angel hasn't been seen on this plane of existence since …"

Richard interjected: "Since forever. They don't exist. But that doesn't mean Goodmind isn't a threat most dire."

"So how do we get the key?"

"All in good time," Richard said. "The greater problem for us will be delivering the key to the infernal vault."

Letta: "Isn't that why we have the bear? Sorry—Mister Bradley?"

"You can just call me Bixby. I honestly don't give a fuck."

"Fair enough. Can't you take the key to your hell?"

"Things like us can't touch the key. I'd go up like a Roman Candle. I can guide one of you, but an actual human soul will need to turn it."

Frith gave him a wide-eyed frown. "What do you mean a 'human *soul*'?"

Bixby looked at Richard, said: "It's been a long time since I reviewed the rules for this shit. They're not gonna be able to go there unless they're dead, right?"

Francois erupted with laughter. "It is the great unknown, the undiscovered country, the end of existence. You'll never be able to do it. Failure is your birthright, your doom, your destiny. Unless you want to retreat into your dreams? I can prolong a single instant into eternity. Give you a life to—"

Matthias closed his fist; the act slammed Francois's mouth shut. "That is enough."

Francois wrestled his mouth back open. "You would *dare* befoul the Master of Dreams with your parlor tricks, old man?" He spat black bile onto Matthias's hand, which caused him to reel backward, his flesh suddenly sprouting a inky latticework of veins. He balled his fist, bared his teeth, and banished the Dream Master's magic from his body. Darkness drained from his hand, but he gasped for breath and staggered into a chair. Most everyone rallied to his defense:

Nicky yelled, "Lay offa Matty, asshole!"

Frith simply stormed at Francois, but Traxler blocked her path and and brandished his Faraday cattle-prod in the demon's face. "Want more of this, weirdo?"

Francois's spuming eyes narrowed. He gave them all a wicked grin. "You will *all* need respite before tomorrow's sunset. And I'll be waiting."

Traxler shrugged. "So long as you keep your weird fuckin' eyes on those magical screens of yours, that's fine by me."

Letta shouted: "That's enough! Richard, what did you mean when you said we have to be dead?"

"Humans   may   enter   the   uppermost   infernal downfall—Stercorebubulus—and survive, but in order to travel to any others, you will need to be dead."

Letta, Frith, and Traxler were silent for a moment before Nicky stood forth, flashing a peace sign.

"It ain't no *thaaaaaaaaaaaaaaaaaang.*"

Nicky's five-and-a-half-second utterance of the word "thang" echoed through the Fortress.

Pulling a Keifer

L ET ME GUESS," FRITH SAID. "Your *other* motto is, 'always carry a set of defibrillators'?"

"Very funny, Winnie," Nicky said with an exaggerated wink. "But it's not just a defibrillator. It's a device of my own invention." She laid out the device, which included defibrillator paddles, as well as several IV lines. "Didja ever read *A Prayer For Owen Meany?*"

"The John Irving novel?" Frith said. "No, only *Garp.*"

"Does anyone mind if I spoil it?" Without waiting, she continued: "*Anyway,* the whole story is about this kid who thinks he's been touched by God. He has premonitions about a disaster that's going to happen later in his life, and he spends years preparing for it, going through the motions of what he'll need to do. He calls himself an instrument of God."

"I think they call him 'Old Father,'" Frith said, indicating Richard and Matthias.

Matthias shrugged. "He has no name, he has many names. That is simply what he *feels* like to those of us who have glimpsed or felt the iridescent ether."

Nicky smiled. "That was really cool, Matty," she said before turning to indicate the device. "I've only got one of these, but it has several 'inputs,' okay? The key to pulling a keifer is killing the brain while keeping the body basically alive."

Matthias: "I beg your pardon, but pulling a what?"

Nicky held up a palm. "Pulling a keifer! Like Keifer Sutherland in *Flatliners?*" She started knocking on her head. "No, no, no! Of course you haven't seen *Flatliners!* Use your head, Nicky, use your head! So, it's a movie about people who explore the afterlife by killing themselves. Wait! Do you even know what movies are? Shit! Ack, sorry for swearing!"

"We are aware of motion pictures, child."

"Okay, phew. Well, to tie all this together, I think Old Father sent me here to help us pull keifers."

Richard's expression softened a few perceptible degrees at this.

Nicky blushed and continued: "You attach these electrodes to your temple and chest, while the IV goes in your arm. Push the Cutie Patootie—" (she indicated a big, red button labeled, *THE CUTIE PATOOTIE*) "—to go under. You can set a timer to bring yourself back up again, or someone can watch you."

Traxler leaned in. "If I'm looking at this right, and I like to think I am, you've basically built a portable life-support system." He indicated several readouts: "You're tracking blood pressure, pulse rate, and EEG?"

She popped her eyes wide: "Don't you mean your *braaaaaainnn-waaaaves?!*"

"Right," Traxler said with a chuckle. "But what's this third number?" He tapped the third readout, two LED digits.

Nicky raised a finger. "Ahhhh! This is a metric I learned about on the Dark Web. It measures something called *Vital Essence,* or VE. I had to special order the module from some kook in Australia.

It's a measurement of your soul's foothold on the earthly plane. I experimented with all kinds of ranges for it, but after mucho trial and error, I settled on a range of one to sixty-seven. One, you're totally kaput and croaked; sixty-seven you're alive and probably very, very high. Anything from fifty-seven to sixty-*fouuuur?* is alive and pretty much normal, while anything lower than two ain't coming back from the beyond."

"Why one to sixty-seven?" Frith asked. "Why not one to seventy?"

Nicky whooped: *"Ha!* Gross." Everyone gave her a confused look, so she added: "Because sixty-seven's a prime number, y'all? I mean, *seventy?* Ugh, what kinda number is *that?!* It's divisible by, like, everything!"

"Shoulda seen that coming," Frith said. "So this thing actually works?"

"Yes, of course! I mean, maybe! Maybe? Maybe yes? I'm not sure, honestly. Any time I went under, I just saw the goofiest stuff."

"Can you give us an example?" Letta asked.

"It was just episodes of *The Simpsons*," she said with a shrug. "But I was definitely dead."

Letta examined the device. "Okay, so next step: Francois, what can you tell us about this camel-bingo guy?"

"Camerlengo," Richard corrected.

"Camel-bingo, right."

Francois, who had been mostly silent, emitted a rattling hiss. Giggling.

"I can tell you all about him. *Voir!*"

He flicked his fan closed and open again, bringing up dozens of pictures of the Camerlengo. Arbogast carried a few dozen extra pounds, with a double chin, five-o'clock shadow, and thick wire-frame glasses. He wore the red raiment of a Catholic cardinal, complete with zuccheto and various jewelry. He went about his business like normal, despite the inclement weather, scurrying from building to building to meet with church leaders.

Until night fell. Then his activity took an unusual turn.

Letta smiled. "Would you look at that. Vatican City has an underworld."

"Vraiment, mamzelle Letta. He is a naughty, naughty little man."

Vatican City was mostly dedicated to the apparatus of the church, but it also included small residential and commercial areas. Adjacent to this area and immediately to the north of the Papal residence stood the Vatican Archives. The building resembled Versailles, with pillars, ramparts, and stone frontage, all of it centered around an ancient wooden door.

Arbogast visited the archives every night, but not through that door.

"Behold," Francois said as he rotated his left hand back and forth to "rewind" and "fast-forward" the image. Every night, Arbogast snuck from his residence to the Archives, where he circled around the building to what appeared to be a blank brick wall, which he tapped in rapid succession, revealing a secret door.

"Where does this lead?" Letta asked.

"A *bar clandestin*. In addition to his more *carnal* vices, the good Camerlengo is a man of spirits."

"He's a boozehound," Frith said.

Francois nodded. "Every night he enjoys one, single glass of liquor, which he has flown in from all over the globe."

Frith leaned in. "So do we break into his place while he's out? Get the key then?"

"Non. Ever does he wear the key around his neck, against his beating black heart."

His skeletal fingers did a dance through the air, causing the rifts to open and close and strobe and flash rhythmically. When he stopped, the rift before her showed Arbogast leaning forward. A leather lanyard was cinched around his neck, but it came loose and revealed a golden disc.

"That's the key?" Letta asked. "Doesn't look like a key."

"I believe it is a locket of some kind," Francois said.

Traxler nodded, pointing. "He wears it close."

Frith: "And that's leather. Not like he won't notice if someone yanks it off him."

Nicky sidled her way next to them. "What we need is a master pickpocket."

"You have one."

Matthias had spoken. They all looked.

Frith shook her head. "Aren't you a little old for field work?"

"Not I. Him."

He pointed at Richard the Cartographer, who was scowling.

Letta crossed her arms. "Mister Mallestratos, I think it's time you regaled us with a story about your earthly exploits."

"Very well, but first you should know that my complete earthly name is Richard Pudlicotte. And I masterminded the most lucrative heist in the history of mankind."

1303: Westminster Abbey
May 1, approximately 2:31 a.m.

HE WAS SEVERAL INCHES SHORTER, with a full head of auburn hair and a voice that was at least two octaves higher. But if anyone from the Fortress of Maximum Suffering had met him, they would've recognized Richard the Cartographer instantly, even as he was carrying out the night's labor, the final test of a crucial component in what would come to be known as the Great Crown Jewels Robbery of 1303.

Richard and another man lay sprawled on a steep staircase leading down to the Abbey's crypt, where the spoils awaited behind a heavy wooden door laden with fortified locks. Stone ceilings vaulted overhead, while the only light came from cresset torches flickering on the walls and a pair of oil lamps set on the floor. The men lay on their backs, doublets soaked with sweat, arms extended before them, both of them slowly belaying ropes. The ropes were secured to posts at the top of the stairs on a retaining wall that encircled the Abbey and lashed to a wooden construction that, at a glance, resembled a small boat. Closer examination would reveal that it was actually a ten-foot section of stairs.

This was the key component being tested tonight, a "bridge of stairs." The Abbey's Crypt, which held the Crown's vast treasure, was protected by several measures, including a treacherous staircase that was bisected by a three-yard gap.

"Easy, easy," Richard whispered.

"Shut it, Dick. I know damn well to keep it easy." His compatriot bore a craggy visage, with black hair he kept cut close because of his work. As he put it, "I don't want any blackguards catching hold of my locks as I turn my rounds."

This was Bill Palmer, better known as William of the Palace. His haircut not only served him well as deputy Keeper of Fleet Prison, but it also let him better blend in with their conspirators at the Abbey, the Black Monks, so named for their robes.

Through clenched teeth, Richard said: "If it drops down that gully, it'll take us weeks to fashion a new one."

The Crown had its own stairbridge, of course. Stealing it was beyond even the means of Richard's network of brigands, spies, and tell-tales, but King Edward I—better known as Edward Longshanks— had in all his wrathful arrogance moved the apparatus of state from London to York to more conveniently prosecute his war against William Wallace and the Scot. Doing so had left Westminster Abbey's Crypt vulnerable to enterprising scoundrels like Richard, who learned of the dimensions of the stairbridge thanks to a loose-tongued city clerk named Bakewell. Bill's whore had plied Bakewell with a tincture of something exotic she said would "bathe the world in a wonder of wind."

Straining from the effort, William said: "It ain't dropping down no gully."

They let the stairbridge down a few more inches. One of their other conspirators, Adam de Fentlok, had suggested simply jumping across the divide, but Richard had dismissed that notion.

"Shall we toss the Rod of Moses back across that gulf then, along with all the other great tonnage of treasure?" Richard asked. "Legend says it has no bottom. If one of us should trip, we'll fall until Gabriel's trumpet sounds."

"Closer, closer," Richard said as he belayed the stairbridge down a few more inches. His rope was lashed to the structure's rear, while his partner's was tied to the front, letting him lift it like a drawbridge until it spanned the gap. In the dim-glimmering light, they couldn't see the far side, leaving William to delicately lower it over and over, hoping to find purchase.

"I think I've got it. Just a few more—"

A woman's voice came braying down: *"On the twelfth night of Dec-e-e-e-mberrr, yadda da dadda da dadda da-da!"*

Another voice, this one male, kept up the tune: *"On the eleventh night of Dec-e-e-e-mberrr, yadda da dadda da dadda da-da!"*

A startled William let slip the rope, which sent the stairbridge falling. The sudden motion scorched both men's palms, causing them to cry out in pain and protest:

"S'blood!"

"Bolts and shackles!"

SLAM! The stairbridge fell into place perfectly. Richard and William exhaled and clambered to their feet in anticipation of their fellow conspirators, who came skipping down the stairs, tipsy as you please. The first was a woman, clad in a low-cut surcote she'd customized with her own stitchings, along with her prize and joy: a brass brooch she'd inlaid with a single emerald. Her hair, which she'd neatly pinned back that morning, had fallen into ringlet'ed disarray. She bore a perpetually wide and wolfish grin.

This was Edelina Cookson, known to her friends as Edie.

The second conspirator to stagger down the stairs would be familiar to Letta, Frith, Nicky, and Traxler. Clad in the black robes of his order with his hair cut in the traditional tonsure, he waved about a tankard of ale, sloshing half its contents down the stairs.

This was Matthias de Rilesford, who would, before the year was out, become the seventy-seventh Guildmaster of Lord Morningstar's Menagerie, but for the time being, he was simply a Black Monk of the Abbey—a very, very drunk one. With an arm looped around Edie's waist, he sang:

"On the tenth night of Dec-e-e-e-mberrr, yadda da dadda da dadda da-da!"

She slapped his chest. "You filched the stanz from me!"

"Bugger it all," he laughed, unlooping his arm and presenting her to the other men. "After you, my dear!"

She sang: *"On the tenth night of Decem—"*

William shushed them. "Shut it, the both of you! You'll wake up everyone from here to Thames with your caterwauling."

Edie and Matthias immediately shifted into a mock performance for an audience of two, turning to each other with gogging eyes as they pressed fingers to their lips and shushed each other, theatrically checking over their shoulders. Matthias slipped on his spilled ale and sat down hard, sloshing another draught into his face. Edie sat down next to him, the both of them giggling. Richard crossed his arms, smiling.

"You're a little late for Twelfthtide. It's May Day."

Edie covered her mouth. "Is it, now?" She stood. "So you're saying you don't want me gift?"

William's posture shifted. "You got it?"

She dipped into her cleavage and produced a pouch, about three inches in diameter and sealed with wax. William swiped for it, but she held it out of his reach. "Give love a kiss, first."

Stomping up the stairs, he swept her into his arms and kissed her deeply, taking hold of her hair. She gasped. He laughed. "I'll always have a kiss for my little Edie. Now let's have it."

Breathless and smiling, she dropped the pouch in his hand.

Richard leaned in for a look. "He gave it up willingly, the clerk?" he asked, referring to the wardrobe clerk tasked with guarding the crypt's key.

Edie cackled. "He thinks I've got sugar in me heels. He even offered to reseal it when we's finished our work."

William said, "Not that it'll matter when the crypt's bare. O, to see the look on ol' Longshanks' face when he finds out."

Matthias cast a bleary-eyed gaze down at the stairbridge. "It fit, then? Well, I owe Fentlok a groat."

Richard nodded. "That is, if he remembers what we're about. Bedlam near to unmanned that poor soul."

A new voice, faint and shaky, warbled from above like a wounded bird.

"Was it to scope?"

A silhouette stood at the top of the stairs, cast in darkness by starshine and the moony glimmer of cloudhaze. He took a tentative step down, and firelight brought into view a thirtysomething man with prematurely graying hair and thick spectacles.

Richard's eyebrows rose. He smiled. "Adam! We weren't expecting you."

Matthias lurched to his feet, his eyes suddenly clear, and bounded up the stairs, offering his arm to their old friend Adam de Fentlok. He escorted him down one delicate step at a time.

As they approached, William scoffed lightly and muttered, "I still say it's foolish to leave such a great task in his hands. His mind's like to a chaos."

Edie shushed him.

Matthias and Adam stopped a few steps above. They had all freed him from Bethlem Hospital back in February, both for his all-encompassing knowledge of London's waterways but mainly because they couldn't bear to think of their dear friend suffering behind its walls.

Richard stood to the side, sidling ever so slightly closer to Bill Castle, and presented the wooden section of stairs.

"It fits perfectly, my old friend," he said to Adam.

Matthias produced a groat to honor his wager, but Adam waved it away, saying, "You owe me nothing, brother." He blinked owlishly, his eyes magnified to great white disks. "And the key?"

"Here," William said, holding up the pouch. "Let me open the—what the blazes!"

William looked at his empty palms in a bluster—the pouch had appeared in Richard's hand like magic. William would later tell the inquisitors that Richard was the best cracksman and buzzer in Europe.

But that awful time wouldn't come until the summer.

After they'd all been caught.

Richard grinned. "Should we test the key?"

Matthias frowned. "But Adam—" he stopped and corrected himself: "Beg pardon, *you* won't be ready to move the gold till Friday, yes?"

Adam's eyes rose. He seemed to go somewhere else. William and Richard shared a concerned look, but after a moment, their friend seemed to return. "We'll have the barges on the Thames by Friday, with enough souls lively to do the pass-along." To Richard he added: "We *should* test the key, though."

Matthias nodded. "I'd hate to come back tomorrow night and find Edie nicked the wrong one."

She punched his shoulder. "I didn't nick the wrong key, you gull!"

Richard broke the pouch's seal and held up the key to the greatest store of wealth on the face of the earth. Torchlight twinkled in his eyes.

"Let's go look at some gold, shall we?"

Present Day: Faraday Delivers

RICHARD FELL SILENT.

"So you were a man back in 1303?" Frith asked. "Doesn't that make you kind of young for a hell-lord?"

"I am more than seven hundred years old."

"You don't look a day over six hundred ninety-nine," Nicky cooed.

Letta held up her palms. "Well, what happened next? That was just starting to get good!"

He shook his head. "We've no time to waste, Letta Starchild. We must make arrangements to travel to Vatican City, and as I told my master earlier, it will involve considerable risk for me—and thereby, the mission as a whole."

"What's the risk to you?" Frith asked.

Francois was already giggling. "Ohhh, but you must let me tell them, O Great Cartographer."

Richard: "Silence, creature." He addressed everyone: "A few of you have already seen an example of my ability to transform my appearance. Successor, Catalyst, Master Traxler, you bore witness to me in a partially-transformed state. I was able to look mostly human while still retaining the ability to invoke my powers as needed. But if I am to aid you on holy ground, I will have to perform the rite of *Maladenudation.*"

A wide-eyed Nicky whispered: "Did I hear the word 'nude' in there?"

Richard rolled his eyes. "In a manner of speaking, mortal. I have the ability to completely cast off my powers and return to my human form for precisely one earth hour."

"That's not a lot of time," Letta said. "How long until the Altar-Boy-Fucker goes to get soused?"

Francois consulted his array of rifts. "According to my intelligence, he'll arrive at the speakeasy within the hour."

"And we only have until sunset tomorrow to pull off the *entire* heist, or … well, everything goes kablooey?"

Matthias nodded. "Correct."

"Got it," Letta said. "Then we have to move on this right now. Let's go pull a hell heist."

Part Five
1993: The Third Maxim

IT TURNED OUT TYLER DIDN'T need to do anything.

He'd already provided the crucial intel they needed—where the reporter was staying—but Athena ordered the bigwigs to bring him along, "for edification and illumination," whatever that meant. Nicky, as the production's eye in the sky, stayed back at the schoolhouse with little Letta to coordinate communications.

They headed toward Gloversville, a small town in the foothills of the Adirondacks, riding trucks: Athena, Frith, Franco, and Tyler in their main truck, a four-seater; Bayard in the second; Stanton in the third. Mountain mist rolled in from the north and bathed the blue-black scene, the trucks jet-streaming through the murk and kicking up tornadoes of wake. Stars shone overhead but didn't glitter;

the barometric pressure was ticking higher and higher. Everyone had a faint headache.

Finally, the Super 8 sign emerged from the darkness. They pulled off the road.

"Turn off your lights and don't use your hazards," Athena told everyone through her walkies, one walkie for each channel she needed to monitor. Nicky had fashioned a special set of headphones that let Athena listen to each channel but prevented the other channels from talking over one another. Nicky had an analogous set of headphones with a mouthpiece.

They wheeled the trucks behind some hay bales a few dozen yards off the road. "Bayard, ride ahead and do what needs to be done. Stanton, provide discreet backup and execute like usual."

The other two trucks rumbled out of the field and down the road. They waited. Tyler fidgeted.

"What is he going to do? He's not going to hurt anyone, is he?"

Athena squeezed his thigh hard enough to make him flinch.

"Have you ever counted casualty?"

Tyler shook his head. "Counted … casually?"

"No, no, no. *Counted casualty.*"

"I don't know what that means."

"It means—"

Bayard's voice interrupted, speaking in her ear: "All set, Foundation."

"Bayard's done his labor," Athena told everyone in the truck. Frith and Franco nodded their acknowledgments. Athena changed channels: "Stanton, report in."

"I've got the key."

"Very good. You and Bayard stand sentinel outside her room and await our arrival."

Athena spoke in her ear: "Very good. You and Bayard stand sentinel outside her room and await our arrival."

Nicky sat cross-legged on a desk, cupping two sets of headphones to her ears and listening carefully. A CB-radio exchange box sat before her. She'd custom built it just for occasions like these. It had several input and output ports, as well as support for ten different audio channels, and only Nicky knew exactly how to use it. Their Foundation called her "eye in the sky," but she was less eye and more *ear*.

Letta sat next to her, trying to eavesdrop in on the excitement. Nicky had, with Athena's blessing, dismissed the rest of the ranch so she could work in privacy.

Letta leaned in. "What's going on, what's going on?"

Nicky pressed a finger to her lips but whispered: "What's happening is some smartypants is about to get taught a lesson. You don't mess with the Starchildren."

"It was that lady you saw earlier, right? Out back of the theater?"

Nicky nodded, monitoring her headphones, her face cycling through an array of expressions: her brow creased as she frowned; her eyes flickered wide; a huge smile spread across her face. She looked over, biting her lower lip.

"You're darn tootin' it was that lady," she whispered. "You wanna hear Athena and the bigwigs give her the business?"

Letta smiled and nodded, even though she didn't know what it meant to give someone any kind of "business." Nicky plugged in another set of headphones, which she handed to Letta.

Back at the schoolhouse, crosstalk and chatter sounded against the backdrop growl of truck engines.

"Keep your headlights off, Franco."

"Roger that, Foundation."

"What's the plan here?" This was Frith speaking. "We're just going to put a scare into her, right? Get the network off our asses?"

"I don't want anyone to get hurt." This was Tyler.

Athena ignored them both. "Pull around back, Franco."

The truck's engine shut off.

Letta whispered: "What *are* we going to do to her?"

"Just what Frith said," Nicky said, covering her mouthpiece. "Put a scare into her."

Athena spoke: "My children, this is an auspicious occasion. A new Starchild is crowning before our very eyes, and on his first new birthday, he will get to bear witness to our collective strength in the face of adversity. He will see, with his own true-blue eyes, the might of the bigwigs and the power of our hearts united as one. I expect total silence until we make contact with the target. Tyler, do you understand, my child?"

"I … I think so."

Franco spoke: "Kid, all we're saying is don't say a single word until we can get in there and talk some sense into this lady. That's it. You're safe. We're all safe. Foundation wouldn't put any of us in harm's way."

"Okay," Tyler said, barely audible.

Car doors slammed through their headphones. Faint footsteps padded through grass then onto pavement. No one spoke, but everyone breathed heavily. The schoolroom's walls seemed to draw closer as Letta's entire world narrowed around her headphones. She glanced at Nicky, who wore a bizarre smile; she looked less happy or delighted and more like she was simply baring her teeth. It reminded Letta of illustrations she'd seen of dragons or werewolves.

Metal slid against metal.

"Stanny must be unlocking the door," Nicky whispered, tapping Letta's shoulder rapidly. "It's all about to come due."

"What's about to come due?" Letta asked.

"The bill."

More heavy breathing, then chaos. Bedsprings squeaked. A woman cried out only for her voice to be suddenly muffled. Wood thumped against carpet as furniture got overturned. Glass shattered and crunched. Footfalls slammed around. The woman wheezed and rasped through her nose faster and faster, hyperventilating.

"Slow your breathing, notper." This was Athena. "Slow your breathing. This will all unfold without incident if you slow your breathing and stay with us in this moment. Will you try to slow your breathing?" A moment's silence, then: "Good. Bayard, please show her the instrument of your subjugation."

The woman shrieked through someone's hand, presumably Franco's or Frith's.

Athena continued: "Quiet, *quiet yourself,* notper. No one can hear you. We've seen to that. There's no one else in the motel, and we've subjugated the clerk. Silence and stillness take you, notper, and know that in this distending moment, thou art safe. You are. Bayard is subjugation, nothing more. He does not deploy his implement with lethal force. He never has, and he never will. But we need you to know that if you scream, no one will come to your aid. You are axiomatically with us now, in this time and place. An object-entity with us all. Do you pledge utter silence, notper?" A moment passed, then: "Frith, you may uncover her mouth."

The woman gasped and heaved several breaths. "What do you want?"

"We know you're with the media. Yes?"

"I wanted to see the show. Aren't you doing *Othello?*"

Ten seconds passed. The only sound was everyone's breathing. Letta's chest constricted. Tears welled up in her chest. She looked to Nicky, but she still bore that same strange smile.

Over the headphones, Athena spoke: "You're frightened, notper, which is understandable. But know this solemnly: I will only ask twice more. I will ask the same question. Here is the first repeated instance of it: Are you with the media?"

"I'm a huge Shakespeare fan, up from Syracuse for a class. I'm sorry I walked in on your rehearsal, okay? I'm sorry!"

Nicky flicked a switch on her radio and spoke: "Foundation, would you mind if I had a word with Miss Culpepper?"

"We have this well in hand, eye in the sky."

Nicky shifted to a tone Letta had never heard from her. Her voice dropped into her chest, her delivery slowing precipitously. She sounded twenty years older and a hundred years wiser, all in an instant: "Foundation, I know I'm a handful. I get it. The silly jokes, the cameras. Me being a hyperactive headcase. But when I had to leave my family, you took me in. You became my family. And I can never repay you for what you've given me: home and hearth, security and soul. Foundation, I hereby invoke our third maxim, and I ask permission to speak with the notper Ashley Culpepper."

A moment's silence, then Athena quoted the third maxim: "Secrets are forever. Protect them even into the afterworld and past all the Infernal Downfalls. How is that relevant to the matter at hand?"

"Foundation, I have protected a secret for a long time, and I've got to talk about it. Forgive me for not telling you sooner, but *please* let me speak with her. I wouldn't ask if it wasn't important."

More silence. "Very well."

Letta hadn't breathed for a full minute. She clutched the headphones to her head, hanging on every sound and utterance. Rustles and thuds presumably signaled the transfer of headphones to Ashley Culpepper, who spoke next.

"Who is this?"

Nicky's voice, so staid moments before, leapt into her nose in a wheedling taunt: "Hi there, Ashie. Remember me? Remember your baby sister?"

Thirty Years Later: The Predecessor

MATTHIAS RARELY VENTURED TO THE Fortress's lowest floors. The atrium containing the Apparatus took up the top seven of the building's ten storeys, while the lowest three housed an archive and memorial to the previous seventy-six Guildmasters, whose members went back to the dawn of recorded time. These three floors had a hivelike structure and arrangement, with dozens of small staircases, balconies, and interior windows looking up and down to various statues, bookshelves, and displays dedicated to Matthias's order.

In the waning moments before the Successor was to begin her initiation, Matthias found himself standing before two statues. One depicted his predecessor, while the other depicted Richard's predecessor, a woman known only as Illyria. Matthias never learned much about her; only that she was a fearsome warlord around the time of Christ's supposed birth and that she oversaw the Menagerie during an era of relative stability. Monsters and murderers had little to fear in the more ancient world, but as the Menagerie's source of sustenance became more resistant, resilient, and tenacious, the order's ranks fell closer and closer to that fabled, unholy number of six hundred and sixty-six.

They fell below that number on the night of Friday, May 3, 1303.

1303: Streets of London
May 3, approximately 10:59 p.m.

THE TOLL OF A DISTANT bell signaled something was amiss.

The key had worked. Two nights previous, when they placed the stairbridge, Richard de Pudlicotte, Matthias de Rilesford, Bill Palmer, and Edie Cookson had spent a glorious half hour touring the royal crypt, marveling at the endless dunes of silver and gold. Much to the dismay of Bill Palace, Edie unlaced her surcote and pretended to bathe herself with pearls and emeralds. Richard slipped on a sapphire-studded gold ring that had once adorned the finger of Saint Dunstan while Matthias swung around the sword that had knighted Henry II.

It was the greatest night of Matthias's life. He was now at the beginning of his worst.

He was pelting down an alleyway past stonefaced buildings, inns, and pubs, their rear walls streaked with piss stains, the smell of boiled cabbage and pork on the air. He'd strapped two satchels to his back, both of them laden with more wealth than he could spend in a thousand lifetimes. Behind him was one of the Abbey's pages, a lad of twelve summers who had agreed to the job for a price of ten pounds. They tried to offer him more, but he refused.

"It's more'n I'll ever need. All's I care 'bout is for Tall Edward to pay dearly for sending me brother to die for naught."

Matthias and the pageboy halted at the top of the alley, which ended in a T-intersection with a dirt road lined with more stone- and wood-faced buildings. The pageboy bore the same burden: two satchels packed with gold and jewels, but he'd added a touch of whimsy in the form of a crown that bobbled on his head. While keeping an eye on the road, Matthias snatched it off.

"Watch it, boy," Matthias whispered. "We're not clear yet." He examined the crown with widening eyes. "By'r lady, but I think this belonged to King Lionheart."

"It's about to belong to King Bridgeford," the boy said, referring to his employer.

Wagon wheels squeaked and clattered toward them. Two wagons, both empty, came rattling up to the alleyway, one of them pushed barrow-style by Adam de Fentlok, whose owlish eyes popped brightly, while the other was horsedrawn and being driven by a habit-wearing sister who Matthias instantly recognized.

"*Edie?* God's bones, what're you wearing?"

She pressed a finger to her lips. "Shh! I'm testing to see if I'd catch fire when I put it on." She emitted a faint cackle. "C'mon now, dearie, we're losing the dark."

Adam, his brow twinkling with sweat, halted his wheelbarrow and muttered: "Ferries and barges be the order of the night, yes, indeed they are. What be the cargo, neighbors? Plaguerot, I presume?"

Matthias touched his hand and whispered: "It's gold, Adam. All from Longshanks' coffers."

Adam adjusted his spectacles, seeming to understand. "Ay, that's a good turn. That rascal, he's had it coming since Lucifer fell."

Matthias and the pageboy both slung their cargo onto the wagons just as the mastermind himself arrived, Richard Pudlicotte, who pushed a cart laden with treasure hidden under a burlap covering. Richard greeted his coconspirators and surveyed the scene.

Bill Palmer sidled next to him and intoned: "It's not enough. Like to a chaos, I said."

Richard shook his head at Bill to say *be quiet,* but inside, he couldn't admit he was wrong. It *wasn't* enough. He approached Adam and spoke to him gently, keenly aware of the man's fragile mental state:

"Adam, is this all you brought? One wheelbarrow? We've tons of treasure to move, and all of it must make it to Thames before sunrise. Weren't you supposed to bring more help?"

At that moment, the streets around them burst to life, silently and vibrantly. From every alleyway, corner, and even some rooftops emerged dozens, no, *scores* of people, all of them wearing the black cloaks of Matthias's order. Richard, William, Matthias, and Edie looked around in growing astonishment. In the space of five minutes, the crowd of people swarmed across the carts, taking up the treasure in parcels large and small. To a person, each and every one of them paused to thank the lead conspirators.

An old man said: "I thank'ee, sir, and I'll get this cargo to its rightful place."

A woman not older than sixteen summers said: "Grammercy, grammercy, good sirs. And lady!"

Another woman, this one bearing a mother's kind eyes and weary face, approached them and said with a hitching voice: "My child was so sick. No surgeon would see him. But Adam prepared a dram of something miraculous and made him well."

Another simply tipped his hat and said, "Adam's a dear, and Longshanks can fuck a goat."

Dozens of others were at a loss for words, their eyes also brimming with tears. A massive man, one of the few men taller than six-foot they'd ever seen, simply squeezed Richard's and Matthias's shoulders and hugged Edie before he pounded over to Adam's cart and took his hand.

"Thank you for this, old friend. Maybe Longshanks will stop sending our sons to die up north." The huge man pointed at the conspirators and jerked his chin at Adam, saying: "I owe this man me life. You look after him, or I'll hear of it."

Another said: "And I."

"And I."

Richard, Matthias, and Edie exchanged looks and nodded.

"You have my word."

"And mine."

"And mine," Edie said.

The weary-faced mother spoke in a hushed whisper: "He's an angel. He always was."

Edie agreed: "He *is* an angel, that one. He holds all our hearts."

Adam's confederates, accompanied by the pageboy, bid them farewell and vanished in every direction, stealing down alleyways, slipping into shadows, and bounding across rooftops. They left the carts without so much as a farthing, shilling, or groat.

Richard crossed to Adam and said, "This is well done, my friend."

"Aye," Adam said, staring into the distance, smiling. "The Thames is so beautiful at night."

"Indeed it is. And your friends—they know where to go?"

Adam's magnified eyes swung over to him, instantly clear. "To the very fingerbreadth. And they know to meet back here in an hour for the next ton of treasure."

"That's splendid news, my old—"

They mistook the sound for a moan at first.

Everyone startled, turning around or checking over their shoulders. Someone moaned again. Everyone exchanged spooked looks for a moment before Edie figured out what it was.

"It's the tower," she said, pointing across the city. The Thames river could be seen glittering in the distance, while beyond stood the Tower of London. Its bell tower didn't sound on the hour, instead only tolling once an afternoon as means of calling the city's prisoners back inside from the yard. And yet, here it was, sounding twice, thrice, four times in the late evening.

Matthias frowned. "Why are they sounding—" His skull was suddenly the tower, his brain the bell, his mind a pulsing drumbeat of agony. Somewhere miles away, Matthias's friends were calling to him, but they no longer existed. He'd collapsed to his knees, clutching his head and scrabbling at his face. With every beat of his heart, his skull seemed to squeeze a few inches smaller, threatening to blast his brains out his eye sockets.

What deviltry is this?

Hallucinations of stomach-turning horrors beset him—of war crimes, child slaughter, babies spit upon pikes, rapings and pillagings—but these visions also included more remarkable sights: basilisks and gryphons and all manner of monstrosities he'd only seen in paintings or illuminated texts. As the bell chimed once more, he sensed with absolute certainty that someone had, in that very same moment, met their fate—a redheaded woman from the north. *Ireland,* he thought through searing pain.

The bell's final toll echoed across the sleepy cityscape. The torment had ceased.

Richard was at his side. "My friend, what vexes you?"

Matthias opened his mouth to speak but screamed instead. From everyone else's perspective, the old monk suddenly behaved in a most bizarre manner. His entire form quavered at an insane speed, shaking faster than anyone they'd seen with the palsy. This only lasted a single second for them, but from his own perspective, Matthias experienced an entire day's worth of memories—starting with the arrival of the stonework woman.

Illyria.

"Matthias?"

The voice caught him by surprise. He turned to find the eccentric young woman—the one as enamored of modern technology as she was of Richard—standing on one of the statuary's many small staircases. He felt simultaneously embarrassed and welcoming; his embarrassment sprang from a deep-seated and long-held shame of his office, while another part of him felt a kinship with this strange soul who had shown him inordinate kindness from the moment they met.

But it's more than that, isn't it?

Yes, it was, because Nicodemus reminded him both of his old friend Adam de Fentlok and also of the woman whose death brought about his ascension to the head of the Menagerie.

Alice Kyeteler, the Witch of Killkenny.

"Uh, hello? Earth to Matthias, come in, Matthias?"

"Forgive me, my child. I was merely countenancing the reality that my powers may elude me at a key moment and that I may fail you all and doom the multiverse to chaos and dissolution."

"Oh. Got it, cool. Yeah, that's what I figured. Same here!" She inched closer. "Uhhh, hey."

"Yes?"

"Uhh, what's up?"

"I beg your pardon?"

"I was wondering if I could ask you a favor?"

Matthias's brow creased. But he smiled. "I'm not sure what favor I could grant you, but please ask it."

Nicky fidgeted. She blushed, crossed and uncrossed her arms, chuckled, then crossed her feet and propped her hand against one of the statues—which immediately tipped over and collapsed with an ear-splitting *CRRR-A-A-A-SSSSH!* Carvings of arms, legs, and other body parts disintegrated across the floor. She covered her mouth, mortified. She took up the statue's stone head, newly severed—a scowling man with a braided beard—and tried to place it back on its pedestal.

"Ohmygawd, ohmygawd, ohmygawd, I'm so sorry! Gosh!"

Matthias crossed to her and touched her hands. She fell silent.

"Don't trouble yourself, child," he said. Gingerly, he took the stone head and peered into its eyes. "This was a likeness of Acrisius the Accursed, my predecessor as Guildmaster. He was a sadistic ghoul."

"Oh," she said, barely audible. "But don't you have his same job?"

Matthias nodded, his eyes downcast. "Well met." He set aside the stone head before looking up, his face clenched in woe. "The past seven hundred years have been but the beginning of my penance. Though I have come to learn that the difference between angels and demons is often a matter of perspective, I believe that there exists true good and true evil, true heavens and true hells. And I shall be consigned to the latter once your friend takes command of the Menagerie. I have earned my eternity of suffering."

Nicky's lower lip trembled. "Sounds like you're being pretty hard on yourself."

From far above came a calling voice: *"Nickyyy? Where the fuck are youuuuu? We gotta goooooo!"*

Matthias cleared his throat. "What favor did you want to ask?"

"Oh, right. Gosh. Sheesh. Shucks. Um, so, you know how you and Richard have these sort of nickname-y kinda codename-y codenames for Letta and Frith? 'Successor' and 'Catalyst'?"

"Yes, for that is who they are."

"Well, I was hoping you could give *me* one of those cool codenames. And I … um, I kinda had one in mind."

The New Codenames

THEY HADN'T SEEN MATTHIAS LAUGH, but when he and Nicky came walking up the staircase, they were both laughing so hard they had tears in their eyes. Richard's demeanor softened again, allowing some of his more human features to bubble to the surface. He actually had *dimples*. Letta, Frith, and Traxler all shared pleasantly confused looks as Nicky and Matthias wandered over to Francois's command center, arm in arm, giggling like old friends.

"My child, that is such a remarkable coincidence."

"I know, right?!" Nicky burst into a merry gale of laughter as they unlinked arms. Hot hail peppered the stained-glass overhead. Nicky crossed the room, her laughter trailing off to a light chuckle. She could've been at a house party, or a wedding reception, or any of a hundred places that weren't teetering on the precipice of universal Armageddon. She took up a spot by Letta, Frith, and Traxler, whispering, "All righty, then. Let's have a good hell heist, everyone."

Letta smiled and slowly said: "What the fuck is *up* with you two?"

"Yeah," Frith said. "You're freaking me out *and* getting on my nerves at the same time, which I didn't think was possible. What gives?"

Nicky, still giggling, shook her head. "Oh, me and Matty just had a little heart to heart, didn't we?"

"Indeed we did," Matthias said, turning to Richard. "Have you made preparations?"

Richard nodded. "I have. Successor, with your permission, I will proceed."

"You are permission'ed."

"Successor Letta Starchild, Catalyst Frith Starchild, all who the fates have brought to this place—I will open a portal between the Fortress and the outskirts of Vatican City. Once that portal is open, I will divest myself of my covenant with Lord Morningstar for one earth hour. During that hour, I will be able to traverse sacred ground, but I will have none of my powers."

Francois chuckled deep within his chest. Traxler shot him a nasty look then addressed Richard: "You sure you want to take that risk?"

"Unless one of you feels confident enough in your buzzery to remove the key from the camerlengo's person, we don't have much choice."

Letta smiled. "Buzzery?"

Richard realized his error and nodded. "The art of pickpocketing. A former colleague of ours, Adam de Fentlok, used to praise my skill in the art. Long ago." His eyes got a faraway look for a moment before he righted himself. "Very well. If you will all stand back, I will—"

"Mistress Nicodemus?" Matthias had spoken. "Isn't there something you're forgetting?"

Everyone turned to Nicky who stood arms akimbo and looking puzzled for a full five seconds before slapping her forehead and shouting, *"Oh, my god! Right!"* She jumped up and down. "Oh, my GAWD guys! Abort, abort! Hold *everything!* We almost just completely fucked absolutely everything totally the fuck *UP!*" She waved to Richard, who was about ten feet away. "Richard! Hey! It's Nicky!"

"I know who you are."

She sawed at her neck with a flat palm. "Close any and all portals to any and all hells or hellish domains or dimensions—or zones!—that are currently open or opening!"

"I haven't opened any yet."

She continued to wave and saw at her neck. "Abort, abort! Discontinue or cancel any and all hell heists that may be currently transpiring!"

"This is the only one, and it has yet to begin."

Nicky finally relaxed. "Oh, good. Thanks. Oh, my GAWD, you guys. That was close! *Phew!*" She theatrically wiped sweat from her brow. "We almost forgot to do the most important thing ya gotta do to ensure a good hell heist!"

Letta glared at Nicky. "Listen, I think we—"

Frith touched Letta's arm, discreetly shaking her head. She addressed Nicky: "This sounds like it's important. Tell us, but can we make it quick?"

"You got it!" Nicky said. "Matthias, would you care to tell them?"

Letta, Frith, and Traxler all shared a baffled smile. Even Richard's dimples sank deeper into his cheeks. Bixby stood patiently, while Francois sat at his command center surrounded by empty rifts. Matthias clasped his hands behind him and stepped forward.

"We must all, as Mistress Nicodemus put it, decide which member of the Ace Team we are."

Nicky corrected him: "A-Team, Matty! It's just 'A,' like the first word in the *Alphabet Song!*"

Traxler smiled. "You mean the first letter in the alphabet?"

"That too!" Nicky said. "Matty, continue." Matthias opened his mouth to speak, but Nicky bulled ahead, pulling out her little notebook: "*Anyway,* Letta, you're *totally* a Hannibal, *obviously.* See, most A-Teamers multitask, but Hannibals kinda don't. They share the most DNA with our *old* great owl, Athena, even thought you're not her, and she's definitely *not* you. You're the leader and mastermind. All you need is a good cigar!"

Frith crossed her arms. "But—and I can't believe I suddenly have an opinion about this—wouldn't you want to use ... well, our old codenames? Like great owl, early entry, subjugation, muscle—"

Nicky's response came accompanied by a jabbing finger. "*No. No.* Just, no. Never again. I'm sorry I even brought those up. Those nicknames are *shitty. Fucking shitty.* They were only for a frame of reference." She indicated her notebook. "I've been keeping track of our strengths and weaknesses and personalities and overall hotness—someone's pulled into a clear lead there, and sorry Bixby, but it ain't you—" (she mouthed at Richard, *It's you*) "—and we're getting new A-Team codenames because most of us multitask, right? No one is *only* early entry or *only* subjugation or *only* eyes in the sky."

Traxler raised a hand. "This is fine with me, but can I ask a favor?"

"I dunno," Nicky said with a wink. "Can you?"

"Touche," he said, pointing at her. "Can you guys please not say I'm B.A.? I used to get that all the time in school."

Nicky was outraged. "*What? No!* That's crazy! B.A.? Are you *crazy?!*"

She hooked her thumb at Traxler and called: "Matty, you believe this guy? Thinks he's a B.A.! No, no, no, you're *clearly* a Faceman."

Traxler blushed, flattered in spite of himself. "Oh. Okay. Thanks."

Richard's dimples vanished. "What does it mean, to be a 'Faceman'?"

Frith said, "He's the pretty one."

"Oh." Whatever smile he had faded in tune with his insides flashing with smolders of heat lightning.

Nicky pounced, jumping up and down and pointing. "Wait, what?! Busted!" She pressed her fingers to her lips and gave a poor impression of a police whistle: *"B-b-r-r-r-r-b-b-btttt!* Sorry to pull ya over, sir, but you are *busted* for being jealous. I'm afraid the sentence is mandatory," she said, her delivery and tone lowering into a husky whisper: "A hundred years hard … lovemaking. Gentle but firm, passionate and caring—"

Frith leaned in. "Oh-*kay,* then! Nicky, I *love* these new codenames. Can we get on with the hell heist?"

"No, not yet! Sheesh! Matty, sorry for cutting you off. Mind telling Richard my new codename?"

"Gladly, my child. Richard, henceforth, Mistress Nicodemus is our *Murdock.*"

"I know not what that means."

"In the annals of *A-Team* lore, before their mission could begin, the … well, *team* had to free Master Murdock from Bedlam."

Richard's heat lightning vanished. He rotated toward Nicky.

"Really?" He seemed to address no one in particular.

Nicky answered: "Well, it was a different mental hospital every week, and they never went to London, but yeah. That's Murdock."

Richard surprised the humans once again. He floated toward Nicky, his face melting between human and hell-lord. His black eyes softened as he looked down at her, his expression caught between awe and pity.

"Did your friends free *you* from Bedlam?"

Nicky shrugged. "May as well have. I've definitely had better years. Or decades."

Frith crossed over and hooked an arm around her shoulder. "You look fine to me."

Nicky hugged her back. "Thanks, Winnie."

Bixby asked Richard: "I take it one of your boys was in lockup, back in the day?"

"Aye. He who I named before, Adam de Fentlok, and a most remarkable soul he was. He worked with Matthias to transport Longshanks' gold from the Abbey to the River Thames."

Letta: "Why was he in the hospital?"

Richard shook his head. "Not a man among us could say. He spoke strangely, of tombs and gateways and directions no compass could con, and yet he saw the world with eyes most wondrous." Richard's dimples reappeared. "Our efforts to free him from Bedlam were actually a more complex endeavor than breaching the Abbey's crypt."

Matthias chuckled. "All *that* took was a few fistfuls of hemp-seed and Edie's décolletage. But we would have roundly failed without him and his legions of dear friends."

The heavens bellowed thunder. Bloody-bright light flooded the world. The hot hail, which had been peppering the Fortress, started tommy-gunning it. It sounded like a stadium packed with a hundred thousand banshees cheering for their demise. Black clouds absorbed all ambient light, broken only by intermittent rubyflashes. Save for Francois, everyone's mood darkened.

"We're not gonna get a tech rehearsal for this one, people." Letta said. She nodded to the Infernal Cartographer. "Richard, open that creepy-crawly staircase and get into costume. Nicky, prep your Keifer-er. Frith, Traxler—fire up your Hard-ons."

"Hauberks."

"I'm not learning that word. Francois, do whatever it is you do."

He greedily drywashed his skeletal hands. "Oui, mon petit Successeur."

"That's mon petit *Hannibal,* from now on, ya fuckin' degenerate. Traxler, you're our Faceman. Nicky, you're Murdock. Frith, I think that makes you our B.A. by default."

"I think I can find some pity in my heart. Let's do this."

Richard clawed his hands into talons and activated his dark host, which swarmed across the mezzanine and whirlpooled into a staircase. Black, bamboo-like reeds sprouted from the opening and locked together into banisters. That done, Richard touched his shoulders, unclasped his chestplate, and prepared to lift it over his head. Letta raised a hand.

"Richard! Wait, don't you want some privacy?!"

Frith whispered: "I'm pretty sure Nicky's about to pass out."

"I have never been more conscious in my fucking life," Nicky said. "As you were, Richard! Please feel free to take off your pants. I swear to Jesus I won't peek at your buns. Much."

But when he revealed his nakedness, his groin was smooth and genderless. Nicky seemed deflated but her eyes were still sparkling. Richard and Matthias faced each other and joined hands, muttering an incantation. Richard dropped to his knees, his jaw unhinging, his insides disgorging thousands, millions, *billions* of the bizarre black insectoids that composed his damned corporeal form. As they departed, he shrank, his limbs shortening, his head bristling to life with a shock of auburn hair that settled to his shoulders.

It was done.

On his hands and knees, Richard heaved air into his lungs. Matthias quickly crossed the room and brought back a blanket to cover his nakedness. Nicky quietly snapped her fingers.

"Way to cock-block, Matty," she whispered.

Matthias helped Richard to his feet, smiling.

"Hello there, old friend," he said, his voice heavy.

Richard beheld him. And hugged him. If Francois had eyes to roll, he would have, but the others gave them a moment's peace. Releasing him, Richard said: "You're not drunk."

"I gave it up. I thought you noticed."

"A lot has escaped my notice in the past seven centuries." He turned to the others. "Hello." He was instantly blushing under Nicky's gaze. "Um, forgive my attire. I seem to have misplaced the clothes I wore when I died."

Traxler: "What're you, about six foot one? I've got some extra clothes in the trunk. Might have to roll up the sleeves, but they should fit okay." He headed over to the Prius.

"Thank you."

Traxler returned with a change of clothes. "Let me know how these fit."

Richard nodded and retired to a side chamber, prompting Nicky to mouth *shit* to herself. The energy of preparation overtook the room. Francois swiveled toward his command center and slashed open several rifts that gave view to different parts of Vatican City, including the speakeasy. Nicky ran and grabbed her keifering rig. Bixby sharpened a butcher knife he'd stowed on his person. Richard returned wearing a denim button-down, beige chinos, and a vest that emphasized his V-shaped torso. He'd pulled his hair into a ponytail. Nicky bore a slack-jawed gape; she could've been looking into the face of god.

Letta prodded her, said: "Focus, Nicodemus. Remember, you're about to *test murder* me, and I don't want you getting stuck on cloud nine."

Nicky nodded and whispered, "Okie-dokie" in a daze.

Frith, Traxler, and Richard all arrayed themselves around the staircase. Francois swiveled to face everyone.

"His eminence *l'mariné* departed the holy residence only moments ago. I shall provide you with a, como se parlez, scouting report."

"He will soon arrive at the bar clandestin. I shall first guide you there."

"Can't we just use GPS?" Traxler said, adding to Nicky: "And that was the proper usage of 'can.'"

"Non, Monsieur Garcon de l'gran Catalysuer. The unholy storm has disabled all such devices. You will be required to use the mobile phones I have … como se parlez … *awakened*. I will guide you to the bar, after which I will modify the Dark Nightingale's soul." Francois raised a finger. "Ah, but attendez! You will also need something else!" He nodded to Frith, who was standing next to a table appointed with quill and paper. "Mon gran mamzelle, would you hand me a piece of parchment, si vous plais?"

Frith grabbed a sheet and took a step toward Francois before she stopped and assumed pose that a ballerina would recognize as a *first arabesque*: she leaned forward, standing on one leg while extending the other behind her and stretching her arm to its limit.

"Here ya go, freak," she said.

"Oh, but you have nothing to fear—why not come closer?"

"Just take the fucking paper."

He plucked it from her hand with a chuckle and slashed open a rift that revealed a sleeping man: the camerlengo. Francois reached through the rift and into the man's head, which rippled open like slippery oil paints. Francois's teeth chattered and clicked as his fingers lanced and probed and snaked around inside the camerlengo's mind.

"Ahhh, a neverending parade of sorrow are his dreams. The merest peek into this man's black soul begets a limerance most *lyrique*." He retracted his hand. His skeletal fingers swarmed with images of screaming mouths—young ones. The humans all winced. Bixby growled. Richard's brow darkened.

Francois peered at his hand, searching for something. "Toutefois, I seek not his appetites *carnal* but *gourmand*. Aha! Et viola." He caught an image of a tiny bottle between his thumb and forefinger. He "crushed" the image in his fist, then smeared it across the paper, which suddenly danced with Asian characters that formed into place under a stylized sketch of an arched bridge. Francois presented the paper, saying: "This is the label for a Miyota whiskey, one of the rarest in all the world, distilled and aged at the foot of a volcano in rural Japan. Its supplies are thought to be exhausted, and our good camerlengo has spent the past decade trying to locate a cask of it. Simply wrap this paper around any bottle, and it will become a Miyota."

Frith performed another first arabesque to retrieve the paper.

"Wow, Francois, this is actually pretty helpful," she said.

The Dream Master's eyes narrowed. "De rien, mamzelle, but *forget me not*, Monsieur Traxler: I expect to be fed come break of dawn."

"Don't worry," he said. "It's coming."

"Great," Letta said. "Is everyone ready?"

Heartrates thumped faster and faster. Everyone exchanged looks that asked, *You ready for this?* Even Matthias's jaw was clenched, his eyes flinty and alert. Nicky balled her fist.

"Game faces, ladies," she said. "Oh! And gentlemen. Oh! And bears. Oh! And whatever the fuck Francois is. Oh! And Master of Anguishes."

Richard and Traxler simultaneously said, "'*Masters* of Anguish.'"

They shared a smile. Nicky was suddenly on the verge of tears again. "I'm not afraid. I'm not afraid. I'm not afraid. I'm not afraid because you guys are here with me. And I love you."

Frith touched her shoulder. "We love you, too." She gave Letta a significant look.

"Love you, Nicky," Letta whispered.

Nicky gave a nervous chuckle and wiped away her tears. "Thanks. Should we, like, synchronize our watches or something?"

"Nah," Letta said. "Just remember, if we fuck up, the universe explodes. *Let's go!*"

Richard, Traxler, and Frith vanished down the staircase.

After a stomach-turning jaunt down and then back up Richard's staircase-portal, they emerged into what looked like the past. An ancient castle wall rose around them, complete with ramparts. Beyond the wall behind them was a McDonald's sign—and thousands of shouting voices. Uniformed gendarmes stood along the ramparts, guns drawn. People speaking hundreds of different languages cried:

"Entrare, entrare!"

"Dejanos entrar!"

"Tuingie ndani!"

The message was the same: *"Let us in!"*

Richard slipped into some shade, out of sight of the gendarmes. Frith and Traxler joined him. A few pellets of hot hail struck and sizzled into the earth nearby, while a drizzle of rain fell from the red-flashing sky. To their right stood a set of deep green double doors, both steel and inlaid with rivets. Each bore a curved brass handle.

"Clement the Fifth ordered the rite of consecration performed not long after the construction of the first infernal vault. Its radius extended to this gate, the Porta Viridaria, now called Porta San Pellegrino. This marks the boundary of consecrated ground and beyond which I could not have passed before."

Behind them, Richard's staircase vanished.

"Whoa, where'd it go?" Frith said, pointing.

"Worry not," Richard said. "Matthias concealed the passageway with an enchantment so as not to tempt any curious mortals."

Traxler jerked his chin at the city. "What about your buddy the Centurion? Mister Goodmind? Will it hide it from him?"

"I know not. We've never done this before."

Thunder growled across the city.

Frith: "Tick-tock, guys."

Richard looked around. "I hear no timepiece, Catalyst."

"Sorry," she said. "It's modern parlance for 'let's hurry the fuck up.'"

Richard gripped one of the brass handles. "Quite right. Let us make some fucking haste!"

Lightning flashed. The door yawned open, and they plunged inside. Behind them, Richard's staircase flickered back into view before vanishing again.

Nicky had set up her keifering rig on a faded, cracked wooden table. The Apparatus's map of hell waxed and waned like a lava lamp, the various Infernal Downfalls floating in lazy circles. Matthias stood near the staircase, his brow knit and sparkling with sweat as he muttered an incantation over and over. In response, the staircase phased in and out of sight. Nicky looked on with concern.

"You okay over there, Matty? Anything I can do? Need me to Murdock those stairs for ya?"

"Not unless you can learn seven hundred years' worth of sorcery and conjuring in the next day, but thank you, my child."

"Okay! You just holler if you need to tap out!"

Meanwhile, as Francois monitored Team Vatican's progress, Bixby accompanied Letta to the table.

"You sure we can trust that guy?" Bixby whisper-rasped, jerking his nonexistent chin at Francois.

"Nope," Letta said. "That's why I need you to guard us while Nicky performs her test." She addressed Nicky: "How's this work?"

Nicky slapped the table. "First, get those buns up here and get comfy."

Letta climbed on and stretched out. Francois could be heard directing Team Vatican: "Once you pass the papal residence, make a left onto Belvedere, then a right onto Pio X."

Nicky attached the electrodes to Letta's temple but hesitated with her blouse. "You mind unbuttoning a few?"

"It's a little late in the game to get bashful," Letta said, opening her blouse a few inches.

"Oh, it's not that, sheesh. It's just … sometimes you still feel like a kid to me."

As Nicky applied the electrodes to her chest, Letta chewed on silent words for a moment before asking, "How much do you remember about that night?"

A stethoscope somehow appeared on Nicky's head. She pressed the diaphragm to Letta's chest and answered, "Which night?"

"The night ... well, our last night on the Ranch."

"Oh. Hmmm," Nicky said, preparing the IV needle. "Not much. Flashes, really. I remember those goofy codenames Foundation gave us. I remember waking up at ... that place where they took us. The ... big play room?"

Letta gave her a concerned look. "The big play room?"

Nicky gave her head a quick shake. "Anyway, who cares? It was a long time ago. You ready for this needle?"

Letta nodded. Nicky flicked her bicep until a vessel rose and she could slide the needle in.

"Easy there, chief. This machine's kinda twitchy."

"How twitchy are we talki—"

But Nicky had already pressed the Cutie Patootie. Letta convulsed once and froze into a grimace-faced tableau, like she'd stuck a fork into a wall socket. She flumped to the table, still.

"How twitchy are we talki—"

Letta perceived the moment of her death as a great uncoupling of her consciousness from the world. Her last word—"talking"— got cut off at the letter *I*, which stretched into infinity, *"iiiiiiii,"* its sound distorted and derezzed. Her vision doubled, like someone had applied drops to both eyes, while all color drained from existence. Simultaneously, her vision degraded as she lost the ability to see a third dimension; her view of Nicky and the Fortress looked as flat as a monochrome watercolor painted by a novice. Nicky's face faded into cartoony generalities: she was nothing but a smear of orange hair and the vague contour of a nose. All else was blank. That image fluttered away on a sheet of parchment, leaving behind nothing but diving darkness. Letta tipped forward, a sense of incredible *distance* before her, as if she was peering down a million-mile passageway.

"I swear if my phone sprouts labia, Francois, I'm kicking your ass."

Frith had spoken. They sprinted down Via della Tipografia, alongside antiquity and modernity: museums from the 900s stood alongside modern office buildings. Night had fallen. A layer of pitch-opaque clouds hung overhead and flashed with occasional veins of red, like a ceiling of black concrete inlaid with sputtering neon. Bits of hot hail sprinkled and spat down—flakes and marble-sized grains—small but still redhot. The rain had stopped for the time being.

Francois's response was a slurpy chuckle. "I wouldn't *dream* of it, mon grande mamzelle." He wailed with laughter. Too hilarious. "Once you pass the papal residence, make a left onto Belvedere, then a right onto Pio X."

"Got it," she said.

"Have you chosen my Turkish delight yet, mon amis?"

"Yeah," Traxler said, coming to a stop. "Across the alleyway stood a residential complex, a yellow-brick building from the seventies. A window illuminated and cast the silhouette a person into view. At a glance, it appeared to be a young woman putting on her habit. Traxler activated his phone's video feed and trained it on the window, saying, "Yeah. I've got your Turkish fucking delight. Right here. I'll bring her with us when we come back. That good enough?"

"She looks *delectable,* and the faithful always pack a particular, je ne sais—*saveur.*"

"Yeah, I'm with you," Traxler said. "Nuns are yummy. You happy?"

"Quite, monsieur."

Traxler deactivated his phone. "God, shut *up*." He took off running, followed by the others.

Frith ran alongside him and hissed: "Trax, what the fuck was that talk about the girl, the Turkish delight? You're not actually gonna—"

"No, of course not, but I can't explain now. Just trust me."

They ran on.

Nicky was counting the seconds on her phone's stopwatch: "Ninety-one, ninety-two, ninety-three …" Letta had been "dead" for a minute and a half. A few yards away, one of Francois's rifts showed Team Vatican running along a narrow city street flanked by yellow-brick buildings.

"Two minutes." She checked Letta's vitals. Brainwaves were nil, while her blood pressure was holding steady: nice as low, with about one heartbeat per minute. Letta's was currently flipping between 3 and 7. Bixby's snout suddenly poked over the tabletop. He stood on tiptoes and gestured with the butcher knife.

"How's she doing?"

Letta's VE dipped to 3, then climbed back up to 4. Nicky said, "The key to a good keifering is maintaining a steady VE. Anything lower than two, and she might be a goner, but if it climbs above ten, she won't be 'dead' enough to reach the afterworld. Basically, she'd wake up."

Across the way, Francois wheedled:

"Do you need my aid, Guildmaster?" Francois asked. "I need only dip the tippy-tips of my fingers into your morpheal depths in order to—"

"Silence, beast," Matthias said, his brow dripping. "Haven't you a mission to carry out? To modify the soul of the Dark Nightingale?"

The VE meter flipped to 4, then back to 3.

"Ahhh, monsieur, that mission can wait." Francois stood and approached Matthias. "Let me—"

Nicky looked up. "Hey! Leave him alone, Fran—"

Tap-tappitty-tap-tap-tap. Francois ripped off a progression, spun on his heel, and faced her, his eyes pumping smoke in fat, audible bursts: *choom, choom, choom.* Behind the smoke smoldered twin embers that drew her gaze—she looked into his endless delights.

The meter jumped to 5 and then 6 before dipping to 2.

Matthias stood over the staircase, still. Silence reigned. A streak of white light caught her eye. She pulled her gaze from the Dream Master's smoldering eternities as she circled around the table—*who was lying here?*—and approached the streak. It looked like a tiny comet: a glowing red pellet, about the size of a pencil eraser, trailed a streak of white mist.

She realized it was chunk of hot hail that had penetrated the stained-glass ceiling and now hung frozen in mid-air, as still as Matthias. Francois's chuckle was a low drumbeat that rumbled all around her.

Oh no, oh no, oh no, she thought. *I fell asleep. I'm dreaming.*

Team Vatican stopped in some shadows. Frith checked her phone's clock, but because they'd lost global GPS, it was stuck on eastern time,

2 p.m. "Jeez, do we know which timezone is gonna count for sunset tomorrow?"

"I know not what a 'time zone' is," Richard said.

Traxler: "Let's just assume Greenwich mean to be safe, so we've got about twenty-four hours until—" He stopped short and held up a hand for silence. Footsteps were approaching from the north. A man wearing a black pea coat, jeans, and a black stocking cap rounded the corner, heading their way. The three hell-heisters hunkered down in the shadows. When the stranger's face came into the light, they all exchanged glances.

Frith nodded. "Target acquired."

Their phones crackled again, but it wasn't Francois who spoke: "Team Vatican, it's Bradley. Y'know, the fuckin' teddy bear. Something's wrong. I think Francois's got 'em."

After Team Vatican departed, Bixby called on his training as the Dark Nightgale's lead enforcer.

He took stock: the room was a shitshow—there was no way to keep an overwatch in a fucking atrium. Matthias was struggling with that staircase-portal, while the sole hostile, the Dream Master, was fixated on his command center. Or at least he was *pretending* to fixate on it. Bixby had never faced off against a creature like Francois, but he figured, *Hey, if I stab him in the face enough, that's bound to slow him down, right?*

Bixby was just starting to feel safe when Nicky started speaking in gibberish.

"Siren, siren, siren, sir. Is there a room forpty plain? Clothes? Huh, there are voices nearby. Okay, okay."

She was carrying out a dumbshow of fiddling with her defibrillator thingamajig, but her mind was clearly elsewhere. He speed-waddled over to the table and quietly lifted Nicky's iPhone. He figured Francois would glom on to the ruse as soon as he opened a channel, but he had to chance it.

Swiping open the phone brought up a mobile interface themed around Francois himself: a cartoony rendering of his visage smiled from the screen's top-middle, while bones composed the text and bloody organs replaced the buttons. Only two options were available: the first was a human heart labeled *1-900-FRANCOIS,* while the other simply read *Team Vatican.* (Its background icon was a pancreas, for some reason.) When Bixby went to press it, the *1-900* button chased his fingertip around the screen until he managed to evade it and dial Frith and the others.

"Team Vatican, it's Bradley. Y'know, the fuckin' teddy bear …"

Letta fell.

Faster and faster she plummeted, feeling no wind at her face, only an inexorable sense of velocity that carried her down, down, down toward a boundless black void across which massive shapes gradually faded into view—thousands of them, all spherical or elliptical, like a galaxy of black bubbles.

But within this galaxy, five elliptical bubbles hove into view, larger than the others by several orders of magnitude. Their surfaces were faintly iridescent and translucent, giving view to insides that churned and swarmed and seethed with activity; a froth of mayhem.

Oh, my god, Letta thought. *This is hell. This is actually hell. I'm dead and I'm going to hell.*

She screamed.

Richard snatched Frith's phone and, unsure of its function, held it with both hands like a sandwich, hissing into its end, "What do you mean, 'he's got her?!'"

"I think they fell asleep and he's, y'know, got 'em both trapped in one of his fuckin' nightmares."

Traxler shushed everyone. Arbogast was approaching. He got within seven or eight yards before turning toward the brownstone and facing what appeared to be a solid wall. He knocked five times—four in quick succession, followed by one. Seams sliced into the stones, and a secret door slid into the wall. The camerlengo vanished into a dark passage.

Frith leaned in to whisper into the phone. "How could they fall asleep? Did they lie down?"

"Guys, have you ever seen anyone drop off with their eyes sittin' open? My ma did it all the time back in the day. Creepiest fuckin' thing. That's what Nicky's doing, and the boss lady, Letta, is out, too, but she's fuckin' *out*-out."

"Letta's been … uh, keifered?"

"Yeah, she's fucking dead."

Traxler: "Can you wake her back up?"

"I'm not touchin' that keifering rig, man. I'm worried if I work it wrong, I'll punch her ticket for good."

Richard returned Frith's phone. "Leave this to me."

He started to leave, but Traxler caught his arm. "What?!"

"Only I, with my full complement of powers, have any hope of stopping the Master of Dreams. I must return to the Fortress to aid Matthias the Guildmaster and the Nicky the Murdock. Here." He produced a tin box from his pocket, opening it to reveal a wedge of wax. "This is a wax blank. Use this to take a mold of the camerlengo's key."

Traxler: "How are we supposed to get close to him, the camerlengo guy? Isn't that your department?"

"It's a simple matter of buzzery. You have the enchanted parchment. Use it to get the camerlengo's attention. Get close to him, and create some manner of diversion, a fakement or some other ruse. Follow the Murdock's lead."

"Murdock?" Frith asked. "Oh, Nicky. Follow her lead *how?*"

"She insinuated that whimsical missive on my person? The woman depicted as a great cat?"

"The valentine."

"Quite right. Perfect buzzery. She drew close while I was distracted and carried out the pass. Do the same with the Camerlengo."

Traxler hissed: "How? You're looking at the only guy who got cut from his junior high drama department. I'm not exactly Denzel over here."

Frith elbowed him. "Don't sell yourself short, sweets."

"I don't mean in terms of overall good-looks, honey, I mean—"

Richard: "Your banter is charming, but to your question, Master Traxler …" he thought. "Let me see, what was the name of the old brigand who taught me buzzery as a boy …" His face scrunched up. "Forgive me. Some of my life-memories from before my death remain bathed in mist." Frith and Traxler blanched. Not noticing, Richard continued: "Ah, yes. Sammy Hagar. That was his name."

They gaped at him. "You were friends with Sammy Hagar?"

"Yes. Samuel Hagar, from Stratford-On." He smiled. "Has his name lived on to this era?"

Traxler: "In a manner of speaking. Sorry to interrupt. Go ahead."

"He told me that when it comes to theatrics, it matters not whether the fools in the penny-pit believe it. It matters if *you* believe it." He straightened up and checked to make sure the coast was clear. "I must make haste. Distract the camerlengo, lift the key, take the mold, and return it before he notices. Good luck and farewell."

He took off. Frith and Traxler stared at the speakeasy's entrance, then at each other for a moment before Frith's brow furrowed. Smiling, she crossed the street and turned around, her face catching the red light of a neon sign. She pointed.

"I've gotta duck into the drug store for a minute, honey. Be right back."

Nicky found herself in a high school basketball gym. Strange letters splashed across the far wall. For some reason, the bleachers had been pushed back to make room for a bunch of beds, all of which stood empty.

This is the play room.

That's what she'd said to Letta earlier. *Play room.* Their last night on the Ranch, after everything was … over, they'd all been taken to a play room. A gymnasium. But where was everyone else? Where was Letta, Frith, Franco, and Stanton? If they'd brought everyone here, why wasn't this place packed with people?

A voice sang from all around:

"There was a young girl named Nicky—" (tap) *"—whose sister was ever so tricky—"* (tap-tap) *"—So when Nicky was able—"* (boom) *"—She quick turned the tables—"* (boom boom) *"So …"*

None of this made sense to her, of course. Nicky didn't *have* a sister. Did she?

Spectral voices—not Francois's—echoed around her: "Subjugation. Early entry. Intelligence. Wheeljack. Eye in the sky." The voices grew louder: "Muscle king. *Muscle king. MUSCLE KING.*" Windows rattled. Light fixtures swayed. The domed ceiling bowed inward. Nicky reared back, covering her ears and gritting her teeth. Light flickered—her peripheral vision caught it. Spinning to her right brought into view a small office that adjoined the gymnasium. The office had a picture window adorned with more gibberish letters that arced across the glass.

A voice inside her head whispered, *Coach. That's what it says. Coach.*

Inside was *her* coach. That much she knew. It was a plain fact. But someone had drawn the curtains—deep red ones—so she couldn't *see* her coach. Might as well go knock on the door, right? Nicky took a tentative step forward and stopped.

Nicky muttered to herself, "Which podcast was that?" Some paranormal podcast had rented out a studio for a special episode that featured her and half a dozen other of the conspiracy theorist world's best and brightest. They'd sat in a room with walls of soundproof foam.

Those aren't curtains. That's soundproofing foam.

And this all happened the night of the tech rehearsal. In 1993.

She concentrated, trying to lure the full memory of that night out of hiding, but it evaded her mental grasp—she'd repressed it too entirely.

"Nooooon, you didn't repress it," Francois taunted her.

"I know I didn't," Nicky told the room. "Didn't repress the memories, that is. Someone else did. But I *did* choose to *keep* them repressed." She crossed to the office and gripped the doorknob. "I hereby invoke the Eighth Maxim of the Starchild-Nicodemus Fellowship."

She opened the door—and Francois sprung his trap.

Matthias had fallen into a fugue state while trying to conceal Richard's passage. Francois had no interest in feeding on the dying old man, so he ignored him.

Matthias' dream was a memory: He sat in a stone cell. Water dripped from the ceiling into a puddle inches from his feet, both of which were missing their final two toes, the wounds having been cauterized with a redhot iron.

It was June of 1303, and the red lightning had been striking 'round the compass for weeks.

Longshanks has tasked his most trusted inquisitor, Drokensford, to corral them, which he did with incredible speed. Only Matthias de Rilesford, Edie Cookson, Richard Pudlicotte, and Adam de Fentlok remained alive. Of those four, only the latter—sweet and kind

Adam—had evaded capture so far, thanks to his many friends and allies all around London.

Edie's screams floated down the corridor. They'd put the screws to them first, but they'd weathered that. A few had fallen while being cooked in the Bull. More spoke after having their toes lopped off. Still others were split asunder by the Pear. Matthias still couldn't close his mouth all the way after his encounter with the Pear, although he knew they'd only put it in his mouth—and not the other way—because they thought he had information.

Which he did.

Richard and Matthias had sworn each other to secrecy. Part of the treasure they'd divvied up among the conspirators, but the bulk of it they'd hidden away. Despite Drokensford's worst efforts, no one talked, because even though Richard and Matthias might've known the location of the treasure, the *collective* knew the full truth: that all of London was a conspirator. Hundreds, if not thousands, of monks, innkeeps, merchants, sellswords, and clergy had all pitched in. Fentlok had masterminded their involvement when he conjured the great convoy from the Abbey to the river.

If they gave up one, they gave up *all.*

And that included Adam, who had already endured so many horrors behind the walls of Bedlam.

Matthias twined his fingers, about to pray, when the floor started clacking and chattering. Thousands of stones, large and small, shifted and slid and jumped skyward, assembling themselves into some manner of statue. Bloody and befouled water sluiced down the statue's sides as it took shape, the blocks subdividing by the tens of thousands as they cascaded upward and brought into view a woman rendered in stone. She wore a kirtle that was laced to her wrists, the skirt melting into the floor. Her eye sockets stood empty, her head covered in a coif. As she finished taking shape, darkness bled into her attire, rendering it in black, all while her sides unseamed and spewed forth millions of clicking and chittering insects that swarmed around her body and assembled into a three-foot-tall black hawk that perched on her forearm and blinked at Matthias with glowing red eyes.

This was the Anti-God adherent most magnificent, her unholy eminence the Lady Illyria Mallestratos, mistress of anguish, princess of pain, and infernal cartographer.

"Time is short, Successor," she said. "But the fates have granted you a boon: the Catalyst perished yesterday. The wounds he sustained while slaying Alice Kyeteler proved mortal."

"Kyeteler," Matthias whispered. "Alice Kyeteler, the Witch of Kilkenny?"

Illyria chuckled and nodded. "Indeed she was, Successor." She extended an arm and revealed that her kirtle included a cape that hung from her collar and connected to her wrists like bat wings. A living image materialized onto it, rising in a relief assembled by thousands of tiny stones and tinted by fluids lifted from her surroundings: blood, filth, oils, and rot. A young woman glared at him, her hair bloodred, her eyes so wide they seemed lidless. Her hair hung to her shoulders. "With the Catalyst dead, now you need only nearest and truest friend."

"Never," Matthias said. "I won't betray him."

"Then you must breach the heart of Leviathasmodeus to retrieve … *him*."

Matthias winced at her words. *Him*. The monster who broke him as a young acolyte. Down the passageway, Edie shrieked. Illyria grew a few inches, her stone teeth scraping together as she smiled and soaked up the misery surrounding her. Matthias spat; it struck her skirt and sizzled away.

"Back to the pits with thee, fell creature," he said. "I'll have none of your witchcraft."

Her hawk cried and lunged at him, but she held it back. "Quiet, my dear, quiet," she said, stroking its hood. She spoke with surprising compassion: "Your predecessor was a coward, too, but a coward's way is the only path through this, Successor. Pudlicotte's your first and best, your dearest and truest. Drokensford needs only a name and a location. You have both. Hand them over, and you'll end this cataclysm in a stroke."

Grief broke him in half. He held his face, sobbing so hard he could barely breathe. "Why, of all the countless souls he could have chosen, did the almighty's wrath fall upon mine?"

She shook her head. "That is neither the tale nor the truth. You'll learn all in time, but for the moment, know that not you, not I, not Pudlicotte, the King, neither Drokensford nor indeed any single one of the world's teeming masses—nor the breadth of creation itself— matters the slightest grise to Old Father. He dreamt us and forgot us, all in a passing eternal moment, ages ago. And we're all left to clean up His mess. You have my sympathies, but I suggest you make your decision with celerity, or all is lost."

Matthias's tears dried up. His chest emptied. His legs relaxed before him. All feeling and energy drained from his body. He was about to speak when someone else did.

"Matt?"

He knew the voice at once. Illyria drew to the side, revealing that her dark host had carved an opening to the neighboring cell, which held his friend, who now stood before him. Matthias sat up.

"Dick?"

"I'm ready. Call in the guard. They'll roust Drokensford, and he'll be here within the hour."

"How did you—"

"She came to me last night. Explained it all. Matt, it's time. I'm ready."

"No, old friend. I can't."

Richard shrugged. "It's a simple exchange. I'll be put to death, you'll take over this Menagerie she speaks of, and the world lives on. Unless you want to make this brazen attempt upon hell itself?"

Matthias shook his head. "Nay." His lips quivered. "My friend, Longshanks will show you no mercy."

Richard grinned, rakish and gentle. "I didn't show *him* any." For a moment, Matthias remembered first meeting the young scamp at the Old Queen's Head. Richard crossed over and hefted the old monk to his feet, pulling him into an embrace. "Come, let's bring a close to this business. For Edie. For Adam. For them all."

Matthias released him, weeping. "Forgive me for what I'm about to do."

"It's done." He crossed to the magical opening and paused with a foot propped on its rim. "But soft, we truly made quake the pillars of Olympus, didn't we?"

He returned to his cell. Illyria closed the passage and melted back into the floor. Matthias crossed to the door and called for the guard.

Letta felt like a satellite plunging toward Jupiter.

Her view was this: the "highway to hell" slashed across the middle-center of her line of sight. Looming up and to her left was Leviathan, while much farther up and to her right floated two more of the major Infernal Downfalls, both of them mostly concealed behind Leviathan's massive, smoldering silhouette. She tried to remember which ones they were, but her memory had gone understandably blank, plus she was focused on the mission's target: Asmo.

She tried in vain to rotate her body but had to rely instead on straining her neck to its limit, which turned out to be easy, as she had no physical form. Her head spun around like an owl's, giving her a clear look at Asmo, which floated at the far end of the Highway to Hell. The scope was immense. It looked like a neighboring galaxy, dark and distant and—

THOOM … THOOM-THOOM-THOOM. She didn't hear but *feel* the impacts. Owl-turning her head back around, Letta realized she was but one of a million-million meteors. All around her, countless other souls streaked to their doom. The vast majority showered into Leviathan, peppering its outer membrane with surging starbursts, while others hooked around the massive Hell and landed in one of a million others.

But none struck Asmo. None even headed toward it.

Richard said the only way into Asmo was from Balaam, but he also said there was a second *way in. Is the Highway to Hell the second way i—*

CLANG. It turned out she *did* have some kind of physical form, because she smashed into it at thousands of miles per hour. Her head ringing and her whole body smarting from the collision, Letta found herself hugging a black signpost that floated in the endless void. Above, the post terminated in a figure-eight. The 8's top opening was empty—a simple hoop—while its bottom was filled with some kind of preternatural orange fluid that bubbled and churned. Below, the post terminated in millions of wriggling jet-black bugs.

Reminds me of Richard, Letta thought.

Indeed, the signpost was composed of the same chattering black insectoid host that filled the Cartographer's innards. Suddenly remembering her comms device, Letta hugged the post and tried to reach into her pocket.

That's when the train passed.

The signpost floated some ten or twenty "miles" to the port side of the Highway to Hell, which hung about fifty "miles" below her. At a glance, the Highway looked like a cylindrical aqueduct cast in cement, but further examination revealed that its surface danced with millions of interlocking panels in all manner of shapes; some were familiar, like hexagons and octagons, but others defied description— non-Euclidean supershapes and polygons with *omega* number of sides. Hulking rivets and bolts held it all together, but *those* were fucking weird, too; their surfaces shivered and shimmered like the three-dimensional shadows of four-dimensional shapes. (Which is what they probably were.) The Highway looked less like cement and more like an ultra-exotic, extra-dimensional lifeform—a python-caterpillar—whose flesh fizzed and effervesced.

Letta held on.

Frith and Traxler crept along cobblestones. Arbogast's secret knock had (thankfully, luckily) admitted them into the speakeasy. A shapely young woman wearing a revealing variant on papal raiment had opened the door, which led directly down a steep staircase that smelled of mildew and fermenting sugars. Wood paneling covered the walls, the beams slanted at forty-five degree angles pointing down, down, down. At the bottom, a cobblestone-floor hallway stretched into darkness.

Light glimmered and glass clinked ahead. They rounded a corner into a small chamber that was about twenty feet across. The cobblestone floors continued, while the wood panel walls terminated in favor of ancient scattered stone. Wood beams spanned a low, vaulted stone ceiling whose construction dated back to the mid-700s AD. A half-dozen wooden tables, graying from age, dotted the room. The bar was the only modern feature. It stood against the far wall and was fronted with underlit stainless steel. A young man, perhaps nineteen or twenty, wiped down the bar against a backdrop of hundreds of bottles of fine bourbons and whiskeys.

The two hell-heisters huddled in the shadows, taking in the space. Traxler shoulder-bumped his wife and jerked his chin. Only one patron was there, Arbogast. He'd doffed his cap and coat and was fiddling with his smartphone. The contents of his table: a tumbler of something brown and a bespoke velvet bed that held his current bottle, something called Kentucky Owl. Frith produced the enchanted paper. She and Traxler communicated in a silent code that only they could decipher; the encryption key was their yearslong intimacy.

What about the bartender? Frith asked. *How are we going to get back there to use the enchanted label?*

Traxler nodded, then asked: *WWBNIBHC2D?* He communicated this unusual series of letters with a combination of an elbow prod and a waggle of his eyebrows.

WWBNIBHC2D? Are you fucking kidding?

He whispered, "Yeah, What Would Brigitte Nielsen in *Beverly Hills Cop Two* Do?"

I'm not flashing my cleavage at this guy to distract him! Besides, look at what I'm wearing! (To Frith's point, she was still wearing her houseclothes: jeans and a sweatshirt.) *And what if he's not even into women?*

We've got to get back there somehow! If you're not going to pull a Brigitte Nielsen, then—

Wait, look!

She pointed. The bartender was vanishing into a back room. Frith seized the opportunity and strode across the bar, stealing a glance at Arbogast. He didn't notice her. She picked a bottle at random, applied the label, and scooted back across the bar to a table, waving Traxler into the room. He joined her, his presence drawing a look from Arbogast. He cooly regarded Traxler, then went back to his phone. Frith and Traxler shared a look.

I guess they don't get many in here, he communicated with a look.

The bartender reappeared and, taking note of the new arrivals, crossed over.

"Cosa desiderate voi?"

"Oh," Frith said. "No parlez Italian? Ingeles?"

Arbogast looked up, briefly taking note of the English-speakers. The bartender frowned slightly but nodded. "Yes, of course. You haven't been here before." It wasn't a question. "Do you need to know about the prices?"

Blood drained from both their faces. The prices. How could they have overlooked such a crucial detail? They were about to order a whiskey that cost thousands of bucks a shot, and neither of them had that kind of cash on them. Frith was about to speak when something strange happened.

Her phone rang.

The device's kooky "Francois" interface vanished in favor of a standard iPhone ring screen. It read simply, YOU NEED TO TAKE THIS CALL. She did.

A familiar voice growled: "I just wired thirty grand to your PayPal. They accept it here."

Arbogast looked up. "You have Wi-Fi?"

The voice continued, "Just nod at him. I bounced a signal off an old Russian satellite. Pay the bartender now, or we all kick the bucket. I'll be around. Signing off."

Frith lowered her phone and brought up the PayPal app. Traxler leaned in.

"Was that who I think it was?"

Frith gave him a look. "Yeah, Goldberg. How'd you know?"

"Wild guess." She faced the bartender. "Two shots of Miyota, please."

It was like she'd sounded an airhorn in the small space. Arbogast's phone clunked to his table. He spun his chair toward them, smiling incredulously. Meanwhile, the bartender covered a huge smile spreading across his face. Laughter spurted between his lips.

"I am so sorry, madam. If we *had* such a fine whiskey, it would be more than five thousand dollars a shot."

A gog-eyed Arbogast unwittingly came to their aid: "Ma hai Miyota, signore."

He pointed. The bartender turned—and sighed in astonishment. As thunder rumbled, he slowly crossed to the bar, where he cradled the enchanted bottle like it was the Holy Grail. "Dio mio," he muttered, before catching himself. "Perdoname, padre!" Arbogast's finger flew to his lips in a *shush*. The bartender bowed his head in apology, walked over, and set the Miyota in the table's built-in velvet bed. "Signore and signora said two shots?"

"Yes, indeed," Frith said,

"Goodness, you need glasses. One moment," the bartender said, turning away.

Arbogast immediately protested. "Con permiso, con permiso!" Chair legs scraped cobblestone. Uninvited, he joined Frith and Traxler, snapping fingers at the bartender. "*Three* glasses, Giovanni, per favore."

"Of course, signore," the young man said, ducking behind the bar.

Arbogast smiled, revealing a mouth of veneers so shockingly white that Frith and Traxler cringed inwardly; he looked like he'd crammed an ivory bear-trap into his skull. "Feels like the world's ending, doesn't it?"

Frith whooped laughter and slapped a hand over her mouth, nodding. "Yeah, kind of."

The camerlengo cocked an eyebrow at her strange response, but Traxler knew she'd done it on purpose so she could surreptitiously reach into her pocket. She set her hand on the table, palming something out of sight. Arbogast continued, his accent bearing a whiff of Brooklyn: "I see so many fucking American tourists, but hardly anyone touches this place deeper than the travel guides." He leaned closer. "You must let me split this with you."

Thunk-thunk-thunk. The hell-heisters jolted. Three tumblers sat before them, one still spinning on its base thanks to the bartender's shaky hands. Arbogast looked at him like a cut of meat.

"Are you feeling well, mi Gio?"

When the bartender grinned, the sweat along his upper lip condensed and cut a pair of ellipsis around his mouth like a gleaming van dyke. His face had nary a wrinkle or a blemish.

"Of course, signore. It's just that I've never broken the seal on a Miyota before."

Frith gently prodded her husband and tilted her head at the camerlengo. A leather lanyard peeked out from his collar, wrapped tightly around his neck.

Traxler acknowledged her with his eyes and addressed Arbogast: "We wouldn't dream of splitting this with you. We've been saving up for this for—"

"Sorry, I wasn't being clear. I was talking to the lady."

Frith noted the flex in Traxler's jawline and touched his hand. "We'd be delighted, but like my husband was saying: we've been saving up for this for years. It's too much to share."

"Oh, but I insist."

Frith and Traxler shrugged and shared a quick laugh, pretending to make a decision.

She smiled. "Are you absolutely certain?"

"Of course. This is your first Miyota?"

"It is."

"First times are so special and beautiful," Arbogast said. "Don't you think?"

"Sure," she said, her gorge rising at the thought of Arbogast's sordid history. She addressed the bartender: "I'll send the money for our share now."

Only Traxler saw Frith's sleight-of-hand. She raised her iPhone to pay, palming a small plastic bottle to its bottom, which she held over the camerlengo's tumbler, deftly squeezing a squirt of fluid into it. Arbogast produced a wad of cash and thumbed out his share of the cost. The bartender pocketed the cash, quickly checked his phone, and nodded.

"Very good, signores and signora. Con permiso ..."

He opened the phony bottle of Miyota and let three glistering brown ribbons pour forth. Frith and Traxler watched Arbogast with unblinking eyes. He swirled his drink and raised it.

"To new friends and first times."

They drank, and Frith stowed away the small plastic bottle.

Its label read, *Ipecac*.

But back to the train.

Its arrival was heralded by an incredible gravitational *suck* that yanked Letta's feet away from the signpost. She held on for dear life, her body billowing like a flag. A silly part of her felt embarrassed at her Buster Keaton-esque pose before she remembered vanity had little use in such an ill-defined netherscape. The train grew closer and closer, making no sound but kicking up a quivering, radial wake that encircled the Highway. As it approached, the gravitational suck abated until Letta was once again hugging the signpost. Letta still couldn't hear the train, but she *felt* it. The vehicle's wake squeezed her heart and compressed her lungs, even though she had neither. It barreled past underneath, banking laterally around the curved inner surface of the organism-aqueduct like a body on a canola-slick slide. Letta's feet started to pull free of the signpost in the *other* direction as the rear of the train came into view. She grit her teeth and held the signpost so tight her pectorals burned.

A sudden burst of light blinded her.

From the train's top came flying a fireball, a *comet* that hurtled right at her. Letta's eyes bulged as she contemplated her choices: release the signpost (and get pulled to her assigned Infernal Downfall), or hold on (and get incinerated; if one could even *get* incinerated in this place). Supernatural physics pre-empted her decision; the comet covered the distance in milliseconds and smashed into the signpost's empty hoop, where it lodged in place, radiating heat so incredible Letta barely even *felt* it. If she'd had a pyrometer on hand, she'd have known the comet's temperature was about ten thousand degrees Fahrenheit, or roughly equal to the surface of the sun. Her noncorporeal body was liquefying in its presence, the agony so beyond anything humans were evolved to feel, she only felt a light sting.

For now. All newcomers to the Infernal Downfalls enjoyed a similar transition period during which the manifestations of their mental selves learned to process any and all kinds of pain, no matter the magnitude.

Then it was gone, with a *pop.*

Even in this nether-realm, an overwhelming coolness washed over her. Overhead, the signpost's figure-eight was once again empty. She heaved a sigh of relief before she noticed her situation had changed; the aqueduct had moved; or rather, *she* had moved, the signpost having spontaneously shifted its position by several hundred thousand "miles." Moments earlier, the train tracks had hung in space almost directly below, now the tracks were little more than a thread that flickered like a fiber optic in the deep distance. The train continued on its way to Asmo, its hectic wake fading into the distance. Letta clung to the signpost, feeling the inexorable pull of her Infernal Downfall, whichever one it was. Tears beaded in the corners of her eyes.

Was this it? Was this her fate? What happens if she, as the Successor, should die? *Really* die? Would the mission fail? Would all of existence disintegrate?

Letta indulged a moment's utter despair. It came and went in a heartbeat, but it lasted long enough for her to release the signpost and continue her journey to hell. She closed her eyes, not caring to know which hell was calling her name. All feeling faded away except for a sense of increasing velocity. As she fell, her face grew warmer and warmer. *I must be close,* she thought, relishing not only the prospect of letting go—but also of a reckoning. She thought of a woman who emptied out her child's college fund to pay the entry fee into LodEx … and Letta had allowed it; cheered the woman on, even. There were countless such people, mostly desperate or lonely women who wanted independence, a job, or something new and exciting in their lives.

And I preyed on them, she thought.

She was close now. Her face burned like she'd stuck it into a raging fire. (This level of pain was "mild" enough for her noncorporeal self to register.) At what felt like the last possible moment, she opened her eyes and was greeted with a blinding white flash.

She had gone to Hell.

They had failed.

Part Six
1993: The New Sect

Hi THERE, ASHIE. REMEMBER ME? Remember your baby sister?"

Athena took off her glasses and closed her eyes. "That's a remarkable admission, Nicodemus."

Blood trickled from the corner of Ashley's mouth. One of her eyes was already swelling shut. Frith held her fast, while the others flanked their Foundation.

Ashley's face stretched in horror. "Nicky? Please listen to me."

"Shut up!" Nicky yelled so loud her voice fritzed. "You owe me a fucking apology, Ashie!"

"Nicky. You've got 'em. I'm sorry I'm sorry I'm sorry. Please come home. I—I'm not even here with the network. I came on my own to—"

"Bullshit you're not here with the news." Nicky's voice dropped into an idiot's drawl: "'This is Ashley Culpepper with Action News Channel Nine,' you fucking arrogant bitch. I needed you to stay with me. Begged you to. You knew what it was like at home. With them. But you ran off to school and *left* me."

"Come home. Nicky, I'm not here with the network. I've been trying to find you for years, and I got word you landed with this—"

"Do not fucking call us a cult!" Nicky was shrieking. *"We are a family and a fellowship but you wouldn't understand!"*

Ashley tried to mount a response but was sobbing too hard. Frith glanced at Tyler, who stood in the corner, covering his mouth in shock, tears streaming down his face.

"Foundation?" Frith said. "Maybe we should put the brakes on this."

Athena stood still as a statue for a full five seconds. Sound seemed to drain away, leaving only Ashley's cries. Their Foundation tilted her head and bared her teeth. She ground them together audibly, the sound like the squeal of Styrofoam. Frith grimaced.

Athena pointed at her and said: "You know all about the mucilage, don't you?"

"The—what?"

Athena deactivated her microphone. "Francis, Bayard, Stanton, I hereby invoke the sixth maxim."

What happened next always reminded Frith of the first funeral she'd attended. A friend's mother had unexpectedly passed, and Frith was the only one from her class to go to the viewing, at the behest of her poor, long-suffering mother. She was only ten years old. Someone at the funeral had guided her to the front, even though she tried to say she didn't want to go. The sight stuck in her mind like a spike. It was her friend's mother, but it also *wasn't* her. The mortician had slathered lipstick on her, even though she never wore makeup; but worse than that was her skin; all of her flesh sagged and drooped from her bones, like she'd been deflated.

That's what the men looked like when Athena invoked the sixth maxim: deflated.

Still holding Ashley, Frith looked around in growing alarm. "Foundation, what is—"

"The sixth maxim is the most sacred of our edicts, Winifrith. What's most useful about it is, *one cannot fake* adherence to it. You always tried your best to mimic adherence, but ..." She crossed to Franco and pinched his cheek, stretching it to reveal his teeth in a grotesque grin until she released it with a *snap*. "I always knew you weren't a true believer, Winifrith. Or should I address you by your real name, your *true* name?"

"Winifrith *is* my—"

Her world flashed a sudden, blinding white. A firecracker exploded inside her head, *bang!* She heard nothing but a distant ringing. Dimly, she sensed that she'd released Ashley and was staggering backward. A clattering wall stopped her. She tasted twin rivulets of blood—*My nose is broken*—and slid along the wall to the floor. She saw white, then a kind of swimming snow (like TV static), then a shadow blocking the light. A familiar silhouette hulked over her, a man standing with his left arm bent, his fist balled.

Franco.

Her hearing returned next. There was screaming, and a lot of it. Multiple voices, a man and a woman. The woman's screaming stopped, stifled by a heavy hand—Bayard, probably—while the man's, the *teenager's,* specifically, continued. Hand scrabbled at her shoulders. She had fallen against the door, and Tyler—*right, that was the kid's name*—was trying to move her out of the way. A futile effort, of course, given she was half-unconscious and weighed upwards of two hundred pounds.

"Francis. Him, please."

Franco grabbed Tyler's shoulder and slung him into the wall. Tyler raised a hand to protect his face.

"Stop! N—"

Wearing a pantsuit, Frith strode down the halls of the J. Edgar Hoover building. Always prompt, she'd prepped a full dossier on her new subject. She stopped outside the door of the assistant director who was overseeing her case. Hanging on the wall was a photo of the current U.S. President, a surprise winner the previous year.

Bill Clinton.

The door opened, and another FBI agent stepped out, nodding to Frith as he passed.

"Go on in," he said.

Frith entered, sat down, and opened her file. The assistant director, a man who'd been ushering her up the ranks of the Bureau since the Kentucky Devil case, twined his fingers.

"Go ahead, Hastings."

She nodded. "We have reports of disappearances all over the upstate New York area. I think they can be traced to this commune."

"I read your report. It's … eccentric, like most of your cases. But after Kentucky, I've learned to give you the benefit of the doubt. How are you going to infiltrate?"

"I'll pose as a runaway teenager. Change my hair, my makeup."

The assistant director smiled. "Wish I had your baby face."

"It's a blessing and a curse," said Frith, who was twenty-eight in 1993.

"Right," he said with a chuckle as he stood. "Good luck, Agent Hastings."

They shook hands.

Athena was loath to lose Franco's abilities as an artist, so when she invoked the sixth maxim, he always punched with his left. Franco wasn't huge, by any means, but he'd been a powerlifter all his life, as well as an amateur boxer in his youth.

So when he struck Tyler, the results didn't make sense. They didn't make sense because they didn't seem *possible*.

"Stop! N—"

Franco flashed with instant savagery. His fist drove Tyler's hand into his skull with a wet *smatchssshhh,* like a sledgehammer crushing a bowling ball. Tyler's eyes rolled back to whites, his fingers and thumb jutting from his caved-in head like duckbills. He clumped to the floor. His lungs, on reflex, sucked in one last breath—*slurrrrthhp*—and he was gone. Franco awaited his next command, his left hand once again beet-red and smashed to a gnarled mess.

Ashley shrieked through Stanton's hand.

Athena touched her ear. "What was that, Nicodemus? Oh, we were just cleaning things up. Would you like to say goodbye to your sister?"

Nicky clutched her headphones to her head, frowning.

"Say goodbye?" she asked. "Whadda you mean, Foundation?"

"I mean exactly what I said. Doesn't that bring you a measure of peace, to know she's about to pass beyond the veil?"

Nicky's lower lip curled in horror. She was breathing redhot air. "Foundation, I'm so sorry. I can't tell if you're joshin' me or not."

Letta tugged on Nicky's sleeve. "What's going on, what's going on?"

Athena: "Is that Letta?"

No one answered for a moment until Nicky ventured: "I'm sorry, Foundation. She wanted to listen in on the production, and—"

"It's fine. I'm glad she's there. She should start to learn what our true aims and intentions are here. Letta, pay attention to everything that's about to happen. Nicodemus, this was your choice. For all intents and purposes, you sent us here, and now that we're here, I intend to cast your sister in *Othello.* She'll make a nice feature in the rear."

Athena deactivated the radio and faced Ashley. She was about to speak when someone moaned from across the room. Frith.

"Athena." Her nose gushed blood, the middle of her face already smeared with blue and yellow bruising. "Please don't do this."

Athena sat back on her feet, like a girl at a slumber party, before Frith. "I pegged you for a burrower the moment you set food on the lands. I never had to tell you a tale of thunder and vengeance."

"We can work out a deal. You'll do time, but it'll be easy."

"Do you know where the mucilage comes from?"

"I don't—"

"My supplier's from Savannah. Says she has a line on it from overseas. She ships it to me in special containers that can hold anything. The notpers who cross us, I've been sculpting them into various decorations: furniture, objects d'art." She stood and reactivated her radio. "Nicodemus?" A pause, then: "I'm afraid there's nothing that can be done. I'm being forced to count casualty. Sometimes you have to take stock of your enemies and align your soul with the reality that they need to be removed from your life."

Lights flashed across the ceiling: red and blue, interspersed with yellow. Various voices shouted from everywhere. Nicky was frozen. Letta set down her headphones and approached the window.

"What are all those lights?"

Athena spoke again: "Nicodemus? Did you hear me?"

Nicky ran to the window and pulled Letta away from it. Her breath caught in her chest as her pulserate skyrocketed. She found herself in a living nightmare where she forgot how to walk or run. A gunshot blasted nearby, the muzzleflash casting the ceiling a sudden bright gold. Nicky fell to her knees, pulling Letta down with her.

Athena: "Nicodemus, what was that noise? Is something wrong?"

Down the hill, someone shouted: *"Get on the ground, now!"*

More gunfire. Screaming and footfalls sounded everywhere. A few silhouettes bolted past outside. Nicky left her microphone on, trapped between two impulses: either to actively warn Athena about the raid—and risk her killing Ashley—or to shut off her audio, let the police catch her, and possibly save her sister; "possibly" being the operative word. Her brain calculated all the potential outcomes, and unless the cops busted into that hotel room right that instant, her sister was most likely doomed.

And it was her fault.

A gunshot shattered the schoolhouse's picture window. Letta screamed. SWAT officers heaved into view, wielding riot shields and rifles.

"Get down! Lie flat on your stomachs and put your hands on top of your head!"

"You're on your own," Nicky said and yanked off her headphones.

It was in that moment that the Starchild-Nicodemus Fellowship was born.

Franco's violence had obliterated Frith's sensory apparatus, so she registered the next thirty seconds only as flashes of imagery and sound.

Athena wheeled toward Franco, said: "Her, now."

Frith screamed.

Red and blue lights ignited outside.

In a cartoony smear of action, Franco struck Ashley.

Stanton had moved his hand, leaving no barrier between Franco's fist and her.

Ashley fell to her knees, still alive. Her lungs continued working, spraying aerosolized blood. Franco had flattened her face, driving her nose deep into her nasal cavity, which in turn pulled her upper lip away from her teeth. Blood dotted her exposed incisors and canines. She collapsed to her side.

Booted feet kicked in the door, which flew off its hinges.

"Get on the ground!"

Athena wailed: "Franco, again!"

Franco raised his fist, presumably to piledrive it onto Ashley's skull, but a single gunshot—silent to Frith's ears and only marked by shadows on the ceiling—sent Franco barrel-rolling over the bed.

Stanton and Bayard broke into dead sprints toward the door, but a strobing hail of firepower dropped them both. The top of Bayard's head exploded and disgorged a gout of gore that splattered the wall and ceiling, while Stanton took a round to the top of his shoulder.

Only Athena was left standing.

"Get your hands on your head!"

Letta was sobbing. "What's happening, Nicky, what's happening?"

"Shh. Sweetie, just be quiet and do what they say."

Nicky held Letta close, protecting her with her body. They pressed their faces to the hardwood, the smell of floorwax filling their noses. Glass tinkled as the SWAT members stepped through the window. Footfalls stomped all around them.

"Secure the room."

More footfalls. Doors slammed open and shut. Gunshots blossomed in a sudden, violent exchange of fire farther down the hill, followed by more shouting and a smattering of *bangs* and *booms*. Nicky flashed on the previous July, when she told the bigwigs she'd put down Marjorie; the fireworks just never stopped around the mountains.

Boots crunched glass inches from Nicky's head.

"Stand up." It was a man's voice, one she'd come to know well years later.

"C-c-can I use my hands to stand?"

"I don't know. Can you?"

Nicky rolled halfway on her side to get a look. He stood six-two, with dark black hair that had yet to take on the dusting of gray he'd have later in life, when he'd meet Nicky again at the Fortress of Maximum Suffering. But even back in 1993, Bowden Traxler could've been a stand-in for Tony Todd.

Nicky gave him an *are you kidding me* smirk. "Weird time for a grammar lesson, dude."

He smiled down at her.

"Sorry," he said. "Point taken." He extended his hand. Nicky took it, and he helped her up. Another SWAT member, a white guy, helped Letta to her feet.

"My god. Another kid."

"I know. Let's get 'em outta here."

Despite a concussion, Frith fought off the EMTs and made her way across the holding area, an abandoned high school gymnasium they'd converted into a processing area and triage ward. On her warnings, they'd sequestered Athena into an adjoining office they'd soundproofed.

At the Super 8, they lost the boy, Tyler, as well as Bayard. At the ranch, they used nonlethal measures but still killed one cult member.

Franco was gone. Ashley Culpepper was gone.

Frith stood before the office where they were holding Athena. The word COACH arched across a glass window that was packed with soundproofing foam. The SAC, a man named Dobbs, appeared at her shoulder.

"You should get some rest."

"I need to talk to her."

"Okay," he said. "Make it quick."

Frith slipped into the office with her sidearm drawn. Athena sat at a small desk, smiling.

"Egg on everyone's faces. The bureau's having a good year, aren't they?"

Frith sat. "I'm going to make you a deal. You're going to use the sixth maxim on Nicky."

Athena crossed her arms. "Hm. What a fascinating proposition. In what manner shall I deploy the sixth maxim?"

"You're going to make her forget she had a hand in her sister's death."

"That's not how it works."

"I don't fucking care how it works. Nicky's a sweet kid who fell in with the wrong crowd, and she doesn't deserve to spend the rest of her life thinking she killed her own sister."

"Winifrith—or is it Agent Hastings? You heard the spite in her voice. What I gave her was a perfect moment. And oh, I can't take full credit for it, no not at all, because I had no idea Miss Culpepper was related to Nicodemus. But a cast of fate brought her to us so that

Nicky could purge herself of her hatred and send her sister's soul to the Infernal Downfalls."

"Do it, and I'll make sure the death penalty's off the table."

"New York doesn't have the death penalty."

"You're not from New York. You're from Pennsylvania. And we're going to try you there."

Blood drained from Athena's cheeks. "That's not possible."

"We're *making* it possible." Frith smirked.

Athena closed her eyes. "You don't believe in the afterlife do you?"

"I don't know. I've seen a lot of weird stuff over the last few years. But no, I don't think anything happens after we die."

"You will." It wasn't a question. Athena's eyes changed density as she soft-focused on a distant horizon. "But you don't now. That's why it wouldn't matter if I told you your father wound up trapped in the massive, gaping maw of Hades himself, carrying all his worldly wealth on his back for all time, the ground slippery as a tongue, the air rancid with bile."

Invisible fingertips tickled the inside of Frith's skull. She'd already seen the Kentucky Devil. What if there was more?

For now, she dismissed the thought.

"That's a lovely fairy tale. Do we have a deal?"

Athena nodded. "We do. Bring her to me."

Thirty Years Later: The Impromptu Fakement

THANK GOD SHE GOT IPECAC, Traxler thought as he slunk into the speakeasy's bathroom and into a stall. Arbogast had excused himself moments after tasting the phony Miyota ("overwhelmingly complex and engaging"), and Traxler waited a discreet moment before following. A cobblestone and scattered stone hallway that flickered with brass fixtures led back to the restrooms. Traxler's stomach lurched when it occurred to him they might be single-occupancy. If he was forced to incapacitate the camerlengo, it might jeopardize the mission.

Fortunately, the bathroom—there was only one—included two stalls and an airplane-sized sink. Arbogast's retches sounded like screams interspersed with bouts of heavy, wheezing breaths. Traxler stood on the toilet and peered over the side. Traxler's stomach lurched *again* when he didn't see the key at first, but a glint caught his eye.

There you are.

The leather lanyard hung from a hook. As Arbogast launched into his fifth bout of barfing, Traxler reached over the partition and lifted the key, but when he saw it, his expression said, *What the fuck?* Dangling before him was a golden disc with no discernible markings, openings, or function. He was about to call back to base when his thumb grazed the disc's center—and it *blossomed*. He had to stifle an awestruck gasp at the sight: metal melted and unfolded according to a preternatural, super-scientific technological principle he couldn't fathom. The end result was a golden sun with glimmering, quivering sunrays. It had a handmade, hand-*drawn* quality, as if it were living animation.

Bzzzz. Traxler almost swore aloud; his phone was vibrating.

At a loss, Traxler took molds of both sides of it and tapped the center of the "star," exhaling with relief when it folded itself back into its original shape. As he leaned back over the partition, his phone vibrated again, *bzzzz*, and he paused, expecting the camerlengo to look up … but he didn't. Traxler hung the key back on its hook and extricated himself from the bathroom silently, measuring every step and every movement. Arbogast was still vomiting when the door closed.

He jogged back up the hall to find Frith gone and continued running up the staircase. A message from Frith blinked on his phone: *GET BACK TO FORTRESS NOW.* He shouldered his way past the doormaid and ran outside—where he immediately heard rapid-fire footfalls. Frith was sprinting away from him. Traxler gave chase, awkwardly running with one hand clutching the wax mold in his pocket while his other arm pumped away. Ahead, Frith shoved her way through the Porta Viridaria, the action accompanied by a blinding flash of lightning. He quickened his pace—just as a tremblor jostled him off balance and sent him staggering into a wall. Shaking his head, he looked around. Red lightning flashed, and more rain drizzled down.

Great, more earthquakes, he thought.

Another tremblor rattled all the windows on the block. Light glimmered on the horizon, but that was impossible; it wasn't even midnight yet. *Boom.* Another tremblor. And another. It occurred to Traxler that what he was feeling weren't small earthquakes.

They were *footsteps.*

Suddenly it was 1993 again and he and his FBI buddies were crowding into a theater to see *Jurassic Park.* They were a bunch of chuckleheaded young guns, but when the T-Rex's footfalls shook that glass of water, they fell dead silent, each of them as awestruck and terrified as the kids onscreen.

Years later, Traxler looked to the south. The creature's silhouette, wreathed in a borealis-like gleam, hunched over the palazzo. Whatever it was, it must've landed in Saint Peter's Square—and it was headed their way. The Porta San Pellegrino stood between the square and him, and if Frith was still here …

He ran.

The green gateway of the Porta bounced closer and closer, while over the skyline, the creature grew as it approached one thunderous step at a time. Its head emerged from a shroud of mist like a waxing moon. A centurion's helmet, with cheek guards, bracketed the creature's face, which was as smooth as newly buffed marble. Its nose was doric and aquiline, its eyes cauldrons that cradled a pair of blazing white dwarf stars.

"Holy fucking *shit,*" Traxler hissed as he dashed through the gate, where Frith's seemingly severed head sat on the ground. The image made his heart boom before he realized she was peeking out of Richard's passageway.

"Come on, come on!" she whispered. He dove into the opening. They both pelted down the staircase as a massive foot smashed into the earth above and cast them in chattering darkness. "I've seen everything from a level one to a level five preternatural, but that thing was, like, level eleven! What the hell was *that?!*"

"I think that was Arbogast's guardian angel. What's going on at the Fortress?!"

"Letta's awake, and she wants to execute Francois."

Nicky had avoided the truth for all these years.

The sixth maxim was Athena's secret weapon. She used it not only to control her acolytes, but also to make them forget the crimes they committed—the murders, the mayhem, the horrors.

After Nicky left the Ranch, she added the eighth maxim as a means to countermand the sixth. To her, it was the *true* final maxim of the Starchildren—Athena had simply forgotten to add it.

But Nicky had yet to invoke it.

Years later, trapped in Francois's nightmare, Nicky stood before the door to her coach's office and thought of its words:

> *Eight: Show kindness, remember, and speak honestly, for these are the triune paths to friendship.*

Remember. It was a simple revision to Athena's religion, made by a faithful protestant. Nicky never stopped believing in Athena's teachings or her power, but she disagreed with her Foundation on certain points. One was the sixth maxim. It *needed* a back door, a means to un-delete the forgotten memories.

But Nicky had never invoked it.

She'd come close. Sometime she'd wake screaming from a nightmare with fading memories of blood and bits of bone dancing across her consciousness, and she'd begin to invoke her new maxim. Something always stopped her, though; she always backed away from the intention, too terrified to look behind the wall Athena had erected. She knew something terrible happened that night. Over the years, she'd even read news stories about it. A few Starchildren had died in the raid on the ranch, while Franco and Bayard had perished in a related raid on a motel in Gloversville. Two civilians had died, too: a college kid named Tyler Bates and a news reporter, Ashley Culpepper.

Culpepper had loomed large in Nicky's imagination for many years. There was something so familiar about her, but any time she tried to look into her identity, she'd forget what she was working on, or get dizzy, or lose time. When websites like Facebook came around, Nicky tried to look up Culpepper's family, but all the search results were written in gibberish. All she found out were the basics: she was a news reporter who died that night.

All the same, a part of her knew.

She may not have suspected the actual, horrible truth, but she knew *something* terrible was hidden away from her. After all, why would Frith have gone to such lengths to make sure Athena invoked the sixth maxim?

That night, when she fell into Francois's trap, Nicky made a fateful miscalculation. She saw the dream as a puzzle, an escape room with only one way out: *remember.* If she'd known Francois's plan—to exploit the back door into her mind—she would never have dared invoke the eighth maxim in such a setting.

When she did, her mind turned into hell.

A geyser of purest new-moon-midnight-black erupted across the Fortress and boiled away to leave only Tormentos Mallestratos, Infernal Cartographer and Master of Anguish, his face a portrait of righteously evil rage.

Bixby came running up: "Thank fuckin' god! Or y'know, Satan! What took ya so long?! He's got Nicky and Matty, and Letta's still under."

Bixby indicated the table where Nicky stood babbling over an unconscious Letta. Richard flowed on a black wave over to them, his innards spewing forth dozens of black tentacles, one of which gently lifted Nicky's chin.

"Here's not where plaid and paisley fall," she said with a distant gaze. "Put up and put away those handlebars and magic spiders ..."

"Morningstar be kind." The Infernal Cartographer spun toward Francois, who sat at his control center, ignoring him and appearing to carry out his duties. Images of Vatican City filled his rifts. In one, Frith and Traxler vanished into the speakeasy, a detail Richard noted with hope.

Tik-tik. It was Bixby, tapping his armored skirt. "Don't forget about the old-timer." He indicated Matthias, who had collapsed to the floor.

The Infernal Cartographer hesitated. There were two of him: Richard and Tormentos. They'd occupied the same mind and body for seven hundred years. The latter—the hell-lord—had taken full control moments after assuming the mantle of his predecessor, Illyria. He spent the better part of those seven centuries raging at Old Father and performing his duties as Master of Anguish. He lost himself, both in his work and his soul.

But the Rite of Succession had reawakened Richard.

"I must act fast," he said. Richard cast forth his consciousness into the vast beyond. The Fortress fell away, leaving only himself and the map of the Infernal Downfalls, still rendered in wood, stone, and steel. They floated over the center of the Bermuda Triangle, the titanic whirlpool spinning into darkness below. He spoke in a thundercracking tongue known only to the deepest denizens of New Abbadon, and his voice banished the skies, earth, and stars in favor of a *true* view of the five major Infernal Downfalls and their millions of smaller progeny. His hands swam and flashed as he searched the boundless hellscape for his target.

He knew it would be small.

He knew it would be swimming in a foam that emanated from the minds of every living human: the Ocean of Dreams.

Only a select few preternatural beings—like Richard and Francois—knew of it, and Richard was counting on Francois being unaware that he, *Richard,* knew of it. It might be his only advantage. Each individual dream was itself a tiny bubble universe, generated by the hopes and dreams and horrors of every living slumbering soul. Taken together, all those dreams were like an ocean with tides, currents, and shores. *Good* dreams washed ashore on the banks of heaven, while nightmares seeped into the netherspaces between and among the many Infernal Downfalls.

This region of the Ocean of Dreams was called the Dark Inlets.

Some unknowable and arcane cocktail of unseen forces determined the Inlets' location at any one moment. On a whim, Richard had spent the 1500s researching its movements. One popular hypothesis held Old Father and Lord Morningstar played dice every several-thrice millennia to change its location. Another maintained that our entire existence was merely the fevered visions of a slumbering celestial from a higher plane.

But Richard's preferred hypothesis argued that the world's foremost collective downfall—or "sin," in more common theological parlance—would attract the Inlets to its coequal realm. If the majority of people were dreaming about wrath, their nightmares would act as a tidal force that pulled the Inlets closer to mighty Leviathan.

He was right.

Francois's dream realm stood out like a flicker of bright red amongst a tertiary-color rainbow. Richard "zoomed in" and brought it into clear view.

"Dream Master! I have found thee!"

Francois's face rose from the membrane like an iridescent crystal carving.

"Ahhh, bon soir, Monsieur Cartographer! Forgive me, but I had no choice. Monsieur Garcon de l'gran Catalysuer failed to bring me my supper, so I simply *had* to feast on your friend, le Mamzelle … *Murdock?* Would you like a taste?"

When Richard saw what Francois had done to her, his rage was boundless.

That it was a lie was obvious. He lacked a deep knowledge of dream magicks, but he didn't need it. The membrane decoded Francois's glammer. In her nightmare, Nicky was murdering her sister. Brutally. She kneeled over her in some manner of contemporary inn, surrounded by a few other people: three large men, a teenage boy, and one diminutive woman whose resemblance to Letta was immediately apparent. Nicky straddled another woman, her elder sister, raining down blows upon her, punch after punch, breaking both her hands, and reducing her sister's face to a flattened, pulpy mass of blood and viscera.

But flickering underneath Nicky's nightmare, like a dumbshow in parallel, was the truth: one of the men had murdered her sister, having delivered a crushing blow that knocked her dead in a stroke. Nicky was dreaming a lie, but her face told a different story—she was a portrait of anguish, guilt, and shame, all of which commingled with her rage.

Morningstar be kind, Richard thought. *He's tapped into a real memory and rewritten it somehow. This is no mere nightmare. She thinks this is real, that it truly happened.*

If he was being honest with himself, the arrival of the Murdock—of Nicky—had awakened old feelings in him. As a mortal, he had never married, maintaining a strict bachelor's lifestyle. Women came and went, enhancing his reputation as a rake, but none had ever been as open about their attraction as she. None had ever captured his imagination the way she had, either.

He was Richard and Tormentos … and he called upon Richard to speak for him, for only he could summon the emotions needed to help Nicky: love and empathy.

Richard wailed unearthly words that reverberated across the hellscape. In every corner of every Downfall, the Cartographer's commands shook the damned skies. Existence itself strained at its seams around his form: inkvine scars opened and gave view to demented nearby universes where non-Euclidean hyperbeasts roared. In response, Richard's dark host *emptied his body,* leaving only the remnants of his flesh behind. They floated in space, sketching his basic shape, while his insectoids morphed into millions of tentacles that lanced into Francois's bubble universe.

And *moved* it.

Hulking nearby was the titanic curve of Leviathan's boundary. Richard shoved Francois's universe a few "inches" closer to it. Francois's smirk vanished.

"Non. You cannot."

"It is my right and power as Master of Anguish."

His billowing eyes narrowed. "But I would perish, and you would need to replace me in the Menagerie, to say nothing of your precious *whirligig,* oui?"

Time telescoped. Silence reigned. Richard had no desire to send Nicky to Leviathan, and he had forgotten about their need to modify the Dark Nightingale's soul.

"Richard?"

She sounded like she was whispering from the depths of an oubliette, so distant and tiny was her voice. But she was there. In her nightmare, she'd collapsed to the floor and curled into a fetal pose, her eyes glassy and streaming tears, her hands shattered and shaking.

Richard called to her: "Nicodemus?"

"Don't you fucking dare hesitate. Not for me. The stakes are too high. And I know what I did. I deserve it."

Hell-lords don't cry that often, but Richard sensed those feelings welling within him for the first time since his execution. His throat—or the noncorporeal simulacrum of it—tightened, forcing him to choke out the final unholy words that would send Francois's bubble universe hurling into Leviathan. His dark host contracted like a mortar cannon and blasted the tiny universe forward. The bubble ignited as it began its descent. Strictly speaking, gravity didn't exist here, so it plummeted on a straight line, not a curve. Richard called back his dark host, which flooded his form, and watched in growing despair.

Francois was right. If the Master of Dreams perished, they would have to find another creature to take his place in the Menagerie. The Rite of Succession only accounted for *one* such replacement; any more would complicate the Rite by an order of magnitude.

Richard had committed his energies to carrying out the so-called hell heist … but now the prospect of sacrificing the Catalyst once again held tremendous appeal, and—

It was gone.

Richard cast his sight into the distance. Francois's bubble universe had vanished. Had great Leviathan already absorbed it? Impossible. He was about to investigate when somehow, someone spoke in his ear.

Goldberg.

"I think you better get back here," he said. "The situation has grown evermore dire, or as they say, 'Shit just got very, very real.'"

Lightning flooded darkness and awakened her in a searing, stomach-turning jolt. She snapped upright on the table, tears streaming down her cheeks, clutching her chest and wheezing. Her vision faded in from the periphery: thousands of bookshelves came into view—*Am I back in college?*—followed by a face that was simultaneously familiar and surprising: Nicky, her old friend from the Ranch. *Did Nicky go to U Montana with me? Are we studying for finals? Where am I?*

Sobbing and chattering stoked her memorycenters.

Nicky hunched over the table, shoulders shaking. Tears *tap-tap-tapped* the wood. A strange device—Nicky's device, Letta knew—sat next to her and emitted faint wisps of smoke. Nicky's fingertips lay on a big red button. She must've pressed it only moments before.

The Keifering device.

The whimsical name whispered from a distant corner of her memory, but that damn *chattering* was drowning it out. A thousand-million insects, a swarm of something, chittered and clicked and clacked to her left, where rising from the floor was a seven-foot colossus, a patchwork of flesh and metal and bone. He wore an armored skirt and rose on a roiling cloud of those insects.

Her memorycenters flared once more as it all came back to her:

The nightmare she was living.

The Menagerie.

Her mother.

The heist.

Nicky had tested the device on her; the colossus was Richard,

Master of Anguish; and she was in the Fortress of Maximum Suffering. She shook her head, trying to regain her mental footing. First: where the hell *is* everyone? Richard, Frith, and Traxler had left on the mission to Vatican City, while Matthias and … *the small one* had remained here to stand guard.

But who was the *small one?*

Someone squeaked: "Yo, chief!"

Letta looked around. Matthias, the old sorcerer, kneeled on the floor, eyes closed. Francois was rising from his command station, while Richard appeared to be facing off against him. The squeaky voice spoke again:

"Down here!"

She looked. A teddy bear, covered in blood, was hopping up and down and waving a butcher knife. The name came back to her:

"Bixby? What happened?"

Someone touched her shoulder. Nicky. Her face was a downward smear of grief. "I … I killed her. I'm so sorry, Letta. I failed you. I failed the whole Ranch."

Francois spread his hands. "Monsieur Cartographer, I did what you asked. I released her."

Letta coughed. "Released *who?*"

Nicky squeezed Letta's forearm. "I didn't have the courage to look until now. I'm not worthy to be your friend. I'm so sorry."

"Nicky, what the fuck are you *talking* about?"

Richard's dark host flashed from within, his innards rumbling with thunderstrikes that sang in tune with a storm that raged anew, showering the Fortress with steaming hail and lacing the sky with neon-red ribbons.

"You *lied* to her," he said. "You rewrote her memories."

Letta's eyes cleared. "Richard, what happened?"

"The Master of Dreams attempted to feed on Nicodemus. He hoodwinked her with a palimpsest over a true memory."

"Richard, I don't know what the fuck palimpsest means."

"He wrote on top of an *actual* memory with a false one. And tricked her into thinking it was real."

"What … which memory?"

Nicky's sobs had dried up. She stared at nothing. "Her name was Ashley."

Letta froze. "You remember." Not a question. "How?"

"The eighth maxim."

"The eighth—" Letta stopped as she remembered Nicky's addition to the maxims: *Eight: Show kindness, remember, and speak honestly, for these are the triune paths to friendship.*

Remember.

Nicky continued: "We used to take a john boat out to this little island to camp. Spent the whole summer of nineteen-ninety there. Our father … her father, my step-father … was not good. Ashley took me to that island to get away from him. She was getting ready to leave for college. I cried so much on that beach. Held her hand, begged her to take me with her." Her tears returned. "I killed her."

Letta slid off the table. "What?"

 "My sister. At the hotel. I killed her."

Francois moaned with a smile.

Richard slowly approached. "That is the palimpsest, the lie crafted by the Master of Dreams."

On cue, Francois gave a little bow.

Letta shot him a nasty look and took Nicky's hands. "You weren't at the hotel."

"No, no, I was," Nicky said, shaking her head.

"It was Franco. The Sixth Maxim. You and I were back at the Ranch. Remember? In the schoolhouse? It's when we met Traxler. Francois fucked with your head, girl."

Nicky grimaced. "This memory feels pretty fucking real, Lets."

Letta wheeled around. "Matthias! Wake the fuck up!"

He blinked his eyes open and rose. "Forgive me, Successor, I was—"

"I don't care. Did Frith and Traxler get the … key?" She frowned, her memory still foggy.

Francois's words dripped with unctuousness: "Shall I ask them for a, how do you say … *update of status,* mon capitane?"

"*Shut the fuck up.* Where's my phone?"

"Right here, chief," Bixby said, handing it over.

She dialed. "Frith? Get the fuck back here. Shut up. *Shut up.* Forget about the key. We're about to have an execution. We're killing Francois."

"You cannot kill me, mamzelle."

The rest of Team Vatican had returned. Richard closed the portal to Vatican City. Frith had wrapped a shivering Nicky in a blanket; they sat off to the side. Letta stood arms akimbo. She squinted through a bleary-eyed haze but remained defiant.

"You're goddamn right we can. Nicky, what's the ritual to—" she stopped. A glaring Frith gave a single shake of the head that said, *Not now.*

Nicky whispered: "We *can't* kill him. We need him to do the beetle thing."

Letta snapped, "He tried to *kill* you."

Frith stepped over. "Ease off her. And I'm sorry to say this, but Nicky's right. This isn't the time to lose part of the team."

"This is your fucking fault, Miss FBI! If you hadn't told Athena to use the sixth maxim on her, this wouldn't have happened!"

Frith's volume increased: "You don't know that!"

Francois cackled. "Yes, *fight, fight!* Time is waning, mamzelles, and all of existence is ready to perish!"

"Shut the fuck up!" Letta screamed.

"I know how to kill him."

Silence as all heads swiveled toward Traxler.

"What?" Frith said. "How do you know?"

"Someone told me. Someone who's been speaking to me and Richard."

"Quite so, Master Traxler."

Letta looked at both men. "What're you two talking about?"

Traxler addressed everyone: "The guy who's been hacking into Francois's control center." To Frith he said: "The guy who called you in the speakeasy. And Nicky's boyfriend. One of 'em at least. Goldberg." Raising his voice, he called: "I read the book you told me to!"

Once again, red light flooded Francois's rifts, which spat sparks across the mezzanine. Francois whirled and backstepped away. The intruder's full appearance came into view this time: a man in a black-and-white striped clown costume with a tiny hat and a featureless white mask tat covered the top half of his face.

"Greetings," he said.

Nicky shrugged off her blanket and ran in place, waving her hands. *"Goldberg! It's you, it's really you!"*

"It is I."

"You haven't been returning my pings on the Dark Web, mister!"

Traxler nodded. "Thanks for the assist, man."

Frith hooked a thumb at the rift. "You've been talking to this fucking lunatic?"

"He's been helping."

Richard: "Indeed he has." Addressing the rifts, he added: "I cannot fathom how you communicated with me in the Dark Inlets."

"Nanotech with Faraday enhancements," Goldberg said. "Microscopic machines. I swabbed some onto that *Thundercats* valentine she slipped you." He shifted gears: "But we don't have time to share war stories. You fucking idiots are about to destroy all of existence. I'm here to offer my assistance—for a price."

Letta: "What kind of assistance?"

"Yeah," Frith said. "And for what price?"

"The only price I will exact will be a thorough sounding of your hearts and souls. Each of you came to this mission as damaged goods, with traumas untold in your sordid, spotty pasts. I'm here to take a moral accounting of your failures and guide you to both an individual and collective redemption—if you're strong enough to satisfy the very simple tests I will put in your paths."

Frith shook her head. "Thanks but no thanks. I've *seen* your tests."

Nicky's eyes bulged. *"Really?!* Ohmy*gawwwwd* are they as diabolically awesome in person as they are on Netflix?"

Traxler: "Honey, he's *already* been helping us."

Frith sneered. "So he wired us some money because we were too stupid to remember to bring our own. We've already got enough trouble on this mission."

Goldberg chuckled. "I'll say you do. Agent Traxler, why don't you show everyone the mold you took of the key to Clement's Shield?"

"Okay," Traxler said, producing the block of wax. The corners had gotten smushed in the transit, but it was otherwise intact. Letta frowned.

"What am I looking at here? This looks like a kid's art project, not a key."

Richard's dark host flared from within. "Morningstar be kind. I am a fool, an *imbecile*. Master Traxler, was the key of an unusual nature—a *living* metal?"

"Yeah. It was a gold disc that … well, it sort of transformed into a sun."

Letta broke in: "What does that mean, guys? Can we make a copy of the key or not?"

Matthias spoke for the first time since Team Vatican's return: "We cannot. Master Traxler, what you held is known as *sunsmelt*. It is a drop of actual sunshine forged into a key by the Heavenly Host itself, and if you have already unfurled it, then …" He looked to Richard, who nodded.

"All may be lost."

Lightning cracked across the stained-glass atrium in a blinding red X. Francois wailed with laughter. Letta couldn't conjure the energy to yell at him; her lungs had filled with ice.

Matthias: "Master Traxler and Lady Frith, is there something else you need to tell us?"

"Uh, yeah," Traxler said. "I think we saw your buddy, Richard. The angel."

A hush fell over the room, broken only by Francois's chuckles.

Richard's face grew haggard. "You saw Hasdiel Goodmind?"

Frith nodded. "He was the size of a fucking building, so he was hard to miss."

"Did he see the *graduscalariten?*" Richard asked.

"The what?"

Matthias: "The passage. The stairwell manifested by Richard the Cartographer."

Traxler and Frith exchanged looks. She said: "I … honestly don't know. He sort of stepped on it."

"By the boundless torment of Leviathan," Matthias swore. "When you brought the sunsmelt to life, it must have alerted Goodmind to your presence … and our mission."

The sound of cement scraping together drew everyone's eyes to the command center. It was Goldberg clearing his throat.

"Looks like your heist is going exactly according to plan, with no roadblocks or hiccups whatsoever."

Letta stormed toward the command center, ignoring Francois's presence. "So are you gonna *help* or just sit there shooting your fucking mouth off?"

"I will and I have. Mister … Cartographer? Or is it *Richard Pudlicotte?*"

Richard's dark host rumbled at the mention of his name. "What dost thou want with me?"

"Please re-open the passageway to Vatican City."

Everyone (except for Francois) rustled uneasily. Matthias spoke: "Master Goldberg, if Hasdiel Goodmind has detected our actions, we cannot risk re-opening the passage. It would open the Fortress to attack from the heavenly host."

Frith: "They can't *already* attack us? Aren't they, y'know … angels?"

"They are, Catalyst, but this location is one of the very few regions hidden from their powers. When they look this way, all they see is empty sea."

Letta: "A blind spot."

Goldberg broke in: "Trust me. You want to re-open that passage."

Matthias looked to Letta, said: "Successor, I leave the decision to you."

Letta exchanged looks with everyone else. Frith and Traxler both nodded. Nicky did, too.

"Do it," she told Richard.

The hell-lord blanched. "Successor, I have never faced Goodmind in battle and prevailed."

Goldberg: "You won't have to."

Letta and Richard met eyes. She confirmed her order with a nod. Richard cast forth his dark host, which swirled into a living staircase—that was immediately screaming. The very instant he re-opened the passage, a man's voice wailed from it, growing louder and louder in tandem with clattering and clanging footfalls. A heavyset man hurled himself up and out of the staircase. He wore a steel collar, like a rusted tire wheel. The wheel's interior bristled with hundreds of sharp tines that dug into the man's flesh. He stopped before them, covered in sweat and hyperventilating, with blood bubbling around his nostrils.

"I did as you said!" he screamed. "Now get this fucking thing off me!"

Frith gaped. *"You?"*

It was Camerlengo Arbogast.

A chuckling Goldberg proclaimed: "Ladies and gentlemen, may I present the Papal Camerlengo, Tate Terrence Arbogast."

Arbogast's terror somehow increased as he took in his new surroundings. "Oh, my god! *Oh, my god what is happening!* Christ Jesus preserve me, Christ Jesus save me—" *ZZZKKT!* Glowing red threadlines flashed like little lightning bolts within the flesh of his neck. He snapped his teeth together and convulsed a moment before collapsing to his knees.

"That's enough from you," Goldberg said. "Agent Hastings—"

"Hold!" Richard had spoken. He closed the portal, then addressed Goldberg: "Proceed, interloper."

"I will, but you'll soon see there was no need to close the portal." He shifted gears: "Agent Hastings, I believe you'll find your last mission's objective around his neck."

Frith slowly crossed the room, looking around as if she was expecting a trap. As promised, the strange key was still dangling from the camerlengo's neck. She yanked it free and held it up for all to see. Richard and Bixby backed away, the latter waving his butcher knife her way.

"Watch it, stretch. Remember, if one of us touches that thing—"

"Right!" Frith said, lowering the key. "You'll go up like a Roman Candle."

Traxler walked up next to her, looking on in awe.

"That's it," he said.

"Take it!" Arbogast wheezed. "I did what you told me. I prayed him away, then took the stairs that materialized by the Porta Viridaria. Let me go!"

Richard: "What mean'st thou that *'you prayed him away'?"*

"The great titan," Arbogast said. "I sent him away, he who hath beheld the face of the almighty."

"Ha!" Richard's eyes flashed. "Did he tell you that? What a preening, deceiving braggart most mighty is Goodmind. He is but one of the heavenly host's underlings. The *truly* highborne, Gabriel or Michael, would never deign to waste their time on one such as you, mortal."

Frith's eyebrows raised. "But he's kicked your ass every time you've fought?"

"That is of no import," Richard snapped, his eyes flashing a sudden white. "Camerlengo, I demand to know: did you banish Goodmind?"

"Y-y-yes. The almighty himself endowed me with that power, and—"

Both Richard and Matthias laughed, their expressions dark. Shaking his head, Matthias said: "Old Father hasn't looked this way in centuries. None of us would know how to get his attention. No one has since ..." He trailed off, glancing Richard's way. "Well, it hasn't happened in a life-age. But what on earth is this device around your neck, my *good* sir?"

Richard smirked. "Some manner of heretic's fork."

"You're correct," Goldberg said. "Letta Starchild, your mother was one of my greatest inspirations, and I have endeavored to honor her art with my work. When I learned she was the target of this cycle's Rite of Succession, and that the Successor was going to actually make an attempt to free her from the bowels of Asmo, I knew I had to ... participate."

Richard: "But *how* could you know any of these things, mortal? Such knowledge is jealousy guarded."

"Not as jealously as you might think," Goldberg said. "But aren't you all a hurry? Don't you want to know how *else* I've helped you?"

Frith nodded but addressed her husband: "You said he told you to read a book?"

"Yeah," Traxler said, crossing to a table where he took up a leatherbound volume, the same one he'd been reading when Letta and Frith had first brought Nicky to the Fortress. He held it up and addressed Goldberg: "I read the part you told me to."

Frith crossed her arms, her voice tightening with tension. "What part?"

Traxler thumbed open the book. "Nicky, you said that Francois was vulnerable in 'meatspace,' in *our* world. He is, but that doesn't mean you can kill him, right?"

"Right," Nicky said. "He always comes back."

"Unless you challenge him to a Lucid Duel."

Francois, who had been listening quietly, hissed. "There is no such thing!" He bared his talons and teeth, his eyes practically spraying smoke.

Traxler shrugged. "You *know* there is." To everyone he said: "Goldberg showed me where I could learn how to challenge a—" (he addressed his wife) "—what level preternatural is Francois, would you say?"

Frith could barely conjure enough oxygen to speak. "Five."

"Right. He's a level five free-repeating preternatural. They had a different taxonomy back in the—" (he consulted the book) "—two-hundreds. Year 236 AD, to be exact. But a guy named Elishu perfected the art of the Lucid Duel, taking out one of your own predecessors, Francois." He slammed the book shut with one hand. "I hereby call on you to open your greater morpheal depths to me."

Frith stepped in front of him, her eyes pleading. "Honey? Don't do this."

"Winnie, the moment I recognized him, I knew I'd have to kill him."

Nicky had staggered over to them. "But what about the beetle thing?"

Frith nodded. "She's right. Without him, Letta won't be able to enter the infernal vault."

Traxler craned his neck to address Goldberg. "You want to answer that one?"

"With pleasure," Goldberg said. "The original Master of Dreams emerged from the southern straits of Pangaea during the first winters. We weren't yet homo sapiens, but enough of us had evolved the brain centers that govern dreaming. Etchings and cave paintings have survived to this day that depict a woman with smoking eyes. These images appear all over the world. We had no written records, of course, but accompanying these images were depictions of the dead—children, usually—and of the mourning."

Goldberg continued: "But most intriguing: one cave painting shows this strange woman carrying an arachnid-like creature. The artists of the time chewed up prehistoric berberis to produce the purple color." He paused. "The first Master of Dreams, or in her case, Mistress of Dreams, *sired* the whirligigs. They are, in essence, the parents of all monsters; the *conduit* through which hell expressed itself on the earthly plane. Modifying a whirligig can be done by other adepts, occultsmiths, and wizards—but for the Master of Dreams, it comes naturally. On instinct. If Mister Traxler can vanquish the current Master of Dreams in a Lucid Duel, he himself shall become the new Master of Dreams, with all the rights, privileges, and powers therein. It will also forestall the need to replenish the Managerie's ranks with a new creature, because Mister Traxler will instantly become the new initiate."

"Right," Traxler said. "And Francois? If I lose, you get to feed, and you finish out the mission."

"Oh, mon frere, I will not lose."

"Don't call me that," Traxler said before turning to his wife. "You ready? This has to happen now."

Frith rubbed her brow. "You sure we can't just feed him a nun?"

Sitting down, he shook his head. "It's this or nothing, baby."

Francois assumed a meditative lotus pose on the floor. "Ready?"

"Ready."

Simultaneously, Francois's smokestack eyes extinguished as Traxler's rolled to whites. Frith crossed her arms and swallowed back tears. Silence settled over the room. Letta took Frith's forearm and squeezed it with surprising force. She nodded at one of the adjacent rooms.

"We need to talk."

The humidity hit him first. Then the smells. Some were good, others bad. Honeysuckle and freshly mown grass mixed with charred flesh and a sickly sweet aroma he couldn't place at first. He tried to sit up but couldn't. Pain screamed a steady siren from his left shoulder. He was tied up somewhere. No, not tied up—he was *bound* to something, and the heat, the heat was growing. Someone was cooking something, but when he tried to open his eyes, he found he couldn't do that either.

Vinyl.

That was the sickly sweet smell. Vinyl, the kind used in cars. And it was burning.

He forearm-wiped away a bloody film that had coagulated across his brow and blinked his eyes open. A rectangular window wreathed with glass teeth gave view to a dirt crossroads that sat amidst a flat, grassy plain. A white state highway sign bent over the shattered windshield, seeming to peek into the car: MISSISSIPPI STATE RTE 58. Something pressed against his left shoulder, which continued to wail with pain.

Traxler fumbled for his seatbelt, hissed when he touched the scalding metal button, and freed himself.

Winnie, Winnie. Where is Winnie?

Memories mixed in a sudden, sickening cocktail throughout his mind and body. One of his Momma's old sayings came back to him: *Memories are curious cousins and strange bedfellows.* It was one of his first—and last—memories of her. He never quite understood what she meant until this moment-within-a-moment, when he remember-realized he was engaged in a pitched battle against a demon who commanded total control over the subconscious.

He knew that a Master of Dreams could conjure almost any world to entrap its prey. Francois could've dropped him next to a black hole, if he so chose, but he had elected to repurpose *this* memory because it was far more powerful.

Truth was a whetstone in a Lucid Duel, and Francois was using one of the worst nights of Traxler's life as the canvas upon which to paint his doom.

It was the night the Fishmonger almost killed Frith.

As soon as Frith shut the door, Letta laid into her.

"This is *your* fucking fault."

The physical contrast would've been at home on the Vaudeville stage: wee Letta jabbing her finger at a giant, her face red with rage, her teeth gnashing, all while the much larger woman fought back tears, her face a portrait of bafflement: arched eyebrows, slack jaw, palms turned up in protest.

"Letta, my husband is out there right now, risking his—"

"If you'd told Nicky the truth back in 2011, we wouldn't be here right now."

Frith absorbed the blow as the clocked turned back.

Let's mend fences, the subject line read.

Letta and Frith had exchanged a few emails over the years, most of which were cold. Letta never quite forgave Frith for being an undercover agent. Frith acknowledged her friend's hard feelings and explained she was only doing her job.

But when Frith revealed that she had asked Athena to use the sixth maxim on Nicky, Letta had immediately booked a trip to "mend fences," as her email said.

This was in 2011.

Frith hadn't seen Letta in person since she was a kid, and she had to adjust her entire demeanor to interact with this thirty-year-old woman who now stood in her apartment. Traxler was out of town. Frith poured them a glass of red wine and settled onto their sectional couch. She and Traxler were still crammed into a one-bedroom in Arlington, but they'd appointed it well, with hanging greenery, movie posters, and a small tiki bar, where Letta sat on a stool. The evening had gone well to this point; they'd discovered an easy chemistry, sharing inside jokes and anecdotes from the Ranch ... but now a tense expectation hung in the air. Letta swirled her wine, staring at the floor. Frith set down her drink and twined her fingers in her lap, waiting for the shoe to drop. Letta looked up.

"Have you spoken to Nicky?"

"Uh, no. Not since ... well, not really since that night."

"So ... she doesn't ... I don't even know how to ask this. She doesn't know what happened?"

Frith marshaled her thoughts. "After Athena ... did her thing, we had Nicky evaluated. Asked her some questions. We don't really know how it works, but ... no, she doesn't know what happened. Not really. She remembers being at the Ranch, and she has some sense of what happened the night of the raid, but her relationship to her sister is basically erased. Think of it like her sister is a city on an island. The sixth maxim destroyed all the bridges leading to it."

"And ... you did it on purpose?"

Frith nodded. "I did. It was my call. Well, they *let* it be my call because no one really understood what Athena could do."

"Why? Why did you do it?"

Frith leaned forward. "You remember Nicky. Don't you? She's a sensitive soul. There's no way she could've lived with it. With what happened."

"Don't you think she should've been able to make that decision herself?"

"Can I tell you something, Lets? When someone asks me a question that starts with 'don't you think,' they're not *asking* me what I think. They're telling me what *they* think. So—do *you* think Nicky should've made that decision on her own? Nicky, who came from a broken home where god knows what happened to her and who couldn't talk about her childhood without bursting into tears? *That* Nicky?"

"It wasn't your call to make. She should know what happened. We *all* should. Athena stole that from us. She robbed us of our memories."

"Athena? You mean your mother? Susannah Josephine Miller?"

"That's not her *true* name. And neither is Cindy yours."

Frith's heartrate flickered faster, but she banished her rising temper with a shake of her head.

"I don't mind calling you Letta, but I only assumed the name Frith as a part of the op."

"You lied to us from the instant your lips parted in our presence."

"Stop talking like that. Talk normal. *Speak* normally."

"Fine. We should tell Nicky."

"Tell her what? Which parts?"

"All the parts. Tell her everything."

A dark shape on the road drew Traxler's eye.

He extricated himself from the burning car and ran to the shape. It was Frith. They'd been assigned to find and neutralize a strange killer in south Mississippi, a colossus who locals had nicknamed the Fishmonger due to his attire: a bloody apron and surgeon's facemask. They'd tracked him to a small town about twenty miles north of the coast. After the fiasco at Starchild Ranch, Frith and Traxler's little division was once again on the Bureau's shit list, but they'd provided them with enough budget to deepen their research into the strange purple ooze that Athena had used to construct her sunflowers. There had been reports of it showing up at grisly murder scenes all over Mississippi.

Someone, supposedly the Fishmonger, had torn a victim's head in half by gripping their jaw and opening their face like a book.

Someone, supposedly the Fishmonger, had torn a person limb-from-limb using only his bare hands.

It all sounded so outlandish to Traxler; tall tales and local legends growing like fungus on what must have been nothing more than unfortunate accidents.

"When I was a kid working in a factory, I once saw a guy get caught in an industrial lathe," Traxler said on the drive down. "It turned the poor sonofabitch to strawberry jam. These folks must've gotten caught in a threshing machine. That's all."

Though not yet married, they were already madly in love. Frith graced her future husband with a look she often gave him: a cocked eyebrow that said, *You'll see.*

Days later—when they first arrived at that Mississippi crossroads—and years later—when Traxler was forced to relive this night in his Lucid Duel—Traxler realized Frith had been right all along.

There *were* more things in heaven in earth.

Things *did* go bump in the night.

And when he got out of the burning car, he realized that his left shoulder was shattered, but the injury hadn't happened during the wreck. What shattered his shoulder was what *caused* the wreck: the trunk of a newly uprooted evergreen tree. It had smashed through their windshield, crushing his shoulder and lancing through the back seat. They'd been driving normally when the tree rocketed out of a field to their right, as if shot from a cannon. Once again, memories mixed. At first, Traxler assumed they simply hadn't seen the tree; that it had fallen naturally.

This is where his *real* memory and the current nightmare diverged.

In reality, Traxler had reconsidered his assumption calculated the odds that a tree had blasted out of a clear, flat field as if launched by a trebuchet and dismissed the possibility, instead placing his faith and trust in Frith.

The tree hadn't fallen.

Something had *thrown* it.

He pulled his sidearm, which he always wore, and reverse-traced the tree's trajectory, firing off half his magazine into the darkness. Something howled in response and stampeded away, its massive silhouette bouncing toward the horizon. He ran to his wife and found her concussed and banged-up … but basically okay.

But in the Lucid Duel, Francois transformed Traxler into a helpless viewer to his own fate. Instead of pulling his gun, he ran straight to Frith and kneeled over her, unaware of the hulking creature approaching from the darkness. His next sensations happened in strobe-flashes: a speeding wall smashed through him, knocking him skyborne and unconscious; when he came to, a bear-sized silhouette hunched over Frith, hacking at her with a gleaming steel implement that flashed moonlight and sprayed blood. Entrails arced everywhere in drizzling red parabolas.

The creature left him on the side of that lonely Mississippi road, bloodied and beaten—but alive. Traxler shuddered on the ground, in shock, wishing with all heart and all his soul he could relive this moment and do it right.

Someone started a "slow clap" in the near distance. Steel toes clicked and clacked on pavement. Twin smokestacks heralded the arrival of the Master of Dreams, who appeared over him, still applauding with his skeletal hands.

"Mon frere, that was too, too easy! You are like the festering sore of need, of *weakness.* This memory practically pranced up to me, *begging* me to make you my next diddy." *Dee-dee.* "There was an old man named Bowden, whose—"

Strangled wheezes rasped out of Francois like a death rattle.

Traxler had another move to play. The Dream Master had no physical form, but Traxler's wellspring of willpower endowed Francois with one he could touch, grab, and throttle. Traxler's past self remained on the ground, still bleeding and mourning Frith's death, but his present self—his *true* self—had blinked into existence before Francois, his hand slamming into the creature's neck. His flesh crinkled like petrified burlap, spewing out a haze of dust and smoke. Traxler bared his teeth.

"You picked a fight with a grown-up, son." He chuckled and shook his head. "Motherfucker feeds on the vulnerable and thinks he's big-time. The only reason you got the drop on Nicky is because she's been through so much. And this?" He jerked his chin at Frith's corpse. "You think I'm afraid of losing her? Must be your first day on the job. I'm not afraid of losing Frith because *she is invulnerable. Nothing,* least of all your dumb ass, can kill her. No, what I'm afraid of is her outliving *me* because *I am not allowed to die without permission.* If *I* died, that'd mean I failed my mission." Francois's windpipe cracked like glass as Traxler closed his fist and opened wide his jaw, which stretched grotesquely long. An earthquake shook their surroundings and made the earth yawn wide along a dozen faultlines. The horizon disintegrated and showered into empty space until Traxler floated in an endless void, clutching the soul of the Master of Dreams, who he was ready to devour.

But for a moment, he hesitated. Frith's question whispered in his mind:

What'll happen to you when you win?

"Everything? Really?" Frith stood and crossed to the bar. She leaned against it, still a full foot taller than Letta, even though she was sitting in a tall chair. She spoke in a low, grumbling whisper: "Should we say her own sister died that night, and that it's basically her fault? Should we tell her Franco did it? Should we tell her she taunted her own blood right before Athena ordered her execution?"

Letta looked up, lips downturned and practically trembling, her complexion growing pale. Frith backed away.

God, she's still just a kid, she thought, and within her grace and mercy for her old friend began to well up.

Until her old friend spoke.

"It's not your fault you look like that," Letta said.

The words sounded like they'd been spoken over an aging public-address system, the vowels tinny, the consonants muffled. At least that's how Frith remembered it because the insult had upset her so instantly and entirely. Letta felt like family, and like any family member, she knew how to push the right buttons. Frith, who had been the butt of a million jokes since she started towering over her classmates in first grade, fell silent, her skin crackling cold.

Letta tilted her head with a slanting smile. "It's not your fault. But?" She dropped into a whisper: "Is that why you're such a bully?"

The scene grew blurry, but not because Frith was crying. Although she was quick to tears, none came that night. She was simply trying to project herself to another place where she could, in peace and quiet, review her life's actions to prove Letta wrong. She scanned her memories for examples of her being a bully, because why would Letta lie about something like that?

Well, why wouldn't *she lie?* Frith thought. *Her life's work is built on snake oil.*

Frith spat: "You're a fucking *crook.*"

"Oh?" Letta swiveled her stool to face her, looking bored.

"That scheme you've got? The coaching thing? You're a predator. Me and the guys at the office—excuse me, the guys and I—we checked out your website. There was a lady in the comments who said she only had five bucks to her name, and one of your mods chiseled it out of her. Now you're going on television? I watched one of your shows. Crowd full of fanatics and open pocketbooks. Saw someone with a tattoo on their chest: *Emily Miller is my Lodestar.*"

Letta sucked her teeth behind pursed lips. "Hmm. Good word." Shifting her attention to Frith, she said: "There are needs in this world that can't be satisfied by its current state. Religion's useless, god is dead, culture is a wasteland … and it's left us with this gaping fucking *hole* that no one can fill."

"Except you?"

"Except for adepts *like* me, who understand the language and who have been called to *complete.* I'm the only one who can find the keystone, Winifrith. It's out there, and no amount of bullying by wannabe nobodies who can't look their own face in the mirror are going to stop me." She smirked. "You know, we have a line of skin cream that would be great for that acne you've—"

Frith's barstools had low-slung armrests, which she gripped as she bullrushed Letta and slid her stool slamming back against the wall. She hovered over her old friend, nostrils flaring, radiating heat.

A blood vessel throbbed on Letta's neck. Otherwise, she was perfectly still.

"Frith, you're scaring me." The statement's flavor was half manipulation, half truth.

"I'm … I'm sorry," Frith said, her vision fading back into focus. Her temper had blinded her for a moment, but now her apartment came crackling back into view, the image overlaid with bright white specks. "Letta, um." She backed away. "I don't … I don't feel safe in this conversation anymore." She sat on the adjacent stool, her face slack.

Letta slid off the barstool and crossed to the door. "I'm going to tell her, Frith. I swear I'm going to."

She left.

"If you'd told Nicky the truth back in 2011, we wouldn't be here right now," Letta said.

Years later, standing in a floating fortress, Frith absorbed the blow, thought for a moment … and shook her head.

"You don't know that. And besides, do you even care?"

"Of course I care."

"You weren't interested in helping Nicky back then. You just wanted to hurt me—or … not even hurt. *Unmoor* me."

Letta was silent. Another voice broke their impasse:

"I agreed to it."

Nicky was just closing the door.

Frith asked, "So you knew she was invoking the Sixth Maxim? She didn't just spring it on you?"

Nicky shook her head. "She told me exactly what she was going to do and what she was going to erase. But Frith," she added. "You promised her she wouldn't get the death penalty."

"I did."

"But that's exactly what she got."

"I fucking lied."

"Why?"

"Because some people need killing."

Nicky nodded. "I get it. But … she deserved another chance. God whispers to us, Frith. He whispered to Athena, but she just heard him wrong, is all. She should've had a chance to see what I did." She shifted gears. "You both fucked up. I didn't want to know what happened, but Frith, if I'd known you'd go back on your deal with her, I wouldn't have agreed to it. I should've known. She should've lived."

Silence.

Letta touched Nicky's arm, said: "Hey, if she were still alive, someone else would be pulling this hell heist, right?"

They all smiled, not quite ready to laugh.

"Madams?"

It was Matthias, standing at the door with a haggard face.

Frith could barely breathe. "Yeah?"

"The duel is finished."

A mound of dust marked Francois's grave

Letta and Frith emerged to find Traxler sitting up and pointing at the command center, where Francois's remains lay.

"It's done," he said, his voice a rumble from a dark, unknown elsewhere. He stood, but he didn't *stand*. No, he levitated from the table as vaportrails of black smoke whipped around him. His eyes looked normal but incredibly bloodshot. The interior of his mouth was stained a dark black, as if he'd been drinking pitch. He regarded his wife with a curious glance before crossing to Matthias and Letta.

"Matthias. I understand now. I will feed, but first I'll help complete this mission." He faced Richard, said: "Cousin."

Frith had crept closer, lips trembling. "Honey?"

Blood drained from his eyes momentarily as a smile burst across his face. "Winnie." He pulled her into a hug so tight her spine crackled. Pulling back, he held her shoulders. His eyes pulsed red and white in tune with his heartbeat. "I don't understand this, I don't understand what I am, what I can *do,* but I can help us get this done, I can—" His teeth clacked together. He rubbed his brow, backing away and clenching his eyes shut. Frith stepped closer.

"Trax? Honey?"

"We have to keep moving," he said looking up, his eyes once more lividly bloodshot. "You are the love of my life, and you always will be, but ..." he trailed off.

"But what?"

"I'm so ... fucking ... *cold.* Matthias, can you spare a set of those robes?"

The old wizard obliged, returning from his quarters with a black cloak he helped Traxler shrug into. He grimaced, hunching over as his eyes smoldered a sudden and shocking red. He radiated heat in rolling waves. Frith backstepped, watching with a fractured heart as her husband transmogrified. Lava-lines of heat snaked across his flesh, charring the cloak's sleeves up to his elbows. Smoke rose from his neckline and carved up the cloak, lifting the collar into a kind of Elizabethan backsplash. After a moment, the smoke settled into a steady pattern of swoops around him, like electrons circling a nucleus. Red bled entirely through the whites of his eyes. His voice continued to emanate from unknown depths.

Matthias regarded him. "Worthy raiment for the new Master of Dreams."

"Thanks, but please call me by my human name. I don't want any titles. I just want to win."

"Very well," Matthias said, turning to Letta. "Letta Starchild, we await your orders."

Letta, still shaken from her near-death (and near-hell) experience, nodded to Richard.

"You said we can get to Bullshit from here. Open that gate."

"Very well, Successor." He conducted his dark host in an inky symphony, ordering them into twin helices that splashed into the floor and tore wide a yawning chasm from which steaming drops of black oil rose in slow motion. The remaining humans all winced or grimaced.

"Holy cats, y'all," Nicky said from behind her hand. "Smells like someone puked in a porta-potty."

Richard and Matthias discreetly made eye contact and raised their eyebrows in acknowledgment. No one noticed.

"Suck it up," Letta said. "Now, for the rest. Bixby, you and I will take the key into the infernal vault, but we'll need someone in Base Primum when we turn the key or … whatever it is we do with this thing." She indicated the sunsmelt pendant, which Frith handed over.

Goldberg spoke: "I've got that. Most high-ranking members of the world's clergy can get into Base Primum, but the college of cardinals in particular get special treatment—the kind of special treatment that will get you close to Clement's Shield."

Everyone looked to the far wall, where Richard's insectoids kept the camerlengo secured with wrist and ankle manacles. Goldberg's trap drew blood in a circle of dripping dots around his neck.

"The lord is my shepherd, I shall not want," he whispered. "The heavenly host will foil your efforts, sinners. Nothing can stop them, though you've prevented me from prayer, still my thoughts fly up in protest of this treatment."

"Everyone," Goldberg said. "Remember that this man personally and single-handedly raped and abused more than three hundred boys over his career. He's filth, and his filthy visage is our way to Clement's Shield."

"So Frith needs a disguise," Letta said. "Matthias, can you handle that?"

"I can," he said. "At least, I *think* I can. Catalyst, come closer."

Frith crossed over. "Now what?"

"Behold the Camerlengo's face and person. Know it well, and produce it in your mind's eye."

She closed her eyes. "Done."

He produced a pair of ancient-looking spectacles from his robes and placed them on her, instantly transforming her face to the Camerlengo, all while shrinking her by several inches.

Nicky gasped, while Letta cleared her throat.

"Nice job, Matthias," she said. "Do you call that enchantment the 'Clark Kent'?"

"I beg your pardon?" he asked.

"Never mind," Letta said. She crossed to the opening to Stercorebubulus, checked it, then looked to Richard. "We can't use this passage."

"Why not, Successor?"

"Are you insane? Look—we'll fall."

Everyone gathered around. It was like looking through a transparent floor on an airplane. A shimmering membrane separated them from Stercorebubulus. About a "mile" away sat the murky map of a city soaked in pitch and oil. Weather systems of inky clouds and oil-slick rain floated between them and the city below. Flickering streetlamps and buildings gleamed through the haze. Drops of pitch dribbled "down" from Stercorebubulus the membrane and slowly seeped through to the Fortress, where they drifted lazily upward, carrying an unspeakable stench with them. Suddenly, a foot stepped across their view, inches away, its scabby sole pressing directly into the membrane. Everyone drew back, their gorges rising from the smell.

Richard nodded. "It will all make sense once you pass into Stercorebubulus."

"I'll take your word for it. How's the clock?"

Traxler answered: "Assuming Greenwich midnight is the deadline, we have eighteen hours."

Letta nodded. "Got it. Now, what about the keyhole in Optimus Primum? How's Frith supposed to find it?"

Goldberg: "I'll see to that. All I need is for Mister Traxler to get her there."

"Great. Thanks for being helpful and not so … uh, trap-happy," she said, then addressed Traxler: "Start working on that gateway to heaven. Frith, you're on deck. Nicky and Bixby, you're with me."

"Forget it."

Nicky had spoken. Everyone looked to her. Letta propped her arms akimbo. "We need you to run the keifering device on me."

"I'll be alone in there." Her voice was barely a squeak.

"I'll attend you," Richard said to an immediate rebuke.

"No! We need you here. You have to, y'know, balance the Force." She indicated the Apparatus.

"But—"

"*No*," Nicky said with a stamp of her foot. "You saw what happened when you came in there to save me. You *have* to stay here." She turned: "Traxler? You're tough. Can you come with me?"

"I can't, little girl. I have to monitor comms and get Frith into Base Primum."

Nicky faltered, touching her lower lip.

Letta closed her eyes. "Nicky, this is *important,* and we'll take every step to—"

"We need more muscle," Frith said. "Matthias, aren't you the overlord of an entire *army* of creatures? Let's recruit one. And I know just who to call."

"Who?" Traxler asked.

"The man who almost killed me," she said.

He walked right out of Traxler's nightmares, literally.

Moments before, in the depths of Francois's Lucid Duel, Traxler had beheld this goliath's silhouette on the backroads of Mississippi. After Matthias mustered him back to the Fortress, this massive thing that had once been a man forced Richard to widen by threefold the diameter of his *graduscalariten* to admit his passage. His shoulders rose from the enchanted staircase first, so hunched was his back. He wore a faded and threadbare olive-green button-down under a rubber apron splattered with blood. What looked like riot gear concealed his face: black glass shielded his eyes, while a gas mask covered his mouth. Wisps of gray hair indicated a much older man than his build, which was so cartoonishly muscular that even while fully clothed, he could've been the figure model for a classroom of sketch artists perfecting their depiction of the male anatomy. His head was big enough (and misshapen enough) to win blue ribbon at the All-Mississippi Irradiated Gourd Festival. He clutched a home-fashioned weapon, a baseball bat inlaid with the blade of a guillotine. (Local legend held he'd stolen it from a roadside attraction that showcased torture implements.) Blackened blood caked and spotted the blade.

At odds with the rest of his appearance were his pants. Not only were they brand new bluejeans, but he'd apparently had the cuffs tailored into bell-bottoms. Strips of paisley elastic patched up the work.

He stood before them, shoulders heaving. His gas mask emitted hisses and moans.

Traxler: "Braxton J. Merriweather."

"The Fishmonger," Frith said.

Merriweather's shoulders heaved as the pace of his breathing increased. Goldberg entered the conversation with a deep chuckle. "I take it my reading recommendations came in handy against Francois, Mister Traxler?"

"Yep," Traxler said. "I called upon my learnings from *Volume Two of the Malleus Mallefacarum: Dispatching Wights, Wendigos, and other Creatures that Feed Upon the Mortal Mind.*'"

Steel flashed a blinding crimson as the Fishmonger drew back his cleaver—but the cry of an old woman froze him in place. Goldberg made a *tsk-tsk* sound.

"Before you attempt to chop the Dream Master in half, I'd take a look at this."

The rifts blinked like a slot machine until they displayed Goldberg in the top corner, while the others showed a woman, about eighty years old, chained to a bed. A patchwork of bed sores covered her exposed flesh. A frilly nightgown, the same paisley as the Fishmonger's tailoring, covered her modesty. Her arms ended at the elbows, her legs at the knees.

The Fishmonger growled.

"Huff and puff all you want, Merriweather, but this is your test," Goldberg said. "Ever since HyperDivision FullMax made you their guinea pig, you've been a creature of rage and instinct, but your sole remaining spark of humanity is the love you have for your mother—even though your first act upon escaping the lab was to mutilate her. Know this, Merriweather: I have placed an explosive charge in her head. If you harm any of your fellow team-members on this mission, I will detonate it. So please, save your rage for the perils of hell. You'll have ample opportunity to channel it there."

Merriweather lowered his weapon. Nodded.

Richard swept over. "I will hear of it if this young lady comes to harm."

The creature's only answer was a slight shift in posture. Richard seemed to accept it as assent and backed away.

Letta touched Frith, whispered: "You sure this is okay? Having him on the mission?"

"Yeah," Frith said. "We need him."

"Okay," Letta said before standing forward and addressing the team: "Frith, get ready to visit the pearly gates. Bixby, get ready to lead me to your infernal vault. Nicky, pack up the keifer … er. Richard, try to keep hell from blowing up. Matthias, take a knee. Stage one of our hell heist was mostly us fucking up a lot. Badly. But just because you've fucked up a lot badly once doesn't mean the second time isn't the charm. We're going in. Or down. Point is, we're going. Let's get ready."

Part Seven
Turning the Key

A S THE SUN ROSE ON the last day of existence, the storm started anew.

Awestruck vertigo greeted Frith on her arrival to Base Primum.

Rocks and pebbles slid from under each scraping footstep along the mountain trail, skittering and pattering off into endless clouds that surged with innerflashes of red lightning.

Traxler's voice in her ear: "Did it work?"

"Oh yeah."

Her husband's tone deepened with concern. "Everything okay? You sound out of breath."

"That's because it just got taken away," she said, her gaze rising skyward. Richard's map had captured the basic shape of Base Primum … but little else. An undulating canyon of forest rose in a hundred-mile cone that funneled toward the firmament like the interior of a lush volcano. Concentric rings of fire floated lazily around the funnel's circumference, while bucolic greenery and slashes of forest adorned it. The yellow disk labeled *GATEWAY* in Richard's crude map was in reality a blazeburst emanating ribbonlike fingers that caressed the scene.

Frith giggled. "Richard, if I make it back, remind me to give you notes on your map."

Traxler responded: "*When* you get back, baby, *when* you get back."

A gruff voice interrupted them: "[Stand aside in a foreign tongue]!" Shoulders jostled her aside. Her heart lurching, Frith skidded slightly off the path but found her footing. The man who'd just shoved her aside wore an array of robes whose bright colors had faded led a line of pilgrims up the path, waving them along. Like him, they wore colorful robes, but unlike his, theirs were new and vibrant.

He paused, raising a hand to get their attention, and indicated something that floated their way from above. Frith squinted into the light, from which a bouncing silhouette took shape; that of a gondola.

"[Get ready to board!]" the man called, prompting an outburst of joyful tears from his flock. An ornately embossed steel plate sat to the side of the path and magnetically pulled the gondola into station safely. The man and his pilgrims all filed in, everyone hugging and sharing stories in a tongue Frith knew not. The man gave the gondola cable a couple of tugs, and they soared skyward. One of the fiery tendrils from above drifted down, blocking its path, but the gondola passed through it with an audible *whoomp.*

That's when Frith saw the rest of Base Primum.

Her eyes had adjusted to the brilliance, allowing an entire interlocking network of gondolas, ziplines, funiculars, and rickety rope bridges that hung and swung to and from every path. Millions of pilgrims simply walked the spiraling path to the top, while others rode gondolas or braved other means to reach their destination faster.

Frith choked back tears.

A new voice intoned in a seeming gibberish: "Sei vivo-*nnn*d well, sir?"

He stood inches behind her. This guy couldn't have been more than thirty, though the bags under his eyes told the story of a man who hardly slept. He wore a raincoat over a black priest's cassock. Out of habit, Frith started to hunch her shoulders—she always did around shorter men—before remembering her disguise.

"Yes, hello," she said, fumbling for words.

Goldberg, in her ear: "This guy is Giancarlo Donata, Vatican liaison to Base Primum. The good news is you've never met, so you won't have to make small talk. The bad news is he's a fucking degenerate, so be glad you're disguised as a man. Also, I just enabled some realtime translation for you, because he doesn't speak English."

Frith nodded an acknowledgment, then addressed Donata: "Thank you for getting here so fast. I trust your journey was safe."

Donata cocked an eyebrow. "Safe?"

Goldberg: "I said no small talk."

Frith course-corrected: "Never mind. I need a guide to Clement's Scro—to Clement's Shield."

"Yes, I received word to that effect. Shall we—oh my."

He stopped short as another passel of pilgrims passed. One of this group was a shapely young woman who, in her haste, had only been able to pull a single, sheer robe around her naked form, which undulated in sine-wave silhouette. Frith's skin almost crawled right off her frame, so frank and foul was his stare. Frith rolled her eyes.

"Master Donata? I'm in a hurry."

"Then it is fortunate you're with me, or you would never get there." He paused and regarded her, squinting. "Is something bothering you, signior?" He reached over his own shoulder and indicated his back.

Frith realized she was hunching again, but not out of habit. No, she was bent under the weight of something she'd strapped to her back.

The hat-box.

The world pivoted under their feet.

Team Infernal Vault stood over the passage into hell and looked down into what appeared to be a free-fall. Letta, Nicky, Bixby, and the Fishmonger all stepped forward, and the world spun underneath them like a rotating trap door. When it stopped, they found themselves on a city street bathed in fog and saturated with that same floating oil sludge that had leaked into the Fortress. Letta's first impulse was to look *up,* to figure out why they'd seen a mile-long drop to a cityscape far below, and as soon as she did, she realized Richard had been right.

It *did* all make sense now.

Looking up gave the same view: the distant map of a city. But looking *forward* revealed the rest of this hell's nature—the city itself sat on the interior surface of a great ring. The ring was about half a "mile" wide and must've been hundreds of "miles" in diameter. Directly ahead, the ring sloped gently upward, the cityscape vanishing into the black weather systems above, all against the backdrop of empty space.

Only it wasn't *entirely* empty.

"Wowwwww," Nicky whisper-wheezed as she wrapped a bandanna around her mouth.

"There's more than one ring," Letta said, pointing to the right— or to starboard—where another, slightly smaller ring-city floated, a massive wheel with a glimmering interior surface. To the left—or to port—more rings floated, some of them shaped like moebius strips. One of the rings had almost developed a spoke; a causeway spanned the ring's diameter, a gap sundering its middle, its surface seething with hordes of fireflies.

But as remarkable as these sights were, it's worth pausing a moment to emphasize the smell.

"Do *not* under any circumstances reveal, impute, imply, or outright tell them how awful is the reek of Stercorebubulus," Matthias warned Richard in private the day before. "If the mortals, or for that matter the less earthly creatures, had any sense that they were about to swim through a latrine that had been stuff'd with many a maggot-infested corpse, besoaked with pitch, set aflame, stuffed *again* with mountainous heaps of blackened, rotten entrails pulled from every plague-barrow in Christendom, packed with pigshit, doused in piss, infested by lice, swallowed whole by the Forty-Faced Fiend of Brobdingnagian, digested and shat out once more, o'ercrac'k with a single, exquisitely rotten egg, and then left to fester for endless millennia, they would flee from this 'heist' with all haste."

Nicky had tied a bandanna around her nose and mouth, but the smell's true scope hadn't hit them yet. None of their olfactory organs even begin to remotely process the back-breaking stink that engulfed and throttled this realm.

And they wouldn't, at least not for another few moments.

Letta scanned the scene, getting her bearings. Despite the oily weather, the city looked reasonably normal but dated. The architecture was a cross between Victorian London and 1960s Las Vegas, or Ragtime Chicago, perhaps. Iron railings, brownstone frontage, wood-paneled storefronts, wrought-iron porch railings, and colorfully-painted bricks and stones, all of it saturated and soaked with that strange oil, lined the streets. Neon and blinking bulbs adorned nearly every building, but the signage made no sense.

The second letter in your favorite color

The meaning of your name spelled backward

The most common element in the mitochondria of the 96967696676365th fat cell in your right leg

Other signs were written in bizarre glyphs the defied decoding. Letta's eyes hurt just looking at them.

"Don't read the signs—*and stop where you are.*"

Bixby had spoken. He was jogging out ahead, calling over his shoulder, and bounding from one part of the pavement to another, eventually stopping on what appeared to be a clean patch of sidewalk. Letta wrapped a bandanna around her mouth and nose, coughing as she inhaled drop after dripping drop of it.

"Got it," she called, then indicated the everpresent drops of oil. "What *is* this shit?"

Bixby called: "Stop where you are and look down."

At first it looked like a normal sidewalk dotted with black puddles, but closer examination revealed the oil was made up of millions upon millions of *faces*. They rose from the oilslick in bubbles of relief, each one locked in a tableau of suffering and sorrow. Their cries emitted more drops of oil, each one a tiny severed head that itself screamed in torment. Some floated up, others drifted down. Some parts of the city were drenched in this ooze, all of which bubbled and seethed.

Each drop was a damned soul, dissolved to near-nothing.

They were everywhere, moaning and wailing and screeching from every exposed surface. Stercorebubulus was hewn from suffering and buttressed up with misery. And yet even more voices could still be heard murmuring from the storefronts. Nicky blanched and ducked behind Merriweather, whose head was whipping back and forth in confusion.

"I'm keeping you in front of me, big guy," Nicky said. She cupped a hand around her mouth and called: "Bixby! Where the heck're we going?"

Letta was pointing. "Nicky! Your foot!"

Black sludge slithered up and around her foot, the whole mass of it a burbling, babbling, wailing, and keening black cottage cheese of muck and ick and slippery slime, all of it composed of millions of hellbent faces. Bixby came scampering back, hopping from one clean patch of pavement to the next. Using his butcher knife, he cut through the sludge, which fell into slices, almost like meat. Once Nicky's foot was free, he stood.

"I shoulda briefed you before we got here, but the clock was ticking. Don't try to read the signs, don't step in damned, and try not to *breathe*. You humans, the meatsacks still living and breathing, you *kind of* need air, but this place isn't earth. It isn't real, and what you're breathing isn't, strictly speaking, oxygen. Plus, there's another big reason you don't wanna be breathing."

"What?" Letta asked.

"It hasn't hit you yet, has it?"

That's when Letta and Nicky blacked out.

His mind was filled with thunderheads waiting to flash.

The newly christened Master of Dreams beheld his command center, which he'd already rearranged to his liking. Francois's rifts had all been almond-shaped, like rips in a straining burlap sack. Traxler abandoned the literal metaphor and made his rifts into rectangles with a logical flow: each member of the hell heist team had their own visual display with their name in the lower right.

A distant part of his memory whispered, *Aliens. Like in the movie Aliens.*

But then those thunderheads reared up again. Searching his memory was like trying to recover data from a hard drive that had wiped. It was still *there,* but everything from before his Lucid Duel was bathed and buried behind a wall of static.

"Master Traxler?"

Matthias had spoken. Traxler ground his teeth and faced him. "What?"

"They've fallen over. The two women."

Sure enough, they had. Both Letta's and Nicky's displays had gone sideways. Bixby came scampering up to Letta, his posture expressing alarm even if his toy face couldn't.

Traxler stood, barking: "Team Vault? Team Vault? Report, re—"

Bixby's voice crackled through: "It's just the fuckin' stench. Knocked 'em out."

"The *stench?* That makes no sense," Traxler said. "I'm coming in."

Matthias laid a quivering hand on his shoulder. "Calm yourself. We need you here. Merriweather and Bradley are both there to protect them."

"Yeah," Bixby said. "Relax, man. They're lucky; some folks go insane. Thank Crom Herman Munster here's already got a gas mask."

Traxler nodded and sat. Onscreen, Bixby instructed Merriweather to carry both women. This seemed to put Traxler at ease. Goldberg had his own command-center display, which showed him sitting at his schooldesk, using a keyboard and mouse while he presumably watched the action on his own bank of monitors. He noticed this entire interaction and chuckled.

"Matthias, tell me: what happens to you after Letta completes the ritual?"

"I will age approximately seven hundred years in the space of a few moments. The result, from your perspective, will look like I've collapsed into a mound of dust."

"Sounds delightful," Goldberg said. "I once broke into a particle accelerator and constructed a trap that positioned a man's head in the path of the beam. It liquefied him."

This exchange seemed to summon Richard, who floated up behind Matthias, a protective shadow.

Matthias answered: "I know not what a particle accelerator is, but that sounds most dreadful, interloper. Why regale us with such a story?"

"That man readily gave his life to save his daughter. I'm just wondering if you feel like you've done your part for existence."

"Meaning what?"

"The meaning is plain," Goldberg said. "Do you, Matthias de Rilesford, former Black Monk of Westminster Abbey and seventy-seventh Guildmaster of Lord Morningstar's Menagerie, feel as if you've sacrificed enough for the greater good?"

Matthias's gaze grew cold. "If anything, I have sacrificed too—"

Richard spoke up: "Quiet, the lot of you. The Catalyst is about to breach Clement's Shield.

Clement's Shield resided yonder and afield from Base Primum.

Donata led her down six sets of stairs, through several winding hallways, around half a dozen corners and turns, all the way down into a dark, dripping room that rattled and moaned from the conveyances and mechanisms above, but after creeping through a passage of pitchy darkness, Frith emerged into an endless space of sky and cloud. It stretched to infinity, this realm, perfectly flat with no earthly curvature, while behind her hovered a wallface that boundlessly extended above and below, a wall as tall as a galaxy and flat as if sketched with a ruler.

Several stairways snaked away from this plane and into the sky all around, some terminating in small huts and buildings, while others clawed, Babel-like, at the blinding heavens above. Donata raced ahead, jumping from one unevenly mortared step to another, the path terminating in a splatter of ancient brick that bore a single door. He stopped before it and turned.

"Scutum Clementiae is one of the most hallowed places in all of existence. To pass within it is to walk the same steps as the sacred ones themselves." He nodded significantly upward. "Only the keyholder may pass through this gate. I ask thee, Tate Terrence Arbogast, can'st thou present the key?"

Frith reached into her pocket and produced the sunsmelt key, thinking to herself, *The replica you made better be convincing, Goldberg.*

On cue, Goldberg spoke in her ear: "It'll be convincing."

Against the backdrop of limitless sky, Donata turned the key over, nodded, and returned it. "Very well, Master Camerlengo. State your holy business."

"In light of these dark days, I've come to inspect the vault's security and to observe the Chinon Parchment, which may hold clues for how to navigate out of this crisis."

"And why do you have the key with you?"

"To ensure with proof of person that no living being, celestial or earthly, may open the great Scutum Clementiae while I conduct my inspection."

Donata nodded, stepped aside, and opened the door. As Frith passed, he mumbled, "I'm touched you asked whether my journey was safe." His eyes glinted darkly.

She froze, and while she was searching for a response, Goldberg pre-empted her burgeoning panic:

"Don't say shit. Just shrug and walk inside."

Frith did indeed shrug, but before proceeding, she locked eyes with Donata.

"Why won't they make it?"

"Pardon?"

"You said everyone in there was on a hopeless journey. What did you mean by that?"

Goldberg: "Frith, knock it off."

Ignoring him, she pressed Donata: "Well?"

"We both know why, signior. The ways to the Empyrean are known only to a select few. Base Primum is the closest most of them will ever get. But you *know* that, Master Camerlengo, for your ticket was stamped when you took the cloth."

"Yes, of course. I was only confirming."

She stepped inside. Donata, silhouetted by divine borealis, cocked an eyebrow. "You have thirty minutes, Camerlengo." He shut the door behind her with a queer, hissing *shuuuunk*. A magical space enclosed her. Black brick covered the walls and floors, all of it crumbling and worn. Wooden shelves and stacks of old papers packed the room.

Goldberg groused: "That was *an unforced fucking error.* You can't risk any—"

Traxler voice broke in: "Give it a rest, man." To her, he added: "Honey, let's get eyes on the safe so we're ready when Letta turns the key. Or smooshes the key—whatever you do with that thing."

"Right," Frith said, scanning the chamber. Her heart did a tiny somersault.

"Where's Clement's Shield?"

They bounced along the streets of Bullshit, the Fishmonger's boots clomping and splattering through the muck of a million-billion souls. Bixby led the way, headed for the edge of the ring, and while they ran, everyone saw and heard something different.

Braxton J. Merriweather heard old voices calling from every house.

Most were the gruff commands of men in brass:

"You've got the right muscle mass for the shot, son."

"He was born to be a legend, general. He's the one. All we need to do is find a way to make dittos."

"Set the sats to FullMax and proceed, doctors. No matter how much he suffers, remind him he's serving his country and was born to end all wars."

Nicky Starchild saw an old friend.

"Franco?" she whispered. He stood on a Victorian's porchfront, leaning against the bannister like it was a lazy summer afternoon, and indeed it was. A wreath of pink and orange light shone around him and underlined how foolhardy their mission was, how hopeless.

All she had to do was join him, and it would all be over.

Letta Starchild, no stranger to dishonesty herself, heard random taunts and jeers from the houses.

"You're not up to this."

"Leave them behind."

"Abandon them and you'll wake up from this nightmare."

"Your legacy's as dark as your mother's."

The souls of Stercorebubulus had drawn blood, and they knew it. Dark silhouettes rose from every exposed surface—walls, streets, rooftops—bubbles of black, each of them composed of millions of the damned. Distinct shapes emerged from the silhouettes. Some were humanoid, while others took on demonic qualities: batwings and horns and cloven feet and tails. Still others sprouted additional arms and legs. One dark shape resembled an upright silverfish, its thousands of arms and legs shimmering like squick-inducing butterfly wings. They lumbered closer, this dark horde, groaning and painfully detaching themselves from every exposed surface with *slurps* and *thops*.

It was Bixby who realized they were in trouble.

"Okay, guys! It's this way—oh, shit."

Letta, Nicky, and Merriweather had sunk into the supple earth, falling to their knees, their hands planted in the black ooze, which seethed and bubbled its way up their arms and coiled around their torsos. Bixby bounded over and hacked Merriweather free of the slop. He reared up, snorting and whipping his head back and forth.

"Get them up!" Bixby yelled. "Get 'em out of that shit!"

Traxler spoke in their ears: "What the hell's happening? Do you need help? Frith has almost made it to Clement's Shield! What's going—"

Merriweather obeyed the order, hooking his arms under the women's shoulders, but when he pulled, it felt like they'd been cemented to the ground; they didn't budge a micron.

Suddenly, a bolt blazed from the inky night.

Still caught in the ooze, Letta craned her face toward the light and learned another aspect of Stercorebubulus. Some of the rings were stone, while others were the black sludge of the damned. About half a "mile" from their current ring's edge, one of these sludge-rings, about five miles in diameter, exploded when something flew through it. A massive exit wound splashed open, its center a blaze of blinding orange.

Creamsicle dappled this dark world and heralded the arrival of a strange flying contraption.

It soared from the ring's exit wound, the contraption did, its pilot having flown straight through the muck, and as he approached, he carried hundreds of tributaries of ooze in his wake like pitchdark spider-silk, every strand of which flowed into his face. The make of his aircraft recalled fanciful Renaissance sketches in its antiquity and invention. Twin sets of batlike wings formed a perfect cross around a central spherelike grid that held his seat and steering system. There was no single wheel or yoke but an array of levers that controlled the craft's pitch, yaw, and roll. He guided it to their ring and brought it to a scraping, slippery landing. The wings tilted forty-five degrees into an X as the craft came to rest, while the pilot's seat rotated in tandem on a gyroscopic mechanism.

The pilot dismounted and strode their way, revealing as he approached that those hundreds of filaments of spider-silk leading to his face were in fact flowing directly into a pearly white SCUBA-like device that covered his nose; he was *breathing* the souls of the damned. A leather jerkin covered a muscular torso, which was also overstrapped with a chest-guard and accompanied by leather gauntlets, an armored skirt, and sandals. Detritus of the realm filled out the rest of his attire; a helmet carved from a skull sat upon his head, which was buried under a millennia's worth of hair- and beard-growth, all of it a kinky dark black. He'd slathered more of the damned across his body—as protection or salve, the hell-heisters didn't know—but all across his person bubbled and moaned the souls of Stercorebubulus. Bixby slid his butcher knife into his fur and raised his palms.

"Izzy! About fuckin' time! I sent word *hours* ago we'd be here!"

The man, Izzy, strode to Letta and Nicky and drew a gleaming short sword.

"Hold your head back, woman," he said to Letta. She did, and he raised his sword. They bared their teeth in anticipation of a big swing, but instead, he simply dipped the tip into the puddle of black sludge. More orange light flared around his blade and spread through the puddle and up the women's arms. They both hissed and pulled themselves free as the puddle boiled away into an orange mist.

"Wow. What just happened?"

Izzy ignored her and produced a length of wine-colored fabric from his person and cleaned his blade. Glowing orange fluid saturated the fabric, which he pressed into Nicky's face.

"Inhale. Now."

She coughed but managed to suck down a breath. He stepped over to Letta and presented the cloth.

She hesitated. "What's that orange shit?"

"The bewithered extract of the dying damned," Izzy said. "When a soul perishes, it leaves behind a nectar that can protect you in this realm."

Nicky's voice dropped to a whisper: "Dying damned? Souls can ... die?"

"Most assuredly," Izzy said, turning to Letta. "Woman, if I understand your mandate, time is fleeting. Breathe deeply."

Letta sucked down a big whiff, coughed, the shook her head to clear it. She regarded Izzy with sharpening eyes and a creased brow.

Who is this guy? Who is he really?

Izzy addressed Merriweather: "You can breathe through that contrivance?" Merriweather nodded. Izzy re-sheathed his sword. "Now, to matters." He crossed to his flying machine, where he slung a pair of ropes their way. "Take hold of those," he added, producing a pair of glider-like batwings, both adorned with shoulder straps. "I suggest the great wall wear one set of wings, with the little ones astride his back. You—" (he indicated Nicky) "—hold the other line."

"Hold it for what?"

"I'm going to tow you all across the gulf to the outer bolgia."

Letta's eyes grew wide. "The *fuck* you say?"

The outer ring, or *bolgia* as Izzy called it, was uninhabited.

After a hair-raising flight back through the massive ring of the damned, Izzy landed his aircraft on a moebius-strip-shaped ring near the outer membrane of Stercorebubulus. The occasional doomed soul struck it with a *thoom*, lighting the sky with a brief splattering flare. Nicky jogged up next to Izzy, plucking at her lower lip.

"Did you really need to ... uh, murder all those souls just so we could breathe?"

He gave no answer for a moment, instead scooping a few fistfuls of the black ooze off his aircraft and spreading it across his body, slathering some under his nose and into his mouth. He respirated it as they walked the city.

"If Old Father called them here, they matter not," he said, unsheathing his sword.

"Well, didn't he call *you* here?" Nicky asked, prompting an elbow prod from Letta, who gave her a look that said, *Knock it off.*

More city streets spread before them, but the architecture had fallen back several centuries. Adobe pueblo-style houses and buildings stood alongside rondavels, medieval huts, domed stone structures, thatched roofs, and soaring ramparts. Shattered walls separated street from street, all of it soaking wet, as if a heavy rain had stopped only moments earlier. The ring's other half—the reverse of the moebius strip—hung a scant hundred feet overhead, catching light from the inner rings.

Izzy led them to a walled-in adobe that was the only splash of primary colors in the realm. Bright tiles of emerald blue and green, with the occasional lacings of gold filigree, covered its exterior. An arched gateway led to an inner courtyard, followed by another arched gate to the interior, where more bright tile covered the walls and ceiling. Hardwood panels, seemingly new, covered the floors. Merriweather stood guard at the doorway, while Bixby stood next to the fireplace. Over the mantle hung an ancient longbow, double-concave with an inlaid brass grip. A quiverfull of arrows sat underneath it.

Letta looked around in growing impatience. "When are we gonna head over to the next hell? Funk-whore? What was it called?"

Izzy examined the blade of his sword. "If you're referring to the Downfall of Phaegor, we have reached the gateway to it. I built my home upon its threshold."

Nicky looked around. "Do we gotta say *alakazam* or something?" she asked as she unpacked the keifering device onto a broad round table, which she patted. "Upsy-daisy, *mon petit Hannibal*."

Letta laid down next to the keifer-er. "Please don't add him to your repertoire of impressions."

"Got it, chief," she said before addressing Bixby: "But seriously, where's the gate?"

"It'll make sense once you knock her out, girl."

Nicky nodded. Letta stretched out while her old friend affixed the IV and electrodes to her chest and arm. Bixby peeked inside her backpack.

"How'd you carry it? The whirligig?"

Izzy's sandals scraped stone as he spun their way. Shadows danced across his brow. Letta waved away Bixby's question and focused on her work.

"Wait," Nicky whispered, turning to Letta. "You ready?"

She nodded, slipping in a plastic mouthguard she'd brought. Nicky pressed the Big Fucker. Letta jolted, clenched her teeth, and fell still. Nicky looked around. "Um …"

"It didn't work!" Letta said, walking across the room to Nicky's astonishment. She looked back at the table, where Letta lay, and ahead, where Letta stood. Bixby shook his head and handed Izzy a gold coin.

"A bet's a bet," he said. "I can't believe that worked."

"Can't believe *what* worrr—oh, wow." Letta finally saw herself on the table. Looking down, she patted her body, which appeared solid. "Shouldn't I be glowing or more, y'know, *Haunted Mansion-y?*"

Izzy's fingered the edge of his sword, his lip curling. "Do I look like a specter to you?"

"No," Letta said. "But then what I don't understand is: why are you … well, *normal* while everyone else here is reduced to fucking motor oil?"

"Boss," Bixby whispered. "You might wanna have a look over here."

"Where's Clement's Shield?" Frith had asked.

"You should be looking right at it," Goldberg said.

Against the far wall stood an easel-like display case. Foggy glass enclosed the Chinon Parchment, which was about twenty inches tall and covered with browning quillwritten script. Frith scanned the room again. She patted down the walls, checking behind the easel-display. All she found were more bookshelves and stacks—but nothing that resembled a safe or strongbox of any kind. She tapped her earbud.

"Team Fortress, we've got a problem. Clement's Shield isn't fucking here." She waited for a response that didn't come. "Hello? Hell—"

Gold glinted and drew her attention. Behind the Chinon Parchment sat a strange-looking box: about three feet across, with an octagonal shape, like a long STOP sign rendered in matte black with inlaid gold details. Her earbud fritzed and emitted a strange hum that tickled her inner ear before falling silent again. She kneeled by the device and reached out to touch it, seeming to trigger some internal mechanism that whirred to life. The box seamlessly lotus-blossomed open, splaying wide to reveal a miniature staircase, bathtub, and other whimsical props, all of which were linked together with various pulleys, ramps, and servos.

This manner of machine had a name. A Rube—

"Goldberg," Frith whispered before jumping to her feet and touching her ear: "Team, Goldberg's been here, and—"

A small glass cup ascended from the device and filled with water. At the top of the tiny staircase, a boot kicked a ball, which made a circuit around the box before returning to the top of the stairs to get kicked down again. As the ball made each trip around the contraption, the water sank a few millimeters.

"It's a fucking countdown," she whispered before shouting: "Team, can you hear me? Goldberg's planted a bomb in Clement's Shield!"

In Stercorebubulus, the fireplace shimmered. Letta approached it, and awe blossomed across her face. The gateway to Phaegor racked into focus with each step until she had to squint into the haze of a noontide desert. A dusty expanse spread beyond the fireplace's charred bricks. She bent and ducked her head into the opening and through a barrier that banished the stench of Stercorebubulus in favor of a sterile, alkaline dustiness. There was no sun, but rather an oppressive light that emanated from everywhere. In the distance sat a small building—*a train station?*—with a porch and overhang.

But most remarkable was what hung in her periphery: nothing.

Below her ran the ragged edge of a continent that curved away to either side. In order to gain entry to Phaegor, she'd have to carefully step through the fireplace and over a three-foot chasm that plunged into nothingness. She stood back into Izzy's house.

"I take it that's Phaegor?"

Bixby said, "That's it."

Nicky leaned over to look but frowned. "I don't see anythi—oh, you've gotta be keifered. Cool."

She sounded as excited as a kid waiting on a root canal. Bixby and Letta shared a look. She raised her eyebrows to say, *We've got to keep moving.*

He nodded and faced Nicky. "Girl, you got the ripcords?"

Nicky nodded. "And the whirligig."

The members of Team Fortress all manned their stations, unaware of Frith's distress. Her rift display showed her standing patiently by the Chinon Parchment with Donata still in the room, while in

Stercorebubulus, Nicky was reaching into her backpack. Traxler touched his earbud.

"Nicky, make sure you're wearing the Faraday gloves when you handle it."

Richard floated over, accompanied by Matthias, whose brow furrowed.

"I should have attended them," he said, prompting a chuckle from Goldberg.

Richard flared: "Silence, interloper."

Onscreen—or on-rift—Nicky pulled on a pair of purple gloves. From her backpack, she produced what looked like a large Ziploc bag, about a foot across. She opened it, shoved her fist inside, and produced the amethyst beetle they'd extracted from Claudia Castle. She held it wriggling over Letta's chest, biting her lower lip.

"So how do I … uh, put it in her?"

"Nicky?" Traxler began. "My knowledge of this still feels new. It's all gut instinct, like before."

Gut instinct. Hours earlier, when they'd prepped for this stage of the mission, Traxler had, over his wife's objections, held the whirligig in his bare hands. His body, somehow surviving contact with the preternatural organism, *melted* into it until his hands vanished inside its exoskeleton. (He looked like he was wearing the whirligig as a muff.) He cast his thoughts back to their encounter with Claudia Castle, reciting her entire life's story under his breath as a muttered litany.

Bixby had watched all this in silent awe. "Buddy, you still with us?"

"I'm still with you. What now, Bradley?"

"You've gotta juke it. It can't *only* be her soul. It has to be part of mine, too."

Traxler nodded, but after a few moments, nothing seemed to have progressed. He bared his teeth, sweat breaking out across his brow. "I don't know how to do this."

Danger rose on the winds. Letta stirred, checking over her shoulder. Had someone joined them? She shook her head, feeling silly and superstitious … but had someone (or something) *whispered* to her? She checked over her shoulder again. Behind her sat Nicky's backpack.

Nicky. She knows how to revise.

The turn of phrase made her smile in spite of the situation. It brought her back to the Ranch's schoolhouse, with its polished floors and fifties-era light-fixtures; it brought her back to her 'marms scolding her for not taking her studies seriously enough; it brought her back to that awful night when they both cowered on the floor and Traxler stepped through the shattered window.

She didn't understand her next actions, but she found herself crossing to Nicky.

Letta whispered to her: "Where'd we meet?"

Nicky's face whipped toward her, as open and dilated as if she'd just took a hit of smelling salts.

"You heard it too?"

Letta nodded. "He needs help with the *revision*."

Nicky rushed up beside Traxler, laying her hand on his forearm. The others present reacted in alarmed protest—Matthias clenched his teeth, Richard's dark host grumbled, Frith made a vain attempt to stop her—but the end result was the two of them, Traxler and Nicky, standing together.

She whispered, "You need to write *over* it. You need another maxim."

That was all it took. The whirligig's change was nearly imperceptible, but its shade of purple lightened by several degrees. It was done.

But hours later, when Nicky was holding the whirligig over the temporarily dead body of her old friend, she hesitated, wishing Traxler could've come with them, feeling certain she'd never be able to do *any* of this magic crap on her own.

That's when a ghostly hand guided hers.

Letta's soul, or essence, or astral projection, had walked over to gently touch her hand and press the whirligig down onto her corporeal chest. No one had whispered to her this time; she'd simply made an educated guess that these creatures behaved according to their own innate sense of instinct—and she was right. When Nicky pressed down, the creature immediately burrowed into Letta, slipping through her flesh as if it were fluid. A faint rippling wake marked its entry.

Letta squeezed Nicky's hand. "Good work, girl."

Nicky, her breath ragged, nodded and managed a shaky smile. "You better get going."

Letta held up her forearm. "You remember how Richard explained these?"

A bracelet of pure emerald encircled her wrist. Richard had provided them hours earlier before they departed. He'd cited some long, medieval-sounding name for them—"vee-chee" something— but Letta had immediately rechristened them the *ripcords.*

In response to Letta's question, Nicky nodded and raised her forearm, which bore a similar emerald bracelet. She clawed her fingers, spurring the bracelet to sprout three tendrils that snaked between her fingers.

"Just like Spider-Man's web-slingers," she whispered, forcing a smile.

Letta smiled. "Right. But please don't play with those. If you trigger the ripcord—"

"—it'll bring us right back to Bullshit, next to the exit, one time use only, *I know,*" Nicky said.

Izzy rustled. They all looked to him. He manned the door alongside Merriweather, who'd fallen into a silent stupor. Letta craned her neck.

"Everything okay?"

"There is no one, Successor. Proceed with your mission."

Letta nodded and faced Nicky, saying: "Can you do this? I need you to tell me you can, Nicky, or we'll have to figure something else out."

"We don't have time to figure something else out, and you know it," Nicky whispered. "You better go. Are you ready to use Goldberg's parachute-bungee thing?"

Letta reached into her corporeal self's pocket and produced a small polyhedra, a dodecahedron of pure steel that Goldberg had shipped to the Fortress via a quadcopter drone he'd outfitted to withstand the rigors of the Bermuda Triangle. Letta had looked at it with dubiety, but Goldberg had assured them they'd need it to gain entrance to the infernal vault. Bixby had propped his little arms on his hips at that.

"How would *you* know what my infernal vault even looks like, pal?"

"You'll both need to be present to enter the vault, and to actually reach its gateway, you'll need to perform a kind of high-dive through the nethervoid in which the various Infernal Downfalls all swim." Bixby stood silent, but his hands slowly dropped from his hips. Goldberg continued: "If I'm mistaken in my research, I'll happily leave you all and go aid another hell heist."

Bixby had relented, and now they both stood on the threshold of Phaegor together.

"Come on," he told Letta. "It's not far."

Letta gave Nicky one last look of encouragement before she ducked through the fireplace with Bixby.

"Team Fortress, did you read me? I said there's a fucking *bomb in fucking Clement's Shield.*"

Silence.

She seems really ... patient, Traxler thought, fighting through the thunderheads in his mind that concealed his old life. *Normally, she'd be complaining about how long this is all taking or telling that old guy to beat it.*

He swiveled toward Richard and indicated Frith's rift display. "How long has she been down there?"

The Cartographer floated forward. "Three-quarters of an hour, I believe."

"Why is that man, the representative from the Vatican, just standing there? Shouldn't he have left by now?"

Richard leaned forward, his dark host flashing red from within. Overhead, hot hail pattered the stained-glass dome like handfuls of buckshot. "Well observed, cousin. She won't be able to access Clement's Shield with him in the room. Why hasn't he left yet?"

Traxler nodded, said: "Goldberg, do you have anything to add?"

"I sure do. Better pay attention: your boss and the teddy bear are getting close to the jump point."

Even as an undead walking soul, Letta still felt the need to breathe, as well as all the sensations that attended it. Walking across the plains of Phaegor felt like walking across a lunar surface that sat mere miles from a nearby sun. Incredible heat bore down, while redhot winds bit through her flesh. She wrapped a scarf around her face and scanned the terrain, wishing she'd brought a pair of—

"Sunglasses?" Bixby said, as if reading her mind. He'd stretched to his tiptoes to offer her a pair of tanning eyeshields. She wedged them into her sockets.

"Thanks. So what's the big deal with Leviathan, anyway?"

They were approaching the train station she'd noticed earlier, but as they got closer, it seemed to diminish in size. Letta soon realized it wasn't getting smaller; they were somehow getting bigger, or rather, that the senses of scale and distance were reversed here.

"Don't worry. You don't need to know about Leviathan."

"Let's say I'm curious. Why is it any more dangerous than any other hell?"

Bixby indicated the way-station. "Come on, it's this way." Shifting gears, he said: "Okay, Leviathan. It's weird, but my old boss—y'know, the Dark Nightingale—seemed to know all about it. She used to scare the almighty shit out of us with these stories of hell and damnation. She'd read her Dante, so she knew about the different circles, but she always talked about one in particular. Later, after she … well, fuckin' cursed me, and I learned about infernal vaults and all that shit, I heard about Leviathan, and thought, *Mighty fuck, that's what she was talking about.*"

They had almost reached the little way station she'd seen earlier, and as before, it seemed to diminish in size. Pavement rose from the sand and curved toward it. Strange letters jigged across its frontage. Somehow, Letta could understand them. It wasn't a train station but a bus stop. The sense of scale rendered everything in Phaegor slightly Lilliputian to Letta's eyes; the realm was built for a population that topped out at three feet.

A bench sat under the overhang, which provided no shade from the ever-saturating, omnidirectional lightsource. Three of Phaegor's denizens, two men and a woman, sat there, all of them trapped in a state of constant *fidget.* They shielded their eyes against the light, but their hands cast no shadows. Wind blew dust into their mouths, but no matter how many scarves or fabric they wrapped around their faces, nothing stopped it. They kept shoving each other back and forth, battling for bench space.

"Move over, move over."

"I can barely even fit."

"It's late. *Again.*"

Their bodies lacked solidity, as if sculpted from water and burlap. Attempts to shove one another resulted in corporeal invasion: hands slipped into midsections, elbows into heads, every infraction kicking up mounds of dust. They were angry anthills, their flesh bright red from eternal sunburn, their faces masks of annoyance and irritation. One of them, the woman, stood.

"I didn't spend four thousand points for this nonsense," she muttered, stepping past Letta, whose leg inadvertently brushed her—and keyed off a keening wail. Letta's flesh was like knives to the small woman, who whirled into the dirt to the cackling amusement of the other two men.

"Someone had a whoopsie-daisy!"

"Need a plaster for that, bitch?"

The collision had splayed the woman's left arm wide open, as if to be dissected. Her bones, soaked in blood and dotted with gristle, gleamed for an instant before desert dust caked them over. Her flesh sealed shut around the mess, leaving her arm grotesquely inflated with gunk and grit. She ground her teeth and gripped the wound.

She shrieked: *"You came here on the bus, didn't you? You're one of them!"*

Letta backed away. "I don't know what you're talking ab—"

Bixby stood forward. "You're goddamn right we came here on the bus! And we'll take you back with us if you all don't fuck *right off—now!*"

The men bared their teeth in unison, twin snakes trapped in torment. The woman kicked her legs in a desperate churn to propel herself away. They pelted off in different directions, one of them headed toward a square shape on the horizon that swam and shimmered in heat mirage.

They were alone.

"What was she talking about? What bus? Weren't they *waiting* for one?"

Bixby shrugged. "Hell if I know. But come on. We're losing time." He led her past the bus stop toward the edge of the continent. Gesturing with his knife, he said: "So: Leviathan. What makes it so dangerous are the souls there. You've seen two Downfalls so far. Most souls who wind up in a downfall barely have enough moxie to hold a shape together. In Bullshit, they dissolve into slime, here they can't so much as bump into a *real* soul without flying to pieces. But Leviathan? Different fucking story. The souls there'll cut through you like butter. It's the shitcan for every asshole who just won't shut the fuck up about how right they were about everything. Think of all the worst abusers, wife-beaters, murderers—they all wind up in Leviathan. Their national anthem oughta be *They Just Wouldn't Listen!* It's supposed to be the hell of wrath, but it's absorbed a lot of the other hells over the years. Think of every storybook image of hell, with the fire and brimstone and people getting pitchforks up the ass. That's Leviathan, and we're not going anywhere near it, thank fuckin' god."

They were nearing the continent's edge. Letta hooked her thumb back the way they came.

"What about your friend, Izzy? Why's he so … uh, solid? Shouldn't *he* be in Leviathan?"

"I think he almost got sent there, but there's some other reason he wound up in Bullshit."

"Who was he in life?"

"I dunno, but he died a helluva long time ago. And there are 'solid' souls in every Downfall. Some more than others. I dunno how it all works, but there are other factors at play. Whether you're solid or not depends on how fucking pissed off you are combined with … *something* else."

"What else?"

Bixby held up a paw. Earth crumbled underneath his outstretched footpad as he tested the edge of the world. Peering over the side, he shook his little head and chuckled. "Right where they said it'd be."

Planted into the ground by his foot was a tiny flag: half white, half yellow, with two keys—one gold, one silver—crossing under a trio of crowns. The banner of the Vatican. Letta inched closer to the edge, looking back and forth.

"Where is it?"

"Look down."

About a thousand "feet" below shimmered Phaegor's outer membrane. Floating beyond it, another thousand "feet" farther down, was a gleaming sphere. Letta looked over, her face stretched in alarm, but before she could speak, Bixby touched his ear.

"Goldberg, we're in position. How's this bungee thing work?"

"It's quite simple," Goldberg's voice came crackling back. "But first, why don't we check in with the Catalyst? Miss Hastings, can you hear me?"

"Miss Hastings, can you hear me?"

Frith spun around, wincing at the sudden outburst in her ear.

"Where the fuck have you all *been*? Everybody listen to me! Goldberg's planted a bomb!"

"How can you be so sure it's a bomb?"

Frith hesitated. "Well, I guess—"

"I'm fucking with you. It's totally a bomb."

"Fantastic. And what did you do with Clement's Shield? It isn't here."

"I assure you it's there, Agent Hastings, and your friend the Successor is in position to open it. To do so …"

"To do so, she'll need to leap through the nethervoid between Downfalls to reach Mister Bradley's infernal vault."

Back at the Fortress, everyone had heard the previous exchange, all while Traxler's video displays suddenly shifted: the image of Frith and Donata fritzed out. Donata vanished, and Frith quantum-leaped across the room. Traxler backed a few inches away from his control center, his anger growing. Coils of smoke whipped around him as his eyes filled with blood. Richard's dark host rumbled. Matthias came up alongside them both, his face ashen.

"The interloper showed us a false image of the Catalyst."

"That I did," Goldberg said.

Onscreen, Frith raised her palms. "What the fuck *is* this, Goldberg?"

"I promised to help this mission, and I am. But for a price. Do as I say, or we all kick the bucket."

A sloppy roar followed his warning, heralding the arrival of another drone quadcopter, misfiring and soaked from the rain. It listed through the atrium and came to a landing before Richard. An encasement unfolded from its top to reveal a solid-steel rendition of a Rube Goldberg device. As it rose from its casing, its mechanism triggered: a boot kicked a bucket, which sent a ball clattering down a tiny staircase that fed into a merry-go-round and a half dozen other quaint details (a bathtub, a tiny balloon that inflated and popped), culminating in a jack-in-the-box that bobbled forth and pressed a button that had been in plain view the whole time. Two openings shuttered wide, from which slid a pair of golden manacles.

Goldberg continued: "Faraday tech can only get you so far in the Infernal Downfalls. In order to deliver the energy needed for my device, I'll need to call upon one of the Menagerie himself, Richard Pudlicotte, also known as Tormentos Mallestratos, our redoubtable Infernal Cartographer. Would you please place your arms in the capacitors?"

"And what will happen if I do?"

Nicky's voice blared over the line: "Richard, wait. Don't do it."

Nicky's palms were planted on the table to either side of Letta's head. She wiped away a dribble of brow-sweat and squinted in concentration. Merriweather emitted a small growl. Izzy palmed his hilt and stepped closer.

In her earbud, Richard spoke: "I don't think I have a choice, Murdock."

She swallowed a happy sob upon hearing her nickname. "Goldberg's a genius. He plays a dozen moves and ten dimensions deep into the game."

Goldberg: "Miss Nicodemus, you're right. But remember: I am also a citizen of this plane of existence. I have a vested interest in the success of this mission."

Nicky bared her teeth. "Richard? I was wrong, he's right. You've got to do it."

"Very well," Richard said.

Back at the Fortress, Richard nodded and lowered himself to the ground, his armored skirt spreading wide around him like a steel flower. He slid his arms into the manacles—or "capacitors," as Goldberg called them—and waited. After a moment, hot needles dug into his wrists, and he winced. In the seven centuries since his execution, he had experienced untold, ceaseless pain. It was a constant in his existence, the steady drumbeat of suffering. His flayed flesh always felt newly raw and cut, the patches his remaining skin each burning as hot as a newborn sun.

It was exquisite. And it was what powered him, motivated him. He *was* pain. His suffering helped him maintain the rage he needed to maintain balance across the Infernal Downfalls; it was his engine. Only while he maintained maximum levels of self-torment could he possibly hope to discharge his duties.

But there was *another* kind of pain; the kind of pain he remembered from being human. He had last felt it near the Temple Mount, during his most recent bout with Hasdiel Goodmind, he of the Righteous Dagger, Benefactor of Abraham and Prelate Centurion of the Empty Throne. Richard had traveled there to learn how to better balance the Infernal Downfalls—an ancient library buried deep under the Mount held magicks and knowledge he needed—but Goodmind was awaiting his arrival. His stature varied depending on the need and the scene. Richard knew Goodmind had assumed a massive size to intimidate the mortals, but when facing a cousin, he needn't resort to such theatrics.

Richard emerged from the subterranean library, his dark host cradling a stackful of books, when Goodmind attacked. Looking back, he knew he should've detected Goodmind's presence based on the wild changes in the earth's gravity. Like all the Heavenly Host, Goodmind was armed with a blade forged from the heart of a neutron star, its weight and density unmeasurable. Light and spacetime bent around it; heat mirages giving view to the recent past quavered around its length. Richard's perineum sensed its swing before it hit, and when it did, it split him in twain. Goodmind expanded himself to a greater stature to underline his triumph, blocking out the moon and stars as he towered over his conquest. When he spoke, his words rang across the desert like church bells; if illuminated text could speak, it would've sounded like him:

"*The Menagerie's ranks are dwindling. And when they fall below the unholy number, I and my brothers shall thwart the Rite of Succession and bring an end to your unholy realm.*"

Richard lay struck in half as Goodmind drove his blade into the earth and opened a passage to Heaven, hurling himself into an endless sky of silver glass. It took Richard weeks to fully heal, and when he did, he vowed vengeance against Goodmind, even though the prospect of facing him again was terrifying.

But regardless: the pain Goodmind inflicted on him felt the same as what Goldberg's manacles were causing him now.

The dodecahedron unfurled into a squiggly, squick-inducing mess.

Standing on the precipice of Phaegor, Letta coughed on dust and touched her earbud. "Looks like your thingamajig's come online, Goldberg. How's this thing work?"

Clicks and clunks echoed through her commlink, reminding Letta of a landline phone changing hands. The last thing she'd heard was Richard saying "Very well," then silence.

Is Goldberg up to something again?

A hiss, like someone activating a microphone, and Goldberg spoke: "Just step closer to the device. It'll do the rest."

Letta hesitated. It looked like an intricately carved ivory lantern that had burst open to reveal a nest of eels, or a rat king.

Goldberg repeated: "*Clo*-ser. And I'd take Bixby into your arms first."

Letta scooped him up. He brandished his butcher knife, holding it at the ready.

"Let's do this, boss. Got no time for doubts."

She nodded, swallowed, and stepped closer. The rat king transformed into several dozen ivory serpents that slithered up her body and encoiled themselves around hers and Bixby's shoulders. She checked their tightness and nodded.

"Pretty clever, Goldberg," she said. "Hey, any reason why the rest of the team's gone silent?"

"They're … busy," Goldberg said. "You better make this jump before it's too late."

"Got it," Letta said, resigning herself to the task and inching closer to the edge. "Bixby, have you ever made this jump before?"

"Nope. I always wondered how the Vatican built this thing. All I gave them was the password."

"What's the password?"

"Never mind. You better get going."

She jumped, and the instant she left the relatively stable ground of Phaegor, screaming erupted in her ear—Richard's screaming.

Goldberg's device was draining him.

Traxler and Matthias had both jumped to attention, flanking Richard as he kneeled, bound to Goldberg's manacles. White light flared from both, seeping up into his body and siphoning his dark host into itself. Without his dark host of insectoids, Richard was little more than a bizarre art project. The flesh of his face and forearms, along with a smattering of other patches, floated in mid-air, as if glued to a glass figure of himself. Traxler tried to grab hold of him, but there was nothing to grab hold *to*.

"Stop it! Stop it!"

"RELEASE ME, INTERLOPER!" Richard cried in a hollow voice; *hollow* because he had no insides to give it power.

"I can't release you, O Great Cartographer," Goldberg said, shifting his posture as he tapped a few keys on his command station. "Successor, are you reading all this?"

An echo accompanied Letta's screaming voice: "Goldberg?! What the fuck's going on?!"

They passed painlessly through the membrane, plunging toward the infernal vault in the senseless, smell-less, feeling-less nethervoid, their passage accompanied by the shouts and mayhem back at the Fortress.

Traxler's voice: "He's dying! *You're killing him! Stop!*"

Matthias started reciting some old enchantment, but Letta knew the old-timer wasn't up for a battle. She was about to pull her ripcord when they reached the limit of the bungee's range and snapped to a teeth-clattering stop. Letta hugged Bixby tight.

"That was fuckin' close," he said. "Almost fell into the long goodnight."

"I've got you, but—" (she checked their bearings) "—something's wrong." The bungee device had stopped about a hundred "feet" above the infernal vault. She touched her earbud. "Goldberg? We're short, man. I mean, I know we're both short, but I mean we're not *there*. You need to lower us about another seventy-five or a hundred feet." No answer came. "Goldberg, you there?"

An unexpected voice joined the commlink: "About that. Mark me,

Successor. I'm afraid you'll have to make other arrangements tonight, because you're no longer able to access the Infernal Vault."

"Who the fuck is this? *Izzy?*"

Bixby spoke, his voice icy with fear: "Izz, man, what's going on? We had a deal."

Izzy had struck in a flash, his hand plunging into Letta's chest in a strobe blur. Nicky hadn't even detected the movement until a purple glow drew her gaze. Izzy held Claudia Castle's whirligig in a shaking fist, his teeth clenched. He'd motioned to his ear, and Nicky handed over her commlink. She only faintly heard Letta's voice—*"Nicky! What's happening back there?"*—as she backed away, turning to alert Merriweather, but before she'd so much as opened her mouth, Izzy drew his sword and brought it around in a glittering arc straight through the goliath's middle.

Merriweather stood stunned for a moment before his body slid apart, cleanly cut. His upper half thudded to the floor, arms twitching, while his lower half erupted with a geyser of blood that could only be characterized as *Argento-esque.* Squiggling up and out of his lower half was another amethyst beetle—a whirligig—which Izzy impaled on his blade, instantly blasting it into a phosphorescent orange paste that splattered across the wall. Merriweather's remains desaturated and transformed to ash. Izzy brought his sword under his nose and inhaled the Fishmonger's bewithered soul in twin *snortches,* exhaling harshly.

"The great beast's soul is extinguished, woman. There is no one to come to your aid. You shall remove that emerald band and give it to me."

Letta screamed in instant response: *"Nicky, do NOT give him your ripcord!"* She shifted gears: "Goldberg, is this your handiwork?"

Goldberg: "In a manner of speaking. I'm about to end this heist and this crisis. Right now."

Goldberg continued: "I have indeed planted a bomb in Base Primum. Its tonnage is trivial, but its construct is divine. Infernal agents brought me the ordnance from the bowels of Leviathan itself. If detonated, the explosion would vanish in a flash, its power absorbed by its proximity to the peripheral pulsebeat of the Empyrean. The blast would only claim the lives of those whose souls still belong on this side of the spectral divide."

Frith touched her ear: "What?!"

Letta, ignoring her, screamed: "Goldberg, no! *No! Don't do it! I did not choose that Rite!*"

Frith: "Rite? What're you talking about, Lets? What—" she stopped. "There's another Rite of Succession, isn't there?"

Goldberg: "There is. Letta didn't tell you about it, did she?"

"No," Frith said.

"Then I shall. Letta Starchild elected for the *second* Rite of Succession. The *first* Rite calls for the Successor to sacrifice two souls: the Catalyst, as well as her nearest and truest friend."

"Then how the hell is killing *me* going to end this, Goldberg? I'm only the Catalyst." Silence. Frith thought for a moment, doing the math in her head, and as it dawned on her, she touched her brow. "God, Lets. That breaks my fucking heart." Her chest grew heavy. "Do what he says. I'm ready."

"Oh, I'm afraid that time has come and gone, Catalyst," Goldberg said. "I'm afraid, Successor, that the decision for this falls to your Infernal Cartographer."

"Me?" Richard said. "How can this fall to me? Only the Successor may perform these sacrifices."

"You're *almost* right, but in the Rearmost Appendices of the Chronicles of Haborym, there is recorded a deeper magic. When the Rite of Succession teeters on the precipice of calamity, and if the Successor finds themself in a mortal danger that only the Infernal Cartographer can rectify by sacrificing the Catalyst, he may elect to do so, provided the Cartographer themself is also in a mortal danger."

Letta's voice came over: "What?! If we're *both* in danger, and if *he* can sacrifice the Catalyst, he can?!"

"That is the deeper magic laid down in the Rearmost Appendice of—"

"Shut the fuck up! Richard don't you dare—"

Her voice cut out. Silence fell over the Fortress. Traxler stood and faced Richard, his eyes boring into him.

Goldberg: "It falls to you, Cartographer. To end this crisis, all you have to do is sacrifice Frith Starchild. Will you do it?"

"I will not."

Traxler's shoulders relaxed.

Goldberg: "All of existence hangs in the balance, and you say no?"

Matthias watched his old friend with expectance.

"I'll have no part in the death of any of these brave souls. Letta Starchild, Guildmaster Successor-Initiate to Matthias de Rilesford, has chosen her rite, and I shall see it done."

"Even if it means you pass into oblivion?"

"Even past the great veil and the veil beyond that, beyond even the boundary of Old Father's final dreams."

Letta and Bixby hung in the neverending nethervoid, while millions of "miles" away, the express train to Asmo hurtled by, it passage marked only by a slight pull on her inner ear. Bixby fidgeted.

"You think you can jump it?"

"Do *you* think I could jump it?"

"Nope."

"Well, then don't ask me such stupid—" *Bzzzzzzz!* Their heads snapped back as the bungee device reengaged and they began their descent once more. Letta called into her commlink: "Goldberg?! Give me an update, and it better be 'My best friend Frith's still alive,' you sonofabitch!"

"I'm still alive, big girl."

"Frith?! You're okay?!"

"I'm okay, but I don't have much time. Donata's due back soon. Someone's got to open Clement's Scrotum in the next few minutes, or we're screwed."

Back at the Fortress, Richard's dark host began to flow from Goldberg's manacle device back into his form—but not entirely. The process stopped when he was about halfway replenished, leaving him as a semi-transparent shell of himself that swarmed with black static.

"Interloper," he wheezed. "Release me, so that I may aid the Murdock against Bradley's turncoat confederate."

"I'm afraid I can't do that, Cartographer. Your energy is needed to power the belaying device that currently holds the Successor and Bradley. If you remove yourself, the device will pull them back up to shores of Phaegor." Traxler immediately started toward the portal, only for Goldberg to *tsk, tsk, tsk* him to a halt: "And if you remove yourself from the command center, Master of Dreams, we'll lose communications contact. You'll all be lost."

All eyes turned to Matthias, but he was already gone.

"Letta, it's Traxler. Matthias is on his way down to help."

"*Matthias?*" Letta said in disbelief. "He's gonna get himself killed! Trax, go and—"

"Give me the key."

Bixby had spoken. He'd made up his mind minutes earlier. They were out of time.

Letta shook her head. "No, we can still find a way to—"

"And if Matthias gets killed and Izzy steals your whirly-thing? What then?"

They dangled in a darkness that was only broken by the haze of his infernal vault and the continual collisions of newly damned souls all across the hellscape. Letta closed her eyes.

"I thought you said you'd go up like a Roman Candle."

"I *will*. But not right away."

She thought. "Are … are you sure you want to do this?"

"I am absolutely fucking sure I *do not* want to do this, but what the hell *else* can we do? The bigger problem you've got to worry about is how to replace me. If I do this, I'm helping your mission but fucking up the Menagerie's number."

"We'll figure it out. Thank you. *Thank you.*"

Bixby's tiny head nodded. He quietly said, "You're welcome."

"Have you been in there before? Like, do you know where to go?"

"Oh, yeah. I know where to go."

She produced the key. "Do *not* fucking drop this."

"No fuckin' shit." He palmed the lanyard, but the key's magic suffused even it; his fur crackled and smoked upon contact. "You'll need to throw me."

"Got it," she said, uncoiling the device's cords from his shoulders. "Are you ready to, uh, say 'open sesame' or whatever?"

"Just chuck me right at my name."

She gripped his midsection as more smoke rose from his paw. He really was light as a teddy bear.

"One, two, *three!*"

As he flew, he cried: *"Jonathan James Bradley!"*

An orifice telescoped open like an alien mouth to admit his passage into the infernal vault, but when Letta saw inside, she thought they'd made a mistake. Inside wasn't fire and brimstone or barbed wire or chains or any implements of torment.

Inside was the most beautiful day she'd ever seen.

"Everyone read me?!" Letta's voice blared over the commlink. "Get ready. Bixby's gonna unlock Clement's Scrotum."

In Base Primum, Frith touched her ear. "Bixby? I thought he couldn't touch one of those things, the key."

"He can't."

Frith looked up, her heart sinking. "If he dies, what does that mean for the ritual?"

"I can't think about that right now," Letta said, shifting gears. *"Okay,* Goldberg! You had your fun! Get me outta here!"

The instant his dark host had fully returned to him, Richard yanked his hands free of the device and stood, pointing at Goldberg.

"You shall answer for this treachery another time." To Traxler: "Master of Dreams, hold fast here." As his dark host of insectoids carried him through the passage to Stercorebubulus, he shouted, "Murdock! Matthias! I am on my way!"

At Izzy's home, three things happened at once: Letta's essence came crawling back through the fireplace; Izzy spun his sword and held it pointed down at the chest of her unconscious body, ready to plunge it through; and a sludge-spattered and thoroughly exhausted Matthias staggered through the front door, his hair smoking for some reason. He came to a stop among Merriweather's ashy remains.

Nicky, standing by the mantle, broke into a smile. "Matty?"

"Yes, Murdock. I am here."

"*Silence!*" Izzy shouted. "Successor, I am ready to extinguish your soul with a single—"

His voice was eerily calm: "Stay thy hand."

In unwilling response, Izzy's sword froze in place and rose a few inches away from Letta's prone form. Matthias shuffled out of Merriweather's cremains, leaving streaking gray tracks, and crossed to face Izzy, his palm raised and quailing with palsy. Nothing visual marked his magicks; he was simply overpowering this strange old hero with the sheer force of his will. Izzy bared his teeth as muscles jumped across his frame, his triceps coming into relief as he tried in vain to overpower Matthias's magic.

Izzy hissed: "No one ever thanked me for my brilliance. For decades the old fool stormed those walls, throwing man after man at it as if we had an infinite supply back in Ithaca. If I hadn't acted, we'd still be there, Priam laughing at us from his palace. I should be celebrated but instead, Penny and the rest all wound up drinking ambrosia in the sunset while I woke here alone, my legacy one of contagion, my name *escheat,* despite all the Singer's songs that grant me power in this place. Well, if you *die* here, you *stay* here, so I suppose I'm about to have neighbors, but tell me—*have you harnessed enough belief to breathe here with me?*"

He was as cunning as the stories told. Releasing his blade, he hurled himself back a step, breaking the spell long enough to send Matthias staggering forward. Letta made a desperate lunge for him, but it was too late: as his blade fell, Izzy used a fingertip to gently redirect its point forward, counting on the old man to reassert his magic, which he did, locking the blade back in place.

Just as he impaled himself upon it.

Nicky screamed. Letta froze.

Matthias's arms fell limp. As with Merriweather, his remaining form turned to ash, starting with his fingertips, which rained to the floor. No whirligig emerged from his insides, but nevertheless, the remains of his essence stained the blade a bright orange. Matthias craned his neck and presented the women with a sorrowful portrait that combined seven centuries of exhaustion with a sweet, pained relief at being unburdened.

"Tell Richard … I lied to Illyria."

His body burst into a gray cloud. Izzy snatched his blade from the air, sneering in triumph, but when he brought the blade toward his nose, he unleashed a screaming hell-beast that had, until that moment, been safely tethered to the earth. The beast spanned the room in two great strides, leaping onto Letta's table and using it as a springboard to drive a massive spear through his chest and impale him to the wall.

Ash settled.

Izzy looked into the beast's wild eyes, only to discover it was the same small, terrified woman he had greeted not an hour before. She had used a strange clockwork to temporarily slay her friend, the Successor, whose essence stood watching this unfold, her face stretched in an expression of sheer shock.

"You," Izzy wheezed. "H—?"

He was trying to ask *How,* but his own tongue was already dissolving into ash. That's when he noticed his mantle was empty. She hadn't stabbed him with a spear; no, the woman had somehow grabbed his bow and *used* it as one. Then, in nearly the same motion, she'd disarmed him and driven his enchanted blade through his heart. Ages had passed since he first felt the black veil fall across his being. That had been on the shores of Ithaca, hand-in-hand with his loyal beloved, sun dappling the courtyard, his banners flickering. He had expected to awake in the foothills of Olympus, not consigned to this accursed outshore of Hades. After all these years and so many wars won and foes bested, his very essence had been extinguished by a small, frail woman. As he lost consciousness and his body fell apart, he wished Thetis's strange son could've been there to see it—they would've shared a good laugh—but he also found a fleeting and fond admiration for his vanquisher.

She has fire, he thought. *Anyone who lacks such spirit isn't worth*

Jonathan James Bradley found his original form waiting for him among the sweeping plains of his infernal vault. For years his corporeal prison, Bixby the Bear, had saddled him with creaking synthetic joints and bathed him with the musk of wet felt, but the moment he landed in the shimmering emerald fields of his hell, his body returned. It wasn't much to speak of. He topped out at five-seven and constantly battled a beer gut, but he was strong enough to crush a shot glass with his bare hand.

He knew he didn't have much time, so he took off running, barely cognizant of the otherworldly light emanating from his hand. Holding the key caused him no pain; on the contrary, the feel of sunsmelt filled him with incredible peace.

Only the sight of her children disturbed that peace.

They came running from every corner of this little world he'd sired, smiling and laughing, their minds fixed no further ahead than a sunny afternoon chasing butterflies and building forts. As he ran, grief overtook him in a crushing wave. It was all that remained of him, grief and regret—for helping her, the Dark Nightingale, hunt these innocent souls.

Whatever Old Father was, his almighty power had failed these young souls. Their fates were too cruel; *too cruel* to be allowed.

Bradley's arm was a cylinder of solid sunfire that radiated incredible heat and illuminated an already blindingly beautiful day as he ran and ran, faster and faster, his destination finally heaving into view over a hillock. It looked like nothing more than a stone pillar—perhaps an outdoor oven—but it was built from an extradimensional mortarcraft the Vatican had specially made on the outskirts of Heaven itself.

To say he was weeping would understate the guilt Bradley felt by many orders of magnitude.

It wouldn't have worked for Letta. This place was made for one person. Me.

He was struck silent with repentance as the victims he'd helped send to their graves surrounded him, still laughing and cheering and sharing silly jokes, their childish chatter blending into a plaintive hymn that accompanied his last moments. He tapped the key's center and placed it against the pillar, where it unfurled and enwrapped it in millions of silky strands of sunlight. As his essence dissolved into a sparkling cloud, he cast his final thought into eternity:

If anyone can hear me, I make a humble prayer.
This is my final wish …

Jonathan James Bradley vanished into oblivion, as did his infernal vault.

But his prayer was heard.

No, not heard. It was *read.*

She'd been looking at it the whole time.

The last thing anyone heard from Bixby was his name, his *real* name, shouted as Letta chucked him into his infernal vault. A blast of static had silenced his commlink, or so Frith thought, though over the intervening moments, a kind of minor-key laughter had echoed through everyone's ears, followed by a deep, throbbing hum.

That's when she discovered the Chinon Parchment was a ruse.

The display case folded into itself, a three-dimensional shadow resting against a four-dimensional wall, its wooden panels retracting into nothingness to reveal a shelf so ancient that its wood had faded to a cracked, crumbling gray. Frith stepped closer, bringing another "dimension" into view: dozens of hand-written lines slipped into sight the closer she got, all of them written in a variety of tongues. She recognized Italian, Latin, Sanskrit, what she thought was Korean, as well as Arabic and another she guessed was Aramaic. None was in English, and although she spoke some Italian, she couldn't make out the scrawl. Maybe they were a protective ward, or perhaps the ancient equivalent of *High Voltage! Don't Touch!* She inched closer to Clement's Shield, squinting past the enchanted script, and found the prize:

The Keystone to the Arch of Scourgian Mists.

Its shape was unexpected, hexagonal instead of a wedge. No matter—she had to hurry. She unstrapped the hat-box and let it thump to the ground. Angry red strapmarks arced over her shoulders. Ignoring the pain in her back, she tapped the box's top-center. Glowing white threadlines cut into its surface, which unseamed and blossomed open, revealing her equipment: the Hauberk of Havoc, which she strapped on, slipping into its protective gloves. Richard had donated a segment of his dark host to act as a divider between the hauberk and the pool of enchanted purple mucilage, which bubbled below. The swarm of insectoids seemed to recognize Frith, flowing up her arm and coiling around her neck like a choker. Part of her grimly thought the ensemble—preternatural armor topped off with a hell-lord's onyx-glittering necklace—would make a good club look.

When she gripped the keystone, purple and orange sparks flew from her hands and sizzled against her exposed flesh. Wincing, she stowed it in the hat-box.

She touched her ear, said: "Team, I've got the keystone and am about to—"

Something else in Clement's Shield caught her eye: a scroll. She snatched it. A wax seal that bore the Vatican's cross-key coat of arms held the scroll shut. More magical gilded letters danced across it, but unlike the others she was able to read these:

FOR THE CATALYST'S EYES ONLY.

"There's something else in Clement's Scrotum," she said.

Traxler's voice: "Something else? What is it?"

"Looks like a message … for me? There's a seal on it."

"Weird. Read it and get back here. Richard's on his way to retrieve Letta, Nicky, and Matthias."

Sobbing sounded over the commlink. It was Nicky: "He's gone."

Frith broke the seal and unfurled the scroll. "Nicky? Is that you? What happened? Who's gone?"

"Matthias. He's gone."

"Matthias?" Frith said, and as she read … and re-read … and *re*-re-read … the scroll, her face fell in horror. She pocketed it and strapped the hat-box to her back again with a grunt. Clement's Shield returned to its original shape. She whispered into her commlink: "I'm on my way back, and guys: We need to talk. Everyone get back to the Fortress as fast as you can."

"Who are you talking to?"

She froze. Donata was back early.

"Signior?"

Frith, still touching her earbud, spun around. Donata stood at the door, his face a furrowing scowl of suspicion.

He bared his teeth. "I knew this was a ruse. No one has ever asked me if my journey was *safe*. Who are you?"

In her earbud, Nicky was telling Richard he had to follow Goldberg's orders.

"Richard? He's right. You've got to do it."

Frith's mind, suddenly a supercomputer, calculated the risk

proposition. She removed the enchanted glasses and presented him with her true form. The hauberk had a corseting effect on her midsection and décolletage. Her bosom swelled over its steel rim, creating a rippling pool of flesh, the sight of which struck Donata suddenly silent.

She slowly approached him, swallowing her gorge and dropping her voice a husky octave: "I've been watching you for months, Signior. I need a … *teacher*, to show me the ways of the world. I'm so lonely, and I have such … needs." She backed him against the wall, discreetly flicking a switch on her hauberk's gauntlet, which activated with a low *whump*. She planted her hand on the wall behind him, bringing her lips within inches of his. "Wanna get out of here?"

Before he could respond, she gave him the slightest tap from her Hauberk-powered gauntlets, sending a tiny purple lightning bolt snaking from her finger to his neck. His eyes flashed an instant, blinding violet, and he slammed to the floor, unconscious. Frith reactivated her earbud and unleashed a torrent of shouting:

"*Stop it! Stop it!*"

"*RELEASE ME, INTERLOPER!*"

Frith hissed: "Guys, what the fuck is happening?!"

"Nicky? Nicky, we have to go."

Her fists were full of ash, her shoulders heaving, her face drawn in woe. Letta stood over her old friend, moments after she'd revived her body. Outside, otherworldly light slanted through the empty streets of Izzy's bolgia, the top coil of its moebius-strip structure hovering overhead. In response to her friend's words—the tenth time she'd said them already—Nicky, still clutching Izzy's bow, shook her head.

"I'll stay here," she said. "I can't do this. I don't *want* to fucking do this."

Letta laid a hand on her shoulder. "Nick? Nicky, we need you. We need you to—"

Nicky jerked away. "I *should* be here. In one of these places. I deserve to be here."

Another voice: "That's the second time you've said that, and I won't stand for it."

He stood in the doorway, and only because they'd grown so used to his presence were they not terrified. Richard Pudlicotte, also known as

Tormentos Mallestratos, hovered upon his dark host, his flayed flesh drawn taught across the interlocking mechanized nightmare that were his insides, his eyes pitchdark nightstones, his face a mummer's mask. Luminescent gold slashes on his wrists marked where Goldberg's device had held him in thrall—a sight that pulled Nicky to her feet. She crossed to him and cradled his forearm, gently touching his wounds with her forefinger. Black ichor sluiced to the floor.

"You're bleeding."

"I'll mend." He looked to Letta: "Successor, we must make haste. The Catalyst—Mistress Frith—is en route from Base Primum."

"I know. We heard, and ..." she trailed off, her eyes growing distant. She seemed to wander across the room to Richard, where she laid hands on his wounded wrists. Smoke rose from his flesh, and when she took away her hands, he was healed. Letta swooned and staggered into Nicky's arms.

"Chief, chief! I mean, *Hannibal! Great Owl!* Are you okay?"

Letta was silent for a moment, her eyelids fluttering. She took a breath, blinked, and looked into Richard's eyes.

"How'd I know how to do that?"

"It is beginning," Richard said, feeling his wrists. "The Rite of Succession is gaining speed now that ..." he trailed off. The sight of a hell-lord's lips trembling on the edge of tears sent Nicky into emergency hug mode. She held him close, and he hugged her back, his dark host swirling around them like an embrace of leaves on a windy autumn afternoon.

"He had a message for you," Nicky said.

"What was it?"

Nicky looked up. "He said to tell you he lied to someone named ... uh, The Eerie something?"

"Illyria?"

"Yeah, that was it."

He emitted a small sigh. "Did he? Did he indeed?"

In spite of the circumstances, Letta smiled. "What does that mean?"

"'Tis a tale for another time. You should retrieve your listening bell, Successor."

Letta nodded, plucked her earbud from Izzy remains, and replaced it. "Team, Richard's here, and we're on our way back." She surveyed the scene. "But we're coming back with three less than we started—"

Screaming erupted in everyone's ears. Richard snatched out his commlink and stared at it like it was an angry viper. "What means this rude eruption?"

"Team!" Letta screamed. "Report!"

Traxler spoke next: "Frith! Are you there? Come in!"

Frith's voice was breathless: "Motherfucker must've prayed! It's Goodmind! He's—"

On the far side of the rifts sat Goldberg in his command center.

The view around him was one of incredible craftsmanship. He sat in the loft of a great warehouse, surrounded by shelves and shelves all packed with his myriad traps and snares. These would be roughly comprehensible to the hell heisters: wrought-iron devices build from hundreds of smaller ones, each one an elaborate series of whimsical widgets, staircases, levers, and servos.

But what Goldberg was *looking at* might seem unusual.

Instead of a bank of computer monitors, an array of crystals floated before him. Some were spheres, while others were rough-hewn polyhedra that still bore pickaxe-marks from being dug out of the earth. Below them sat several computer towers, one of which was connected to both a crystal and a monochrome CRT monitor. The crystals displayed mostly the same information Traxler saw—the hell heist team across their various locations—while another housed a series of glimmering data readouts labeled in a tongue only Goldberg knew. Draped to the wall over his display was the banner of a nation that no longer existed.

When Frith knocked Donata unconscious, one of these readouts changed from a friendly red to an alarming blue. (The colors signified different things in Goldberg's original time.) Another readout spat out a series of letters that made Goldberg mutter, "Damn." His gaze fell on Arbogast, who was still cowering in the Fortress, wearing his deadly collar.

"No need for you anymore," Goldberg said, tapping out a series of commands. Onscreen—or on-crystal—Arbogast seized, his face turning first red, then purple before his head burst apart in a blossoming spray of blood, brains, and gore.

Sheez, I wish we could've had Richard along the whole time, Letta thought as the Infernal Cartographer led them back to Stercorebubulus's inner bolgia, or rings. He slung his dark host across the massive divides, essentially transforming himself into a living bridge that arced through the endless darkness as a series of glittering black parabolas. The two women stared straight ahead as they ran through the void, not daring to look down, both of them exhaling with relief when they reached the inner ring. Nicky had Izzy's bow strapped to her back, while Letta had taken his soul-killing blade for herself. Richard floated ahead, fashioning his dark host into a wedge that splashed through the oilslick of damned souls.

"The gateway is close!" he cried, pointing the way.

"Frith!" Letta yelled into her commlink. "Report! Are you okay? Where are you?"

Richard stopped at the gate, crafting an insectoid blade he used to slash at an oilslick beast.

Traxler voice was quiet: "Lets? You better get back here. Frith is … she's asleep."

He was waiting for her at the head of the trail.

She'd only caught the slightest glimpse of him before—little more than the silhouette of his profile in the sky—but it was hard to miss a living, breathing angel in person. Hasdiel Goodmind had shrunk to roughly human size, about seven and a half feet, and was clad in armor that, upon closer examination, wasn't metal or leather or any other earthly make. It could've been fashioned from the innards of some extra-terrestrial creature that made its home on a black hole's event horizon. His attire had no visible edges; it was all contour, similar to the perfect curves of his face. His armor's detailing swam in a semi-luminescent soup like molten mother-of-pearl. At first, a Christian cross emblazoned his chest, but the symbol—whatever it was—quickly changed shape, language, and dimension. She perceived the emblems of a dozen other earthly faiths before it slipped the confines of her understanding; it never settled into one shape but was all shapes at once.

But the main event was his sword.

Cartoonishly huge, it would've looked at home in Japanese animation; it was less "sword" and more "massive wedge of unimaginably sharp ultrametal." Light bent around it, and it exerted a gravitational field that pulled Frith's intestines, heart, and lungs against the inside of her torso. When Goodmind spoke, his face was motionless but for a slight increase in haughtiness. He drew himself up and looked down his Doric nose at her, his face wreathed in flame, his eyes starbursts, his words attended by hosannas, the *clang-clang-clang* of his voice echoing from sea to shining sea.

"*Mark me, mortal, for I am—*"

Frith wailed and leapt at him, devil-may-care.

Traxler, in her commlink: "Frith! Are you there? Come in!"

"Motherfucker must've prayed! It's Goodmind! He's—" Her last word coincided with Frith landing a haymaker across the jaw of one of the oldest beings in all of existence. The collision-point emitted an earthcracking purple-orange disc of destruction. Sound vanished. Something exploded with a *cruntchhhshh* in Frith's mouth. As she reeled back from the punch, she spat a mouthful of blood peppered with the shattered remains of half her teeth. Red tinted her blurred vision. Her heart lurched back to life, having stopped for three full seconds. Her knees ached. She figured her right hand had been reduced to dust and several internal organs had ruptured—but the Faraday tech had held. She was still upright and ambulatory.

And the gate back to the Fortress was a scant few yards away.

Behind the angel.

Goodmind faded back into view. He stood touching his cheek, where four gold circles shimmered, the outlines of Frith's knucklefronts. She'd left a mark, but she didn't count on being able to survive another pass. Pilgrims scurried away from the conflict, hustling up the path, their eyes nevertheless glowing in awe of an actual, flesh-and-blood angel.

Frith scanned the terrain. There was but one way back to the Fortress, and it was through Goodmind. Calling on moves from her field hockey days, she juked left and dove for the gateway, feeling the incredible pull of Goodmind's sword over her, its swinging arc singing with a *thrummmm* she felt in the center of her skull. Her midsection felt cold for an instant, like someone strapped a belt made of ice to her, but the sensation passed. As she fell through Richard's portal, she jealously clutched her backpack's straps to keep hold of her precious cargo.

She flew up and out of the portal, landing in the Fortress seemingly unburdened of all her life's worries. She was light as a feather, sliding across the marble on her stomach and unstrapping the hat-box.

"I got it, I got it," she said, though her voice sounded strange to her; empty and airless. And she felt so *light*. Maybe fighting an angel had helped her work off a few pounds! She laughed inwardly at her own joke, trying to roll over so she could jump to her feet and keep this mission going, but rolling over carried with it the sensation of *twisting*, like she'd gotten wrapped up in her bed blankets. Her legs were crossed at an absurd angle and positively covered with blood. More blood roiled up from her lungs, and she grabbed at her legs, again overcome with that sense of being in bed and unable to get fully covered up.

They're so far away, she thought before whispering to Traxler: "Help me pull them up, would you? I'm cold, and I've got bad news."

She produced the scroll from the hauberk. Her husband kneeled over her, his face a portrait of compassion.

"Winnie?"

"Did I get it back? The keystone? It's here, right?"

"It's here. You did good, but I need you to do something for me. I need you to go to sleep."

It wasn't hard to obey. Unconsciousness was pulling her under anyway. As she drifted off, Frith thought of the funniest thing: *My blankets are my legs, and that's why I feel so cold. My legs are ten feet away, clear across the room.*

Letta, Nicky, and Richard returned to a scene out of a horror movie. Frith's body lay in two halves, a string of intestines their only connection. Goldberg was working away at something, his fingers flying across his keyboard. Arbogast was dead, his body slumped against the wall, his head splayed open into a bloody blossom. Traxler was kneeling over his wife, who had stopped breathing. Nicky covered her mouth, fighting back tears, and tugged Letta's sleeve.

"Oh god, oh god, oh *gawwwd*, Letta, make her better. Do what you did for Richard. Make her better."

Letta stepped forward and stopped. "I … I don't know how."

Richard had hovered up next to her. "You won't be able to. She has been cleaved by a blade of the Heavenly Host."

"Right. Goldberg, I don't suppose you've got a trick up your sleeve for this?"

He ignored her, still typing away. Letta wanted to scream, but she compartmentalized her feelings … and took stock.

Frith was dying.

Merriweather and Bixby's deaths dropped the Menagerie's number to 663, meaning they had to come up with two more creatures along with Athena to bring its number back up to 666.

But the hat-box had made it. Had their prize?

"Did we at least get the keystone?"

Richard crossed to the hat-box and tapped it open. He nodded, but his eyes fell on the scroll.

"What is this?"

Traxler, lost in concentration, shrugged. "She brought it back from Clement's Shield. Said it was a message for her."

Richard took it up and read it—in growing horror. "Letta, you must read this."

"In a minute." She approached Traxler. "What the fuck are you doing? She's gone."

"Wait," he hissed. "Rich, slide the hat-box over here, now." Richard obliged, and Traxler overturned it, spilling out the keystone and gallons of mucilage. Traxler scooped a few handfuls, which he slathered across Frith's midsection as he muttered an incantation and his eyes rolled back.

Sudden, shining beacons of purple light blasted from Frith's eyes, fingers, and toes.

Her two sundered halves slid across the floor and stitched themselves back together. She levitated on an upswelling cloud of purple intershot with flecks and flashes of orange. She was a natural six foot two, but whatever Traxler had done added another six inches to that tally, along with an extra two hundred pounds of pure muscle. The hauberk strained against her expanding flesh, which somehow made her neckline even more insanely alluring. Richard's insectoid choker still encircled her neck. Her eyes opened, and she regarded herself. Tears streamed down her cheeks.

"You saved me."

"You're damn right I did."

They hugged. Letta just stared at them, too numb to feel joy. Nicky inched closer, scratching her chin.

"*Psst* … Traxler. Hey."

"Why are you whispering?" he asked.

"It's a parallel universe, right?"

Traxler nodded and whispered back: "Dreams are windows into parallel realities. I thought if I could retrieve Merriweather's whirligig from my nightmares, I could transfer it into her." He spoke in a normal voice: "And Richard, I don't know all the rules, but I think this means she can replace Merriweather as a member of the Menagerie, right?"

As in if in answer, over in the atrium, the Apparatus' master counter ticked up one, to six-hundred sixty-four.

Richard nodded. "It does indeed, Master Traxler. We need only replace Master Bradley and retrieve Letta's mother to forestall the Apocalypse."

Letta: "How'd you know that would work? The dream-whirligig thing?"

He indicated Frith. "I didn't, but then my lady's something special. She was worth the hail mary."

Frith smiled. "Thank you, and—" She crossed to Letta and hugged her. Hard.

"Frith? I can't breathe."

Frith released her. "Did you even think about performing the second Rite?"

"Fuck no."

She nodded, eyes glistening, while sparks and smoke spat and leaked from her hauberk's righthand gauntlet.

Richard indicated the damage. "Lady Frith, did you cross swords with Goodmind?"

Frith: "Well, I socked him one, but we didn't exactly 'cross swords.' Except for him chopping me in half, I guess."

"Oh. He did that to me, as well, but … you laid hands on him?"

He beheld Frith with a look that could only be described as longing.

She tilted her head. "I was wearing the Faraday gauntlets, but yeah. Why? What's it matter?"

Before Richard could answer, lightning flashed outside for a full ten seconds, the conflagration accompanied by a chorus of ear-splitting roars. The storm's output had fully converted from rain to hot hail.

Overhead, the stained-glass dome hissed and sizzled and steamed with each stone-strike. In the atrium, the infernal map was practically spinning. Infernal downfalls sped around the Fortress in a hectic, mad dance, all of them growing closer and closer to Leviathan, which had swollen in size yet again.

Letta pointed. "Richard!"

"Understood, but Successor—*read*." He handed her the scroll and hurried to the mezzanine's edge to see to his duties. Letta read the scroll, looking less terrified by its contents and more simply *resigned*. Nicky hovered at her shoulder.

"What's it say, what's it say?"

Frith approached, her every footstep a looming *thud*. "I think we all know what it says."

Letta handed the scroll to Nicky, whose face fell in grief as she read it. "Oh, no. Matty."

Traxler's shoulders sagged. "Do I even want to know what it says?"

Letta handed it over. "It says we're going to Leviathan."

On-rift, Goldberg finished his work with a flourish of clattering keys. "There! Done!"

Everyone turned. Letta held up the scroll. "Did you know about this shit?"

"Did I know about *what* shit, Successor?"

"That—" (she read from the scroll) "—the gateway from Balaam to Asmo can only be opened by Matthias de Rilesford, Seventy-Seventh Guildmaster of Lord Morningstar's Menagerie?"

"I had my suspicions, but I didn't need to explore that route."

"What the hell does that—"

"But," Goldberg continued, "now that you know you'll have to pass through Leviathan to complete your mission, won't you need help to do so?"

She sighed, digging her fingers into her hair. "Sure. Yes. I'd *love* more help."

The command-center's rifts flashed like a slot machine before a single image filled every rift: the face of a middle-aged woman standing in a woodsy cabin wearing a Delaware Fightin' Blue Hens sweatshirt. Frith inhaled sharply.

"*You.*"

"That's right, little boys and girls! Someone told me y'all were having a hootenanny!" It was Claudia Castle. She pointed at someone in the room. "And I need to talk to that little lady in the back!"

Everyone looked around for a moment before they realized who she was talking about.

Nicky pointed at herself. "Me?"

"Damn tootin', cutie! You're our key into Asmo."

The Brimstone Express

EVERYONE PEERED AT THE PORTRAIT, which shimmered in one of Traxler's rifts.

"Wow, are you two related?" Frith asked Nicky.

"Separated at birth," Traxler said as he tapped a few keys to enhance the image.

Letta hooked a thumb at the portrait and addressed Richard: "So she kicked this off for you and Matthias back in the day?"

"Correct. The death of Alice Kyeteler decreased the number of Lord Morningstar's Menagerie below the fateful sum of six-hundred-sixty-six." He addressed the rift: "Lady Castle, you're certain this likeness is accurate?"

On-rift, Claudia Castle snatched away the portrait, her wrinkled face filling the view.

"Damn skippy, junior. She and I work together down here. I'm your sweet, silver-haired old fox on the inside."

Nicky, her face still streaked with tears, spoke in a hushed tone: "So … what do I need to do?"

Castle crossed her cabin, where a red-and-black checkered curtain blocked the window. She pulled it, revealing what at first glance resembled the inner digestive system of a supermassive interstellar beast. Ribbed, angry red flesh composed the walls, all of it interspersed with a striping of pus-yellow details. Splashes of pseudo-medieval stonework complemented the chamber in the form of archways, balconies, and buttressing. Other details were more advanced: stainless steel panels inlaid with blinking lights covered one far wall, the metal spreading to the floor, where a podium rose. Still another layer of detailing looked like milky marble, though upon closer examination, its surface quivered and effervesced, while its interior was filled with snaky red tendrils that formed into millions upon millions of letters from an endless array of unspeakable tongues. Hundreds of flickering torches dotted the walls and floor alongside an equal number of what appeared to be fluorescent lights, lamps, and lanterns. Spheres of otherworldly, bioluminescent flame floated all around the room. Behind the podium yawned a massive, throatlike orifice, about thirty feet in diameter, that led into darkness. A half-cylinder, similar to an aqueduct and hewn from that same milky marble material, slashed out and vanished through another, similar opening. Thousands of suffering souls packed the space.

Nicky leaned in and pointed at the edge of the display. "What are these guys wearing?"

What appeared to be guards hovered around the chamber's periphery, all of them wearing different kinds of respirating modules. One mongol hordian wore a simple gas mask, while another soul, this one a seemingly pleasant-looking fifties housewife (complete with gingham apron) had a module sprouting from her back like an oozing black growth.

Castle cackled. "They're like me. We were famous back home, so we get to do this. If you've *got* the juice, you *get* the juice." Into the rift's frame she produced what looked like a SCUBA-diving mask and rig, only instead of covering her nose and mouth, she draped it around her neck like a scarf and unhooked a pair of cordlike inputs that she fed into her ears. Made of the same milky, otherworldly marble as the aqueduct track, the device transformed her eyes into the same strange material. Her eyes, in turn, sprouted thousands of tendrils that coiled around her body. The end result was a mummified version of Claudia Castle whose chest pulsed with a queer orange light.

Frith's face dawned. "You're demons."

"Not exactly," Castle said. "Rumor has it we used to have 'em down here, but not for ages."

"You breathe the bewithered extract of the dying damned," Letta said.

"Righto. Though I wouldn't call it *breathing* so much as *metabolizing*."

Nicky nodded. "Just like Odysseus."

Letta threw up a hand. "*That's* who that was!"

"Lets, you need to crack a fuckin' book sometime," Frith said with a grin.

Removing the apparatus, Castle said, "Yeah, if ol' Ody was here, he'd be jabbing pitchforks with the rest of us—just like someone you'll recognize."

In the chamber, the podium stretched skyward, while on the ceiling, a new orifice slurped open and disgorged a familiar face: a red-haired woman who was a perfect double for Nicky in appearance, but whose animating energy was undistilled malice; her eyes glinted as she scanned the room, her smile a vulpine V. A variant of Castle's soul-respirator was mounted on her back, its inputs snaking directly into her vagina. She was naked but for a loincloth and wrap fashioned from various bits of viscera and bone. Twin hemispheres of a human heart clung to the sides of her neck and beat out a mad pulse. Her eyes glowed the same strange orange as the bewithered extract of the dying damned.

Castle jerked her chin. "That's Kyeteler. If we're gonna get on the skrimsli, you're gonna have to imitate her, little chickadee."

"If we're going to get on the what?" Traxler asked.

"Oh, ha ha. Tourists! The skrimsli, the *train* that runs from here to Asmo. Kyeteler's sky boss for Asmo this millennia. Chooses which unlucky fucks from Leviathan get shunted down there."

Nicky's eyes gogged. "Oh, okay. Um … am I gonna have to put one of those things up my cooch?"

Castle cackled again. "No, sweetie, but you're gonna have to make everyone *believe* you're her, at least as long as it takes for us to get our asses on that train. Then I can take over."

"You?" Letta asked.

"You betcha! Your friend Goldie filled me in. You need to breach the gates of Asmo, and the train's the only way. Problem is, without Kyeteler piloting the skrimsli, you won't even be able to get close." She paused for effect. "Unless …"

"Yes?" Letta snapped.

"Unless you happened to bring back the bow of Odysseus."

Nicky looked up. "Yeah, we brought it back."

"Outstanding!" Castle said. "Little Lew and I used to train on the Lagoon's range before those *dumb fucking filthy stupid cunt* kids let him drown. I thought *I* was Annie-Oakley-Robin-Hood, but he made me look like I couldn't hit the broad side of my own ass, hah! But if I've got the bow of Odysseus, we *juuust* might have a chance of pullin' this off."

Traxler tilted his head. "Why do you need the bow?"

Letta interrupted: "The railroad switch."

Castle pointed in affirmation: "There ya go. *Exactly.*"

Letta addressed the room: "When Nicky tested the keifering device on me, I … uh, well, I slammed into a railroad switch. Or the afterworld equivalent of one."

"That's right," Castle said. "It's some of the oldest magic in existence. Pre-dates our universe. So far as we know, the skrimsli's the only *living* thing to have evolved in the hellscape. It's literally fucking *from* the infinite void. The first architects trained it to carry souls from Leviathan to Asmo after the realm split in two."

Frith: "Why are there two ways into Asmo, and howcome Matthias was the only person who could open the other gate?"

Castle shrugged. "Beats the shit outta me! I think the Vatican dropped in that little detail to fuck with the next Successor when the Rite began again. Looks like it worked, hah!"

Goldberg tapped his microphone. "But there's something else you need to know: Heaven's on Martial Alert. Agent Hastings, you were right: he *did* pray, and now that the Heavenly Host knows we've breached Clement's Shield, they're gonna send everything they've got to stop us."

Frith scoffed. "Oh, it's 'us,' now? I thought we were just pawns in your little morality play?"

"As I've said before: I have a vested interest in the continuing existence of this realm."

Nicky looked around. "What does this all mean? Can we still do this?"

That was seconds before they found they had no choice but to move forward, because the Fortress of Maximum Suffering was about to be lost for all time.

A blinding blaze of crimson lightning thunderflashed across the sky and keyed off another volley of hot hail. A wave crashed into the Fortress and sent it listing. Everyone scrabbled for a handhold. The Apparatus groaned in protest of the change in altitude and tilt. Richard dispatched his dark host in an arachnid spread; dozens of pseudopods raced around the Fortress, buttressing it up, but it was too much for him. The stained glass finally shattered with a scream, admitting a torrent of rain so thick it may as well have been a column of solid water.

Richard beckoned to Letta and Traxler, calling: "I need help! We shall lose the fortress!"

They looked at each other in a panic. Traxler looked to Goldberg and called: "Got any ideas, man?!"

"It isn't Greenwich mean!" Goldberg said with a chuckle. The Fortress tilted another dozen perilous degrees. Everyone skidded across the floor. Nicky fell into Frith's arms. Soaking wet, everyone gaped at Goldberg. A levitating Traxler had taken hold of the hat-box.

"Tell us, Goldberg! When is the deadline?!"

The atrium's first three levels had flooded. A churning floor of water inexorably rose a dozen feet at a time. A load-bearing member splintered in two with a shriek, bringing half the roof down in an avalanche of plaster, brick, and stone. Goldberg's face filled the rifts.

"Leviathan has grown beyond your control, Richard! There's no stopping it. You have less than ten hours hour before it consumes Asmo and dooms us all! You must get back to Stercorebubulus and establish a new command center at the gates of Phaegor. Don't forget the keifering device! I'll be in touch!"

Goldberg vanished, leaving Claudia Castle's astonished face.

"Well, that sounded like some butt-fuckingly bad news! Okay, kiddos—there's a gateway from Balaam into Leviathan. Head straight for the uvula, ya can't miss it! Y'all better get your hustle on if you wanna make this hootenanny! Time to awake your faith, motherfuckers!"

Everyone grabbed their equipment and dove through the passageway to Stercorebubulus. The Fortress of Maximum Suffering collapsed into the whirlpool below.

Avoiding the Heavenly host in Stercorebubulus proved to be surprisingly easy.

Richard had explained that the circles of hell had been changing over the ages, and now they were changing again—thanks to the hell heist. The instant they entered Stercorebubulus, a black curtain enshrouded them. Everyone protested, but a chorus of minor-key laughter interrupted them. Whispering, childlike voices calmed them.

"He's gone, he's gone!"

"Look! They bear the Extinguisher's sword!"

Richard and Traxler muttered enchantments that generated twin spheres of flickering light. Millions upon millions of faces surrounded them, all of them bubbling from the black sheet. They were the damned souls of Bullshit, and they were *growing*. During their last visit, most of the faces they saw were barely the size of a pencil eraser; these were larger, almost human-sized. Steam rose from the sheet and choked the space. Letta and Nicky both coughed, but Richard, Traxler, and Frith didn't.

"It's the stench," Richard said.

"Yeah," Traxler said. "I can … I dunno, *sense* it, but it's not hitting me as bad."

Nicky's eyes got big. She touched Frith. "How about you, Winnie?"

Frith shook her head. "Same with me. It's there, the smell, but it's not … I'm changing."

The faces danced around the oily sheet in interweaving spirals.

"She belongs to Lord Morningstar's stable now." More laughter.

"Stable?" Frith said.

Richard nodded. "The Menagerie. You and Master Traxler are part of the unholy number now."

Frith's expression faltered. Traxler was about to speak when an ear-shattering voice bellowed from above: "WE SEEK A GROUP OF FUGITIVES FROM DIVINE JUSTICE. KNOW THEM BY THESE VISAGES AND BY THE DEMONIC COMPANY THEY KEEP! AIDING AND ABETTING THESE FUGITIVES WILL RESULT IN BANISHMENT TO LOWER, MORE DREADFUL DOWNFALLS."

A slit unseamed in the sheet and parted slightly to give them a view of a pair of titans. Marching through the space around Stercorebubulus were a pair of gleaming, heavenly centurions, both of them clad in the same otherworldly armor as Goodmind. Their helmets were of a different make than Goodmind's; a feather cascaded from one centurion's helmet, sparkling and gleaming in the ambient haze, while the other had a Terra Cotta make and profile, with layers of shielding that hung to his shoulders.

In response to the angels's warnings, the damned giggled. *"We're already in hell. They think threatening us with another hell will scare us."* They sealed the sheet once more.

Richard nodded. "We thank you, O thrice-accursed souls, and we request your aid. Our needs are dual: We need to reach the gateway to Phaegor—the home of Odysseus—and once established there, we will decamp for the Temple of Dissemble, where we will complete the Arch of Scourgian Mists."

"Impossible. The agents of Heaven sealed away the keystone."

Richard nodded to Frith, who unstrapped the hat-box and opened it.

"Look familiar?" she asked.

The voices of Stercorebubulus cooed. *"We will take you where you need."*

While the souls of Stercorebubulus erected a protective barrier around Izzy's house, the team re-established their command center. Nicky fretted over how she's lost her slide projector, but Letta assured her they wouldn't need it. Traxler pulled up a small desk and chair and set up his command center next to the fireplace/gate to Phaegor and re-opened the matrix of rifts. Goldberg reappeared in the upper-left, while Claudia Castle filled the rest.

"Ya made it!" she laughed. "Nice work. I figured you were goners."

Letta leaned over the desk. "So how do we sneak onto that train, Castle?"

"Goldie and I worked it all out." On cue, Goldberg tapped out a few keys and brought of a schematic of the five major infernal downfalls. The display zoomed in on Leviathan. Its interior architecture looked like someone had built a massive rectangular solid inside an ellipsoid.

Castle continued: "First, get your buns down here to Leviathan. Then, your Master of Dreams will use me as a beacon to broadcast the phony train station to Kyeteler."

The display zoomed in on the very lower corner of the rectangular structure. A digital readout marked it as THE SKRIMSLI (TRAIN) STATION. The aqueduct track cut through it, on its way down to Asmo.

"Kyeteler's quarters are across from mine," Castle said, pulling open her curtain again to give view across the chamber, where a medieval holdfast, about a twenty-five yards square, spattered in blood and latticed with gore, floated about a "mile" from the train station.

Nicky: "Why do you two have your own homes? Aren't you in hell?"

Castle said, "Haw! The stronger the soul's *infamy* back earthside, the more perks you get down here. But back to the plan—"

"Wait," Letta broke in. "What do you mean by *infamy* on earth?"

"The bigger the fanclub on earth, the more power we get here. No fuckin' idea why it happens, but it's our caste system. Happens in every hell, but Leviathan's the home base for it all. Folks who wind up here aren't just the angriest—they left the biggest blast radius back home. And it's not just famous people. An abusive father? Haw! They leave behind trauma and damage, and every time one of their victims has a nightmare about them, or hears the front door open and thinks they're back from the dead, they get more juice down here."

"That's what Izzy was talking about," Letta muttered to herself. "All that crap about people singing songs about him." She wheeled on Richard, said: "Did you know about this?"

"I did," he said.

"You know my mother's still a fucking celebrity on earth, right?"

Richard nodded.

"So does that mean she's got power here?" No answer. Letta's tone hardened. "What's waiting for us down in Asmo, Richard? I don't want to hijack this train right into a fucking trap."

"We haven't the time to discuss it now."

Letta fell silent, her eyes shifting in density around her thoughts. Facing the command center, she asked: "What happens after we knock out this Kyeteler person?"

Castle: "You sure you got all your ducks in order?"

Letta whispered: "Shut … the *fuck* up … and keep running through the plan."

Castle shrugged. "Okay! While she's out of commission, your little chickadee'll come in, take her place at the podium, and direct the rest of y'all onto the train in place of some other souls." Her eyes narrowed. "This is where it gets tricky."

Frith scoffed. "Oh, because up till now, it's been completely *non*-tricky."

Castle: "Quite right, big lady. Unless you plan on leaving the little lady behind, she's gonna have to find a way onto the train before it takes off, and as soon as she leaves that podium, all fucking hell's gonna break loose, pun *very* much intended, haw!"

Goldberg, silent for several minutes, finally spoke: "And that's the funny part. She won't be able to get inside the train. She'll have to be on *top* of it when it pulls out."

Nicky seemed to wilt, all the air seeping out of her. Letta and Frith shared a look. The latter was about to speak when the smaller woman spoke:

"Abort mission. This hell heist is over."

Nicky looked up with gleaming eyes. "What?"

Letta crossed her arms, shaking her head. "You've been jumped by a Dream Master, tricked into thinking you killed your own sister, attacked by *fucking Odysseus himself,* killed the fucker, and now I'm supposed to ask you to impersonate one of the worst killers of all time, *literally in literal hell,* and then somehow jump onto the roof of a speeding, Ghibli-esque caterpillar, all so we can go down to the deepest circle of hell and find out my crazy fucking mom runs the place?" Letta closed her eyes. "Forget it. It's too much. I'm asking too much."

Traxler put an arm around his wife, who said: "Does this mean what I think it means?"

Letta swallowed a sob. "I … I don't know. I can't ask that of you, either."

The voice was unmistakable: *"Tsk-tsk."* On-rift, Goldberg had removed his mask to reveal a patch of flesh that wasn't any living tone but as gray as sunfaded pavement. He produced a washcloth and cleaned away the rest of his makeup. He looked less human and more like a living statue carved from weathered, crumbling stone. Cracks and crevices lined his face, which bore a dusting of white hair. He removed his fascinator-hat and set it on his desk. His clown suit came off next. Underneath was a leather jerkin and pantaloons from some unknown era. Despite his bloodshot eyes, his expression was one of compassion. He mumbled, "That's no longer an option."

Letta lowered her head and rubbed her brow. "Of *course* it isn't. Let me guess: Because Frith's already died?"

Goldberg nodded. "I'm sorry. There's only one way out of this, and it's on that train."

Letta sat down, her gaze growing distant. Richard hovered over and placed a hand on her shoulder. Traxler and Frith came closer, too, and kneeled before her.

"Maybe we can find another way."

Letta shook her head. "I can't ask this of you." She mouthed, *Of Nicky.*

"Isn't anyone going to ask me what *I* want to do?"

Nicky had spoken. She crossed the room and set a hand on Frith's shoulder, her eyes brimming with tears. "Listen, I'm not Miss Super-Expert On Hell Heists or anything, but so far, we've managed to break into the Vatican, punch an angel, and kill Odysseus, right?" Richard took her hand, sending a thrill through her. Her smile grew. "When y'all came to get me, I told you I was in. And I'm in. *In-in.* To the very end, hell or high water, come on tits."

Letta stood and blinked owlishly. *"Whhhat?"*

Nicky shrugged. "That line from *Moulin Rouge?* Come on tits?"

"Come what *may?"*

"Nah, that's from part two."

"Got it. So you're up for this?"

Nicky nodded. Letta squeezed her hand and turned back to the command center. "Okay, mission officially un-aborted. Now tell us why she has to be on top of the train?"

As Goldberg explained, the schematic updated its view: "Miss Nicodemus will have to order the train to leave from the podium. The doors seal shut. You'll all have to be inside, but—"

Castle interjected: *"But* there's another important wrinkle in this nutsack. We'll need someone on top of the train to open this hatch to let us out."

The schematic zoomed in on the train's top, about midway down its length, where a marsupial-like pouch rose from the skrimsli's flesh.

Letta frowned. "Why do we need to get out?"

"Two reasons," Castle said. "One, you'll need me on top to hit those switches. Two, once we get to Asmo, we don't wanna be inside that train unless we're planning on staying, haw! The skrimsli—the train—digests all the passengers and shits them into Asmo, where they get shunted to their respective eternity of suffering and existential torment."

Goldberg rested his face in his hand. "It's such a beautiful system. I wish I had come up with it."

"Haw!" Castle laughed. "They should've done a better job of training the skrimsli! They've only had six hundred fucking years."

Nicky: "What do you mean by that?"

Castle addressed Goldberg: "Hey buddy! You wanna zoom in on the skrimsli's ass for me?" The image zoomed in on the creature's rear, which curled up like a scorpion's and terminated in a puckering orifice.

She continued: "This is the crux of the whole thing, this creature's asshole. Once it leaves the station, it ignites." The orifice suddenly spewed a white-bright flame. "You'll have to get us out of the train, escort *my* fat ass back to the *skrimsli's* ass, where I can light the first of two arrows."

The display widened to show all of Leviathan. The train cut across its far side, headed for a tunnel out into the nethervoid.

Castle: "There are *two* railroad switches. The first is *inside* Leviathan. If I *miss* that switch, the skrimsli—the train—won't be able to make escape velocity out of Leviathan and we'll have to take another turn around the joint."

The display pivoted over top of Leviathan to show the oval track, which encircled the realm.

Castle: "Trust me when I tell ya we wanna amscray the fuck outta here ay-sap. But assuming I hit the first switch, we'll shoot out along the Styx down to Asmo."

"The Styx?" Frith asked. "You mean the *River* Styx?"

"You wanna field big Janie Mansfield's question, Mister Cartographer?"

Richard had fallen strangely silent. He looked up. "I beg your pardon?"

Nicky squeezed his hand. "She's asking you about the train tracks."

"Forgive me," he said. "My mind has been elsewhere."

"I get it," Nicky said. "If I'd lost my best friend and my home all in one day, I'd be curled up in a ball on the floor."

Richard smiled. "I have enough spirit left to complete this mission, my lady."

Nicky sighed so nakedly and joyfully that Letta felt suddenly sure they'd pull this off.

"Thanks, Richard," Letta said.

He nodded. "But to answer the Lady Frith's question: yes, once upon a time, the skrimsli and its warren ran all around and through the Infernal Downfalls, sometimes even unmooring one from another, and for many ages, it served as the boundary between the living and dying realms, at least for the damned."

Goldberg gave a small salute. "I couldn't have explained it better myself. Miss Castle, would you care to explain the second switch?"

"You bet," she said. "The second switch is the real bitch of the bunch. Every time the skrimsli makes a trip to Asmo, the second switch moves around the nethervoid. It's the moving target to end all moving targets. If I miss *that* shot, then …"

"Then *what?*" Letta said.

"Then the skrimsli escapes into the nothingness and cuts us off from Asmo forever."

"Or at least until existence comes to an end," Goldberg said. "Master Cartographer, would you care to explain what happens when you reach the gates of Asmo?"

"We shall walk right in. The gates stand open to all who wish to enter."

Letta rolled her eyes. "Well, at least *that* part'll be easy. How will we find my mom once we get in there?"

Silence for a moment until Goldberg spoke.

"You will know the way. I did."

Letta stepped forward. "Who are you?"

He fell silent, his eyes widening as something illuminated his displays.

"Goldberg?" Nicky asked. "What's wrong?"

"They found me. My god, they *found*—"

White light flashed across his rift before it faded to darkness.

Nicky screamed: *"Goldberg!"* When there was no answer, she spun toward the others: "What happened, what happened?!"

"The Prelate Centurions," Richard said. "They must have detected him somehow."

Frith touched her forehead. "Fuck. He was useful, but we gotta keep moving."

"Agreed. Traxler, what's the clock?"

"According to Goldberg's assessment of Leviathan's growth, we've got only hours. Richard, does that … well, *feel* right to you?"

"That assessment is accurate. And to that end, I've made an addition to our ripcords."

Everyone checked their emerald bracelets to find they'd been outfitted with analog clocks that showed their remaining times.

Nicky smiled. "Richard, these are great. And they're already synchronized." Without thinking about it, she stood on her tip-toes and gave him a peck on the cheek. "And I thought you said you couldn't conjure stuff!"

He touched his cheek, his mouth falling open. "Thank you." He was barely audible. "And my lady, I believe you have some of my dark host on your … beauteous lips."

"Huh?" She touched her lips and found her fingers swarming with insectoids. She jumped slightly in response before looking at Richard with a lambent face. "They're kinda cute. Did you say I had a 'beauteous' something?" She dropped into a whisper: "Were you talking about my buns?"

Letta started to speak, to interrupt the moment, but didn't.

Richard floated closer to Nicky, said: "I spoke of your lips, but you're far more than any of my trifling, tongue-tied compliments. You're a sonnet of bravery."

She rushed into his arms. They held each other, kissing, until Castle's cackle broke the spell. "Well, if this isn't the weirdest fuckin' match I've ever seen! If we get outta this, I'm officiating the wedding!"

Frith smiled. "Nah, I've got dibs on that, but—Nicky? Your skin."

The insectoids, about a half dozen, had burrowed into her flesh ·equidistant around her neck. She hissed in momentary pain but relaxed. "Oh! Richard, is this okay? It feels … kinda cool?"

Letta clapped. "And they *look* even cooler. But it's time to go. Nicky, you need to hook me, Frith, and yourself up to the keifering device."

She did.

The three women, bound by destiny, stood and beheld each other in awe.

"It doesn't *feel* weird to be a ghost," Frith said. "I still feel pretty much like myself."

"Me too," Nicky said, immediately running back into Richard's arms. They kissed. Frith, Traxler, and Letta all shared looks. Frith started to speak, but this time, *Letta* stopped *her* with a gentle hand. She crossed to the two lovebirds.

"You'll have plenty of time for that once this is over," she lied.

Nicky nodded. "Okay, chief. Where we off to first?"

"First, we have to complete the arch and get into Balaam."

Richard, still holding Nicky, held up a hand. "There is the matter of your souls. If we are to brave the perils of Leviathan, two of you will need protection."

"Only two?" Letta asked.

"Lady Frith, as a member of the Menagerie, is already protected."

"Got it. So … do me and Nicky need to—"

"Nicky and I," Traxler said.

Letta rolled her eyes. "Do *Nicky and I* need to get chopped in half by an angel, too?"

"No, but as of now, only *I* can provide the armor you'll need. Two of you are already wearing a small fraction of … well, of me." He indicated Frith's and Nicky's insectoid neckwear.

Nicky touched hers and vamped like a fashion model. "Oh, this old thing?"

"Indeed, my lady, but I'm afraid that won't be enough. I will need to sacrifice some third or half of my being to the cause in order to protect you and the Successor."

Nicky's voice jumped an octave: "What? What do you mean 'sacrifice'?"

"You shall see. Time is fleeting, my lady."

Frith held up a hand. "Wait. Do you need this back?" She indicated her choker.

"No," he said with a smile. "It suits you. Prepare yourselves. Once I share my dark host, you will each feel approximately one minuscule fraction of the glorious torment I feel every moment of every day. Are you ready?"

"No, I am not," Letta said. "But do it."

Richard kneeled and muttered an incantation similar to his *Maladenudation* ritual. Nicky kneeled with him, their fingers intertwined. A moment passed. Nothing happened. Nicky prodded him.

"Did you say it right?"

He wailed. Nicky flinched back but kept hold of his hand. His dark host spewed from his mouth in a mad rush, flowing and flashing around the room at Nicky and Letta, showering and peppering every inch of their bodies. They both fell to the floor, their mouths stretched in silent screams, all while Richard diminished slightly, his body once again growing more transparent and gray as he emptied out. When the ritual was complete, Letta and Nicky both struggled to their feet on shaking legs, their appearances changed as follows:

Nicky's six-insectoid neckpiece had sprouted millions of tendrils that braided themselves through her red hair, transforming each strand into steely filaments that lanced and laced through her flesh, outfitting her in a demented evening gown, with bustle, all of it composed of black insectoids and her shimmering emerald hair. She looked like a leatherbound Queen Elizabeth, with a cleavage window that gave view to her heart and lungs, and a daring slash up the front of her dress that showed off her muscular legs, both of which were aswarm with a pantyhoselike layer of insectoids. Her hamstring tendons snaked from her flesh to act as makeshift garters.

Letta's dark ensemble, although comparably racy, was more utilitarian. The dark host formed a layer of form-fitting armor that hugged her curves and carved up her flesh. She bared her teeth as hundreds of black plates sliced away the flesh from her skull, forming a protective barrier that her likeness rested upon. A mandarin collar rose around her neck, while gauntlets clanked together on her hands. Wedge heels gave her a few extra inches. She looked ready to carry out a black-ops mission in a BDSM club.

Before anyone could speak, Nicky spread her hands. "Wait, wait, *just hold up and whoa.* So ... we're supposed to feel, like, one percent of the pain you feel, Richard?"

"That is a rough estimate, but yes."

"Really," Letta asked. "Funny, I don't feel a thing."

"Yeah," Nicky said. "I don't feel—*OH MY HOLY FUCKING SHIIIIIIIIT!*"

"AAAAARRRRR RGGGGHHHHH FUCK SHITFUCK SHIT AAAAA!"

Frith jolted in surprise of the outburst, but Richard simply crossed his arms as Letta and Nicky dropped to their knees, holding their heads and clawing at their flesh, screaming at the tops of their lungs.

Letta: *"OH GOD OH GOD OH GOD I FEEL LIKE I JUMPED ON A BICYCLE WITH THE SEAT MISSING!"*

Nicky: *"I JUST JUMPED IN A WOODCHIPPER HEAD FIRST! NO, FEET FIRST! NO, NO I'M DEFINITELY GETTING CHOPPED UP FEET FIRST AND HEAD FIRST AT THE SAME TIME!"*

"Okay, okay … getting my second wind," Letta said, taking Richard's hand. He hefted her to her feet and crossed to kneel before Nicky. He took her face in his hands. Her eyes gleamed.

"You go through this every day?" she whispered through tears.

"Every moment's breath."

She caressed his face. "You're so brave."

He helped her up, shaking his head. "In this company, that title falls to you."

"I couldn't agree more," Letta said, sounding winded. Through a wince, she turned to Frith, said: "Strap on the keystone, we're going to Balaam."

The damned equivalent of a ticker-tape parade awaited them upon completing the Arch of Scourgian Mists—or at least a very surreptitious version of one.

The Temple of Dissemble floated beyond the outermost bolgia, adrift in a sea of boiling souls, millions of who contributed their bodies to the temple itself. Hundreds of billions of arms, legs, torsos, and plaintively wailing faces composed the temple, from its foundation to its soaring ramparts. A cathedral of suffering it was, hovering near the Downfall's outer membrane and silhouetted in a halo of ghostly light cast by its neighboring hells.

Richard carried them there while Traxler maintained comms back at the command center. He'd insisted on coming—"I can't imagine my lady love doing this without me"—but Frith had overruled his objections.

The Temple's bolgia, like some others, was composed entirely of souls. When they arrived, they stepped onto a soft island of seething faces, but instead of stymieing them, they carried them to the Arch on an undulating wave, all while the colossal figures of the Heavenly guard marched in the distance, their eyes casting slashing spotlights across the Downfall.

"There it is," Letta said.

The Arch was the one structure on the bolgia not made of souls. Millions of Stercorebublus's denizens buttressed it up against the backdrop of the Temple's gothic facade. Two sets of crumbling stones rose, arcing toward each other, wreathed in floating bits and chunks of stone. The top-middle segment was indeed missing. Letta nodded to Frith, who opened the hat-box. The instant she did, the stone ignited from within. Orange light blazed from its center, and it shot skyward, spinning faster and faster as the orange light shattered it, scattering its pieces across the arch, which blazed with that same bright orange until the whole thing caught fire, only it wasn't fire but *plasma*. The Arch transformed from stone to sunfire, a solar prominence burning before them.

They all checked over their shoulders.

"They're gonna see this," Frith said, indicating the patrolling Prelate Centurions.

A new voice cried: "Letta? *Letta Starchild?!*"

They turned to find the Arch had opened the gateway to Balaam, where bedlam awaited.

The united forces of both Stercorebubulus and Balaam shielded the team's movements from the Prelate Centurions. The souls of Bullshit rose up, their bodies becoming whole again with the influx of power from the completed Arch. Corporeal forms struggled out of the muck in a million different configurations: some looked like they'd died that century, wearing more recent attire from around the world—button-downs and slacks and dresses and wraps and turbans and headdresses and headwear—while others hailed from ages past and wore armor, kirtles, jerkins, kimonos. Some were clad only in rags, while others were naked but for a coating of oilslick. Steam rose off everyone, their skin bright red and bubbling.

But they were whole again.

The metamorphosis halted at the edge of the Temple's floating island. As the damned changed from sludge to human, they revealed a stone bedrock upon which the Temple rested. Even more souls boiled away from the Temple itself, which teetered and shook as its load-bearing members changed back to human bodies and scurried toward the hell heist team.

Back to Balaam: the flaming archway shone blinding white for an instant before fading to unveil a realm that, like Stercorebubulus, resembled a city, but in contrast, it was built almost entirely from a strange organic architecture, all of it a glistening, slippery red. Thousands of gog-eyed acolytes streamed from the gateway and surrounded the team.

"Letta? *Letta Starchild?!*"

"It's her! It's her!"

"You changed my life, Letta, and for the better, too!"

Stark naked and covered in blood and gore, the damned of Balaam all surrounded them, wincing as they inhaled the realm's stench and hissing as their non-corporeal flesh sizzled with each step farther into an Internal Downfall where they didn't belong. Suffering and mania attended their every move. One Balaamite, who had carved thousands of instances of the LodEx logo into his flesh, rushed over to Letta, hugged her, then pulled back and gestured at the gate.

"Quickly, quickly! Before they see! *Before they see!*"

The Prelates's searchlights swung their way—but were blocked by a sudden wave of oilslick bodies. A few hundred Stercorebubulusians transformed back to sludge and hurled themselves skyward as a makeshift shield, all while thousands of Letta's blithering acolytes escorted the team into Balaam.

Letta said: "We headed for the gateway to Leviathan! Can you get us there?!"

"In *style!*"

Balaam reminded Letta of an old joke she'd heard about summer weather in Florida: "It feels like being inside someone's mouth." The analogy held because Balaam had literally been constructed inside the mouth of a massive titan of old. "Miles" overhead soared the roof of the creature's mouth, a double-vaulted gothic arch the same deep, apple-red of a palate. The gateway from Stercorebubulus let them out on the far side of Balaam, directly onto one of the titan's molars. A cavity burrowed into it like a coral reef infesting a yellowing marble floor. The titan, whatever it was, still respirated, bathing the realm in a steady weather pattern of humid gusts. Balaam's denizens all walked with the same curious, listing gait, as they'd grown so used to these breaths pushing and pulling them back and forth. After enduring the stench of Stercorebubulus, the air of Balaam was relatively sweet, though it reminded Letta of her grandfather.

Thousands of buildings, hovels, shacks, shanties, and lean-tos clung to every exposed surface like barnacles. Some structures dangled from the walls on hooks that dug deep into the titan's flesh, the entry wounds encrusted with black-red scabs. Others made use of imperfections: an ingrown wisdom tooth provided the foundation for a cock-eyed, tilting skyscraper hewn from enamel and scavenged wood. Their guides were a stampede of naked, bloody bodies who rushed them off the molar and toward the back of the titan's mouth—toward its throat.

As they ran, one naked man sprinted up beside her with bulging-insane eyes. He'd carved the LodEx logo into his chest. "I've fantasized about this moment for years, ever since my suicide!"

"Your *what?!*"

"Hold!" the man yelled, raising his hand. Everyone stopped, chests heaving. Letta's unease grew as she saw what she had made of the hell of avarice. LodEx wasn't the only logo on display, but in this corner of Balaam, it dominated. Thousands upon thousands of *LodExes* blared from every exposed surface, some in neon, some in blinking lightbulbs, some carved into wood or chipped from stone. An array of writhing bodies had been nailed to one wall in the shape of her logo, while another several hundred groups danced in the LodEx logo in a gyrating churn.

Their guide crept back toward Balaam's front, alternating between leaning back and tilting forward as he rode the old titan's breaths. A yawning chasm, thousands of miles in diameter, gave view to the hellscape. Steamy winds burst out with each of the titan's exhalations. The whole crowd of naked Balaamites fells suddenly and eerily silent as they peered ahead and out of the titan's mouth.

Letta crept up beside their presumed leader and whispered: "Did you say you killed yourself?"

He shushed her and added, "Yes. For you."

"For me? Why?"

"I ran out of money. I donated my life insurance to you."

Letta's stomach dropped, and she shivered, like an arctic front had just blown in. She thought back to the keifering test. She had *almost* gone to hell, only for Nicky to revive her instants before she did. Now she knew which one had been calling her to condemnation.

The lead Balaamite grabbed her wrist and pointed: "Look."

Twin searchlights pierced the endless darkness outside, slanting at first from the lower left to the upper right. Like a moonrise, a gleaming centurion's helmet crested into view, followed by the dual sunblasts that were its eyes. The lead Balaamite turned to run just as Richard grabbed Letta, pulling her along.

"That is one of the Highguard!" he cried.

"A what?!"

"An Archangel! *Run!*"

They did, but as they rushed toward the titan's throat, Letta stopped cold. Frith was hunched over a pile of junk; a heaping mass of steel boxes, wooden chests, keys, and chains, all of it glittering gold. Her face was a desolate clench, a drawn browline of seeping, bone-deep grief. Something in that pile of junk had drawn her attention, and Letta wasn't sure if she was strong enough to pull her away from it— so she called on reinforcements.

"Traxler? You need to kick your wife in the ass."

After a terrifying, distending moment, Frith jolted upright and followed along.

They pelted toward the titan's massive throat, each step a squishy, slurpy bounce. Nicky tripped on a taste bud, but a helpful Balaamite caught her and hurried her along. The Archangel's eyes turned the realm to black-and-white: their silhouettes danced like a line of pistons across the back of the titan's throat, where a massive bulb of tissue hung.

Head straight for the uvula.

They reached the back of the tongue, which curled into darkness below like a massive waterslide crafted from flesh. That "grandfather" smell increased to a nearly Stercorebublusian intensity. Letta, Frith, and Nicky held their breath as Richard drew up alongside. Letta tapped her earbud.

"Trax! You still getting a signal in here?"

"Copy that, Letta."

"Castle said to come this way, but is there a staircase or something?"

Claudia Castle's voice broke in: "You gotta jump it!"

"Are you fucking kidding me?!"

Richard pointed: *"Look!"*

As the archangel's giant hand reached into the titan's mouth, Letta, Frith, Nicky, and Richard all hurled themselves down its great gullet.

Birdsong and bacon awoke them.

Something sizzled in the next room. Richard Pudlicotte hadn't smelled anything so heavenly in ages. He found himself lying on a bed—an actual bed—when he hadn't slept since becoming Infernal Cartographer. He rose. A room they'd seen before surrounded them— Castle's cabin—but when he pulled the curtain, a small lake glittered outside surrounded by more cabins and rolling forest hills, not the terrors of Leviathan.

He had awoken in a shared bedroom; three other bunks lined the walls, each holding the other hell heisters. Shadows moved in a doorway. Richard followed them to a kitchen, where Castle, clad in her full bewithered extract breathing suit, stood over an oven range, frying bacon in a cast-iron skillet. Noticing him, she pulled the apparatus's mask down and grinned with crazyglazed eyes.

"Wakey, wakey, eggs and let's get the fuck down to the train station! *Ladies! Up and at 'em!*"

Bedsprings squeaked. Richard pulled another curtain only to find the same idyllic woodsy view. It could've been the wilds of Scotland. Letta and Frith filed in with Nicky, who was rubbing her eyes.

"How long were we asleep?"

"Fuck if I know," Castle said. "No real concept of time here."

They checked their emerald timepieces. Letta cried out in frustration.

"We were out for *hours!* We've only got two hours left! Fuck!"

Castle pulled on a comically oversized potholder and presented the bacon, which wasn't bacon but strips of glimmering orange bewithered extract.

"Then eat up, ladies, because you'll need the protection. Kyeteler's about to report for duty, so we better broadcast that signal prontissimo." They all took strips and chewed.

"Hm," Nicky said. "Kinda tastes like orange Fruit Roll-Up. No, tangerine! No, definitely orange. Hmmm, maybe both? With a hint of …" (she lowered her voice) "… *butt?*"

Castle cackled. "All of the above, little girl." She extended her arm, pinched the air, and unzipped a rift that revealed Traxler back at the command center. Frith's face lit up.

"Baby, it's you. Hi!"

"Hey you," he said, exhaling a pent-up breath. "You made it. I lost your signal for a few hours and figured it was all over. Are you ready? Castle shared the train station's schematics with me. All she has to do is fall asleep, and we can get this going."

As the others ate, Castle stretched out on her kitchen floor. Nicky hooked her thumb at the bedroom.

"Don't you wanna be more comfortable?"

"Haw! I always sleep on the hardwood floor. I call 'em 'Samurai naps!' Helps keep me frosty in case any of those sorry fucks out there try and break in." She addressed Traxler: "Okay, Mister Tall Dark 'n' Handsome. Get ready. It doesn't take me long to—"

She was out.

Castle's snores were surprisingly musical: *hum-HUMMM-hum-HUMMM*. On-rift, Traxler tapped some keys and split the display. In another chamber, this one a medieval dungeon, Alice Kyeteler lay on a wooden cot. In the cabin, Castle's eyelids rippled. On-rift, Traxler's eyes rolled to whites.

"It's time," he said, adding a third segment to the display labeled:

KYETELER, ALICE | INTERNAL NARRATIVE

The display mirrored her dungeon chamber but diverged when she awoke. In her "real" display, Kyeteler remained asleep, but inside of Castle's dream, she stood and pulled on her bewithered apparatus.

Traxler smiled. "Castle and Goldberg delivered. We've got a clean signal."

Kyeteler continued her routine, opening a door onto utter, mind-bending chaos. A red storm like the eye of Jupiter raged overhead, showering a blasted desert landscape with bolt after bolt of red and yellow lightning. Black mesas and mountains and arches of stone carved up the horizon as millions of thunderous flashes marked the arrival of Leviathan's newest souls. They each blazed to the earth, an endless meteor shower of comets that struck the earth and disintegrated. Most exploded in orange splats—a color the hell heisters recognized all too well—but many others found their footing and sought out passage on one of the millions of bizarre vehicles that raged across the land.

All of this happened in Kyeteler's dream, but in her "reality," she was still sleeping in her quarters.

Letta prodded Nicky, indicating the far wall. A duplicate of Kyeteler's bewithered apparatus hung on a hook.

"Nicky. Curtain."

Frith squeezed her arm, said: "Break a leg."

Richard kissed her and held her face gently: "You're redoubtable."

Traxler, his eyes still rolled to whites, whispered: "Do you remember when we met?"

"In the schoolhouse at the Ranch?" she laughed. "Yeah. The sixth maxim didn't mess with *those* memories."

"You were on top of Letta, protecting her. Do you remember doing that?"

"Yeah."

"It was the first thing I noticed." He chuckled and added: "And the way you spoke to me—" (his tone shifted from otherworldly to earthly) "—the way you *mouthed off* at me? I remember thinking, 'I'd want this girl on my team any day of the week and twice on Sundays.'"

Nicky swallowed a happy lump in her throat and pulled on the bewithered gear. She crossed to the front door, and stopped, looking down at herself.

Frith: "You all right, girl?"

Nicky shrugged. "I'm just like, so embarrassed. I mean *gawd*, what if Ashley saw me doing this? I bet she totally went to Heaven."

Instead of heat, a blast of freezing air greeted Nicky when she left Castle's cabin. The view was pure mayhem; the world's largest demolition derby being held on the interior of an erupting volcano. A thousand-foot-high brickwork tower scurried along on steam-powered spider legs. A school bus packed with hundreds of white-eyed, zombified children zoomed past, its side splattered with strange glyphs. A motorcycle gang roared past, and Nicky was sure she recognized Charlie Manson. A regiment of Nazi panzers rumbled her way, their tops dotted with leering soldiers in full SS regalia. Dark figures bled over a distant sand dune as the Mongol Horde crested it and ran pell-mell toward the Nazis in a battle of world's biggest fucking assholes.

The damned souls of Leviathan parted like the sea before her, moaning the name of their tormentor:

"Alice Kyeteler. It's her!"

"It is she!"

"Alice, Alice, Alice."

They all existed in various states of dismemberment, disintegration, or deresolution, each one a a roughly humanoid shape always trapped mid-destruction. They burned, dissolved, exploded, and liquefied in a constant churn all around her, their bodily systems flashing in and out of view as quickly as the soul reconstituted itself. The train station rose ahead, about a hundred yards distant, like a giant scab. Nicky marched ahead, avoiding eye contact with everyone.

Traxler's voice rumbled warmly in her ear:

"Castle briefed me. It's easier to fly here, so you should give that a shot. Plus, they'll be expecting her to."

"How do I do *that?*"

A pause, then: "You might have to consume one of the damned."

Nicky stopped, surrounded by millions of moaning keening souls, all of them caught between liquefication and completion, their bodies surrounded by an everpresent haze of gore, blood, viscera, and fire.

"I have to eat one of them?

Hot hands braced her shoulders. A face bubbling with boils and barbed wire filled her line of sight, the poor creature's teeth sliding into view as its face melted away. Its remaining skin was a patchwork of fleshtones—had it stolen some from others?—while its heart and lungs had merged into one distended mass that throbbed in its chest.

"Take … me," it hissed.

But she didn't, instead lingering in a moment's hesitation until Letta spoke:

"Nicky, this guy was probably a fucking school shooter."

She looked into its gogging eyes, which burst and spewed retinal fluid across her face. Still, she hesitated.

Letta whispered in her ear: "You can't murder a guilty person, right?"

The act was instinctual. Nicky's maw yawned forth, and

accompanied by the wild cheers of all the damned, she ingested the soul and soared into the air.

From the command center, Traxler brought up a schematic of the train station rendered in vector graphics that would've been at home in an eighties arcade game. His face appeared on one of the rifts.

"Here's where the timing gets hinky," he said. "We're going to need Castle on board to shoot the railroad switches, but as soon as she wakes up, Kyeteler will too, so you'll only have as much time as it takes for a hate-filled rage-demon to realize she's been duped and to travel from her quarters down to the station."

Frith: "Can you show us where her quarters are again? I want to get a sense of the distance."

Traxler nodded. "She lives up here."

The schematic panned out to reveal Kyeteler's quarters, the stone holdfast.

"Castle says she moves really fucking fast, but she'll be waking up. We'll have maybe a few minutes after Castle wakes up before Kyeteler gets to the station and blows our cover."

"You mean *my* cover."

Nicky had spoken. All heads swiveled to her rift, where she floated in the air over the teeming masses of Leviathan. A strange control panel slid into view. Its interface looked like Aleister Crowley had designed the new iMac: the monitor was a pentagonal sheet of blood mist. Offset were a pair of smoldering black jewels—extra-terrestrial eyes, perhaps?—that projected data and telemetry into the mist. Dozens of other buttons surrounded the monitor. Most were various gemstones or organ meat from an array of unidentifiable creatures and species, although in the corner sat an IBM numeric keypad circa 1982, its numbers long since worn away and replaced with what appeared to be Sharpie.

"I'm in position," Nicky said just as indecipherable glyphs started to roll across the bloodmist monitor. She grimaced. "I wish we still had Goldberg."

Richard leaned in: "Nicodemus, if my studies of the *Third Chronicle of LeviathAsmodantenora* are correct, you should be able to read those letters, but you'll have to … well, *ask* the letters to behave themselves."

"*Ask* them? I don't speak 'ancient arcane letter-ese.'"

"That is what the *Third Chronicle* sa—"

"I got it!" she whispered, while below, millions of souls flowed in and out of the chamber—most of them heading *out*. Nicky scanned the readout and reported: "It says, 'Monarch Lynchpin Outstanding.'" She stammered on the next word: "'Uh-Ah-asmoSkrimsli Payload Under Weight. Danger of Derailing.'"

Traxler: "Matthias explained that. Lucifer's abdicated his throne, so Hell has no monarch. Without Lucifer to back them up, Leviathan's demonguard has a harder time corraling souls into the train station, which works to our advantage."

"How?" Frith asked.

"We need to sneak onto that train in place of other souls. Without the demonguard forcing souls onto the train, that'll be a lot easier."

Letta: "Wait, what do you mean *forcing*? Don't people *want* to get out of here?"

Richard shook his head. "Asmo is Hell's deepest circle and most feared domain. No one would volunteer to pass through its gates."

"Got it," Letta said. "But what about that warning? 'Danger of derailing'? That doesn't sound good."

Frith raised a hand: "Should we take over as demonguard? Force more souls onto the train so it won't fly off the track and into … y'know, the eternal void?"

Traxler touched his ear. "I think this is academic, y'all. The train's pulling into the station in about three minutes. You better wake up Castle and get moving. And—Letta?"

"Yes?"

"All my hopes."

Their eagerness caught everyone's attention.

At the gates of the train station, the skies of Leviathan churned like a whirlpool of blood intershot with orange lightning. It cast the realm in a perpetual magic hour that might've been pretty had it not been for the hundreds of thousands of writhing anatomical diagrams that wailed from every direction, every surface.

Frith and Richard cleared a path—Frith with her Faraday-enhanced fists, Richard with his dark host. Flashes of purple-orange accompanied Frith's blows, while Richard's entire form splattered across the blasted plains between Castle's cabin—which sat on an oasis of grass and evergreens—and the station. Letta scampered along in her body armor, her breath misting, while a bleary-eyed Castle brought up the rear, the Bow of Odysseus strapped to her back.

"Keep a move on, little girl," she whispered. "We don't have much time before the Supreme Cunt wakes up." She brandished the bow at the fleeing souls, saying: *"Oh, no ya don't! Turn the fuck back around and get into that station!"* Her voice thundered like she was shouting into a three-story bank of stadium speakers. A few thousand souls turned tail and rushed back through the station's gates, a hundred-foot archway composed of the same preternaturally pearly-white material they'd seen before. The team rushed into the chamber, which spanned about three hundred yards. Frith jerked her chin at the ceiling.

"There she is."

Nicky floated before the control panel. When she saw the team, she burst into a smile and waved like a kid at Disneyland. Letta slapped a hand to her earbud.

"Nicky! Be cool!"

Nicky covered her mouth and nodded, her voice echoing in everyone's ears: "What do I do now?"

Castle clotheslined a few dozen souls back into the train station and answered, "We put people on the train, but only if they're destined for the deepest circle. Nicky, that buncha gizmos and thingamajigs in front of you will tell ya who's supposed to go! Start filing souls onto that damn train so it doesn't derail!"

Nicky froze up.

The control panel's bizarre technology bubbled under her fingertips like a tableful of organ meat shocked back to life. Onyx gemstones bulged and viscera seethed in tune with an invisible heartbeat, all while gemstones smoldered with an oracular, dark light. Data spilled across her bloodmist monitor as the hell heist team pushed more souls into a holding area near the train tracks: thousands of silhouettes rose in relief from the mist, each of them accompanied by a dossier-like readout written in that same strange tongue that only she could read.

It was too much information—until Castle gave her an assist.

"Look for the icon, sweetie, the icon!"

"What icon?! What's it look like?"

"A head eating a body. Should be obvious."

Sure enough, some of the souls were marked with a sleek, modernized icon straight from a Renaissance painting: a horned head swallowing a human headfirst. Nicky tapped those silhouettes, which in turn activated an array of tartarean machinery across the station floor: blistery, chapped mouths yawned wide to take hold of souls with thousands of jagged fangs; sections of floor detached and rose under other souls; arms capped with hawklike talons extended from nowhere to take hold of others. Still others found themselves trapped in extradimensional snares—millions of tesseracts appeared in a blinding froth around a group of souls and pulled them apart like three-dimensional shadows. All of these devices had one purpose: to load the train.

Which just so happened to arrive in the station at the exact same time as someone else.

But first, the train. Letta sensed it before anyone else: "Do you feel that? It's coming!"

If was as if they were metal, and a massive electromagnet had just been activated outside, pulling their very essences toward the entry tunnel. Everyone's faces and flesh stretched toward the approaching vehicle, which blasted into the station shrouded in a fog that smelled of cremains. At a glance, the skrimsli looked like a cylinder cast in cement, but further examination revealed that its surface danced with millions of interlocking panels in all manner of shapes; some were familiar, like hexagons and octagons, but others defied description— non-Euclidean supershapes and polygons with *omega* number of sides. Hulking rivets and bolts held it all together, but *those* were fucking weird, too; their surfaces shivered and shimmered like the three-dimensional shadows of four-dimensional shapes. (Which is what they probably were.) The skrimsli looked less like cement and more like an ultra-exotic, extra-dimensional lifeform—a python-caterpillar—whose flesh fizzed and effervesced.

The doomed souls of Leviathan cried out at its arrival, scrambling away from it in every direction and along every surface. Castle led the effort to keep them in the chamber, coaching the others.

"Grab 'em by the jibblies!" she screamed.

Above, Nicky categorized the souls, in turn activating more

infernal machinery that deposited them howling into the train. Her bloodmist monitor displayed a progress bar that slowly filled as more souls landed in the train. A line blinked at the seventy-five percent mark, labeled *Minimum payload.* She shouted out its percentage to the others:

"Forty-five percent, fifty percent!"

But below, tens of thousands of souls slipped past the team's defenses. Castle, clad in her blood-spattered sweatshirt and jeans, slammed the bow into the ground in frustration.

"We're losing 'em!"

Nicky: "We're not even *close* to capacity, guys! We're barely at fifty—"

There were millions of them.

Millions. Millions upon millions of disintegrating souls exploded back into the station in a gushy gout of gore. It was like a dam the height of the sun had given way, releasing the pressure of a century's flooding all at once. The damned swallowed up the hell heisters, causing Nicky a moment's panic before Richard lifted everyone above the fray on several obsidian insectoid platforms.

Nicky exhaled in relief. "Guys! Guys! *There* you are!"

Richard's dark host dissipated and deposited the team beside the train and right into a jumping havoc-swarm of furious souls. Frith shoulder-checked a pair of souls so hard they flew apart in a blossom of limbs and gristle. Richard conducted his dark host into a pair of giant hands pressed palm-to-palm; the hands slid into the mass of souls that packed the train and spread them apart—Moses parting the Damned Sea. The team, now soaked in gore and viscera, hustled onboard, jostling against the other denizens of Leviathan.

Letta touched her earbud. "Okay, we're on!"

Castle screamed: "Keep filling the train, little girl!"

"I am, I am!" Nicky said, her fingers a blur across the control panel. The progress bar filled to sixty percent, sixty five, sixty-six. "Why did they all start coming back in?"

Her wail shook the firmament. The skies of Leviathan flickered at her call, so terrible was its likeness to that of dark immortal goddesses. Everyone turned, and floating over the gateway boiled a red pool, as if they were looking down into a cauldron of blood and gore. She emerged from it, her eyes starkwhite, her teeth gnashing, her red hair billowing majestically around her surcote-clad form.

Castle bared her teeth. "Fuck! It's Kyeteler! We need to get on that train!"

Letta touched her earbud: "Nicky, start the train and get down here!"

Above, Nicky pressed a few buttons, and in response, an array of cattleprod-like spikes emerged from the tracks and lanced into the skrimsli's flank. The creature squealed. Nicky hurled herself down toward the train just as Kyeteler blasted across the room on a column of flaming blood. Letta and the rest rushed onboard the train, dodging around the infernal loading devices, all of which tried to block their path. The skrimsli lurched forward, its gravitational field tugging on everyone's innards. Nicky had already reached the train when two things happened at once:

Kyeteler slammed into her.

And the rest of the damned realized they'd been duped.

"That isn't her!"

"She isn't she!"

"She merely PLAYED the witch!"

"GET HER!"

The Leviathan train station always looked like a riot, but now its mayhem trebled. Rage swept the room. Ancient powers had enacted and erected the arcane machinery to load the train, and for untold millennia that system had held, even during the previous Rites of Succession, but on the day Letta Starchild and her retinue hijacked the skrimsli, that system broke down.

As the train pulled out, Kyeteler drove Nicky into the side of the train in a splash of blood that spattered everyone inside. Letta, Richard, and Frith all moved to help, but a glaring mob of the damned blocked their way. They screamed.

"Nicky, no!"

"Take my hand, take it, take it!"

"Nicodemus!"

But the crowd outside had already swallowed her up. Kyeteler's hands—claws, really—swiped over the top of the mass of bodies, her every slash drawing Nicky's blood. The skrimsli picked up speed, knocking everyone backward, spurring Richard to action.

He pointed to Letta, said: "Stay on the mission! I'm going back for her!"

Letta elbowed a soul in the neck, shouted: "Richard, no—*don't!*"

The infernal cartographer transformed into a chattering black ribbon and coiled out the skrimsli's door instants before it sealed shut, leaving Letta, Frith, and Castle trapped on the train.

Letta shrieked. She said no words but only wailed in frustration. Frith took her in arm and nearly squeezed the life out of her, all while Castle looked on with a dark brow.

"We're gonna get shit straight into Asmo. I've been building up juice here for *years,* just to blow it all for you libertine fuckin' whores!"

"That's *enough,* Castle!" Frith yelled as a familiar voice crackled in her ear:

"Team, team! Come in, come in!"

Frith touched her ear. "Trax! Baby, you're there?"

Letta found an open space and slid to the ground, tears streaming down her cheeks. Frith crossed to her and kneeled.

Traxler continued: "I'm here! I saw what happened."

"What happened to Nicky and Richard?"

"The signal's spotty, but he's still there. I can see his, uh, his tentacles, but …" He trailed off.

Frith shoved away a dissolving soul. "But *what*?"

"I can't see Nicky."

"Fuck!" She looked to Letta, said: "We're circling back around."

Letta kept crying, but Castle responded by shoving the bow's sharp end under Frith's jaw. The Scourge of Camp Crimson Lagoon metamorphosized, her eyes narrowing to slits, her teeth sharpening into fangs, her flesh shrink-wrapping around her skull. The end result was a glaring harpy who hissed with brimstone breath:

"Like. Fucking. Hell. You. Are."

"Get out of my face, Castle, or I'll tear your soul right out of you."

Her voice was steely: "Shut up."

Letta had risen, seeming to grow a couple inches. Orange lightning flashed off the black mirrors that composed her body armor. The skrimsli bellowed as it upshifted to a new realm of speed. Their traincar's passengers, realizing they were outmatched, had retreated to the rear, where they huddled in a tableau out of a lost William Blake: gleaming, sweaty faces gaped with white-wide eyes shot with spaghetti-squiggles of blood, all of them clutching each other, their bodies a shimmering equalizer dancing in tune to their torment, each soul's bodily systems surging in and out of existence as unseen hands clawed away their skin, muscle, gristle, and bones, only for everything to reappear and restart the cycle.

Castle backed away, her appearance returning to normal. "We're not going back around."

"No, we're not," Letta said.

Frith turned. "If Nicky dies here, she's stuck here."

"This is bigger than any one of us. Look." She indicated her emerald timepiece, which read *1:37:00:23*. "We've got barely more than an hour and a half until it's all over. We don't have the fucking *time* to circle back around. We need to get on the roof. *Now get moving!*"

Frith glared for a full five seconds before turning to lead the way.

"It's one more car—uh, well, it's one more *segment* back."

Traxler guided them back through the train. Shivering, bubbling walls separated each segment, forcing Frith to punch her way through, each blow accompanied by a shining shockwave of purple and orange. They made their way through a car packed with grinning grotesques—dark wraiths that clung to every surface—and stopped under what looked like a seam in the skrimsli's flesh.

"Trax?" Frith said, touching her ear. "We're here."

"Go straight up," he said. "You've only got a couple of minutes before the first switch comes in range."

Frith pounded once, twice, thrice before the seam splayed open and sucked everyone toward the opening, which in turn flooded the car with ice-cold air. The other damned souls clung to the walls while Frith hefted Letta and Castle onto the roof, following close behind to find both women laying flat, stomachs pressed to the roof, holding on with white-knuckle grips. Frith dropped to a knee and grabbed a handful of flesh that squished and oozed through her fingers like redhot melting putty.

Fire. Lightning. Sorrow. Suffering.

Those were the sights of Leviathan, as if an endless succession of volcanoes had burst across the arid plains of Mars, with the maelstrom of Jupiter's Great Red Eye churning overhead and Tommy-gunning the land with blinding-fiery slashbolts that heaved great chunks of earth skyward. Skittering legions of madcap vehicle-buildings blackened the land in bleeding eddies. Arachnid contraptions, flame-spewing jalopies, towering holdfasts dotted with torches all roared across the landscape on tank-treads, wheels, jets, and mechanized limbs hewn from bone and gristle. The sight carried Frith back to that fateful night in 1993 when, standing in the Ranch schoolhouse, Athena described this very realm to poor, doomed Tyler.

"Just like she did for all of us."

"*What?!*" Letta yelled, pushing herself to a knee and squinting into the freezing onrush.

"She knew!" Frith said. "She fucking *knew* the whole time!"

"Who did? Knew what?!"

"Athena! She knew everything. She had *seen* everything. All the infernal downfalls. She'd seen it all."

Castle struggled to her feet and helped Letta up. They found their footing as the train hurtled and bounced along at incredible speeds, the landscape a smear of shivering catastrophe. The old woman jerked her chin toward the rear.

"C'mon, ya fuckin' sluts! We gotta get a move on!"

They ran toward the train's rear, hunched over and falling forward with every other step. Howlstorms of backrushing wind shoved them forward again and again. Letta shielded her eyes with a forearm as she interrogated Frith:

"She told us a bunch of stupid fairy-tales! She could've read 'em in Dante or just made them up!"

"I saw my father in Balaam."

Letta's face fell into a new configuration of empathy—open and childlike.

"Your father?" she said as a flaming, airborne contraption barreled past overhead, its engine belching and howling. They leaped over a gap in the skrimsli's segments, its rear only a scant several yards away.

"Yeah," Frith said. "And it was just like Athena said. The stupid fuck was buried in his greed and gold and chests and wealth. His flesh was soaked through, soggy and falling off his skull, which was overflowing with maggots and black fungus."

The skrimsli's rear coiled up before them like a gigantic scorpion shrimp, its anal rictus spitting flame. They all stopped, heaving chestsful of steam.

Letta nodded to Castle, said, "Light 'em up."

Castle nocked an arrow and lit its end with whitehot flame.

Letta touched Frith's forearm, said, "That's why you froze up back in Balaam. You were looking at him. At your father."

Frith nodded.

"I called Traxler to snap you out of it. What'd he say to you?"

On cue, Traxler's deep voice rumbled forth: "She can tell you later. Get ready. You're gonna go through some sharp curves, and then the first switch will come into view."

Back at Izzy's home in Stercorebubulus, Traxler called on old stores of willpower to keep his calm. He still didn't fully understand the magicks he was channeling to power his command center, only that they *worked*. Francois must have seeded every Infernal Downfall with his beacons, all of who broadcast an intermittent signal that varied in quality about as much as dreams did—sometimes the image was blurry, other times crisp, still other times it would shift into absurdity and display the equivalent scene in claymation or Legos. Traxler maintained his focus and parsed it all.

But when Frith saw her father, his focus faltered.

He recognized the son of a bitch instantly, having met him once. Even buried under his wealth, Jacob Marley-style, he still sneered at his daughter.

"Are you still married to that?" he asked, spitting out gold coins every other word, his skull as yellowing and infected as an ingrown toenail.

Frith ignored the question. "Dad, do you know where you are?"

"It's over soon," he said with a cough. "Good behavior, stay of execution. All a big mistake, they told me. I've served more than enough. Job'll be waiting for me. How long have I been here? A century? Ten centuries?"

Letta's plea came over the commlink: "Traxler? You need to kick your wife in the ass."

Traxler silenced everyone's earbuds but his and Frith's, said, "I think you know what to tell him."

Frith's voice dropped to a whisper: "You just got here."

As her father wailed in anguish, Traxler enjoyed a chuckle. Frith, roused to action once more, took off running.

Later, a surprising voice interrupted Traxler's concentration:

"—*only her*—" (crackling static) "—*fail otherwise*—" (crackling static) "—*incoming, incoming*—"

A cold wave washed across Traxler's mind. With the tap of a few keys, he brought up a feed that, although it had been dead for hours, was now broadcasting again. Nondescript city streets and alleyways bounced, the image overrun with snowfalls of static and cascading arcane characters and glyphs. Heavy breathing underscored the feed, which fell still, showing a brick wall strewn with graffiti. The camera flipped and revealed a familiar face.

Goldberg's.

"You're alive," Traxler said.

"For the moment, and I have a vital message for the Successor—for Letta. It has to do with the Bow of Odysseus. It won't work. Listen closely and relay this message to her …"

The skrimsli sine-wove its way through canyons of hundred-foot stalagmites, a steady peppering of lightning accompanying every twist and turn. Castle assumed a wide stance, her knees slightly bent, and readied herself. Frith stood close by, ready to steady her. Letta was waiting a few feet farther back, waiting for the switch to appear, when Traxler spoke:

"Letta, it's Traxler. Don't react. I've got a message from Goldberg."

"*Gol*—" Letta hissed before stopping herself and whispering: "He's still alive?"

"Yeah, and he has a message for you. It's a prayer."

"A prayer?"

"A prayer … from Jonathan James Bradley, and if you don't answer it, we're fucked."

Letta recognized the railroad switch immediately.

Hours earlier, when Nicky had tested the keifering device on her, she'd found herself plummeting toward the infernal downfalls, the view like a satellite's plunging toward Jupiter. She'd somehow slammed into one of the switches and nearly been spiritually incinerated by the passing skrimsli's fireball.

Now as they rounded a corner, the *other* switch—the one they had to hit in order to avoid doing another lap around Leviathan— emerged from behind a mountain hewn from a million faces that spat fire with each moan. The switch looked like someone had sculpted a silverfish bug to look like a crossbuck. Millions of wriggling jet-black insectoids composed a black post that was capped with a figure-eight. The 8's top opening was empty—a simple hoop—while its bottom was filled with some kind of preternatural orange fluid that bubbled and churned. Castle stood directly before her, bow at the ready, while Frith stood to their right.

Letta spoke in an eerily calm tone, given the circumstances.

"I'm sorry I called you a bully."

They passed a wooden water tower whose reservoir overbubbled with flaming feces. Bony arms stretched from the filth and clutched at the sky.

Frith looked over. "What?"

"You're not a bully. You're the bravest person I've ever known. I've always trusted you, even when I was a kid. And I need you to trust me now."

Castle shot Letta an annoyed glance. "This ain't the time for a heart-to-heart, ladies! It's a bulls-eye, or we do this whole thing again!"

Frith ignored her and addressed Letta: "What's happening, big girl?"

"Be ready to catch the bow."

If Castle heard them, she didn't react, so focused was she on her target. Letta drew the Izzy's soul-killing blade and ran forward, plunging it through the old woman's heart. Castle's hands fell limp, letting fly the arrow, which soared over the switch. They barreled past it seconds later. Frith caught the bow in mid-air. Letta retracted the sword and stepped around to bear witness to Claudia Castle's final death. The old woman fell to her knees, gritting her teeth as her temples tinted a dark gray and caved inward like a sand castle at high tide. Her eyes dissolved next, leaving only the slashing sneer of her mouth.

"Whyyy?" she wheezed, crows-feet flaring around her lips. "I *helped* you."

"There's no punishment harsh enough, no circle deep enough for what you did. But Jonathan James Bradley prayed that you'd be erased from existence, so that maybe the souls of all the children you stole might finally find peace."

Castle's cremains scattered to the blazing horizon.

Frith, feeling deja vu, touched Letta's shoulder and said: "I assume there was a good reason for that? We missed the first switch."

"Bixby got a message out before he … left," Letta said, her hair kicking in the wind. "Goldberg picked it up and got word to Traxler."

"Goldberg's still alive?"

Traxler answered: "He's on the run, but he got through to me."

Frith nodded, touching her ear. "Wow. Okay. But why did we kill Castle?"

Traxler: "Goldberg told us to. I don't know how he knows, but there's a new wrinkle to the Rite of Succession. Only Letta can fire the Bow of Odysseus. If Castle had hit that switch, it would've all been over."

The skrimsli sped away from the mountain range and dropped down a twenty-degree descent toward a pitchdark valley that howled with a million-billion keening cries.

Traxler's voice crackled: "Ladies, you're about to go into a dark territory. We'll be out of contact for about ten minutes."

"Got it," Frith said. "How long until we circle back around to the switch?"

Traxler mumbled to himself, calculating. "Ten minutes."

"And how long is the trip from here to Asmo?"

"Hard to say. Maybe another half hour."

Letta and Frith checked their chronometers. Letta winced. "That leaves us less than an hour once we reach Asmo to find my mother and break her out."

"Letta … *how* do we break her out?"

"I hadn't thought that far ahead."

Frith nodded and turned to squint into the wind. Fire arced up from the horizon and slammed down into a basic where a rotund, three-headed beast was shoving souls down its gullet. Frith looked back. "Let's hunker down if we're gonna ride this thing out—" Her focus shifted to a spot in the deep distance. "What the hell's that?"

A meteorite was burning up in the atmosphere, but no—not a meteorite. It was a *comet,* large as a planetoid and bright enough to turn the perpetual night of Leviathan into day. Its heat boiled away the bloodred cloud cover to reveal what appeared to be a glass dome, and Frith had the sudden, insane sense that they were trapped in a snowglobe. The comet struck a towering shantytown—a clumsy-crafted jumble of shacks, Victorian manors, parapets, and ramparts that teetered in the middle of a crimson-smoldering steppe—and smashed it to charred, flaming bits that scattered across a thousand square miles.

But the comet's impact did more than that.

She was gone before Letta could even look back.

A shriek stabbed her eardrum, *Frith's* shriek as she pitched off the train. Letta lunged across the train, landing on her stomach, half her body dangling off the side, screaming, *"Frith!"* Her old friend fell into a mile-wide mouth with fingers for teeth that cackled trackside and swallowed her whole.

"What happened?!"

The train was moments away from entering dark territory. Letta wept.

"She's gone."

"She's—*what?* Letta, what happened?"

"She fell, Bowden. I'm so sorry."

No answer came, only a quick flare of speaker feedback. Then silence.

Letta crawled to the center of the roof and pulled her knees underneath her. The skrimsli sped toward dark territory, while on the far side of Leviathan, the cloud cover was bubbling back into place over the crater that marked the remains of the shantytown. Rising from this crater was a silhouette—a gargantuan one. Steam wafted around the figure, which rose from a knee and stretched to a full thousand-foot height. A centurion's helmet gleamed in the crepuscular light. Although Letta had yet to lay eyes on him, she knew his name immediately.

"Hasdiel Goodmind." When she spoke, she hoped in her deepest heart that someone might answer, but none came. Still she ventured a whisper: "Is anyone there? Frith? Nicky? Richard? Traxler?"

Silence attended her descent into the deepest valley of Leviathan.

She was alone.

Part Eight
1993: The Trap

S HE SAT BEFORE HER FORMER mentor and matriarch, shivering with terror and rage—but more of the former, now that she'd become a protestant.

"Good evening, Nicodemus." Athena sat, wrists manacled, palms flat on the table. "Please, have a seat."

"What am I doing here?"

"You're here so that I may invoke the sixth maxim with you. This is at the behest of the liar Agent Hastings, who burrowed into our ranks as Winifrith."

Nicky's hands shook so bad her elbows ached. But she set her teeth and her courage to say, "You can't invoke the sixth maxim on me, not anymore. I'm no longer a believer."

"Aren't you?" Athena said, and for the first time since they'd met by the Starchild Ranch sign, Nicky saw fear glint darkly in her former master's eyes. "But wouldn't you rather forget tonight ever happened? Forget the role you had in it?"

Nicky had, up to that moment, compartmentalized what she'd done. When she thought about it, truly thought about it, horror gripped her insides. She nodded. "Founda—" she stopped herself and corrected: "Athena. As the sole adherent of the Starchild-Nicodemus Fellowship, I hereby elect to undergo the sixth maxim. To erase tonight's memories."

Athena cocked her head, smiling. "The *Starchild-Nicodemus Fellowship?*"

Nicky whispered: "I just made it up."

"It's charming, my dear. My first splinter sect. I feel like a new mother."

"Let's get this over with."

"Very well, my dear. I hereby invoke the sixth maxim." Nicky's skin fell slack, her eyes rolling to whites. Athena continued, "You shall forget this night, sweet Nicodemus, and you shall not only forget your sister ... you shall forget you ever had a sister. Confusion shall surround her and vex any efforts you might make to uncover her identity. When you contemplate your time with this family, you shall feel a sense of peace." Her voice dropped to a whisper. "Oh, and one more thing. I am hereby adding my voice to the scripture of the Starchild-Nicodemus Fellowship. I suspect you shall adopt our Seven Maxims and possibly even add some of your own. But mine shall reside after and above all others. It shall be the Last Maxim, and its language is thus ..."

Thirty Years Later: The Second Lap

THE SKRIMSLI BULLETED ITS WAY out of the dark territory and began a madcap trip around Leviathan. Letta, clutching the Bow of Odysseus, hunched by the skrimsli's rear, readying herself to light another arrow. Her commlink was a stone in her ear, silent and dead. The wails of a trillion-trillion damned combined for a maddening buzz, like tinnitus broadcast over a loudspeaker. She rode over hills and rises, all while below, tens of thousands of vehicles and convey-ances of deranged make and model raged across the landscape. Millions of hapless souls plunged through the cloud-cover and fizzled to orange nothingness, while others took hold of a million-treaded tank and joined one of the realm's countless warring factions. Letta's focus softened to take it all in, revealing the ever-changing map of a wartorn land; boundaries wriggled and rewrote themselves in an endless dance.

But there was also the angel.

Goodmind moved slowly at this size, casting his gaze about the realm, the cauldrons of his eyes casting twin searchlights everywhere. The damned, insect-like, scattered from his gaze. Letta had no emotional or intellectual bandwith to even consider how she'd evade Goodmind when he found her. She simply practiced nocking an arrow, taking a couple practice shots at passing target with what precious ammunition she had. She had not even the remotest idea how she was going to find, much less *extract*, her mother from Asmo, but as she approached the train station, she set aside those thoughts and, although she wasn't religious, muttered a silent wish that she would escape Leviathan undetected. A tunnel enclosed the station, so she pressed herself to the train's roof and closed her eyes.

What if the train stops? What if Kyeteler's there? What if Goodmind finds me?

All those fears came to fruition as the skrimsli shot through the train station and bucked from a sudden impact that nearly threw Letta from the train. She slid toward the edge, scrabbling with the bow to find purchase only to pitch off the side—

—And float.

She didn't hit the ground. She didn't hit anything. She opened her eyes to a quartet of monstrously smiling faces.

Frith.

Nicky.

Richard.

And Traxler.

"You …" Letta stammered.

"We're here, big girl," Frith said, prodding Richard: "Bring her up."

"What is the *matter* with you all?!" Letta shouted as soon as her feet touched the roof. "I've *got* this!" She waved a finger in Richard's face. "You fucking *ditch* us to save Nicky?!" She wheeled on Traxler: "And *you!* Without you, we've got no comms! Are you telling me you left your station to come all the way down here and find her?!" She pointed at Frith.

Traxler, his eyes tinting black, nodded. "Yeah, I did."

"We are all *expendable! Every last fucking one of us is expendable to make sure this mission is—*" She stopped midsentence. Nicky's face had silenced her. Tears streamed down the cheeks of her old friend, who had grown eerily calm, given the otherworldly circumstances.

In the singsong cadence of a child, Nicky said, "Jesus, Letta. Haven't you ever been in love?" Letta had no response. They stood in silence for a moment, demented scenery barreling by—pus-seething parapets and ramparts bubbling with bloodshot eyeballs. Finally,

Nicky spoke again: "There's something else I need to say while I've still got the nerve. Richard, when you came to save me and we were jostling around with all those scary monster guys and barf skeletons, you kind of accidentally touched my boob, and I wanted you to know it's totally cool, I'm not mad, and it was actually pretty awesome."

Richard touched her shoulder and said, "My lady, I *know* it was awesome."

The skrimsli wove around a few corners. Richard leveled a finger at the horizon, where a colossus was rotating their way.

"We must prepare for battle. Goodmind has seen us."

"Have you ever shot a bow before?" Nicky asked, quickly shifting gears from fury to friendliness, despite Goodmind's approach.

"I took a few practice shots on my way around."

Traxler blanched. "You've never even *touched* a bow and arrow before?"

Letta bared her teeth and shook her head.

Frith shrugged. "Let's hope for beginner's luck, but in the meantime—what the fuck are we gonna do about *that?*"

She indicated the elephant in the room; the image was semi-comical—or comic-book-*like:* a Gojira-scale man clad in otherworldly preternatural armor, his face bracketed in a helmet, broadsword in hand, striding their way in seeming slow-motion, given his scale. The skrimsli sine-wove once more through the mountains. Goodmind's footfalls sent rumbling shockwaves their way.

Letta's brow furrowed. "Richard, can we make this thing go faster?"

The Infernal Cartographer nodded with a grim smile and dispatched his dark host in an arachnid flare around the skrimsli's sides, into which it stabbed, letting loose great gouts of the creature's black blood, all of which preceded an ear-splitting screech as the express train to hell trebled in speed. The team all jostled backward, finding their footing as they emerged from the mountains and brought the switch into view. Letta lit an arrow as Goodmind strode closer, his neutron-star blade exerting a pull on their insides. He had closed within a mile, his every footstep an earthcracking smash. Letta drew back the bow and fired just as an incredible sight blinded the realm:

Goodmind hurled his sword.

Until that moment, he'd moved in relative slow-motion, but his arm flashed in a blur across his form, the neutron sword sailing straight at the railroad switch. Frith covered her cheeks.

"Oh, my fucking god, *no.*"

Letta's shot appeared to be on target—maybe a little high—but without a target, it'd all be for naught. The four watched in tense silence as Goodmind's sword flew closer and closer ... only to sail over the arrow.

"He missed! *He missed! HE MISSED! He*—oh no, Letta, look!"

Hasdiel may have missed, but so had Letta.

Her arrow was flying on a trajectory directly over the railroad switch. Everyone watched in growing horror as it flew higher and higher ... but at the last moment, Goodmind's blade flew over the switch, and its gravitational power pulled it up a few feet.

And directly into the path of Letta's arrow.

Their cheers vanished into the multimegaton blast that emitted from the skrimsli's hindquarters and sent them sailing out of Leviathan toward Asmo.

Letta's second shot landed without incident and detached their segment from the rest of the train. A comforting silence attended their trip to Asmo. Damned souls sparkled across the void as they found their homes. They expected Goodmind to come smashing out of Leviathan in pursuit, but he made no appearance. In the dark distance, something sung a mournful dirge that grew louder as they approached Asmo.

From a distance, it resembled a planet-sized onyx gemstone, but as they grew closer, it seemed to *lose* dimension. It could've been a giant construction-paper cutout laid flat against the walls of reality, so black and impenetrable was it. The main segments of skrimsli rammed into its side, vanishing in a cinematic wipe. Their segment circled around Asmo until it arrived at an archway of blackness that was somehow even more black than what surrounded it. Stonework hewn from pure nightmatter embossed and emblazoned the archway, carved into unknowable shapes from beyond time and space.

They jumped off the skrimsli and looked down the barrel of a tunnel that only led one way.

"To Asmo," Letta said, pointing.

00:14:57

They had less than fifteen minutes to save existence, and fortunately, the fates provided them with guidance. The tunnel led them through several shimmering rings of ice that bubbled with moaning faces. The tunnel opened onto a pathway onto which grass melted into existence. They began a slow but steady ascent into hills that became more and more familiar to everyone but Richard.

"Where is this?"

"Home," Nicky whispered as the sign came into view from behind a bank of evergreens.

You are entering Starchild Ranch. Welcome.
Forever while you're here, you must honor the Seven Maxims of
Starchild Ranch:

They all stopped, Letta coming to the fore and giving her head a soft shake.

"Of course," she said, turning to the others. "C'mon, let's head up—"

The yelp ended in a squeak. Their heads swiveled toward the sound, which came from the left. Nicky had already taken off running.

"Wait!" Frith yelled to no avail, setting off with the rest at a full sprint, Richard hovering in the rear. They followed Nicky to a wooden shack about ten feet high, which the Starchildren recognized as the old coal shaft. Nicky stood nearby, shouting into the hills:

"Marjorie? Marge! Girl are you there?!"

Letta approached. "She's not here, Nicky."

Something yelped again, only this time the sound was much closer—and attended by an echo. With a *whoosh*, the shack's double doors swung wide, but instead of a bottomless pit, it opened onto the interior of the old schoolhouse.

Where Athena sat.

Marjorie struggled in her lap, the woman's hand clenched around the dog's neck. The four entered the schoolhouse, which it turned out, had no roof and opened up onto a night sky speckled with deadly still stars. Letta crossed her arms.

"Hi, mom. Put her down and get up. You're coming with us."

Athena ignored her and scratched the dog's head. "What's your favorite Beatles song, little Marjorie?"

Nicky glared. "That isn't Marjorie. She went over that stupid bridge. Rainbow. She's in dog heaven, not here."

Their Foundation's eyes were lamplights o'erglimmering with destard.

"What dog?"

Sure enough, Marjorie had vanished, only to be replaced by Franco, whose torso rose from the hardwood floor splattered with pitch and glittering with hoarfrost. His face stretched in agony. Frith cried out, Nicky yelled, the men covered their mouths, but Letta simply maintained eye contact with her mother.

"This isn't real." Her chronometer read *00:09:57.*

"How long until the final sunset?" Athena asked, her voice a reverberation of malice. "Five minutes? Ten? How will you extract me from this realm that I rule?" Off their horrified reactions, Athena rose and added, "Infamy keeps me alive, and my power has granted me access to other downfalls and even an occasional glimpse of heaven itself." She tried to caress Letta's cheek, but she flinched away. Athena smiled. "Your celebrity helped me break through, little Letta. Without your work on earth, I never would've been able to bring them all here, Franco, Bayard … and Marjorie."

"You're lying," Letta said.

"No. I extradited them to these shores, where they serve at my pleasure—and help me communicate."

"Communicate? Communicate with who?"

The world turned white and silent until Letta realized that something had struck the ground nearby.

Goodmind's sword.

The explosion laid flat Athena's illusory recreation of the Ranch. When the dust cleared, all that remained was a flat, white plane. Athena sat in the same chair, while the other four clambered to their feet, their necks craning upward at the sight of Hasdiel Goodmind, who shrank to roughly seven feet tall. He extracted his blade and sheathed it just as two more mammoth creatures descended from a portal of silver glass.

One the team recognized as the archangel that had nearly caught them in Balaam.

The other was clad in armor of a vaguely eastern cut, but they didn't recognize him.

"*Enough, brother,*" the first archangel said. "*It is time to bring this Rite to an end.*"

Goodmind raised his sword at them, and for a terrible-transcendent moment, Letta countenanced the end of all things and prepared herself to experience the majesty of its end as mindfully as possible.

A heavenly cry brought her back to reality.

The first archangel had fallen to a knee, clutching an arm that bled golden ichor. Goodmind stood in the finishing pose of his swordstrike, shoulders low and knees bent. A hysterical chuckle escaped Richard.

The first archangel spoke: "*YOU WOULD DRAW THE BLOOD OF A SIBLING CELESTIAL?*"

Goodmind stood. "*YOU WOULD DRAW THE BLOOD OF A CUSTODIAN?*"

The word, though familiar, drew frowns from everyone else—except Richard.

"Custodian?" he asked. "There hasn't been a custodian in this universe for ages. Who?"

Athena sat motionless, a curious smile on her face.

The second archangel sneered. "*YOU LIE, GOODMIND.*"

Goodmind faced the team … and kneeled, placing his sword on the ground before him.

"*Infernal Cartographer,*" he said. "*FORGIVE ME, COUSIN. I DID NOT KNOW, BUT WHEN SHE LAID HANDS ON ME, I SUSPECTED THAT YOUR MISSION HAD ATTRACTED OLD FATHER'S ATTENTION.*"

Everyone looked to Frith, who backed away a few steps. "What are you saying? What's a 'custodian'?"

Athena stood. "A guardian angel."

"Guardian angel?" Frith said. "Me? What does that even mean? Letta, we need to get her out of here. *Now.*"

Struck with indecision, Letta was pre-empted by the first archangel, who rose, shook off his pain, and brought his blade swinging down on the team—only for it to stop in place, frozen by an unseen hand. Frith had fallen to her knees, arms crisscrossing over her face in defense. Everyone looked around in confusion before their eyes landed on the truth.

It was Nicky.

Her eyes had rolled to whites, all while she'd grown several inches. She held up a protective hand that stayed the archangel's sword—a sight that drove both archangels flat to the ground in supplication. Richard looked on in awe.

"In all the endless ages of time and across the panoply of existences, Old Father has deputized only a handful of custodians. Perhaps three or four. And in service of their charge, their power is second only to his own."

"Indeed," Athena said.

Letta smiled. "I guess this is academic then." She unhooked her emerald bracelet and approached her mother. "This is a ripcord, and we're going to use it to take us home and end this Rite."

Athena smirked. "I hereby invoke the Last Maxim."

Existence shook. From across all of everything screamed the protest of a dying plane. Nicky soared a hundred feet skyward, her eyes ablaze, her back sprouting wings of the same preternatural supermaterial as the archangel's armor. Athena turned to the archangels and motioned for them to stand.

"I shall take a place by your side, then? In exchange for this?"

Letta screamed, "What have you done?!"

Goodmind moved to strike, but Nicky froze him in place with a single wave. He struggled against her power, crying, "BROTHERS! YOU RISK THE DESTRUCTION OF HIS BEST AND FINAL DREAM!"

"OF COURSE WE DO," said the first archangel. "LIFE SEPARATED FROM HIM IS TORMENT. HIS DREAMS ARE THE BARRIER, THE SYMPTOM OF HIS FOLLY, AND WE ARE MOMENTS AWAY FROM BEING DONE WITH THEM AND REUNITED WITH HIM."

"NO!" Goodmind wailed. "WE AREN'T HIS FAVORITES. WE NEVER WERE."

Athena stood forth. "But with all of existence gone, you'll be the only ones left with him. Along with me."

"You cut a deal with the angels," Letta said, checking the time: *00:04:03.*

"I did."

"We bring you the guardian angel, you sabotage our heist at the last minute, and they get to be with God again."

"Along with me."

Letta nodded, hand on her hips. "But there's only one problem."

"Which is?"

"You're going to hell."

"I'm already *in* hell."

"Not this one. Didn't you just say you invoked the 'Last Maxim'? Athena's smile faltered.

Letta went for the kill: "The Starchild Fellowship only has seven maxims. If you believe there are more, then, as an acolyte of the Starchild-*Nicodemus Fellowship*, you are condemned to whatever hell that sect deems fit. *Richard!*"

He balled his fist. "Athena Starchild, I hereby consign you to an infernal vault."

Across their view bristled and burst the landscape of western New York as the hills and mountains surrounding the Starchild Ranch replaced the stark white nothingness of before. All three angels had vanished. From nothingness bubbled a pearly white preternatural sphere that enclosed Athena, who leapt at her daughter. Letta's last image of her mother was the trembling claw of her hand as she was sealed away. With Athena imprisoned, Nicky floated back to earth, free of her power. She rushed into Letta's arms and squeezed.

"That was fucking *badass*, Letta!"

Richard floated over. "Well done, Successor."

Frith simply smiled and hugged Traxler, who added: "We've got ninety seconds to get her out of here. What now?"

Letta unhooked her wristband—her ripcord—and fastened it

around Athena's wrist, but before she could activate it, Richard stayed her hand.

"That won't work. But I am the solution."

"What do you mean you're the solution?" Nicky said, barely audible.

Richard produced a piece of folded parchment and handed it over. She unfolded it to reveal a diagram of a section of staircase. The Infernal Cartographer took her hands and smiled into her eyes. "There is an old saying about *keys:* for any robbery, they are the problem and the solution. When Brother Matthias and I burgled the Crown Jewels all those years ago, we faced three problems: two keys, and an empty section of stairwell leading to the crypt. One key we sidestepped by cutting through a wall. The other key we purloined from a drunkard clerk."

Tears beaded in Nicky's eyes. "No. No. I don't want you to do this."

"But the stairs, my dearest Nicodemus, the *stairs* proved too much of a puzzle for us, so we were reduced to thievery, guile, and bribery to obtain this sketch. It's how King Edward Longshanks himself descended to the crypt, and we rebuilt it down to every nail, every hairsbreadth." He faced Letta, said, "And now we face the same challenge. We lie in the deepest circle of hell and have mere moments to ascend to earth."

Letta came closer. "Can you get us out?"

"I can. The power to do so is chronicled in a little known volume I won't trouble you with, but I can open a single passage to take all of you home.

"But not you," Letta said.

"Not I."

Nicky was sobbing. Letta checked her watch: *00:01:01.* "Nicky? It's time. But I won't ask him to do this if you don't want me to."

She grabbed Richard and kissed him deeply. "You are being so fucking romantic right now. *Do it.*"

The heavens opened to admit the passage of the master of anguish. As he cast forth his dark host for the last time, Richard remembered the day of his execution, when to his shock, Longshanks' guards led him down a torchlined hallway … and turned him loose. He tried to ask why but was met with a slammed door. He wandered the streets for hours until a commotion brought him to the center of town, where black-hooded executioners were gathering wood around a stake. A man's sobs drew his attention.

It was Matthias.

"Richard. Forgive me."

"Matt? What happened? Why did Drokensford let me go?"

"Please forgive me when I say … you are not my dearest and truest."

Richard made no response, but his head tilted upward as the answer hit him like a splash of cold, rancid wine. The executioners were leading someone up the stairs to the pyre.

Adam de Fentlok.

"Adam," Richard said. "No. No. Not him."

Her cackle was a cold-cracking screech from the upper ramparts of a nearby holdfast. Illyria, her blackhawk astride her shoulder, laughed down at him as poor, sweet Adam was put to the torch, his skin bubbling. All around Richard and Matthias, the crowd looked on in horror, grief … and anger. Adam had touched all of their lives, and as he burned to death, the city spoke in a single voice: *"No. No. No. Not him. Not this man."*

Richard joined their chorus, lending a prayer to the cries: *God in heaven, hear my plea. Edward Longshanks has condemned a righteous man to undue suffering, and I demand recompense.* All of London made similar prayers, and as Illyria laughed, Richard vanished.

At least it *looked* like he vanished.

The smallest unit of temporal measurement is the Planck time, but if you were to divide one Planck unit into a million-million parts, you wouldn't begin to approach the speed with which Old Father glanced our way. But in this vanishingly small moment, here's what happened:

Gold washed across the world as the universe's darkness lit in a blinding flash.

Pure preternatural energy blasted through Illyria and reduced her to molten stone.

This stone slammed into Richard and, having liquefied him, drove him into a nearby fence made from wrought-iron.

On the plains of York, Edward Longshanks dropped dead.

And back in London, Adam de Fentlok was spared a drawn-out death.

When he regained consciousness, Richard Pudlicotte had replaced Illyria as Infernal Cartographer and Master of Anguish.

The Rite of Succession was complete.

As his essence faded away, Richard thought of Matthias's final message:

I lied to Illyria.

His heart broke for Matthias. The fates had presented him with an impossible choice: betray either Richard or Adam to torture and death. Matthias had delivered up poor, kind Adam because he was the only other conspirator left alive … and yet, his choice had yielded an unexpected result: the combined prayers of London had attracted the attention of Old Father himself. With a fleeting glance, He had brought about Richard's death to ensure the Rite would be fulfilled.

As for Matthias: even though his choice had risked the dissolution of existence itself, he had been willing to perjure himself before the almighty, all in a vain attempt to save Richard's life.

You're goddamn right they were best friends.

Athena Starchild opened her eyes. She was in a conveyance of pure, gleaming white that was hurtling up and up—but somehow *not* up. She was traveling in a direction no compass could con. A circular window opened before her, similar to a porthole, and gave her view to it all. In a single moment, she saw every soul in every hell—saw their crimes, their hatreds, their grudges, their regrets. More important, her noncorporeal mind, briefly endowed with limitless storage capacity, committed to memory the fate of every living soul for the last several million-million years.

She saw this now. She saw this then.

Memories are curious cousins and strange bedfellows. We live our lives one moment at a time but remember them in totality. Sometimes, past and future can whisper to each other.

And whisper they did while Athena Starchild rose out of hell in an infernal vault and carried by the *sanctum corpus* of the Master of Anguish himself.

Final Part
1991: Building the Theater

SUMMERTIME SUN SETTLED OVER THE Starchildren. It was a dog days dusk in mid-August. Athena had ordered the entire Ranch to help with the construction of their new amphitheater. They'd been erecting bleachers all day, and their Foundation allowed them a break. Athena, wearing her usual uniform of sweatshirt and jeans, took a position at the basin's bottom-center, just in front of the house's front door. Golden light washed over the scene and sparked a sense of deep contentment among the Starchildren.

That's when Athena started to sing.

She let loose with an ear-splitting aria, prompting everyone to wince, grimace, or look away to conceal their amusement. Nicky, who had joined the Ranch a few months before, was recording her performance when an unfamiliar voice spoke.

"Should someone tell her she sounds like speaker feedback?"

Nicky covered her mouth and looked over. Kneeling next to her was a heartthrob. Salt and pepper stubble lined his jaw. His profile was dashing perfection, his smile easy and relaxed, his face effortlessly kind. He wore a backpack.

She leaned over. "Hi, I'm Nicky. Are you new?"

"Yeah, hi," he said, offering her a handshake that felt like a friendly vise. "Franco."

Athena finished her performance. Dutiful applause followed. She jogged up the hill and noticed the new arrival.

"I have a million questions for you," she said, pulling him to his feet.

"I'm sorry, what?"

Her eyes sharpened. "What's your name?"

"Franco. Well, Francis."

"Only nine hundred ninety-nine thousand, nine hundred ninety-nine to go! What brings you here?"

Whatever laughter had been brewing among the Starchildren dissipated in favor of a bright and brimming expectation.

Franco: "I heard there was work up here, and …" he hesitated.

"Go on."

Eyes crawled across a suddenly self-conscious Franco, who lowered his voice: "The sign out front. The seven maxims? One of them's blank."

"Yes, the sixth maxim," she said. "What of it?"

He shrugged. "Are you all going to … uh, finish the sign?"

"The sign is a complete object-entity."

"Oh. What's the sixth maxim, then?"

"I'll tell you, but before I do, I need to know something. Is it a he?"

"Is … what?"

Their Foundation's voice jumped into a register they all had heard. Her eyes scanned distant horizons.

"It *is* a he, your most despised. I saw them, the spirits of the deep, drag his soul to the frozen steppes that night, moments after he injected that final, fateful dose. His vision faded to slits before he opened his eyes to the hereafter, the ceiling of his squathouse replaced by a starless sky. The dreadful denizens of acedism, those who don't care they don't care, are walking scarecrows, their dead flesh dried to husks, their clothes tatters, their inner monologues nothing but spite and blame and grudge. The muttering souls of this sorry realm all migrate to one of its countless manors, thinking themselves fortunate to have found such a palatial homecoming, but nothing fits, and everything is out of place. The buses never run on time, the grocery shelves always bare, their thirsts never quenched, their hunger always gnawing. That was the fate levied against your father for his utter lack of interest in the affairs of your heart, and now earthly time, clock time, the time that dances in tune with charm and strange, has no meaning for him as he faces down an eternity of wondering *what did I forget?*"

Franco was sobbing. Athena hugged him.

"Welcome to the fold, Francis Starchild."

Thirty Years Later: The New Fortress

WITH HIS FINAL ACT, RICHARD showed a flair for the dramatic by depositing them where they'd just been: at the gateway to the old Starchild Ranch. Abandoned for many years, a red *FOR SALE* sticker spread across their old engraving. They fanned out around her infernal vault as red lightning continued to flash overhead. Dark clouds concealed the final sunset.

Letta checked her chronometer: *00:00:37.*

"Thirty seconds left, everyone. Say your goodbyes. We tried."

Nicky, still wracked with grief, shook her head. "What? But we're here. We got her."

Letta shook her head. "We're one short. With Athena, the Menagerie only has six-sixty-five. We never replaced Bix—we never replaced Bradley."

A new voice: "I think we can see to that."

A grown man wearing a shitty, 1980s-era store-bought child's Halloween costume strolled up. A plastic-shell devil's mask paired with a vinyl bodysuit bearing crude illustrations of red, pitchfork-wielding demons clothed him. He danced in place and chanted, "Boogitty, boogitty, boogitty!"

"Who are you?" Letta asked, giving her watch a significant glance: *00:00:24.*

"I wouldn't worry about sunset," the stranger said, pulling off his mask to reveal a bald man whose chin ended in a point so sharp it could've been carved from stone. Threadlines of pure white shimmered across his flesh like fiber-optics. "You may check your time devices. I have provided you with, shall we say, a pause."

Letta addressed the team: "Can we confirm?"

Traxler nodded. "They've stopped at two seconds."

Letta turned to the strange man, said, "Are you ... Old Father?"

Frith covered her face. "Letta. Can you *really* not guess who this is?"

"Oh!" Letta yipped. "You're ... well, *we're* your Menagerie?"

"You are indeed, my children," Lucifer said. He waved a hand across his body and replaced the costume with a white linen suit. "Madam Successor, I'm impressed with your performance during this crisis. You sailed into every headwind with heart and hardiness."

"Wow, thanks. So you've been watching us?"

"I have."

"Any fucking reason why you hadn't pitched in till now?"

"Indeed. Forgive me. There are rules ancient and strange that govern this rite. My brother and I drew lots in the early mists before time itself to decide who would oversee each handover, and I'm afraid I drew short."

Letta's posture softened slightly. "Got it. Have you seen everything?"

"Only what he described to me in his missives."

"He? He who?" Letta asked. "Old Father?"

"No. But it's someone else you might recognize."

From nowhere, another man stepped out from behind Lucifer—a man of immeasurable age and wisdom who wore a medieval jerkin.

Nicky's tears changed from grief to joy: *"Goldberg!"*

"Greetings," he said. "Lord Morningstar aided my escape from the Prelate Centurions."

Nicky rushed over and hugged him. "Thank you for all your help. Sorry we shit the bed at the end."

"But you didn't. I myself am a member of the Menagerie … but it has become increasingly difficult for me to carry out my work alone. I need an assistant, an acolyte."

Letta held up a palm. "That's … allowed? We can just point at someone and, *poof!* They're a part of the Menagerie?"

"Not quite," Lucifer said. "You were clever enough to replenish the Menagerie's ranks with the people you had, but in to initiate an entirely new member requires a prayer to be answered."

"A prayer?" Frith asked. "To … uh, well, the man upstairs?"

Lucifer nodded. "I am the one being across all of existence whose every prayer is answered, even though sometimes the answer is no. But I cannot create Miss—is it Nicodemus?"

"Yeah, or just Nicky's fine. I mean, 'Nicky.' You don't need to call me Nicky Fine, Mister Lucifer, unless you feel like it."

Kindly amusement made a silent trip around the circle in the form of warm smiles and stifled laughter.

Lucifer smiled too. "Very well, Nicky it is." He addressed the group:

"I cannot create her a member of the Menagerie without my brother's blessing. I am about to call on Old Father himself to look this way. Brace yourselves."

In the space of one-quadrillionth of a Plank time, they experienced the following:

Someone appeared next to Lucifer, though this person's appearance changed every instant. He or she or they cycled through millions of shapes, looks, and attire. For the purposes of this tale, we shall content ourselves to call it a "he," though his true nature embeggars the imagination. Old Father, having extricated himself from an experiment a million universes away, looked on the face of his brother—sometime nemesis, sometime ally—and silently expressed his thanks for helping to save his most favorite dream.

Lucifer made his request.

Old Father granted it, paused briefly as his ears perked up at another prayer—and was gone.

They had a shared sense that they'd been in the presence of *something,* but they had no memory of it. The clouds dissipated to uncover a perfect full moon. Standing before the grounds of her former cult, Letta Starchild faced her team.

"I, Letta Starchild, now Letta Mallestratos, assume the mantle of Guildmaster from Matthias de Rilesford, as well as the titles of Infernal Cartographer and Mistress of Anguish from Tormentos Mallestratos, formerly Richard Pudlicotte."

"I, Bowden Traxler, assume the mantle of Master of Dreams."

"I, Winifrith Starchild, hereby replace Braxton J. Merriweather."

"I, Nicodemus Starchild, hereby join the hallowed ranks of Lord Morningstar's Menagerie, in assistance of Goldberg, Master of Traps and Snares." She looked over. "But Letta … what about *her?*"

The infernal vault melted open to reveal Athena, trapped in mid-lunge. She staggered forward and found her footing as she realized where she was. Balling her fists before her, she laughed.

"I'm free. I'm free. I'm *free* of that accursed place and its endless chill and sorry simulacra." She wheeled on the team and smiled with dark eyes. "And I, Athena Starchild, hereby assume the mantle of the Scourge of Camp Crimson Lagoon. Ha! But why should I limit myself to there? The LodEx empire is mine for the taking, my child. Just imagine the fame that awaits us when it's revealed I escaped my own execution!"

Letta, her face stony, said, "Turn it back on."

Athena frowned for a moment before her face slowly stretched in horror. Her throat cinched shut except for guttural clicks and moans. She fell to her knees, then to her side, curling into a fetal pose. Frith, on instinct, came to Athena's aid.

"My god. What did you do, Letta?"

"While Old Father was here, I slipped in a prayer of my own. He gave my mother something she'd always lacked: empathy."

Athena convulsed, drool running from the corner of her mouth.

Frith lifted her into her arms. "Empathy. Good move."

Traxler said, "She has to live with it. All of it."

"Is this against the rules?" Nicky asked.

Letta shook her head. "We only needed to replenish the Menagerie. There was nothing in the Rite that said she had to keep on killing. She'll live here, with us." She indicated the Ranch.

"Here?" Frith asked.

"We need a new Fortress of Maximum Suffering, don't we?"

"Fair enough," Frith said. "But … we need to keep expanding the Menagerie. We've only got six hundred sixty-six, and I don't want to pull another hell heist if some random monster gets killed tomorrow."

"We will expand our ranks starting immediately, with a new mandate. I shall request an audience with Lord Morningstar to instruct his demonguard that we no longer have any use for them on earth. They no longer need to *tempt* anyone. This world is teeming with evil as it is. We shall punish the wicked and *only* the wicked."

She rose on a cloud of insectoids and headed toward the Ranch. Nicky, however, stayed behind with Goldberg. Letta turned. "Where are you two headed?"

"Someplace new," Goldberg said. "My new acolyte has a lot of catch-up learning to do."

Frith: "Goldberg, I've got to know—how do you find out so much about all this? How did you know the way into Asmo?"

"Every other potential Guildmaster in history has chosen the *second* Rite of Succession, the sacrifice of their best friend, as well as the Catalyst. Only one other has chosen the first Rite, the hell heist."

"Oh," Frith said quietly. "Who *are* you?"

He shook his head. "I remember so little from that time. I can't even remember how to speak my own language. The Menagerie was quite different back then—wights and warlords and demented intruders of the night—but the job was essentially the same. My predecessor was from the far east. We could barely communicate, but with his waning strength, he outlined the Rites to me. The Catalyst of my era had already died fighting a golem that menaced the steppes."

"Who was your best friend?" Letta asked.

"My wife."

They shared a look of mutual approval. "And ... what was your hell heist like?"

"Terrifying ... and a whole lot of fucking fun." Goldberg smiled and beckoned to Nicky. "We must be off."

"Nicky?" Letta said. "Are you going to be okay? You just lost ..."

"He's with all of us," she said, indicating their hellish new attire. "He's our armor. Let's honor him with our work."

They walked down the road. Traxler rubbed his temples. "Damn. I can feel every dream all across earth *and* the afterworld. Francois left me a mess to clean up."

Frith smiled. "You got this, honey. At least you're not feeling an uncontrollable urge to kill a bunch of horny teenagers."

"You can't kill any horny teenagers, Frith," Letta said.

"What about horny, amoral trust-fund teenagers living off the wealth of others and exploiting the underclass?"

"You can kill *some* horny teenagers."

As the moon waxed across the sky, they made their way up to the ranch. A dark tentacle curled back around the sign, tore off the *FOR SALE* sticker, scored the wood clean, and inscribed a new welcome:

*You are entering the Starchild-Nicodemus Ranch. Welcome.
Forever while you're here, you must honor the Maxims of Starchild
Ranch:*

Punish the Wicked.
Protect the Innocent.
Remember and Honor Those We've Lost:
Bayard Starchild
Franco Starchild
Jonathan James Bradley
Matthias de Rilesford
Adam de Fentlok
Richard Pudlicotte

We were always angels.

Acknowledgments

My fellow California Coldblood author Beth Woodward provided invaluable notes, ideas, and input on an early outline of this work, and to her, I'm deeply grateful. Thank you, Beth.

Discovering the events of the Great Crown Jewels Robbery of 1303 was one of the greatest pleasures of writing this book. The vast majority of my inspiration sprang from Paul Doherty's remarkable account of the incident in his nonfiction book of the same name.

Dale Halvorsen delivered yet another gorgeous cover, and he once again out-thought me when it came to design and inspiration. Thank you.

As always, I am eternally grateful to my lovely wife, Lauren Rock.

About the Author

ROBERT J. PETERSON lives in Nevada City, Calif., with his wife and cat. His other novels include *The Odds*, *The Remnants*, and *Strong Bones*.

www.ingramcontent.com/pod-product-compliance
Lightning Source LLC
Chambersburg PA
CBHW061641190726
48289CB00006B/1697